LOSS OF FLIGHT

Focusing on novels with contemporary concerns, Bantam New Fiction introduces some of the most exciting voices at work today. Look for these titles wherever Bantam New Fiction is sold:

WHITE PALACE by Glenn Savan
SOMEWHERE OFF THE COAST OF MAINE by Ann Hood
COYOTE by Lynn Vannucci
VARIATIONS IN THE NIGHT by Emily Listfield
LIFE DURING WARTIME by Lucius Shepard
THE HALLOWEEN BALL by James Howard Kunstler
PARACHUTE by Richard Lees
THUNDER ISLAND by James Howard Kunstler
WAITING TO VANISH by Ann Hood
BLOCKBUSTER by Patricia A. Marx and
  Douglas G. McGrath
GOOD ROCKIN' TONIGHT by William Hauptman
SLIGHTLY LIKE STRANGERS by Emily Listfield
LOSS OF FLIGHT by Sara Vogan

BANTAM NEW FICTION

LOSS OF FLIGHT

SARA VOGAN

BANTAM BOOKS
NEW YORK · TORONTO · LONDON · SYDNEY · AUCKLAND

LOSS OF FLIGHT
A Bantam Book / April 1989
PRINTING HISTORY
Parts of this book appeared in slightly different form in the following:
Five Fingers Review, No. 5, 1987.

Grateful acknowledgment is made for permission to reprint the lyrics from:
"Eleanor Rigby" by John Lennon and Paul McCartney © 1966 NORTHERN
SONGS LTD. All rights for the U.S., Canada and Mexico controlled and
administered by SBK BLACKWOOD MUSIC INC. Under license from ATV MUSIC
(MACLEN). All rights reserved. International copyright secured. Used by permission.

Library of Congress Cataloging-in-Publication Data

Vogan, Sara.
    Loss of flight.

    (Bantam new fiction)
    I. Title.
PS3572.029L67 1988   813'.54   88-47843

ISBN 0-553-34580-X

Published simultaneously in the United States and Canada

Bantam Books are published by Bantam Books, a division of Bantam Doubleday
Dell Publishing Group, Inc. Its trademark, consisting of the words "Bantam
Books" and the portrayal of a rooster, is Registered in U.S. Patent and Trade-
mark Office and in other countries. Marca Registrada. Bantam Books, 666 Fifth
Avenue, New York, New York 10103.

PRINTED IN THE UNITED STATES OF AMERICA

FG   0 9 8 7 6 5 4 3 2 1

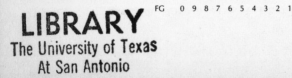

To all those who stood by me
through the long and dark years.

WINTER

JANUARY 3
FRIDAY

Perhaps San Francisco existed outside the weather. After ten years on the West Coast, Dr. Max Bodine still hadn't adjusted to the loss of distinct seasons. It never snowed in the winter. The grass never turned that vivid, new spring-green. There was no heat in the summer. In the fall the trees didn't burst into a riot of yellows and reds to signal the first frost. He could understand why early explorers thought California was an island. Sometimes, to Max, it felt like a separate continent.

He divided the year into his own unique calendar: spring from January to June, fall from July to December. Three days into the new year he began to search for the subtle change-over from one season to the other. Today felt like late April in Virginia, the cool feeling of rain on the air even though the sun was bright, looked hot. As he dressed for his first appointment his attention was drawn to a faint, whirring buzz. He looked out the open window into the courtyard as two hummingbirds darted and danced.

They swirled through parabolas, dropped like dive-bombers, hung motionless in midair. Their cries were tiny chimes. He buttoned his cuffs and knotted his tie while the birds circled through the courtyard performing aerial acrobatics. Finally, wings still beating so fast they were only a blur, the male mounted the female, driving her close to the ground. It was over before Max finished straightening his tie, and then the female soared straight up and disappeared into the morning sun. Can birds do it in the air? Or were her tiny feet resting solidly on the stone courtyard? It must be spring, Max decided. January third and the birds are mating.

Spring was usually the time when most of Max's patients tried to determine if the center would hold, a time when they decided to make changes in their lives. But after several years of practicing his unique brand of therapy, Max knew how few of these plans would pan out. This morning he would meet with Thomas Pierce who suffered from what Max called American loneliness. Thomas had everything: money, a beautiful wife, successful children, a comfortable home. His father had been one of the founders of Merrill Lynch Pierce Fenner & Smith and afforded his son the luxury of being uninterested in money. But Thomas was unhappy. He felt his life held no meaning. Usually as part of their Friday morning sessions, Max and Thomas played golf if the weather was good, or shot pool. But today Thomas wanted Max to accompany him to an orphanage in San José. Max hoped philanthropy would add meaning to Thomas's life, but as he donned his jacket he recognized it was only a faint hope. Thomas, at sixty-eight, had a lifetime of dissatisfaction behind him and seemed quite comfortable complaining about it. Max was his hired audience. If it weren't for the money, Max would have divested himself of Thomas a long time ago, pronounced him cured and been done

4

with it. He knew Thomas didn't really want therapy, just attention. But psychiatrists are free-lancers and Thomas was a steady gig.

He unlocked the Mustang and turned the key in the ignition. He flipped on KJAZ in time to pick up the last, lilting riffs of an Art Tatum tune. Thomas Pierce. As a therapist, Max held the very real impression that people walked into an office for an hour a day with a prepared story to tell to a captive audience. He believed seeing people in their own surroundings gave him a better way of assessing their problems. An office setting was too controlled, didn't allow anything to happen beyond the limits of the prepared story. Their stories seemed to ring more clearly when he could meet the unfaithful wife, the bratty children, see the environments his clients said were driving them crazy.

He met his patients in an atmosphere of their own choice where they felt they could talk. He drew the line at bars and shopping malls. Likewise, he felt the traditional fifty-minute hour was designed as a luxury for the therapist at the expense of the patient. Max treated people in blocks, four hours a day, one day a week, rather than the traditional one hour, four days a week. Sometimes he found himself in art galleries and museums, strolling through exhibits he never really saw. Last year he met a woman at Alcatraz, riding the ferry over and back. Often he visited his patients in their homes, like Barbara Landestoi and Jacob Epter. Vincent Dolack liked to drive out to the country, since his wife was an invalid and Vincent spent most of his time cooped up in the house taking care of her.

This afternoon, after Thomas Pierce, he would have his third session with Sofia Addisge, a native Ethiopian and the wife of a Bechtel engineer. A former patient, who also worked for Bechtel, had recommended Max to Sofia, and she'd been intrigued by his method. They had decided to meet at the zoo today because the zebras and lions reminded her of home. Unlike Thomas Pierce, Max hoped he might truly help Sofia. She was homesick, but involved in her first love affair, and trying to decide whether she would return to Ethiopia with her husband or stay in America.

The day turned hot. Virginia in June. Even with the drive down to San José and a tour of the orphanage Thomas might endow, Max felt, as he usually did when there was no golf game or pool to shoot, as if he were sleepwalking through Thomas's session. He wished Thomas were a more clever man, or at least had a sense of humor. Thomas complained about a toothache, although Max knew Thomas's teeth cost more than the rent on his flat in Pacific Heights. Thomas felt no ardor for his wife, the same complaint that brought him to Max two years ago. In the beginning Max tried to put Thomas and his wife through the paces of sexual counseling. But it soon became apparent Thomas didn't want therapy as much as he simply wanted someone to talk to. American loneliness. A man with money and power and no one to talk to.

As far as Max was concerned, the trip through the orphanage was a bust. Thomas wasn't taken by the children, thought the place quite self-sufficient, and wasn't sure funding an orphanage was the right moral decision. "What do you think?" he asked as they walked back to the car. "Wouldn't you say cancer research is more important than orphans?"

"Depends what interests you, children or health." Max thought Thomas would rather endow a country club.

"I mean," Thomas said, "those orphans could grow up to be parents or terrorists. Bank robbers or accountants. But cancer research would benefit everyone." He slipped behind the wheel of the Citroën. "You know, I've always suspected they could cure cancer any time they want, but they're holding out on us. They cured Reagan, didn't they? Perhaps cancer research is just another money-making venture. And what about the common cold? My wife picked up a wicked cold over the holidays. You're a doctor. Why can't they cure the common cold?"

Perhaps next week Thomas would drag him down to Stanford Medical Center for a tour of the facilities. Still, these trips were probably better than another nine holes of golf. Maybe Thomas was making some progress after all.

Back in the city at one o'clock the warmth of San José turned to gray fog, the color of the inside of an airplane hangar. Max found Sofia, dressed in an expensive sweater and jeans, standing by the giraffe pen. He was struck, as he had been the first time he met her, by her tall, slim bearing and the sheen of her dark skin. She greeted him with a dazzling white smile.

"Good day, Dr. Bodine." There was a slight British accent to her English.

Max smiled. "How are you today?"

She pointed to the flat sky. "The fog and eucalyptus trees remind me very much of home. In the morning the smoke from the fires mixes with the fog from the highlands. It is almost this exact color. I keep looking up expecting to see a Verreaux eagle. When I walked in I passed the colobuses and at first I didn't realize they were in a cage. I don't recall seeing monkeys in cages before. I had a colobus as a pet when I was a child. He lived in the acacia tree outside my bedroom."

Max looked at the dreary fog. Ethiopia. A place Max could barely imagine. The ancient Abyssinian kingdom finding its way into the twentieth century. Yet, Sofia, the wife of a civil engineer, had been engaged by her parents at the age of eight, to a man she did not see until her wedding day ten years later. And now, after fifteen years of marriage, she was actively questioning the wisdom of that arrangement. She'd taken her first lover.

As they strolled toward the elephant house Sofia cleared her throat. "I have done my homework, Dr. Bodine. At least I think I've come up with what you wanted." She fiddled with the rings on her fingers. "When you asked me to describe what I thought about America, I was sure I could never do it. Berhe and I have been here only a few months. And the United States is very different from England, where I went to school. I always think of England as a tea cozy. Small, but self-contained, warming the heart of its history. But America," she threw up her hands in an exaggerated gesture. "I gave the problem much thought during this week. But then I remembered a story from my childhood which I hope will apply."

Max nodded his encouragement. "Good. I'd like to hear it."

Her eyes focused on a point far away, as if she were addressing the tops of the eucalyptus trees. "There is a legend in my country about the Roms, a race of giants who ruled over the country for a long time. The Roms were able to pull a baobab tree up by the roots and snap it over the knee to make a fire. God liked the Roms but saw they were destroying His land. So one day He said to them they must perish to make way for Man. He asked them if they wished to perish by a blessing or a curse. Without considering the decision for even a moment, they asked God for a blessing. God said to them: 'Perish by a blessing then. Your wives shall bring forth men-children unto you and your cows shall bring forth female calves.'

"The Roms rejoiced and celebrated God's choice, and soon all the women gave birth to male babies. The cows were fruitful too. But as time went on the Roms realized there were no bulls for their cows, no wives for their men. A great sadness came over the Roms as they watched the men and cows wither and die. It was finally decided that this could not be endured, and each man dug his grave and put the stones of his tomb together like a hut. Each Rom took all his property, entered his hut, and sealed the tomb from within. Their tombs dot the land to this day. That is part of the way I see America, perishing by a blessing. There is so much here, the beauty and bounty of God. Yet no one seems to rejoice in their good fortune.''

"No one?" Max asked. "You think we're a nation of ungrateful people?''

"Oh, this is just a first impression. But even your television emphasizes the things that are wrong, the things that go bad. You do not celebrate your holidays; instead, we are told of all the people who died in car accidents, how many more or less than last year. This morning on a talk show I listened to experts discuss stress disease. On the news at night, the weatherman apologizes if it is going to rain.''

Max suffered a small pang of cultural guilt. "I imagine complaining about the rain would be quite a luxury in Ethiopia." He'd made a contribution to USA Africa, and tried to talk Thomas Pierce into donating. Thomas didn't believe in sending aid to foreign countries, even when millions were starving.

"There is no point in complaining about anything in Ethiopia. Complaining is a luxury of the Western world though it might be contagious, like a disease. Until I came to America I recognized my duty to stay with Berhe. As an educated Ethiopian, my task was to help my husband and Ethiopia. And yet here I find myself thinking about what I want to do with my life. When I was in school in England I was never tempted by these thoughts. Now that I am in the United States I feel my life opening up. As beautiful as Ethiopia is, I'm not sure I still want to live in a country where most people don't wear shoes. A country where only the wealthy have enough to eat." She looked down at her plum-colored high-heeled boots. "Yet I know, as an Ethiopian wife, there is so little I can do there. I can only serve Berhe. But here I have realized my children no longer need me as a full-time mother. In America I could get a job, start a business, pick my own friends. And yet, with all that freedom I feel more confused than ever."

"Perishing by a blessing," Max repeated. He might use that phrase in the paper he was writing for the APA. Thomas Pierce was perishing by a blessing. No, perishing wasn't the right word. Everything about Thomas Pierce was thriving, flourishing, even his unhappiness, the lack of meaning in his life. "But you're not perishing," he said.

She watched the elephants flick flies with their tails. Sea gulls scavenged for peanuts, keeping a good distance from the elephants' feet. "In Ethiopia perishing is a reality. We have droughts and the biblical plague of locusts. It is hard to imagine anyone perishing in America. Perhaps that's why the car wrecks are so important here. If God wanted to exterminate the Americans, he would stage a giant car wreck, coast to coast." She gave him a wry smile. "It is hard to imagine anyone dying in your country, as if you all could live forever."

They passed the afternoon walking round and round the zoo, turning the story of the Roms over and looking at it from different angles. Perishing by a blessing. A blessing turned into a curse. American loneliness. In a land of plenty, many sons, many cows, something was missing.

Max continued to think about this story after he and Sofia parted at dusk. If that was her description of America, her assignment for next Friday was to come up with a comparable description of Ethiopia. Max didn't know what to do about this patient, whether he should encourage her

10

to leave her husband and stay in America, or whether he should honor her heritage and counsel her to remain faithful to her upbringing. It didn't matter much. One of the things he'd learned in this business was that he rarely influenced a decision one way or the other. He merely provided a frame to think about the problem, offered support as his patient worked through the various options.

Sofia had fallen in love with an American, an engineer who worked with her husband. Love was a luxury too, like complaining, that wasn't part of an Ethiopian marriage. When she talked about her lover, Sofia grew as excited as a young girl. This was the first time she'd ever felt the excitement and passion of love and the experience was wonderful and frightening to her. She turned to Max because she thought this was a uniquely Western dilemma and only a Westerner was equipped to explain it. Caught in a political marriage to a man twelve years her senior, she wanted to know what was happening to her.

When he returned to his apartment on this Friday evening, he felt as if a great weight had settled on his shoulders and was pressing down on his heart. A restlessness took hold of him. Spring fever in January.

Six calls flashed on his answering machine. The first one was an invitation to a dinner party tomorrow night. "Damn, why not tonight," he muttered as he jotted down the time and address in his appointment book. The second voice was faint, quavery, with the threat of tears spilling over before the message could be completed.

"Dr. Bodine. My name is Susan Frazer, Janet Lifton's sister. Elaine's in Kaiser. There's been a terrible accident. Could you please come down? We need to talk to someone about this."

He played the message back twice. Elaine Lifton, eighteen years old, long blonde hair down to the middle of her back. Tuesday afternoons. She'd been in counseling with him for the last month. A terrible accident, or was it an accident? Sometimes you get a feeling about a patient, a bad feeling. Elaine felt responsible for her father's death three months ago. He'd died of a heart attack, at home, probably as painlessly and peacefully as death could be. Elaine was out on a date. Her mother had been playing bridge across town and Elaine found her father and thought he'd fallen asleep in front of the TV. When she tried to rouse him she discovered he was dead.

Oh, God. The young ones were the hardest. An only child still living at home and one evening she discovers what death really means. She'd quit talking, and her mother consulted Max. Each Tuesday afternoon Max would walk with her along the beach. He would talk about death, the meaning of life, yet he felt he wasn't making much progress. After a month he still hadn't heard the sound of her voice.

He whizzed through the other four messages, nothing serious, nothing to raise the hairs on his spine the way Susan Frazer's message had. The weight had slipped from his shoulders to his chest and if this accident was as bad as he thought it might be, he knew the weight would hit his stomach with the force of a blow. He picked up his jacket as he headed back to the car and wished he could bring along something more substantial. A medical doctor could always carry his little black bag. A psychiatrist arrives empty-handed.

Drives like this always made him nervous. The tone of voice told him something was terribly wrong, that the word *accident* didn't come near to describing what really happened. It was like saying someone had "a bit of a drinking problem" after hitting a child while drunk behind the wheel. Sometimes language isn't enough.

His greatest fear was suicide, a botched suicide attempt could be a living death, worse than the finality of death. The suicide of his older sister, Claire, ten years ago made him decide to go into psychiatry. Claire threw herself from the top of a seventeen-story building and Max still dreamed he could stop her before she hit the ground. And now, San Francisco, the suicide capital of the country, the land at the end of the rainbow. He came out here right after Claire's death. He wanted to save them all.

But he hadn't saved them all, although he'd helped many. Very few of his patients were actually suicidal— love and money were more involving than death. But every year or so he treated someone like Elaine, a potential. He could just feel it.

At the hospital he found Susan Frazer sitting quietly and staring out into the night. Elaine's mother had been sedated, in shock. What Max heard sent threads of fear running through his body.

Janet Lifton and Elaine had eaten breakfast together, silently, although Mrs. Lifton kept talking to Elaine, hoping for a response. After breakfast she went out to work in her rose garden since the morning was so lovely, before the fog rolled in. She assumed Elaine was somewhere in the house when she heard the table saw in the garage switch on. Max could clearly hear that high-pitched mechanical hiss. And then Janet Lifton heard screams, Elaine's screams, a man's scream. She ran to the garage to find Elaine on the concrete floor in pools of blood, her bleeding, mangled hands flipping like fish.

The garage door was open, and as Elaine laid her hands on the swirling saw the postman across the street saw the first fountain of blood. He ran over and snapped off the switch, but Elaine had already passed out. The postman called an ambulance while Janet tried to cover Elaine's hands and stop the bleeding. Janet Lifton kept seeing bright white bits of bone floating on the thick surface of blood. Elaine was alive, but the doctors had amputated her hands.

Max sat with Mrs. Lifton's sister through most of the night. Although they talked, he knew he had nothing to say, not all of his knowledge could explain what she'd done. There were so many easier ways, car wrecks, pills, razors, jumping from the bridge. Why a table saw? Except perhaps because it was her father's. But why leave the door open for all to see? Did she know the postman would come by just then? Did she see him across the street?

As Max drove back in the predawn darkness he thought of the Roms watching their wifeless sons, their cows with no bulls. Perishing by a blessing. Taking themselves into their tombs. He hoped Elaine would die, if that's what she wanted. American loneliness. No one to talk to. He wondered what kind of voice she had.

Spring. Spring was here. He consoled himself with the notion spring was a crazy time of year and he, like every other creature on the planet, must endure an unsettling period. History confirmed this. Druids burned their forests in the dead of winter to bring back the sun. Mayan Indians believed there were five evil days in February when the world turned upside down, and the only way to remember what had happened was through nightmares and dreams. The Romans observed the Ides of March. Medieval Germans celebrated Crazy Monday before the Easter fast, twenty-four hours during which murder, rape, adultery, and arson went unpunished and unavenged. Eskimos run in circles on the snow, wearing only shirts made of bird feathers, a spring rite to help the sun rise higher in the sky.

January third and it was already spring.

SPRING

APRIL 7
MONDAY
MORNING

We do things we can't explain as easily as we do things we don't understand. Katlyn Whiston's mother used to say this as if it contained all the wisdom of the world. Katlyn grew up on the phrase, listening to Opal invoke it in response to every whim. All that vagueness, all those negatives rolled into one sentence. Katlyn never liked the phrase but it was always there, coloring her mind like a prism, the way "Have a good day" sits on the tongue of a salesman or "Close cover before striking" decorates a book of matches.

Her mother's little sayings tumbled through Katlyn's thoughts the way other people hear popular tunes. This particular Monday morning the phrase lodged in her head like the refrain of a song. She'd been fighting it since Friday when Royce stormed off to work. One thing about a nasty little phrase like that: if you didn't keep busy the words could overwhelm you, drowning any plan in all that uncertainty. Katlyn worked, driving herself as if Monday were a deadline. This morning she carried four newly designed shirts to drop off at Saving Grace before going to the pool. Zebra, Lion, Giraffe, and Skunk. Four designs in three days. If he didn't come home tonight she'd start another series. Antelope, Elephant.

Work was simply the sane person's way to keep from rocketing off the walls. She was fortunate, she loved to work, to give expression to the odd thoughts and images roaming through her head. Did bank tellers make change in their sleep? Do stock boys dream of filling empty shelves? But she'd dreamed up these shirts and she hoped Charlotte would like them. She always tested her new designs on Charlotte, never quite confident enough to send them off to Bendel's in New York without his approval. But what he liked seemed to sell. It's tough to bitch about success.

Who knew how many shirts she could design before she heard from Royce again? An entire jungle of animal shirts, hanging on the rack at Saving Grace. Not that anyone even needed those shirts, fashion toys, but she needed to work, to keep busy, to keep from rocketing off the walls.

Noe Valley was quiet this morning, looking clean and bright as if washed by the rain last night. Only a few shops on Twenty-fourth Street were open. Most of the traffic clustered around the breakfast and coffee joints as the last of the nine-to-fivers slowly made their way to work. On the street corners, old women bundled up in coats and scarves waited, as quietly as cats in the cool morning sun, for buses to whisk them away to another part of the city. Katlyn noticed a black child, about four, sucking on a Chinese duck foot in front of the Peruvian shop. He was humming something. As she drew closer she realized it was "Jingle Bells." Why a child would hum "Jingle Bells" in April was beyond her. Wishful thinking, she supposed.

It was twenty to nine when Katlyn banged on the glass door of Saving Grace. She put her eyes to the bullet holes, as if peering through binoculars, and watched the interior of the shop filter to aquamarine. Charlotte had found the door on one of his garage sale tours and loved the optic effect. He bought the door as a charm to ward off burglars. The bullet holes made Katlyn think of drug dealers, Chinese Tong wars, gangsters, crimes of passion. Or the shots could have been fired by punks, bored high school students playing with guns. She wondered if someone had been standing inside when the shots were fired.

With her eyelashes fluttering against the glass, Katlyn watched as Charlotte came out of the back and moved through the shop as if he were underwater. Saving Grace had originally been owned by a woman named Grace, a fact which pleased Katlyn whenever she remembered it. It was a second-hand shop before Grace decided to move to Nepal some years ago and sold it to Charles Lawrence, a young Harvard MBA who moved to San Francisco to be part of the gay culture. He was Charlie to his parents and business acquaintances, Charlotte to his friends.

Four years ago Charlotte had been invited to the party Katlyn and Alan threw to celebrate their first wedding anniversary. He had admired the dress Katlyn was wearing, a sarong-style teal blue silk that set off her red hair and long legs. Charlotte said Katlyn looked like Rita Hayworth in that dress. They discussed old forties movies and deco glass and wooden toys, New Guinea birds of paradise and Excaliburs with real leather straps over the hoods. By the end of the party when Alan came up to bed he found Charlotte and Katlyn standing by her closet. Charlotte wore a black T-shirt Katlyn had silk-screened with two purple brontosauruses, long necks entwined, and the neon pink legend *PREHISTORIC LOVERS*. Charlotte commissioned a dozen from Katlyn for Saving Grace, now a boutique, an antique shop, a design originals outlet. *PREHISTORIC LOVERS* became the first in a long series of designs. Four years of profit for both of them. But Katlyn still thought of Saving Grace as a second-hand shop, merely buffed up and overpriced.

Four years ago. An Ides of March party to celebrate their first wedding anniversary. Since last Wednesday her mind seemed to stop, like a dog standing at a door, when she thought about Alan. Do you grieve for someone who deceived you? For someone who left your life? Is grief a choice?

Charlotte opened the door, making sure to keep the Closed sign facing the street. "What have we here?" He was all smiles. "Want some coffee?" He was dressed like a banker today, a three-piece gray herringbone tweed and a gold pocketwatch on a chain. A little mascara darkened his pencil-thin mustache. The banker's outfit made him look older, sturdier, solid as a wall. Last Thursday when she stopped by, he was wearing his ballet tights and a shirt with gauzy balloon sleeves, and Katlyn had marveled at how thin and lithe he was. His body looked as supple as a teenaged boy's. Only the faint crow's-feet around his eyes and a certain slackness in his jaw gave his age away. Lately he'd been talking about getting a face-lift, an idea Katlyn found ridiculous.

She shook her head. "I'm on my way to the pool. I just wanted to drop these off. What do you think?" She put down her shoulder bag and the stack of shirts and held out the first one. Zebra.

Zebra was fashioned as a white satin shirt. Katlyn had sewn diagonal black velvet stripes across the front and back. On the left elbow she'd placed a triangular nose and smaller V stripes to form a face. She'd given it blue eyes complete with fringe for eyelashes. A generous amount of three-inch black fringe ran down the right shoulder, the mane.

Charlotte held it up, flicking the black fringe back and forth. "Oh, I love it," he said in his musical baritone. "But why blue eyes?"

She shrugged. "Being mystic, I guess." Alan's eyes had been blue, cool blue like the depths of ice.

He looked at the shirt from all angles. "I kind of like blue eyes. Makes the face stand out more." He pulled off his coat and tried the Zebra on. "Oh, very nice." He waved his arm to make the fringe dance. "Are they all zebras?"

Katlyn thought it looked quite good on him, the face in sharp relief, the velvet stripes like the herringbone pattern in his trousers, only magnified. Do the stripes of the zebra ever cross? "They're all the same idea." She held up Lion, a beige suede shirt with gold fringe across the body for a big fluffy ruff, eyes and ears on the left shoulder, and just a spit of fringe on the right elbow, the tail. Giraffe was a long-sleeved iridescent gold shirt with rust velvet squares sewn on. The face was down by the left wrist and short copper fringe ran up the shoulder and around the neck. Skunk was black bouclé knit on which Katlyn had bleached a stripe down the shoulder and stenciled a small face level with the left bicep. Charlotte didn't think the Skunk was as successful as the others. He said it didn't have the same spirit of movement.

"But I like these. They could be hot." Charlotte placed the Lion on a mannequin in the store window, his palm stroking the long fringe. "Yes sir. He looks like the MGM lion. Maybe I should set an arch over him." He took the morning paper and stuffed it into the shoulder of the mannequin, beefing up the lion's face. "Grrrrr," he growled at the lion. "They're as fresh as the Hawaiian shirt pillowcases. I'm almost out of those, you know. The green ones with the parrots went quick as lightning. I need about two dozen more."

Katlyn considered this. Making pillowcases was about as easy as sleeping and Charlotte charged a fortune for them. Design Originals. She'd agreed to let him sell the pillowcases exclusively since he was the one who talked Bendel's into handling her work. They were partners, although neither would admit it. Charlotte's latest project was to get her work into a store on Rodeo Drive. He was determined to set her up as the Judy Chicago of San Francisco. She wondered what he would ask for if he got her work displayed in LA. Already he'd demanded a sidebar article and photo if she ever got written up in a national magazine. Charlotte loved big plans. "I'm thinking of taking a trip," she said.

Charlotte gave her a sexy look. "Loverboy taking you off to Mexico again?"

"No." She wondered if Charlotte's reaction would be the same as Royce's. "I'm thinking of going to Africa."

"Africa, is it?" He peeled off the Zebra shirt and held it out at arm's length, making the satin shine in the light, appraising it with a professional air. "Ah, yes. Excellent. Excellent. Such a stud. I know a fellow who'll faint with joy over this. Down in Carmel he bought a nineteen-thousand-dollar chinchilla bedspread. These babies are just the ticket for him."

"I thought I ought to get away for a while. Six months or so." Usually when she brought something new for Charlotte to consider, her spirits would rise with his lavish praise of her work. But not this morning. The antique clothes and toys and knickknacks looked too familiar today. The sparkling glass and sterling silver seemed gaudy. The smell of money drifted in the air. She needed something solid, earthy. "I want to think some things through. Do something different."

Charlotte turned to face her, his eyes sad and knowing. "Six months? We're in business here, love. We could make a lot of money. I could make you famous. There's no time for vacations. Have you started those Halloween masks? Why don't you do that, instead of running off to Africa?"

"I didn't say I was running off to Africa. I said I was thinking of taking a trip up the Nile and down the Congo." But she knew Charlotte could see through her. Charlotte had watched this movie before, when Alan left. And there was no reason to believe he would view things any differently now.

Charlotte tossed the Zebra down as if it had died in his hands. "For a smart woman, you so often talk drivel. Africa. You think going to Africa is going to solve anything? You want me to believe that?" He shook his head. "Africa won't bring Alan back. Africa won't solve your problems with Royce. You'll never learn. I tried to tell you when you first got involved with him. They never leave their wives, trips to Africa or Albuquerque, it makes no difference. That's why they have a wife in the first place, so they never have to take another woman seriously. Believe me, I know. Running off to Africa, won't solve anything."

Katlyn ran the copper fringe of the giraffe through her fingers, an electric feeling as the strands tickled her skin. "It's been two years now. Do you realize that, Charlotte? Two years."

"How time flies, et cetera."

"And I wish you wouldn't refer to it as running off to Africa. I'm just thinking of taking a trip, that's all." She knew Charlotte was right. Africa wouldn't solve her problems with Royce. Africa had nothing to do with Alan. "Making pillowcases won't solve anything either."

Charlotte shrugged absently and began rearranging a vase of silk orchids. "I'm so tempted, Katlyn, but I'm a good friend and I won't, repeat, won't, cite back to you

23

the little litany you used to sing about how getting involved with a married man would be the best thing for you. No responsibilities, you said. Just enjoy each other until something better comes along. But I won't go over all that with you again. It's your song, after all. I'll just say it seems very petulant to consider running off to Africa at this point in time."

"Charlotte, when you straighten out your own life I'll listen to your advice as to how to straighten out mine, okay?"

He turned toward her, as stern as a schoolteacher. "Love is the emotional flu, Katlyn. It hits without warning and runs its course. It's like recreational drugs. Once the rush is over, you're simply left with yourself, plus someone else. It's plain foolishness to run off all the way to Africa if you just want to change things with Royce." He wandered through his store, his hands drifting over the merchandise as if he could collect his thoughts through the tips of his fingers. "Think of me. If you go to Africa I'll be reduced to selling stuff I scrounge at garage sales."

"I just want him out of that marriage. That's all."

"That's all? Honey, why don't you ask if you can bronze his balls?" Charlotte sniffed as if detecting a distasteful odor in the air. "Now listen up, Katlyn." He paced the shop again, deciding what it would be he wanted her to hear. "I'm surprised at you. What do you think you're going to do? Power play Royce now that Alan left you that house? That house doesn't have to change your life. Nothing's different." His eyes clouded with sadness. "Except for Alan."

Last Wednesday when Katlyn dropped by on her way home from the pool, Charlotte had handed her a letter and ushered her through the beaded curtain into the back room. "He didn't know where you were living," Charlotte said, "but he figured I would." The letter was from

Guerrero, Alan's lover, the man he left her for to move to New York. Four lines, typed.

Alan died suddenly the night of March 18.
He wanted you to have the house.
Call Fisk Realty. They've been handling the rental.
We'll all miss him, and I want you to know I'm sorry.

There was the title to the house she and Alan had lived in while they were married, the house out in the Avenues where Alan grew up. Charlotte had called Fisk Realty and discovered Alan rented the house to a Japanese dentist and his family, the Wings, for the past two years, ever since he and Guerrero moved to New York. Guerrero also sent Charlotte Alan's blue-gray Borsalino, his stickpin studded with garnets, and a set of six ruby glass goblets. But Charlotte claimed he knew no more about Alan's death than she did, not how or why. He'd already called New York but hadn't reached Guerrero.

She'd spent five days thinking it over. She tried to remember Alan as a sexy, passionate lover, a husband who would fold her in his arms and kiss away the pain or trouble. Such a fleeting image. Alan's role as a husband and lover hadn't lasted long. Her most persistent image was as if she were watching herself in a movie as she paced through the empty house in the Avenues, her fingers trailing along Alan's father's furniture. "It feels like blood money," Katlyn said. "Finally paying me off after all that cheating and lying and deception. It's not as if I'm going to move back there. But, Jesus, we're all going to die. I just sort of feel it's time for me to do something different."

"Okay, how about this? You want to take a trip, right?" Charlotte performed a little dance step. "I could check this out, but a couple of years ago I heard about the

Panamanian mailboat. It leaves from the Bay Area every week for Central America. There's a small fleet of them, and they stop at all the little towns down the line from here to Panama and back. There's a couple of cabins for passengers, and you can get off anywhere along the line and catch the next boat through. How about if I send you down to Central America to buy some, some, some of whatever they sell down there. You know, cloth, baskets, feathered stuff. You know."

"How about some rifles and machine-guns, Charlotte? I hear they're doing a hell of a business in that stuff these days."

Charlotte picked up the Giraffe. "Okay, I tried. It's just a thought. How about Baffin Bay? I hear things are pretty calm up there."

"Anything particular you'd like from Baffin Bay?"

He ran the fringe through his fingers. "No."

Katlyn flicked at the tiny propeller of a model plane. "Did I ever tell you about my trip to Europe? *That* was a lot of fun. *Very* exciting. I knew a guy from Berkeley who got drafted and ended up serving his hitch in Germany, instead of being sent to Vietnam. He invited me over for the Munich Olympics. The day I was to leave terrorists shot two Israeli athletes. Remember that? Talk about excitement. My soldier boy gets called back to duty, and there I am, sitting at LaGuardia trying to work up the courage to board a plane bound for Munich."

"What'd you do?"

"What would you do? International terrorists are shooting the place up and the German police are playing Gestapo. I lost my sense of adventure, I suppose. So I missed something, not in the ordinary sense of not having a car I wanted, or a baby, which I don't want. But I've missed something. That rental money might help me find out what."

26

"How about this?" Charlotte said. "You run the store and I'll take the Panamanian mailboat. What you need is a little responsibility. You never think of anyone but yourself."

"Coming from you, that's like a clock complaining about time."

His voice was testy. "Well, I fail to see how Africa is going to fix anything."

"It might." She picked up a jar of antique marbles, rolling them inside the glass, the sound like a bad phone connection, amplified static electricity. "I've got to turn it around somehow."

"Dear heart," Charlotte said, "a woman of your age doesn't turn anything around. It's too late for that." He took the jar away from her and replaced it on a shelf. "You go forward, not around in circles."

"It's not enough," Katlyn said. "What if I were to drop dead," she snapped her fingers, "like that. I'm too old to spend my life making overpriced clothes and waiting around for Royce. There's got to be something more to it all than that."

"Like what? You think running a boutique is essential? I mean, maybe a policeman is essential, or a doctor. I'll tell you one thing. Tourist tripping through Africa isn't very essential either." Charlotte donned the herringbone jacket. "Africa. You know, they're shooting people over there too. Talk about dropping dead. And a bunch of them are starving." He shook his head. "I've known only one person who went to Africa, an old lover of mine in Boston who said he wanted to spend a New Year's Eve in Timbuktu. About a year later, I got a postcard from him, about this time of year as I recall. It said: Happy New Year. Life Is Tough And Then You Die But You Don't Have To Be A Wimp About It. That's the last I heard from him."

"I don't really have an itinerary yet. Do you think I should stop in Timbuktu? Look up your friend?"

"No, I don't think you should stop in Timbuktu. I think you've got spaghetti for brains this morning. If you've given this idea more than three minutes of thought your brains are gone completely." He picked up the Zebra again and made it dolphin through the air, watching the light glint off the satin and the toss of the black fringe. He stuck his arm into the sleeve of the Giraffe and played with the shirts as if they were hand puppets. "Only one each, huh? Are you going to do any more? Before you run off to Africa, that is?" He kissed the blue eyes. "I do love these, except for the Skunk. I don't think he'll fly. Make all the eyes blue when you do another batch."

"You're a bitch, Charlotte." She tried to smile, but Charlotte didn't respond. "I'm not going tomorrow. I'm just field-testing the idea. I can see your vote is No."

"Damn straight. You take off for Africa and all you'll be doing is repeating Alan's little drama. And you see what all that came to."

"Did you get in touch with Guerrero yet?" There was so much she wanted to know, so much Guerrero hadn't told them.

"No." Charlotte kept his back to her as he fondled the shirts. "How much do you want for these babies?"

"Charlotte, we all do the same things, only in different degrees." She gathered her shoulder bag and moved toward the door. "I'll talk to you later. I'm going to miss my swim. I figure the shirts at three hundred to four hundred dollars each. If they move fast, I might do another batch for New York."

"Katlyn, who put this Africa idea in your head?"

She shrugged. "It's like getting lost on a trip. Sometimes, when you figure out where you are, you realize you're going in the wrong direction."

"Life is tough and then you die, but you don't have to be a wimp about it."

"When the going gets tough, the tough go shopping."

"We can make beautiful money together," Charlotte said.

Katlyn gave him a wave as she left the shop. He had a point. Why was she even thinking about going to Africa, anyhow? We do things we can't explain as easily as we do things we don't understand. Going to Africa, what did that mean? It was like saying she was going to explore the depths of the Pacific Ocean or go camping at the North Pole.

"Africa?" Royce had said. "Where in the world do you think you're going to go in Africa?"

Where in the world, indeed. So far, all she'd thought about was the trip she and Alan had planned, a dormant memory until last Thursday afternoon when she found her old passport. She'd been looking for her New York Yankees uniform, a surprise to spring on Royce. Baseball season had just started and she thought he might enjoy seeing her in the pin-striped uniform, the black 11 on her back, the gaiters and billed cap. Number 11 fit her perfectly, no alterations except to take in the waist. Nothing delighted Royce like a new costume, and with the taste of summer in the air, Katlyn decided it was time for some new fantasy clothes. Somewhere in her boxes in Royce's garage was the Yankee uniform, bought in a second-hand store years ago for a Halloween party she and Alan attended. Alan used to love watching her wear it around the house. He became passionate when she put it on. At least in the beginning. In the early days of the marriage she believed they were in love, a happily married couple with the future ahead of them.

She leafed through the blank book, staring at the creamy white pages which should have been covered with exotic seals and stamps in various languages and colors. In the same box with the passport were dated slips of paper proving they'd received all their shots, Berlitz books for French, Spanish, and Portuguese. She wondered if Alan had ever visited the Basque country, watched the sun set from the wild Portuguese shore. Strello Mountain was said to have a lake where sunken ships floated to the surface like dead bodies. Alan wanted to see it. The trip was going to revive their marriage. But if Alan went to Spain and Portugal he went with Guerrero.

And now Alan was dead. She would never know what he thought of Portugal, if he ever got there. How had he died? Damn Guerrero. Why was his note so cryptic? He could at least have told them how Alan died.

Now, except for the box in Royce's garage, there was nothing left of Alan but painful memories. The Berlitz books made Katlyn's fingers feel on fire. All those dreams and plans terminated one night by Alan's announcement he was leaving her for Guerrero.

Another of her mother's phrases: Lucky in cards, unlucky in love. Katlyn and Opal were both lucky at cards, at the track, at any kind of gambling that didn't include gambling on a relationship with a man.

Alan's desertion. And now his death. And this house business. What was she going to do with Alan's childhood home? The site of her brief marriage? Somehow that made her angry with Royce. Things she didn't understand. She loved Royce with a feeling as real and intangible as clouds in the sky. A feeling as sure as the way your skin feels the weather. Working with him to finish his house, learning to use his tools, watching him as he expertly handled hundreds of different details from the roof to the floor, she felt a kinship between them. But Royce was never there when she needed him. In that sense he was just like Alan. If only Royce's wife Irene would vanish. She knew it was silly, childish, yet she hoped Irene was as ugly as a cow pie.

Katlyn's eyes lit on the windows of a travel agency covered with posters. And of all the posters, New Zealand, Toronto, Hong Kong, Venice, she found herself staring at a picture of a Masai, ostrich feathers flowering behind his ear, standing on the flat brown plain of East Africa. With his cattle milling in the background, he stood stolidly holding a long pointed horn, which she assumed was used as a trumpet to call to his animals. She thought she could hear the sound the horn would make, like the two-note cry of a foghorn. Africa. She'd read somewhere the Masai lived on blood and milk.

What did she know about Africa? The dusty fossils of Olduvai Gorge. Cool British hotels where every room included a personal laundress. A pride of lions sunning on a rock. Terrorists. Apartheid. The Dark Continent. She looked into the eyes of the Masai, saw nothing. Spaghetti for brains. What did she know about going to Africa?

Katlyn moved away from the Masai staring out of the poster and kept heading for the pool. She felt as if her world were populated with imaginary people, people like the Masai she could see but never know, people like Irene who lived right across the bridge, but whom she'd never meet. People like Alan who just vanished from her life. Warren and Dorre, the closest friends she'd ever had and now they were gone too. That's what getting older must be all about, counting the dead, relating to the imaginary, shuffling through the memories. Yet these phantom people all had their effect on her, driving her toward something she couldn't imagine. Life was too short to do nothing more than imagine it.

Africa. Where in the world do you think you're going to go in Africa?

She thought of her life as a patchwork quilt, garish

shapes and colors butted against each other in random order. Irene's life might look like a seamless piece of silk, but Katlyn's life consisted of assorted leftovers. And she knew better than to tell Royce about her feelings. Royce called this clear sailing and did his best to live with her and love her without involving her in the problems of his marriage. Katlyn took this as a model. She'd never told him about her marriage to Alan, about how he left with Guerrero. How could she now tell him about Alan's death?

Early Friday morning, while she was making breakfast and Royce was packing up so he could drive directly over the bridge after work, she placed the passport next to his coffee. When he asked about it, she said she was thinking of going to Africa.

"Africa? Six months?" Royce looked stunned. "Where in the world do you think you're going in Africa?"

"Up the Nile and down the Congo." The words just popped out. She didn't know she'd even been thinking about Africa. "Or maybe someplace else." As the words rolled off her tongue they sounded like a wonderful idea, a great adventure, a unique experience. Africa, up the Nile and down the Congo. That made the mind jump.

"Did you dream this up in your sleep? Why tell me now when you know I've got a meeting this morning? For Christ's sake, Kat, you've got one hell of a sense of timing. Irene's parents are coming down for Todd's birthday. I can't talk about a trip to Africa just now." He looked as if she'd slapped him for no reason. "What do you want? You want to get yourself killed?"

Later, she realized she'd missed the moment, could have stopped the whole thing with a laugh, a kiss. But instead she said: "That's why I'm telling you now. You'll have the whole weekend to mull it over."

The whole weekend. What kind of relationship did they really have? He was with her every evening, every night, Monday through Thursday. But on Friday he always had to go home, back to Marin and Irene and his kids. Each weekend was like a little death as she waited for his return on Monday night. There was her work, her designs for Charlotte. There was her friend Danny and his movie theater. There was her dog, Dagmar, and long walks in the park. But there was no Royce.

On Friday morning Royce left in a cloud of anger so palpable Katlyn felt the colors in the room change, deepening to reflect his feelings, shadows passing over the furniture. She watched him swing his bag into the back of the Toyota and heard him crank up the radio as loud as a ghetto blaster, rock and roll washing over the quiet neighborhood at seven-thirty in the morning. He drove off as if he were handling a racing Lotus, taking the turn at the corner with a full screech of tires and gears.

We do things we can't explain. Now that she'd announced it as a fact, Africa hung in the air as a real presence. Things we don't understand. She didn't anticipate Royce might take her seriously. All the other options she hadn't thought of that Friday morning swirled through her head as she killed the weekend making shirts for Charlotte. But all weekend long Africa kept popping up. Books by Conrad and Dinesen seemed to leap off the shelves. Zebra. Lion. Giraffe. Alan was dead.

Now all she had to do was get through the day until Royce arrived. Monday, the best day of the week because Royce would be coming home and everything until Friday night would break into light. She hurried through the doors to the locker room, ticking off all the things she could do today to make the hours between now and seven fly. She would swim thirty laps, not her usual twenty. She would clean the house, all the shoes and clothes and scraps and dirty dishes she'd deliberately left lying around each weekend, so Monday would be a busy day while she waited for Royce. As she shucked out of her clothes she decided to tell him the trip to Africa was a joke, a game, a movie. The passport was a prop, not a threat. Maybe she could remember some movie where the heroine threatens to run off to Africa. She should have asked her friend Danny this weekend; he might not know anything about real life but he knew everything about movies. She couldn't think of a single movie where the leading lady threatens to run off to Africa. England, the Continent, even South America. Ingrid Bergman made a couple of films about women in South America. *Notorious*. But never Africa. Women only went to Africa if they happened to be one of Hemingway's wives. It just wasn't something women do.

Getting along in this world is easier with another person by your side. Poor Guerrero. For two years she'd hated that man, but she felt sorry for him now. Now he knew what it felt like to be deserted. How had Alan died? AIDS? A mugging? A subway shooting? Dropped dead of a heart attack, like Earl Lifton up the street?

If she decided to visit Africa it would be without Royce. Without Royce. That thought made her teeth feel as if they were loose in her mouth.

Jody came up to her with a lively smile and a bounce in her step. "So you got through the weekend okay?" She dropped her satchel and stretched, pulling herself up on her toes, her arms a hoop encircling her blonde head, her fingertips touching. Katlyn thought she looked as if she were wearing an immense halo.

Jody, her confidante, soul sister. Jody, who was about Katlyn's age, had a ten-year marriage to Bruce and a fourteen-year-old son and no desire to repeat either experience. But Jody was the kind of woman who could go to Africa. Katlyn could picture the two of them spying on a herd of impala fleeing from a pack of cheetahs.

"Another weekend." Katlyn hooked the strap of her

suit, adjusted the cup to her breast. "Now I'm worried he won't show up tonight."

"He'll show. Curiosity will get the best of him, if nothing else."

"I guess I didn't expect him to believe me." As surprising as a firecracker, her mother used to say. As thoughtful as a forest fire.

"Africa." Jody stepped out of her sneakers. "If I were going to leave Bruce, I'd go to England. Not Africa." She examined her toes, arched her foot as if she were wearing a pair of high heels. "You'll never meet anyone you know."

"I don't know anyone in Africa, that's the point." Katlyn plucked at the elastic in the leg of her suit, snapping it against her skin. "What would you do in England?"

Jody smiled, as if she'd been waiting days for Katlyn to ask. "London. That's where Eric lives now."

Her grin and the light in her eyes made Katlyn smile too. Jody was like that, her moods were common property.

Eric had been Jody's shining star for years. *The* man. A rock musician. After Jody managed to get pregnant she wanted Eric to magically fall in love with her. He didn't, of course.

Jody ran her hands up her calves, the way she would put on stockings. "I mean, that jerk. We lived together in my van for a while, but it never seemed to last with him. I took him to Woodstock, but he left with a girl who'd come up with the Jefferson Airplane. And I loved him anyway. After the kid came, we still kept in touch. Now, for over ten years, I haven't heard a thing. He called this weekend. It's a good thing Bruce wasn't home, my heart was on the ceiling. The same old flutters from fifteen years ago. 'Hi,' he said, 'I'm in town for a convention. I'm a biochemist.' Can you believe it? I mean, he was playing lead guitar last time I saw him. Now they're flying him in from London to Stanford for a convention. I'm going to see him this afternoon."

"After fifteen years?"

Jody smiled. "I told him I was an art dealer. I suppose that's as far from being a pregnant hippie as a biochemist is from a rock star. Anyhow, I'm going to drive down to Stanford this afternoon and listen to him talk about biochemistry and then, with any luck, we'll spend some time in his hotel room."

"You'd go to London on that?" It was as silly as her plan to go to Africa.

"You're the one who's thinking of taking a trip." Jody slipped out of her sweatshirt. "Come on Katlyn. We all got to dream a little."

Katlyn fooled with her straps again. "Now that I've said it, I don't know how to get out of it. Up the Nile and down the Congo. Jesus. Bombs in every airport. Snipers behind every tree. I suppose I could have said I wanted to see the French Revolution."

"Mid-life crisis," Jody said. "More fun than crossword puzzles. You haven't been keeping up with your self-help books. Thirty-five and half your life is over. Mid-life crisis time."

"Nice," Katlyn snapped. "Real nice. I'll just have to see what Royce says this evening." But she was worried, slightly afraid he might not show up.

"You're so disappointing, Katlyn. I mean, it's not like you're married or anything. There are days when I'd leave Bruce in a heartbeat if I had your setup."

"You're always talking about leaving Bruce. But you're no closer to leaving Bruce now than you were two years ago. Eric or no Eric."

Jody cut her eyes to the floor, avoiding Katlyn's look. "Of course I'll never leave Bruce. I love Bruce. But to see our marriage as finite, as if it were the end of something, turns me cold. I need to know I have options."

Katlyn moved to the mirror and began pinning up her long red hair. "Everyone I know sleeps around but me. I'm as loyal as my damn dog. You. Royce. Charlotte. I love the irony of all this. Everyone I know who's happily married is out there happily having affairs." Except Guerrero. Should she write him a condolence card? What would she say? I'm sorry my husband died on you.

"What's your bitch? You're having an affair, one of the better ones I've seen. Don't feel left out."

"Yeah, but it won't last forever."

"So go to Africa, then. Honestly, Katlyn. You and Royce get along beautifully. If you don't think that's enough, go to fucking Africa. That ought to be exciting."

Katlyn removed her earrings and studied the shell of her ear as if the whorls of soft bone and cartilage presented a pattern which would offer a clue. As a child, she'd wanted to believe she was Howdy Doody's sister. She thought they looked alike, big ears framing their freckled faces. Buffalo Bob had been her hero, and she would spend long hours at the window imagining she was sitting on his lap, listening to the secrets he would whisper in her ear. Opal called her Kathy the Catatonic when she dreamed like that, and Katlyn thought a catatonic was a type of lion. Charlotte said she had spaghetti for brains. "Charlotte says that a trip won't solve anything."

"Charlotte might be right. So you and Royce break up, which I think would be sad. But I really don't see what Africa has to do with it either. You're not taking your life seriously. Don't forget, you're thirty-five. Work with what you've got."

If this were a poll, the results were, so far, unanimous. "As the old song says: 'I got plenty of nothing.' "

"Bullshit. The stuff you make for Charlotte is terrific. I mean, my God, you're selling in New York. Why don't you look at yourself as a real designer, instead of Royce's mistress or whatever. Go to Paris and see what real designers are doing."

"Nobody takes California seriously." Katlyn snorted. "A California designer has to do swimsuits and tennis togs."

"Then enjoy what you've got." Jody stepped out of her jeans. "Lower your expectations. They never leave their wives."

"If I lowered my expectations I'd vanish, disappear. Poof! I always set my standards too low. Even in high school, did I care I didn't get asked to the prom? Nooooo. Since I was taller than any boy who wasn't on the basketball team I didn't *expect* to be asked to the prom. And I wasn't."

"This isn't high school, Katlyn." Jody dropped to the floor, looped her arms over her head and pulled on her toes. Jody liked exercise the way dancers like music. "That's all too long ago to think about. Of course, it would be easier to talk you out of all this stupid stuff if I weren't going to see Eric this afternoon. All the junk you're telling me is just the past. You live with that. I mean, Bruce is the past, but I think of him as the present. Eric is the past for sure, but right now I'm thinking of him in the future. Maybe what you're really trying to do is to get Royce to be the past, the present, and the future. I must admit, there ain't much future in a situation like you and Royce have."

"He likes it this way," Katlyn said. "He's all set up, he's got his life worked out the way he wants it. Every weekend in Marin, two Thanksgivings, Christmases, Easters, and one Fourth of July in Marin. And if I need him for something, forget it." How could she suddenly tell Royce about Alan? *By the way, I have a husband who just died.* Christ. What a mess.

"That's so petty, Katlyn. Christmas is for kids. Thanksgiving is for fat. You can't hold that against Royce."

"I feel my life is drifting away from me, like when wine turns to vinegar. You can't get back to vintage burgundy. But Africa, Jesus. Why didn't I pick something easy. I mean, the choice of Africa itself was pretty random. I could have said Antarctica as easily."

"Or Paris." Jody crossed her legs, sailor-style. "So what's easy these days?" She twisted from the waist to loosen her back. "It doesn't matter, though. You take your problems with you. Africa, Sausalito." Jody grinned. "Stanford." She ran her fingers along the crotch of her suit. "Let's go. I want these thighs to glow this afternoon."

"You'll never leave Bruce," Katlyn said as they headed out of the locker room.

"And you'll never go to Africa."

"I'll have to do something if Royce leaves me."

"You forget." Jody tucked her hair up into her cap. "You're the one who's threatening to leave him." She arched on her toes and cut the water with a clean racer's dive.

Katlyn followed her into the water, determined to do thirty laps. Thirty laps would leave her too worn out to worry about whether Royce would leave her, or rather, she would leave him. The distinction in her mind was as subtle as the shading between violet and purple. Slicing through the water, she felt the power in her arms and the strength in her legs. Two years stroking up and down these lanes. Two years as a part-time woman with Royce. No progress on both scores. Alan was dead and she now owned their old house, complete with Japanese dentist and family as tenants. It was all as surprising as if Katlyn had grown wings. With wings, she would certainly have to learn to fly.

What if he didn't come home tonight? He hadn't called all weekend. But as she stroked up and down the lane, Katlyn didn't care about a phone call. She never liked talking to Royce when he was in Marin, always haunted by the fact Irene might be listening on one of the extensions in a remote corner of the house. Maybe Irene had the phones tapped, would take pleasure later in the week listening to her husband say sweet nothings to his lover across the bay. Katlyn wondered if Irene was the type of woman who preferred masturbation.

What if he let her go? What if he let her go? What if he let her go? Swimming beat each thought into the same pattern as the last, the thoughts changing only with the turn at the end of the lane. Thoughts became hypnotic, her mind unable to break their power unless she broke her stroke. Once, right after the film *Jaws* came out, Katlyn had been swimming when she heard that theme, the *DaDaDaDa DaDaDaDa DaDaDaDa* built in her head the way the music punctuated the movie as the giant shark attacked. All she could hear in the chlorine pool was the deep water theme of the movie. Without thinking, Katlyn jumped out of the pool, her legs drawn up to her chin, huddling on the tile walkway. She knew it was silly. She laughed at herself. Yet, her mind's eye kept seeing the girl swirling around in the midnight water, the hand with the ring reaching up.

She tucked for the turn at the end of the lane, determined to think of something else. Forget sex. Forget sex. Forget sex. Nine strokes down the lane she had to abandon that mantra. She could see his eyes warm and bright, the way his 501s hugged his ass like the foil on a Hershey's Chocolate Kiss. The water rushing over her body felt just like his hands. Even the pull of the water through her fingers felt like his thick salt-and-pepper hair. They were all aging, all going to die. Two years ago Royce's hair had been blue-black like a gun barrel. Now his hair reminded her of a raven in a snowstorm. Her heart turned over like an empty cup. The hollow of her pelvis filled as if butter were melting over her bones.

She pulled up to the end of the lane to wash the fog from her goggles. Okay, so what if he let her go? All weekend the idea of going to Africa had been building as if it weren't an impossible thing after all. She could bypass the countries at war. She didn't have to think about *all* of Africa. If she just kept the image of Victoria Falls as solid in her mind as any smaller desire, the whole trip became possible. Just Victoria Falls, everyone's image of the power and majesty of the Dark Continent. Four hundred feet of falling water plummeting over a crack in the surface of the earth, dropping into the narrow gorge. Eternal clouds of mist.

Danny just returned from a trip to Japan, and he'd known no more about Japan than she knew about Africa. His goal had been to see snow on the Japanese mountains, and by maintaining that desire, Japanese snow, he'd gone there and come back with all of the islands of Japan alive in his mind. He now knew temples and the Bullet Train and Japanese Disneyland. He'd visited the locations of all his favorite films. *Woman in the Dunes*. *Ran*. All because he wanted to see snow in the mountains. If Danny could go to Japan, why couldn't she go to Africa? Perhaps even Alan had been to Portugal before he died.

There was something so completely artificial about her life; perhaps only a trip to Africa would help her understand it. The things a death makes you think about. Death reminds you of the quality of your life. A trip to Africa would be different from this endless drifting. She could see the animals, meet the people, look out over primitive landscapes that must certainly be different from pictures in books. Smell something more solid than smog. Her life up to this point could be reviewed in ten minutes, reduced to two words: work and men. She would always have to work, but the men would come and go. Royce's marriage insured the fact that he would some day leave her, like Alan. Certainly, a trip across Africa would be more rewarding than making shirts for Charlotte. She could call it research, study the colorful African patterns, ornaments of shell and bone, work with hides and feathers. So what was left? As she looked at the other women doing laps up and down the lanes she felt an outcast, a nomad, a refugee from the other parts of her life. Perhaps she would feel at home sipping a drink in the Café American, Rick's bar in *Casablanca,* the watering hole for misfits.

The mistress never keeps the prize. Life isn't a dress rehearsal. It goes by every day. Did Alan drop dead, like Earl Lifton? Did he die in his sleep? Or did he have time to think over his life, to list the things undone?

What had she been thinking about for the last two years? Did she expect to go on living only in Royce's spare time? Had she ever really expected him to leave his wife and children?

There was nothing to do but to call his bluff. At least pose the question. She was treading water on a Monday morning. How many laps had she done in this pool? How many shirts and dresses had she designed for Charlotte? How many books had she read, films had she seen? How many bags of groceries had she bought and consumed? How many hours waiting for Royce so she could get on with the good stuff in life? That surely couldn't be the sum of everything. It added up to so little. But if that was the sum, she was still young enough to change it. She would go to Africa. Jody and Charlotte be damned. Let Royce figure out his own life. A woman has to have plans.

It felt tangibly different, a familiar and bitter taste, as if she had soap in her mouth. So far she'd run her life with as much purpose as a drifter wandering through a strange town. She'd depended on others for the directions she'd chosen. Opal. Alan. Charlotte. Royce. But it didn't take many ideas to turn the world around on a Monday morning, if the idea was as big as Africa.

MONDAY
<u>AFTERNOON</u>

Royce Chambers came back from lunch and told his secretary, Donna Moon, to cancel his appointments for the afternoon. "Let's see," he said, "cancel the rest of the week too."

Donna Moon continued typing, the tap of her nails on the keys as consistent as the hum of insects. "The accountant's coming at four."

Outside, Royce had felt the first warmth of summer, a sailor's knowledge the rains were over. He could smell it in the air. "Some other time," he said. "Next week."

"You have Pacific Trust tomorrow."

Below his window, Royce watched eddies of yellows and reds, colors he seemed to have forgotten during the rainy months of winter. No fog hung over any part of the city today. The quiet south of Market Street seemed filled with people on their way to a picnic or parade. Royce felt as irresponsible as a teenager. "Norton can handle them. I need some time off. You won't be able to reach me." Royce never liked the look Donna Moon gave him when he said that. It was a euphemism between them that meant he would be at the house in Noe Valley, rather than at home in Marin County. He kept his back to her, staring out the window.

"What if Mrs. Chambers calls, or wants you?"

Donna Moon didn't care for Irene, who lived in the house in Sausalito, or Kat, who lived in his house off Twenty-fourth Street. Kat said Donna Moon watched too much *Perry Mason* and saw herself as the ever-patient Della Street. "Tell her I've stepped out for baked alaska." He turned and smiled at Donna Moon, hoping to disarm her. Donna Moon's expression was as empty as an un-printed page. "You take the day off too. Look out there. It's a gorgeous day. Cancel the accountant and go have some fun, enjoy yourself."

"I'll handle the accountant. Some one has to run this printing plant." Her eyes were distant and cold, dead stars. Her shining black hair sat on her head like a cap, and for a moment, Royce felt he was looking at a Japa-nese doll sitting perfectly still behind the typewriter. Royce couldn't imagine Donna Moon in love with anything more substantial than a houseplant.

He looked out the window again at the mare's tails racing overhead, wisps of clouds as delicate as painting on Easter eggs. "Whatever." He picked up his briefcase and flight bag and headed for the door. Maybe he would send her flowers tomorrow, let her know he appreciated her work.

As he unlocked the Toyota and threw his bags in the back, Royce felt some of the confusion returning. I have a perfect life, he told himself, so why the hell does it make me so damn miserable? Are these perfectly ordinary problems that just happen to come along with a perfect life? He doubted that. All he knew for sure was that he would feel better once he saw Kat. He would spend a few days with her, his lovely, long-legged, redheaded Katlyn. He'd borrow Frank's boat and they would go sailing. They would spend every morning in bed. They would eat nothing but seafood and drink champagne. Kat would love that. And if she didn't come around then, then he didn't know what he would do.

The one-story house on Elizabeth Street was an investment property, and when Royce bought it, he had hoped he might be able to convince Irene to move to the city some day. He saw no reason why Irene couldn't be as content in the city as she was in Sausalito. But Irene refused to take any interest in the project. Arguing with Irene was like persuading a small child. Lately, since Lindy and Todd were both taller than she, Royce began to think of her as a small child, especially when her voice took on a petulant whine. Her house in Sausalito, her view of the bay, her rock garden out back, her children in school, her club. Irene was determined to stay on the other side of the Golden Gate Bridge. She came to the city for special occasions, nothing like Royce's daily commute. Royce began working on the small Victorian and found there were evenings when he was too tired to drive back across the bridge to Sausalito, only to drive over the bridge again the next morning. He grew to love the little Victorian and took great pleasure in the physical work of restoring it. The house reminded him of a time when the world felt less abstract, when he believed he could feel the pulse of things just beneath his skin.

Royce took pride in a good hinge, a door well hung which closed quietly and didn't bump in the wind. He sanded, painted, caulked window sashes. He took the floors down to the original hardwood, amazed at people who would cover that lovely, even grain with linoleum. He puttied nicks and cracks in the moldings, restoring the house with the same pride and care as a jeweler setting a precious stone. He kept telling Irene he was getting the house ready to rent, but began to think of the Victorian as his bachelor digs. He liked the cozy, close feeling the warren of rooms gave him, a more intimate feeling than the sprawling ranch-style in Sausalito, Irene's domain. He found himself spending weekends working on the house, installing a new shower, planting shrubs in the back. Once he asked Irene to come over and plant flowers, but she was busy and never got around to buying the seed.

Then just about the time when he knew the house could be rented, he met Katlyn. Royce counted himself a lucky man. As he drove through San Francisco this Monday afternoon a pulse throbbed at his temple. He felt his breath come in short, quick puffs. Kat going to Africa. What in the world would a woman like Kat do in Africa? What would he do if she left him?

He let himself in the front door and called to her, but there was no answer. He looked in the back for the dog, and decided Kat had taken Dagmar for a walk. It felt odd to be in the house without Kat. He toured the rooms one by one, noting how different they looked. The bed was unmade. There was no food in the refrigerator, save smeary jars of mayonnaise and mustard and a couple of hard crusts of cheese. There were paper plates tossed on the counter and an open box of Kentucky Fried Chicken that looked like congealed wood shavings. Her clothes were littered from one end of the house to the other, as if she'd scattered them across the rooms. He found an espadrille in the dining room, and its mate in the pantry. Her bathing suit with the purple triangles lay in the kitchen sink like some awful piece of modern art arranged for incongruous effect. A leather cowboy belt hung from the light in the bathroom. There was a container of yogurt in the shower. For one moment Royce worried a thief had broken in, murdered Kat and the dog, and copped the stereo. But the stereo, TV, all hockable goods, remained in the same niches as on Friday. Why would Kat eat yogurt in the shower?

There's nothing to worry about, he told himself. She's out shopping, or down at Charlotte's store. Up the Nile and down the Congo. The house felt empty without her and made Royce lonely deep in his bones, as if she'd already left him. Africa. Maybe he'd take her down to Union Street and buy her that flapper dress, a new costume for their collection.

What would he do if she left him?

The little things came to mind first. The feel of her leg over his as he was dropping off to sleep at night. Most nights she read: current novels, a history of Russia, a book on penguins, poetry. Often the last sound he would hear would be the flick of a page turning or the squeak of her cigarette as she stubbed it out in the ceramic ashtray. These sounds, and the feel of her leg over his, reminded him of how much he hated sleeping alone.

He unpacked his flight bag and wished he'd decided to take this week off before he'd packed back in Sausalito. Nothing but business suits and shirts, as if he were going to work all week and would only see Kat in the evenings, as usual. He wondered if she always kept her bathing suit in the kitchen sink, where she'd gone in the espadrilles and cowboy belt.

In the closet he paused to finger their costumes, the rich velvets, smooth cottons, soft wools. They'd even found a real raccoon coat, which they took turns wearing. His favorite was the World War I fighting ace, complete with goggles and helmet, white silk scarf, bulky leather jacket. When he wore the false mustache Kat told him he looked like Errol Flynn. What would happen to their fantasy clothes if she left him? If he brought the fighting ace outfit home, Irene would laugh at him.

He took off all his clothes and lay back on the unmade bed, staring at the pure white of the ceiling. He couldn't see the answers to any of his problems in the smooth strokes he'd applied to this ceiling three years ago. His lover wanted to go to Africa. His wife refused to divorce him. Between these two women he felt as powerless as a child.

An old feeling seized him, one he hadn't experienced in sixteen years. He got up and stripped the sheets. That panicky feeling when he knew Irene was out on a date with another guy, wondering where they were, what they might be doing. Christ, jealousy. He thought he'd outgrown jealousy when he married Irene. Jealousy was an adolescent feeling which should be left behind when a man is old enough to vote. But here it was again, as fresh and sharp as a razor cut.

Navy blue sheets this time. He loved her hair against the navy blue sheets. Maybe he should put on the fighting ace outfit. But the more he thought about it, the more he worried it might be like expecting a tree to grow after it had been reduced to sawdust. If she'd made a decision a costume wouldn't change her mind.

He heard her key in the door and the click of the dog's nails down the front hall. The Toyota was in the garage, so she had no idea he was here. He wished he smoked or whittled, something to do with his hands. Kat's hands were always in motion, as if she were sculpting the moments of the day from the air in front of her. A man always looked slightly silly alone in a room doing nothing. He'd stay on the bed until she found him. Afternoon delights. She wasn't the only one to engineer a surprise.

The dog gave it away. Dagmar came straight into the bedroom, barking like an animal three times her size. She always reminded Royce of a dwarf Old Yeller. "Hey Dagmar," he said, and she came over to lick his outstretched hand.

Years ago Irene had spent five hundred dollars on a silly Afghan the kids named Wichita, a troublesome animal, but the kids liked her. He couldn't justify spending that kind of money on a dog—a mutt like Dagmar, a good old dog, was more his style. Afghans were pretentious, the dog even had her own goddamned hairdresser. Wichita was more expensive to maintain than his Toyota. Lately he thought about getting a bird or cat, but couldn't decide where to keep it. A third dog, to travel over the bridge with him, seemed excessive.

"What is it Dagmar? Have you caught a pigeon?" Katlyn stood in the doorway, a bag of groceries in her arms. "Oh, it's you. What are you doing here? It's only three-thirty." She seemed annoyed.

"You don't have a corner on surprises. I've taken the rest of the week off. Where've you been?" He didn't like the look in her eye.

Kat turned and went back into the kitchen. "Did I tell you about a month ago, just about when the rains stopped, we came home one day and Dagmar did the same thing? I had the windows open and a bird had flown in. A pigeon. It panicked and couldn't get out. Dagmar and I spent all afternoon trying to shoo it out without scaring it to death. You should see their little hearts go when they're frightened."

"Where were you?" He knew how possessive he sounded. He could hear the clink of bottles and cans as she put away the groceries. Reaching into the closet, he picked out the raccoon coat and slipped into it like a bathrobe. He needed the extra warmth.

"Now you know my worst secret, the one I've been trying to hide from you all this time."

Royce leaned against the doorjamb, watching her swiftly empty the brown paper bag. "What's that?"

She threw her hands in an all-encompassing gesture. "Can't you see? I'm a slob. I knew I was cutting it close this afternoon, but I never thought you'd be here at three-thirty. You've never done that before, you know." She pointed her finger at him, a cocked gun, and tripped her thumb like a firing pin.

"You haven't even kissed me hello." His heart dropped, not the high and happy feeling he usually felt when he saw her, rather, the same kind of feeling he would have if he walked under a ladder, cautious. "You could have kissed me. You could have hopped in bed. But you run into the kitchen to pitch out your paper plates."

"What can I say? It won't take long." She bustled the yogurt cups, Kentucky Fried Chicken box, a milk carton, all in the trashmasher and flipped the switch. "As you can see, the food's in the refrigerator." She swung the door open to prove her point, bottles and jars and packages displayed on the shelves.

While the trashmasher screeched like the air brakes of a train, she rushed into the living room, sweeping clothes and shoes into her arms. "These go in the dirty clothes."

"Your shoes?"

"If I need them I'll remember where they are. You don't like these shoes anyhow. You said so."

"I only said you shouldn't wear them in the rain. Open like that. What about your bathing suit?" He held the damp skimpy suit by the strap, dangling it in the air. "Let's see. Did you go to the beach? Or do you have a job swamping out the Aquarium?"

She snatched it from his hand and moved on to the bathroom. "I swim. Every day from ten to eleven." She reached for the belt on the light fixture. With one motion she dumped all these items into the clothes hamper. She slammed the lid.

In the bedroom she looked at the navy blue sheets. "Ah, the blue sheets." She fell back on the bed with a sigh.

Royce rubbed his palm across his chest. She was so lovely. The pale gold of her dress fanned out over her legs. Her arms, reaching above her head, stretched the silk across her breasts. Her red hair fell in a halo on the pillow, the color of the sunset. Her hazel eyes, one blue, one gray, like an arctic dog. Africa. Why would she want to go to Africa?

He sat on the edge of the bed absently stroking her leg. She smelled like lemons today, as clean as a cut in new glass. He could feel her watching him, thinking about him. At night, when he couldn't sleep, he would draw her into his arms and place his palm over her heart to feel its slow, clocking rhythm. Sometimes she moved her back into the pit of his stomach, and Royce always believed this was a sign from deep in her sleep that she was happy to be wrapped in his arms in the loneliness of night. He could always fall asleep then, his own heart slowing to her rhythm. She was so unlike Irene, who quit sleeping with him after Todd was conceived. It was uncomfortable for her, bad for the baby, she said. And then they moved to Sausalito, a four-bedroom affair where they each slept in their own rooms.

"I thought you wanted me to join you in bed," Kat murmured. Her hand roamed up and down his spine. She drew her long legs around his waist and wrapped them over his thighs. In the delicate arch of her foot a small bruise shone like a sapphire.

She settled against his back, her hands stroking his chest. "So here I am in bed," she said, "and you've sort of disappeared."

"That seems a long time ago," Royce said. "Before I knew you went swimming every day and thought of yourself as a slob."

"You can't hold that against me. I'm very careful to never be a slob when you're here. It would have been all cleaned up by this evening."

"You don't have to clean up for me."

"You've never done this before, you know." Her tone carried more of an edge to it now, not the soft crooning of a moment ago. "Come in without calling. Did you expect to find me with another man?" She kissed him behind his ear.

"I thought about it." There were other men, he was sure of it. She insisted that his marriage gave her the right to see other men. He never dared think who these men might be, but he knew she lived a life more complicated than the fact she ate take-out food and went swimming when he wasn't around. Royce realized he'd trespassed, violated their agreement. It never crossed his mind to call her when he decided to take off today, any more than he would think to call Irene if he were to come home early. He couldn't remember now what he thought she would be doing at three-thirty on a Monday afternoon. Away from her, she remained suspended in his mind, a favorite image held like a photograph. Last week, while lazing in the bathtub, she wore the Prussian officer's helmet with those blue feathers. All weekend he could see her, her red hair flowing from beneath the silver skullcap. Eating Irene's dry roast beef, he saw Kat with those bobbing feathers as she strutted naked through the house. Helping Lindy with her geometry, he saw Kat posed in the bathtub, bubbles foamy as shaving cream all around her, the froth reflecting the silver and blue of the helmet. Shooting baskets with Todd, he remembered Kat tickling his nose with the feathers. Lindy and Todd. At one time they had been the whole world to him, the delights and surprises of their childhood more real to him now than the teenagers they'd grown into. "I guess I thought you'd be wearing the helmet," he said.

"If you want the helmet, you'll get the helmet." She withdrew herself from around him and opened the door to the marble washstand. Inside, where china pitchers and basins had once been kept, sat the silver and blue helmet. She settled it on her hair and kicked off her sandals. "Want to play dress-up?"

He looked at her sadly. The helmet now appeared ridiculous, not spontaneous and natural the way she'd been on Thursday night. "We have to have a talk, Katlyn. About this Africa thing." The silly helmet set off her hair so nicely. When they found it at the flea market he never thought she could make it shine so.

"But I don't want to talk about that right now." She flicked nervously at something invisible on her dress. "After all, we've got the whole afternoon. Did you tell me you've taken some time off? Tomorrow? We could have some fun, do something special." She looked him over, but he felt a wall rising between them.

"I'm taking time off because I think we need to do some serious talking. Not to play games. To work something out."

"Don't you want to have some fun?" She unbuttoned the front of the gold dress. "We never get an afternoon like this. Let's have some fun and worry about Africa later. A nooner, isn't that what they call it?" She ran her finger down the bridge of his nose. "Would you like to do that? A nooner?"

"Where'd you ever hear a term like that? A nooner. You sound like you hang around peep shows. Like you're hustling on a street corner." He grabbed her hand and pulled her down on his lap. He removed the helmet, watching her hair float about her face, and placed the silver helmet on the bed.

"That's unlucky." She moved the helmet to the floor at their feet. "At least hats on a bed are unlucky. I don't know about helmets, but I'm superstitious. It's best to play it safe."

"I'm playing it safe. I want this straightened out. Christ, Kat." He linked his arms around her waist. "We'll go sailing, talk this thing through. We'll eat and drink and screw each other until we're higher than the birds fly. You just can't tell me you're going off to Africa and expect me to wait for postcards."

"Okay, Africa's out." But her eyes lied.

He took her chin in his hands and turned her face so they were staring eye to eye, their noses almost touching. He could feel her heart quicken. "You don't dump news like that on someone and expect them not to want to talk about it. Besides, this isn't some new game you're running here. I know you. If I ignored that passport you'd want to talk about nothing but Africa."

She pulled away from him. "You know, I might have something else planned for this week. I wish you'd told me first."

"What else are you going to do?"

"I have to work, even if you don't."

"I won't interfere with that." He could picture himself on the couch, catching up on his reading while her sewing machine hummed in the other room. He'd run errands for her, walk the dog.

"Still, you can't just waltz in here for a week. That's not fair. How would you like it if I unexpectedly camped with you and Irene for the weekend?"

"That's not the point. You said you were going to Africa because you didn't see enough of me. So now you're going to have all the company you complained of

54

not having last week. Remember that? That was the reason you were going to Africa, because you were sick of sitting around here waiting for me to squeeze you in between business and Irene."

"I'm not sure I said I was 'sick' of this."

"You implied it."

"What do you want?" There was anger in her eyes. "Want to spend the afternoon having a fight? I thought that was an activity reserved strictly for you and Irene." She pulled herself from his lap and stood across the room, her hands planted on her hips.

"Damn it, Kat. I just want to know what you meant about Africa. You tell me that and this whole thing will stop." He moved toward her, a threatening stance. And knew she was right. His first move in every fight with Irene was to crowd her, get in close and back her into a corner. Here he was doing it with Katlyn. He felt as if he'd kicked the dog, sheer meanness against something innocent.

He returned to the bed. He ran his hands through his hair. How could he say his life was perfect, only he was a wreck? She had every right to go to Africa, or any other damn place. He couldn't stop her. Having a fight wouldn't help. They'd never really fought before, not like he did with Irene. He loomed over Irene, as if his height and weight would intimidate her. But with Kat, they stood eye to eye. And Kat never treated him the way Irene did. No pouts or sulks, no threats to call Daddy. He would handle it differently this time, no stock responses. As long as she didn't play games with this one.

Her voice was soothing, placating. "The point of my bitch last Friday was to spend time with you. I'm lonely. Isn't that a scream? I practically live with you and I'm lonely. I feel my life rushing right past me and all I'm doing is waiting for you and making fashion toys. You call that real life?'' She tossed her hair away from her face. ''Maybe we could take a trip. See something of the world. Together. If you're going to stay with me this week, I won't talk about Africa. Okay?''

''Not good enough. That was some fine piece of theater you threw at me Friday morning. You couldn't have timed it better. You didn't bring this up once during the week. You wait until there's no time to talk about it, then say you're going to Africa, passport and all. And now you want to promise not to talk about Africa. Jesus, Kat. Africa. There's a lot of things you won't talk about, Katlyn. It's not the same as not going to Africa.'' Royce ran his hands through his hair again. He hated that habit, a nervous tic. He was sure he would go bald because of it.

She leaned forward and cupped his face in her palms. The unbuttoned silk dress fell open revealing her breasts, close enough to kiss. ''You could come to Africa with me.''

''What the hell would I do in Africa?''

''See the sights. Visit the ruins. We'll get you a bush hat and you can stalk wild game.''

''We can get a bush hat and play wild games right here in the bedroom. We can take the boat out and pretend I'm Mr. Allnutt and you're Rose and we're trying to blow up the Germans. We're sailing down the Ulanga in *The African Queen*. I'm all for that. We can play that one all week if you want. But last Friday I didn't get the feeling we were playing games. You scared me, Kat. I was afraid you might really be serious for a change.''

''Sometimes I am serious, Royce.''

''What about the passport?'' He needed her to reassure him nothing had changed. But for two years now, he'd known there would be a day like this, trips to Africa, or another man, or she might just not be here some Monday night. This trip to Africa could be a game like all the others. He loved the way she became a different woman, stepping into someone else's myth or personality like changing clothes. Kat was Marilyn Monroe, Jean Harlow, Rita Hayworth. Sometimes they kept a personality several days running. Kat as Scarlett O'Hara to his Rhett Butler. He'd never had such fun in his life as he did with Kat, but all that talent, all that imagination, wouldn't always be content with him as the only audience. Perhaps she should have been an actress. But for two years she'd played her parts to him. She was his Kat. His Katlyn.

"Props," she said. "Just props."

He tried to see behind her eyes, beneath her smile, into the secret corners of her heart. Her face was alive with secrets. "I'm afraid you're going to leave me," he said.

"An exercise in turning the tables. You leave me every weekend. You leave me every day. I thought you might like to see how it feels."

He pulled her onto the bed. He kissed her, hoping to convey all the feeling he'd kept bottled up all weekend. He pulled her tongue into his mouth, his hands fondling her breasts. He could feel her heart beating beneath his chest, fluttering harder, quicker, faster than his own. "I don't know what I'd do if you left me." He bit her lip with more force than tenderness. "I don't know what I'd do." He placed his hand beneath her dress, searching for her panties.

She thrust her hips up just far enough so he could slide the panties down her legs. She wiggled around until she worked free of the underwear, then squeezed her knees against his hips. "Would you divorce Irene?"

That was it, what he'd come to hear her say. His erection wilted, power and energy draining out of him like blood from a wound. Her hand slipped between his legs and cradled his balls, holding him tightly, but he couldn't maintain the erection. He rolled off her and away to the other side of the bed. She raised her hand to her mouth and licked each finger salaciously, concentrating as she drew her fingertips across her lips.

"That's what you want, then," he said. "You want to get married?"

"No." She looked at him openly, honestly. "I don't want to get married. I want us to live together. Marriage is a decision about the future and involves all kinds of rules and responsibilities which try to keep the future in line. Living together, every day is a decision, a choice. We aren't tied to each other. People stay together as long as they both feel it's worthwhile." She flipped over on her stomach, her elbows propped and her chin resting in her palms. "I love you. I feel too close to you to watch you walk out of here every weekend and go home to Irene. I feel as if you shit in my heart when you do that. It feels like my life has stopped. I don't think we have many choices, Royce. If you can't leave Irene, and I can't stand to watch you walk out of here every Friday, well, Africa seemed like something to do. You want to work this out. We've got a week together, right? You decide how you feel by the end of the week. If there's no question of divorcing Irene, it's time for me to get on with my life."

He closed his eyes and felt the pounding of blood behind his temples. If only he could divorce Irene.

"You're the one who kicked over work to talk this through," she said softly. "So we have until Friday. Because, you see, you always have to go home on Friday."

"And that's another thing," he snapped. "How were you planning on financing this little jaunt?" A headache was building, just the same as when he fought with Irene. There was the sound of water trapped in his ear, a little murmur inside his skull like a radio signal, a message he couldn't understand.

"If I go it will have nothing to do with you. It won't be any of your business."

"Another man?" His head felt as if a ball bearing were being driven deep into his skull, riveted there, directly between his eyes. He wouldn't be surprised if the pain blinded him.

"It won't be any of your business. Unless you come with me."

Royce pushed his fingertips deep into the tender sockets, hoping to dislodge the pain. He thought he could feel it, physically roll it around between his eyes in the space above his nose. It welled up into the dome of his skull. The pain expanded, penetrating his sinuses and washing across his forehead. He could smell the pain, or his fear, an odor as quick and sharp as the waft of paint thinner. "You don't know what you're asking."

She placed her hand on his shoulder. "Are you all right?"

"Would you get me an aspirin? Maybe something I ate at lunch."

She flounced off the bed and into the bathroom. "Don't try and make me feel sorry for you. Something you ate for lunch. Ha! You're acting as if I want you to change stones into gold. Life is too short to spend all of it waiting. All the things you've said to me, how much you hate being married to Irene. I'm better off on my own than this half-assed relationship." She handed him a glass of water and an aspirin tablet. "In two years something has to change. You didn't expect this to last forever, did you?"

"Yes!" The word made his head ring. "And I thought you did too," he added more quietly. "Remember how you hate it when they stick New and Improved on something you already like to begin with? You like your oatmeal the way you've always liked your oatmeal. New and Improved doesn't make it better."

"I'm not sure I like being compared to oatmeal."

"Okay. Okay." He lay back on the bed. The pain seemed to roll around the corner of his eye, right in line to come spilling out his ear, if only there was such a channel. "Okay. Think of pearls. Sometimes I see my life like that."

"Pearls?"

"Yeah. Pearls." There must be a way to convince her of his feelings, something he could say which would stop this nonsense and put their life back in order. His life. "A baby oyster, or oyster seed I suppose, is free to swim the oceans. But at some point it settles to the ocean floor and builds a shell around itself. It stays there for the rest of its life. If a grain of sand gets into that oyster, the oyster worries at it until a pearl grows around it. Whether an oyster makes a pearl or not is chance. In any case, when the oyster stops swimming, it settles down in one spot. It's even there after the oyster itself dies, the shell lying on the ocean floor."

The look in her eyes told him pearls weren't the answer.

"Perhaps my life won't produce a pearl," she said, "but then, I don't like the idea of lying down on the floor until I die. I'd rather keep swimming."

He could see her as she swam away from the boat when they were in Baja at New Year's, the graceful arcs of her arms as they dipped through the water. "Kat, you are my pearl. But you can't ask me to up and change my life like this." His heart had fallen into the hollow of his stomach. He could feel it disintegrating, being devoured. "Some things aren't changeable. Every year has a winter."

She knelt on the bed next to him and placed her hands on his forehead. Her fingers began massaging his temples. "Every year also has a spring. Things change in the spring."

He let her fingers work their magic. In a few minutes he would still have the pain but wouldn't be able to feel it, the magic of aspirin giving the illusion of painlessness. He wished there were aspirins for the spirit. "Africa," he said again.

Her voice floated somewhere above him as he felt her fingers working across his brow. "It's two years. Nothing stays the same for two years. Not oysters. Not cereals."

"Oh, but Kat. You just don't understand."

"No Royce. You might be able to go on like this forever. You want to live your life in a shell, go right ahead. Me, I can't. We could drop dead any time. Or be hit by a bus. I'm getting desperate to do something besides waiting."

With Kat he found a part of himself he'd never been able to use before. Feelings he'd never acted on were open to him. Working on the house, eating, sleeping, all the ordinary business of life with Kat made him feel he had a place in the world, a feeling he never entertained with Irene. Divorce Irene. Africa. Waiting. Desperate. His bones ached with fear, and he realized his teeth were clenched together so that the muscles in his cheeks and neck were taut as wires. Fear. Loss.

She was asking him to surrender to his sweetest dream. All he had to do would be to go home and tell Irene. Just have the courage to tell Irene. Because within minutes, just the way she did when he first confessed this affair to her, Irene would have images of court struggles, litigation, bankruptcy, hanging in the air between them. Irene accepted his affair. She actually preferred it to their married life. But she wouldn't grant a divorce. She'd cut everything out from under him. All of it. Her father would withdraw his money from the printing business. How much of the world would be left? There would be no place to stand, nothing to do.

Maybe they could take off like Frank, go to Amsterdam or Paris. But even taking off would mean money, and Irene would make certain he wouldn't be able to get his hands on any of that.

Kat's fingers were music, a soft and steady orchestration of his thoughts. He could see them sailing under the Golden Gate Bridge, following the line of the coast south-southwest until the land gradually disappeared and there was nothing but the vastness of the ocean all around them and the coziness of the cabin where they would eat and sleep. He could see the sun sparkling in the red tones of her hair, her pale, freckly skin deepening to a golden tan. They should be on the boat. They would just keep sailing, knot after knot slipping beneath the prow of the *Singing Stars*. Looking into the sun day after day would give her face deep wrinkles and monkey rings where her sunglasses would shade her eyes. Her face would lose the airbrushed gloss of makeup and become weathered. Royce liked that image. He often thought she looked best when asleep, no makeup whatsoever.

Maybe they should just steal the boat. Kat would do it. On the yacht in Baja she slipped over the side into the blue ocean and swam out to touch the back of a whale. Royce watched the huge eye peel open and roll back to try to catch a glimpse of the splashing figure of Kat, stroking through the water toward its basking form. She touched the whale, swam the length of it and passed it, heading west, when the whale gave a great slap of its flukes and sounded. Suddenly she looked very alone and vulnerable with the immensity of the sea all around and the gulls wheeling overhead. When she returned to the boat she was disappointed in him. "How could you just watch?" she had asked. "It's not every day you get to touch a whale." The little dots of her mascara running down her cheeks looked like clown's tears.

He would like to take her to Baja again, take her around the world if that's what she wanted. He knew it was possible, but the preparations and obstacles were impossible. Everything hinged on Irene. No one got away with leaving a wife and kids. Only Frank managed it. Frank left his job, wife, kid, house, the *Singing Stars,* the whole shooting match and got away with it. Frank was wandering the world. Frank was free. But only after months of agonizing and craziness. He'd seen a psychiatrist, an odd fellow no taller than a high school kid, whom Royce had met once at the health club where he and Frank used to work out. No leather couch for this guy, he pumped iron with Frank every Wednesday night while Frank talked through his problems. They'd laughed about him, Dr. Max Bodine, a shrink who made house calls. But Frank swore by him. Said Dr. Bodine made it possible for him to leave it all.

He knew, from those visits to Dr. Sorenson with Irene, just any shrink probably couldn't help him. Hell, most of them would make him wait days before he could even get an appointment, just the way Sorenson did. But Bodine seemed a different breed. And Frank could be in Paris, Juneau, or Kyoto now. Anywhere he wanted to be without Nancy and that squirrelly kid of his. Without the *Singing Stars.* He and Frank always had something in common, a maverick streak neither could indulge with Irene and Nancy by their sides as their lovely, loveless wives. There was just a chance Bodine might help him too.

By Friday. Impossible. If there was just some way he could stall her, maybe the whole thing would blow over. But as he thought about this he knew she'd made a decision and she was ready to follow through. The ball was in his court. She was asking him for his decision, if he could wake up each day and look her in the eye, a simple act he hadn't been able to perform for Irene in years.

Why not give Bodine a try? He could put it on the insurance. Kat would know he was serious, maybe take some of the pressure off. And who knows, maybe the good doctor would have some ideas. With or without Kat his life was certainly a mess. His house of cards had fallen and was about to be scattered by the winds.

He opened his eyes and looked at her lovely face. They held each other's stare for a long moment, then he gave her a wink. He took her hands away from his forehead and kissed each of them. "I've got an idea," he said, and rose from the bed and headed for the phone.

MONDAY
EVENING

That morning Max had worked with Barbara Landestoi, an agoraphobic living in St. Francis Wood. He'd succeeded in getting her to walk with him down to the West Portal post office and hoped next Monday morning they would tackle a more complicated situation, a grocery store or a ride on the Muni. He was pleased with her progress after only two months.

Perhaps he was making progress with Elaine Lifton too. She was home from the nursing home now, after over three months. He'd handled a lot of suicides but never one as damaged as Elaine.

How would she feel when she saw the postman again, the one who saved her? How would the postman feel? Dumb kid. Poor kid, her whole life still ahead of her.

He'd asked her again why she refused the prosthesis. "If I had hands I might try it again." That was progress, she was talking now, telling the story of how she found her father when she came back from a date with a man her father's age. Her parents didn't approve of Carl. He was another sad case, a Vietnam vet who hadn't gotten over the war. He took Elaine to hotels near railroad tracks or airports, noisy places with the feeling of people on the move, and told her stories of napalmed babies, massacres, plunder and theft, until she cried. Saigon fell over ten years ago, in the spring Max noted. For Elaine, death was part of a movie plot, the stories her Vietnam vet told. Yet her father had died sitting in a living room chair. The TV was still on and Elaine couldn't get it out of her head that if she'd been home that night, she could have saved him.

And now Max was trying to help her. If Claire hadn't killed herself he might have done something else with his life, but it was too late now to become a musician or a movie star or a plumber. He was a specialist in divorce and loneliness and madness. A specialist for the survivors of suicide.

He was looking forward to an evening practicing his piano. Several months ago he'd noticed hollow spots in his flat in Pacific Heights, as if something had been stolen from his apartment, but he couldn't say exactly what. He thought of painting the place, but gave that up as too much trouble. The hollow spots were the first sign of trouble. He gladly would have seen patients mornings, afternoons, and evenings, to keep his mind filled with other people's problems. Patients drowned out the white noise of his own thoughts, his dreams and memories of Claire. If he could keep them talking he might help them stay alive.

It had been shortly after Elaine's attempt when Max found a clue as to what his apartment, his life, might be missing. Late in the evening at a friend's party he sat down at the upright piano; and after removing the half-empty glasses and overflowing ashtrays, he lifted the lid covering the keys. He'd never played before, but the sound as he struck the dramatic black and white keys was delightful and soothing all at the same time. He began stopping into music stores to lay his hands on Baldwins, Casios, Rolands, Steinways, Yamahas. A month later he bought an electric piano, no larger than a violin, with switches and buttons to create everything from rhumbas to flutes. He filled the evenings with sound. After buying a few how-to books and tapes, he was even thinking about taking lessons. A good boogie-woogie roll made him grin like a kid. Listening to Mozart piano concertos stretched his emotions the way a good physical workout toned his muscles. A healthy change, he decided, from the often painfully inarticulate people who strung words into stories trying to shed some light on their lives.

With his new piano the hollow spots in his flat disappeared. Max began to feel in balance, sweetly suspended between the words of the stories and the tones of the music. Tonight he'd work on blues, EAB. "Cold Black Night."

Max flipped through the mail and switched on the answering machine. The first call was disappointing. Jacob Epter wanted to cancel tomorrow's appointment to go see his sister in Sacramento who'd just had a baby. Jacob and Max played chess during their sessions, an apt metaphor for the way Jacob viewed his recent divorce. His wife left him for a professional stuntman and a sense of adventure her life with Jacob, an insurance broker, didn't offer. In the seven years of their marriage, Jacob saw their relationship as a series of moves checkmating his life. Her love of playing the horses and driving fast cars forced Jacob into more and more conservative patterns. In the two months Max had been working with Jacob, he'd made good progress handling his grief and guilt over her desertion. Max looked forward to their sessions. He admired the lovely ivory chess pieces set between them and the precision and skill of Jacob's game. Jacob often saw some truth about himself on the heels of a good move and this forced Max to play well. He figured Jacob would no longer need therapy about the time Max would be a truly worthy opponent. Max liked the symmetry of their mutual progress.

"I want to talk about death," the next voice on the machine said. Max loosened his tie and kicked off his shoes. "My legs were paralyzed in a car accident last May, and I can't get over the feeling I should have died. My physical therapist suggested I talk to you since you're about the only shrink in the city who makes house calls. My insurance will pay." Max tried to gauge the age of the voice. "I'd appreciate it if you'd give me a call."

The machine clicked off. What was he supposed to say? *This is Dr. Bodine calling. I'd like to speak to the paraplegic.* It would have helped if he'd left a number.

There was nothing more, two messages. Business was bad, or maybe life was good. Max loved the irony of that. If people didn't have problems he'd be out of a job.

The phone rang. He let the answering machine handle it, that was the best aspect of the thing as far as he was concerned. He could listen as the caller stated the problem and form some cogent remark before dialing back.

The third ring sounded and the machine kicked in. "You've reached the offices of Dr. Max Bodine. I'm sorry I'm not available to speak with you at the moment, but be assured I'll return your call at the first opportunity. The message space after the tone isn't timed, so feel free to tell me as much about the reason for your call as you want to." That last line was a mistake and Max meant to change it one of these days. Barbara Landestoi sometimes talked for forty minutes.

"This is Royce Chambers. We met once through Frank Hennessey. I'm hoping you can take me on for a short while. I've got to solve some problems immediately, a deadline so to speak. Do you have any time this week? I'd be willing to pay, what should we call it, a rush fee? Anyhow, the money isn't the issue and I've got some problems that are. Please call, any time day or night, 285-7945. Thanks so much."

Royce Chambers hung up and the machine clicked off. Max puzzled over the voice and the name. Royce, just like the car. He thought he remembered a tall man with dark hair Frank had introduced to him at the gym, but maybe that was someone else. He could give him Jacob Epter's slot tomorrow afternoon. This would be interesting, Max decided. He'd liked working with Frank Hennessey and wondered if Royce Chambers would take him to the same health club in Sausalito. They'd lifted weights, run in place, pulled on the arm machines, while Frank sorted out his frustrations at being a vice president in his father's construction firm. Max tried to channel Frank's anger into the machines and they joked about whether they would have to take up boxing. Frank's boyhood dream was to hitchhike around the world without a penny in his pocket. The last card Max received was postmarked Hong Kong where Frank was loading and unloading freighters. In this line of work, that was success.

Less than half an hour later, as Max was about to step into the shower, the door buzzer sounded. He considered the swirling steam, how cold the rest of the flat would feel if he went to the door just now. He decided he wouldn't answer, he would just dunk his head into the stream of water and start to sing. Invariably the doorbell meant turning away some religious nut or a kid needing a sponsor for a popsicle contest. The buzzer rang again and Max reluctantly switched off the shower and threw a towel around himself. He was always a sucker for the doorbell, no matter how often he swore to ignore it. He couldn't imagine who it might be but shambled out to the front room anyhow.

A cabdriver stood in the doorway. She carried a large package carefully wrapped in cut-and-taped grocery bags. Max could read the red SAFE part of the Safeway logo pasted over one end. "I feel like a goddamn mailman," she said. "You got to sign this."

"What's this all about?" He wished he had his bathrobe on. The hair on his chest prickled in the cold air. The cabbie eyed him without the slightest trace of modesty.

"Just sign this." She handed Max one of his own business cards, the beige ones from a few years ago, listing only his name, credentials, and a phone number at the hospital. Max made a point of keeping his address to himself. "Sign this," she said, "or I don't get the fare."

His first thought was of letter bombs. Although he couldn't think of any of his patients with enough malice or expertise to want to blow him up on his doorstep, Max knew therapists whose lives had been threatened by their patients. He knew a woman therapist in Berkeley who'd lost her dog to a patient. The man brought steak bones to his session and offered them for the dog. That evening her Irish setter died from convulsions after happily gnawing on the poisoned bones. The man explained he felt his therapist would have more time for him if she spent less time with her dog.

The cabbie looked him over. "You're awfully cute in that towel," she said. "I've always had a thing for short guys. You remind me of Al Pacino. I took him to the St. Francis once."

"How much?" Max took the package from her, letter

bomb or not. At the moment the package was preferable to the woman in his doorway.

"I get paid on the other end if you sign this. But a tip would be nice. Or you could ask me in." She shifted her weight, striking a pose.

Max signed the back of his business card and shut the door in her face. He put the chain on, as if afraid she would try to break her way in. He listened for her steps going down the hall.

He stood in the middle of his living room, holding the package. This must be Patrice's handiwork. Another ambush. Patrice's only psychic gift was an uncanny sense of timing, managing to pop back into his life just when he thought she might be fading quietly into the past. There was no pattern to it, but in the six years since their divorce this was her fourth correspondence. Two years after the divorce he received a box of smashed china, the wedding set her mother had given them. Year before last she returned, with no note, the O gauge train set he'd sent their son Conrad for his birthday. Last spring a telegram arrived stating she'd gone to visit her mother in New York and asking him to pick up Connie at kindergarten and take care of him for two weeks. *Asking.* Max couldn't get over the way she used that word. As if he could refuse and leave Connie at the kindergarten for two weeks. But when Max went to pick him up there was a note: CHANGED MY MIND.

He shook the package, but it didn't rattle. It was soft and pliable in his hands. No metal edges. It felt like cloth and that seemed innocuous enough to him. No one had invented a cloth bomb yet. The grocery sacks were neatly cut and taped together, the big red SAFE arranged to show. Patrice was the kind of woman who could spend an hour signing a birthday card, practicing the formation of the letters of her own name until she had them just right.

Inside were two separately wrapped packages. Max opened the first one.

A handsome three-piece navy suit was carefully folded in tissues. There was a pale pink shirt, black socks, and a black leather belt. All the sizes were correct. Max held them up against his body, admiring the expensive labels. Even the trousers had been shortened to just the right length. He smiled a little, an overture from Pat. And then, as always when he thought of Patrice these days, there was that resigned and defeated feeling, the way a strong runner must feel when he places second in a race he hoped to win. Max believed this would always be his final impression, the only lasting feeling after nine years.

The other package was closer to the mark, a clearer reflection of how they felt about each other. Scraps of his clothes, old shirts, pants, underwear, socks, a jacket, all cut and torn and ripped to shreds. He recognized buttons and fabrics. There was the head and neck of a flamingo from what used to be his favorite Hawaiian shirt, a shirt he'd left in the laundry six years ago when he moved out and never mustered the nerve to ask for. There were scraps of brightly colored jockey shorts, presents from Patrice he'd deliberately left along with the blousey boxer shorts with the hearts all over them, she'd given him for Valentine's Day. The hearts were ripped up too. The toes were cut out of his socks. Oval suede patches from the elbows of his corduroy jacket along with the severed arms and collar. The matching pants had been ripped through the crotch.

There was a note amidst all the rags.

I live with two evil angels on my shoulders.
Between the three of us (my evil angels and me)

I'm sure I will fail my orals, so I decided to
clean out the house. I was going to use these as
washrags, but thought you might want them back.
The suit's much better than the one you left.
Call it an even trade.

Patrice was dead right, evil angels indeed. John Calvin and Sigmund Freud. They made perfect rudders for
her. Max could picture it, Calvin telling Patrice to clean
out the house, Freud taking over as she tore up the clothes.
Calvin making her replace them, Freud writing the note
attempting to explain. Calvin and Freud hovered over
their marriage, their son, their divorce. He always tried to
think of Conrad as his son but knew this was merely a
semantic game. Connie was Pat's son, Pat's baby, Pat's
hopes for a girl. The child was something she felt she had
to do. Max hadn't been consulted.

Patrice had been a June bride, and their divorce was
finalized three years later in December to insure a clean
tax return. The romantic and the pragmatic, another of
those ideas so plausible in the abstract that can work out
so disastrously. A graduate school marriage, and Patrice
never forgave Max for it. Patrice hadn't married a doctor
to be sent off to work.

Max saw the pregnancy as Pat's revenge. Shortly after
he began his practice, Pat announced she'd quit her job
and was going to have a baby, as if that sentimental word,
pregnant, would solve all the problems between them.
Max found it difficult to be happy about this, never quite
getting over the surprise, and being too close to ideas
about children and parenting as they are presented in
textbooks. He was working with a fourteen-year-old
anorexic who'd been abandoned to the welfare department. The last time she saw her mother, they'd gone to a
tattoo parlor where the mother had a shark etched on her

daughter's throat, just below the left ear. As Max talked to the girl, he would watch the shark appear to swim out from underneath her hair, a living image animated by each word the girl said about her mother. The girl haunted Max. He kept thinking of the two of them entering the shop, as if to buy mother-daughter look-alike dresses. Instead, they came out with matching tattoos, a sign only the two of them could share. A livid picture, a design which would form the daughter in the image of the mother.

If Patrice had been a stranger to him before, her pregnancy transformed her into someone utterly foreign, alien to Max's feelings. He would watch her sleeping on her back, some nights believing he could see the baby growing. Their bedroom filled with the blues and greens of the shark in the nighttime light. Patrice would mark that baby as surely as if she had it tattooed. Max felt power-less. He held no illusions his training could help save the child. Or Pat. Or himself. The deep, dark notches under Pat's eyes looked as permanent as the colors on the anorexic's throat. He watched the energy drain out of Patrice's face as her belly swelled. He felt cast off from shore and unable to swim to safety. Deep water.

They had made no plans, although Max once sug-gested a bigger apartment, one that didn't have as many stairs to their flat on the top floor. Pat liked the flat. She still lived in it with her son, near the medical center where Max completed his residency.

As the pregnancy advanced Max fought desires he'd never known before. He wanted to buy a sports car, a two-seater Alfa Romeo which would zip around curves at astonishing speeds. He wanted to drive away, fast. He found himself reading detective novels, following clues that brought each story predictably to its end. Patrice became a woman he'd known long ago, not the woman who moved through the flat humming to herself. Patrice never talked about anything but the baby, and Max always talked about everything else.

Spring, for Max, was a troublesome time, always an echo of the spring when Claire died. All the sad events in his life seemed to happen in the spring, and he breathed a sigh of relief when June arrived. The technical term for periods like this was anniversary grief and Max felt as if he were holding his breath each spring, analyzing the depth of his memories. In February, a week before the baby was born, the anorexic ran away and Max never heard anything about her after that, although he would dream of the tattooed shark swimming beneath her hair. The first week in March Patrice gave birth to a boy, although she'd been convinced the baby would be a girl and planned to name her Constance. In April she asked Max to move out, and he decided he had no choice. The following year in the middle of May, Max's father drowned. Three years ago on the first of June one of his patients killed herself. He'd had one suicide attempt this spring, Elaine. In the spring Max thought he could hear gunfire nearby, the sound muffled by the wind so it was impossible to pinpoint where the shooting came from. Claire had jumped.

Max reread Patrice's note. Evil angels. If he had evil angels he wasn't sure who they would be. Patrice was enough, lurking like a guerrilla, waiting for the moment his guard was down. Voodoo was Pat's style. Once she had her child, Patrice didn't need Max any more, except as a recipient for her anger. Such logic. She was afraid of failing her orals, so she tore up his clothes. When things went well, she only thought of him as she cashed his checks every month.

If only Patrice knew who she was, what she wanted from life. But since the divorce, her only occupation was that of Conrad's mother and a professional graduate student. What was she studying? What did it matter? As long as Max paid her tuition, she'd hop from one department to the next. He wished there were some statute of limitations on how long a grown woman could stay in school.

Enraged by the grandiose gesture, the cabbie driving over from Parnassus Street to his flat in Pacific Heights, plus the return fare, he marched into the kitchen for a grocery sack. *That* was certainly an intelligent way to be spending his money, their only support since Patrice refused to work again. For that matter, who paid for the suit?

He took all the torn and shredded scraps of clothing and wrapped them up, much as Pat had done. No dramatic gestures for him. He'd mail them back to her third class, better yet, COD. Before strapping down the last side he enclosed a note: KEEP YOUR TRASH.

But then he would have to sit and look at the package all evening, pale brown waste sitting in the middle of his living room. He would have to take it to the post office in the morning. And if he was going to send the rags back, what about the suit?

He moved to the desk and took out his list. Since the final fight with Patrice he'd kept a list, at his own psychiatrist's suggestion, of how he would like to retaliate. The list consisted of two parts: the things he'd actually done, and the desires he'd managed to curb.

DONE
1. Canceled all her credit cards, magazine subscriptions, book clubs
2. Had phone disconnected
3. Sent alimony and child support check unsigned (||||)
4. Sent alimony and child support in checks of $5.00 randomly during the month
5. Informed post office she'd died and canceled her mail

REFRAINED FROM
1. Murdering her when she destroyed my stuff
2. Pitching her stuff off the fourth-story porch
3. Ordering one ton of manure to be delivered to her front porch
4. Calling her to yell (卌 卌 卌 卌 ||)
5. Breaking her boyfriend's neck when he came asking for money
6. Canceling her car insurance
7. Mailing her alimony and child support in dimes (5,000)
8. Going to their local bar and causing a scene (卌 ||)
9. Moving to Alaska
10. Having her committed
11. Trying to patch it all back up

Most of the items were from the first year after their divorce. He still added check marks to number 4 on the REFRAINED FROM list, but the last time was after her note a year ago, CHANGED MY MIND. He added number 12 to the REFRAINED FROM list.

     12. Mailing back the rags

He decided to keep the suit. He'd paid for it in blood if not actual money. If Patrice had a boyfriend, as she usually did, no self-respecting lover would buy an expensive suit for his girlfriend's ex-husband. Maybe her mother bought it. Her mother still had hopes for a reconciliation, but then her mother also believed in séances and communicating with the dead.

Max went back into the shower, hoping the rush of water over his body would warm him, wash away some of the mixed feelings Patrice stirred in him. It didn't take much to ruin an evening these days, a Monday evening at that. The package had indeed been a letter bomb. He remembered the story of the girl in San Diego who got out her daddy's shotgun and peppered her high school on a Monday morning in the spring. Her only statement had been *I hate Mondays*. Some punk group made a hit record out of that line. As he shut off the water and rubbed himself briskly with a towel, he wondered if Pat wanted to see him. Patrice wasn't a woman to simply state what she wanted. She probably didn't even know herself.

He put on the suit and the fine material made him feel better. He looked good, just the type of suit he would have bought for himself, tailored exactly to his proportions. Now that he was dressed he really ought to go somewhere, show himself off. Brooding in his apartment was the last thing he should do, isolating himself as if he were emotionally snowbound.

Tucking the package under his arm, he went out. He thought of taking it to the Salvation Army dumpster, but there wasn't enough to give to the poor. Two blocks away he spotted a city trash bin and shoved the package inside. He should have dropped it in the ocean, perhaps he would have felt some satisfaction watching it sink slowly from sight. He wished he were walking in a New England woods in the fall. He wanted to see dead leaves flutter like flags at his feet.

Walking down Union Street, Max listed his options. He could go home and call Royce Chambers, but the effort of explaining his method, the philosophy he worked with, the fee, would take more energy than he possessed at the moment. Call any time, day or night. That was license to wait until the shadow of Patrice melted into some other experience. Something more positive than spitting glass or doing his taxes or waxing his car in the dark.

The sidewalks seemed filled with solitary people skirting each other as if they were all looking at different points on the horizon. He passed a mother dragging a small boy, apparently unaware that she was holding his hand. Overdressed salesgirls tottered on their high heels like birds surprised by the loss of flight. Elderly Oriental men lugging plastic sacks seemed weighted down by their suits, several sizes too large for them. A punker with spiky orange hair and four or five pounds of metal chains ate a cookie in front of a toy store. The Beatles: "All the lonely people." David Reisman: "The lonely crowd." Max wished for a street preacher on a soapbox, telling them they would be all right, just love the Lord.

A couple ahead of him caught his eye. The man was tall and rangy, athletic looking, with distinctive salt-and-pepper hair. He held the arm of an equally tall redheaded woman, who pressed herself against him affectionately. She held her shoulders high and her walk was loose in the hips, her brightly patterned skirt swinging in time with her step. They were involved in an animated discussion, and every few steps the woman gave a kind of skip or hop. Max knew she was smiling, the man returning her warmth.

He decided to follow. There was something pleasing about this couple, a balm to soothe his raw nerves in the wake of Pat's package. They were music conjured up to entertain him for a few moments, to give him access to a place outside himself.

They were window-shopping, stopping in front of boutiques to point at the glitzy merchandise. Once the woman threw her arms in the air and twirled on her toes, sweeping her hand along her skirt as if doing some South American dance step. The man laughed and pulled her away from the window and on down the street. People in love. Max could hear their music. Reggae. Salsa. Rag-time. Boogie-woogie. All those high, fast, happy sounds.

They finally turned into an antique shop, without gazing through the windows. It was dark now and the shop well-lit with light spilling from the show windows. Max knew he should leave them, but instead he took a table at a sidewalk café directly across the street from the antique store. Piano jazz drifted on the spring air, Cedar Walton perhaps. He could stare into the shop as if he were seated in a movie theater.

He often spent evenings like this. Once he sat in his car listening to an argument coming from a second-story flat. It had been autumn and the windows were open and the couple were arguing about buying a monkey. A long time later, after the sun had set, they began to make love, the question of the monkey still undecided, and Max couldn't remember what he'd intended to do with that evening, why he'd parked his car in that block.

Across the street he could see the woman's hands flitting above the display cases like the delicate flight of butterflies over flowers. She disappeared into the back and the clerk plucked several items out of the glass case. He offered them to the man, returned them to the case when declined. The clerk handed over what looked like a black wand the size of a conductor's baton. The man turned it carefully in his hands, held it up to the light. At that moment the woman returned from some place in the back of the shop, light flashing off a silver-sequined flapper dress. She shimmied through the store, a waterfall of light, showing off for the man.

The waiter came for his order, and Max snapped at him, irritated by the disturbance. He ordered a glass of white wine, unable to think of anything more interesting, and secretly afraid the waiter knew exactly what he was doing sitting at that table. Across the street, the woman moved through the antique shop in her sparkling dress.

It caught the light around her breasts and hips. She

glowed in the center of an exotic showcase. Reaching behind the clerk, she pulled out an ostrich feather crown, pale white plumes set into a black band, and placed it on her red hair. She shimmied again, as if following the jazz playing in the bar behind him, the feathers swimming in counterpoint above her head. She turned on one foot in a circle, her hand tapping against the heel of her shoe, a quick shimmery flapper step. The man smiled, clapped his hands enthusiastically, and nodded to the clerk. The clerk made a note. She crossed over to the man and threw her arms around his neck. Max thought she looked like a really good piano melody, the lightness of her mood coloring the air around her.

The waiter returned with his glass of wine, and Max absently placed a bill on the table. He resented every moment his eyes weren't on the window across the street. He wondered if he should have ordered a carafe, if he would be able to sit at this table all evening watching the couple pick over the antique shop.

The man reached for a suit on the rack and disappeared into the back. The clerk handed the woman the black wand. It was a cigarette holder; the clerk supplied the cigarette. She pulled languidly on the mouthpiece, mugging and blowing smoke in a cloud above the plumes set into her red hair. She smiled and smoked, flourishing the black cigarette holder and looking quite elegant, as beautiful and artificial as anything in a movie or dream. She sparkled in the light, as happy as any woman Max had ever seen.

He sipped his wine and felt the heady excitement of their pleasure. And then, with the same certainty one feels when hitting a small animal with a car, the same awful feeling something sad and irreversible has happened, Max knew he'd never made anyone as happy as the redheaded woman in the store across the way.

He wanted to leave, but couldn't bring himself to rise from his chair until the buying spree was over. He was committed to watching the whole play. The man returned in a dark blue pin-striped suit, wide lapels with deep notches, pleated pants. A zoot suit with high, padded shoulders. The woman turned him around with her hands, admiring him, straightening the hang of the jacket. She selected a fedora with a brim as wide as a stereo record. He cocked the hat over one eye. Dapper. Zelda and Scott. They looked at each other, smiling, laughter in their eyes.

She disappeared into the back again and Max wondered what she would be wearing next. A black negligee with seamed silk stockings, or perhaps a fabulous white fur coat. There was a theatrical sense about her, as if she were performing for the whole street to watch. Max envied the man this private show.

The man took out his wallet. It was over. The clerk added up the figures on the bill. Max got a good shot of the man's face as he stood at the counter and thought the man looked like the headmaster of a boys' school, and probably the soccer coach, as well. Max wondered how much the outfits cost, where they would wear them. When the woman stepped out of the back in her sparkling dress, the clerk wrapped up their street clothes. They swooped up the parcels and left the shop.

From his table on the sidewalk with the dregs of his glass of wine, Max watched them go past on the opposite side of the street. They looked like a duet, piano and horns. Max imagined them climbing into a Pierce-Arrow and zooming off into the night. Perhaps they would end up playing faro at a private club. Max wondered what kind of game faro was. He only knew rich people played it.

His teeth began to ache, a cavity, something rotting

in the back of his mouth. Then, as if the store had been open for their private pleasure, the lights went out and the clerk pulled grates over the windows.

Max ordered another glass of wine, solicitous of the waiter this time. He would leave him a good tip, as if bribing the man. The pleasure he felt at viewing the shopping spree was as illicit as if he'd stood beneath their windows watching them undress.

Gasoline fumes rose from the street. The show was over, and Max felt as if he were sitting in an empty theater. As he walked back up the hill, he wondered if the redheaded woman in the sparkling dress would join Claire and the other women in his dreams.

APRIL 8
TUESDAY
AFTERNOON

A woman answered when Max returned Royce Chambers's call around nine-thirty Monday evening. Max suspected she might be listening because Royce Chambers volunteered no information about the nature of his problems. Max explained his four-hour sessions, his philosophy, his fee, and the choice of setting for their meeting. He informed Royce of Jacob Epter's cancellation on Tuesday afternoon, the only spare block this week. Finally Chambers suggested his printing plant south of Market. Max decided it would be something like Lewis Petrie and his office at the College of Marin. A man having problems with his work. After all, that was at the heart of what drove Frank Hennessey off to Hong Kong.

His morning session with Vincent Dolack went very well. Vincent liked to drive, and they cruised up to Santa Rosa and back under a vibrant sky in Vincent's plushy

BMW, commenting on how the green fields of winter grass were beginning to turn gold. Max always thought the hillsides above Petaluma looked like a Japanese painting, the gnarled green trees against the waving gold grass. Vincent said these hills reminded him of Spain, the color of cider.

Vincent's wife, Abby, suffered a stroke four months ago and spent her Tuesday mornings in physical therapy. Vincent had been taking care of her, moving his architectural design firm into his house so he could be near her. The stroke affected her speech and movement on the right side of her body. Lately she'd begun to show signs of improvement, and Vincent entertained hopes she would one day be able to converse with him again. He recited the words she had regained and demonstrated with delight little movements in the fingers of the right hand.

They returned to the city under a bright cold sun, Vincent to pick up Abby from her therapy, Max to meet Royce Chambers. The address was easy to find, a cinderblock warehouse. There would be no sun inside. Max knew the colors would either be dull or painted artificially bright. He wondered if they would talk with the thunder of machinery in the background.

He took the elevator to the top floor and walked in the door marked Office. An Asian woman greeted him stonily and told Max to have a seat. Max couldn't spot a private office, just the gallery running along the side of the building, windows on both sides facing the street and overlooking the floor below, where printing presses hummed and clunked and thumped to various rhythms. Max checked the gallery again. There were two desks, several chairs, a drafting table, telephones, walls of files. Nothing private or conducive to a four-hour talk. A moment later the man with the zoot suit from the antique shop last night walked in and extended his hand. Max felt his stomach drop like the first rush of seasickness.

"Pleased to meet you, Dr. Bodine. I'm Royce Chambers."

Max shook the hand and flashed his most professional smile, then he blushed. He felt like saying: Oh yes, that's a wonderful dress. He wondered if he would be able to resist the image of the redheaded woman for the next four hours.

Royce walked over to the desk facing the Asian woman and pointed to a chair for Max. The Asian woman began typing on a rattling old IBM, the same sound as jingling a pocketful of coins.

"Donna Moon," Royce said loudly. "I'm going to need the office for a while."

Max couldn't identify an expression on her face. "Pacific Trust will be here in half an hour," she said. "What are we supposed to do with them?"

"I need to talk to Dr. Bodine."

"You also need the Pacific Trust account. Norton and I can handle them, but not if we have to conduct business in the bathroom." She returned to her typing.

"Christ." Royce ran his hands through his hair.

Max was sure he would stutter with embarrassment all afternoon. He felt stiff, unable to meet Royce's eyes. He could feel the stare of the Asian woman, the way she would look over his shoulder throughout the session. He was sure to make some slip and say something about last night on Union Street. Max took a breath and gave a weak smile. "This might not be a good setting for our discussion. This shouldn't interfere with your business." He looked out the windows facing the printing presses and watched the men and women moving around their machines from his vantage point one floor above. Their attitudes were as different as people driving cars through the city. One man exercised with HeavyHands while his press hummed beside him. Another seemed to be stroking his machine like a prized animal. A woman, her arms in long rubber gloves, the hands covered with ink, had a makeup mirror on the top of her press. "Perhaps we could go to your house," Max suggested.

Royce bit his lip. "I don't have a house to spare for this kind of thing."

Donna Moon lifted the phone and said: "Norton, you better get up here. I think there's a mistake in this estimate." She shot Royce a look which plainly told him he was interfering with her work.

"There's a quiet kind of bar and restaurant around the corner," Royce said. "Have you had lunch? Would you like a drink?"

Max shook his head. "Places like that get distracting. I've learned bars and restaurants aren't a very good setting for the kind of work we want to do today." He felt a little more in control now, glad to make this decision.

Royce looked out the windows for a moment. He rose quickly then, and made for the door. "Donna Moon, I'm sure you and Norton will handle Pacific Trust perfectly. Make my excuses, okay?"

Donna Moon gave them another utterly blank look and returned to her typing. Max rose to follow Royce, who set off purposefully toward the elevator.

As they descended to the street, Royce asked if Max minded a little drive over to Sausalito. Max felt better. He was sure the sunshine would revive him. He would put the antique shop out of his mind, as forgotten as the taste of last night's dinner.

As Royce led him to a top-of-the-line Toyota, he apologized again. "Donna Moon's not long on personality, but she's a hell of a secretary. I couldn't afford this afternoon without her."

Max took a deep breath and launched into the business at hand. This part he could do in his sleep, as rote as the way a child learns the alphabet. "Where people want to talk sometimes illuminates their problems. I'd never been backstage in a printing plant before, so just getting a look helps."

Royce cut him off. "It has nothing to do with work, if that's what you're thinking. Or Donna Moon." He pulled out into traffic, the Toyota humming as if it had just been tuned. "Like I said on the phone, I've really got the same problem Frank had. In fact, this might be old home week for you. I'm taking you to Frank's boat. I don't know where else to go."

Max had never been on Frank's boat, but the idea of being out on the water, in the sunshine, appealed to him. "Sounds fine. I meet clients in lots of places. This morning I rode up to Santa Rosa because my client likes to drive." Max decided Royce didn't want to take him to his house if he was thinking of leaving his wife, the way Frank left Nancy. He doubted the tall redheaded woman from last night was Royce's wife, just a feeling he had.

"I love this boat. I'd buy it if I could. Nancy lets me sail it and take care of it since Frank's gone. I spent part of last weekend sanding down the deck to reoil it. Teak. Never varnish teak. Just oil it real well once a year. Nancy wants to sell it, but right now I don't have the capital to finance it. It's all my wife's father's dough. He financed that printing business. He put up the down payment on our home in Sausalito. A couple of years ago, I borrowed some money from him for an investment property I was going to fix up and sell. I doubt if he'll finance a boat for me, not at this point." Royce looked saddened by this fact. "That's why I had to see you this week. The long and short of it is by Friday I have to decide between my wife and," he paused, watching the traffic as they passed through the toll booth on the Golden Gate. "You know, this is a funny thing. I've been thinking about how to describe Katlyn. I mean, 'mistress' is so old fashioned. And 'lover' sounds too transitory. 'My friend,' well, that's too vague. And I don't know anyone who can say 'significant other' and keep a straight face. She's just my Kat."

Max saw the woman in the sparkling flapper dress and his stomach took another roll. Kat. "I get the picture. It's a pretty good description, actually, in lieu of a better word." He wondered if he could casually say: Oh yes, she's a redhead, isn't she? Max wanted to confess his voyeuristic evening, share the pleasure with Royce. As they crossed the bridge, Max wished he didn't have to sit passively all afternoon, professionally listening as Royce talked about Kat. He wished they could grab a couple of beers and just talk about the problems of women in general. Patrice. Katlyn. Freud didn't understand women either.

"I'm thinking of getting divorced," Royce said.

Royce parked and led Max to the slip. The *Singing Stars* was a thirty-six-foot ocean-going cruising sloop with a baby-blue mast. As Royce pointed out the various features on the boat, Max could gauge the values Royce held, the care and attention he lavished on a superb piece of workmanship. The *Singing Stars* must be a magnificent sight as she cut through the water and ran before the wind. Sailing her would be a true experience, one Max wasn't prepared for this afternoon. The sun was bright and cold and Max was wearing one of his business suits and wingtips. He wondered if Royce intended to take her out, the two of them in suits, crewing as if they were in a fashion ad. The air as clean as if it had been washed, the blue of the sky so even it might have been painted like a bowl above them.

Royce unlocked the hatch and descended the companionway, his long legs flitting down the short ladder.

Max could hear him rummaging below. He stood on the deck and looked out at the harbor. The slip was squarish and Max couldn't find the channel which would take them out to the bay.

Royce shouted "Here. Catch!" and threw a bright red beanbag chair out of the companionway. Max caught it, wondering what he should do with it, when another bean-bag chair came flying out of the hold. Max set them at his feet and watched as Royce's head emerged from the cabin.

"I've got some sweaters and blankets in case you're cold. But if it's okay with you, I'd like to sit out here for a bit. If you put one of those," he indicated the bean bag chairs, "in the pushpit," he pointed to the corner between the side of the boat and the stern, "you'll find it's actually quite comfortable."

Max felt the gentle roll of the boat as he walked over the deck. He placed one of the beanbag chairs in the corner angle, pulled a sweater over his head, and sat down. It was very comfortable, relaxing, with the warmth of the sun on his face.

Royce settled himself across from Max with the ease of a man who knew this boat intimately, who loved this sloop. Max watched the lines ease out of his face, the telltale tension that collects so easily in the corners of the eyes and mouth. He could imagine Royce sailing like a puppeteer, pulling on the lines and rigging to make the sails fill with wind and carry them away. He saw the woman in the flapper dress, Kat, glitter against the sun and sky.

"You're right. This is more humane than a hard leather couch." Royce smiled, pleased with his access to Frank's boat.

Max stretched his legs, not anxious to start this. He wondered how many masts were in the harbor and thought it would be nice to try to count them all until he fell asleep, lulled by the gentle rocking of the boat and the warmth of the sun on his face. "You've been in therapy before?"

"My wife, Irene, and I were in family counseling for a while. It didn't work out really, although Irene still goes to that therapist."

"Why didn't you get a reference from there?" But Max already knew the answer, especially if Royce Chambers was anything like Frank Hennessey.

"I wanted a fresh start. I didn't want Irene to influence you. Because you see, her problems are exactly the opposite of mine. And to tell you the truth, I didn't care for Dr. Sorenson very much. Irene and I spent a month telling her who we were before she felt she had anything to say."

Max didn't care for Lois Sorenson either, but knew he had to stick up for his own kind. "Maybe she thought the best way to help you and your wife was to have you listen to each other. You'd be surprised how little gets said in some marriages."

"Nothing about marriage would surprise me at this point." Royce let his eyes drift over the boats in the slip. "I wish I'd thought of this before. We could have taken a spin around the bay." He fingered a brass winch. "I wish I could buy this boat."

"Sailing would be interesting," Max agreed, "but it might keep you too busy to talk about what's bothering you."

"Oh yes. That." Royce ran a hand over his face, pulling on his nose. "Kat wants me to make a decision about leaving my wife by Friday."

A sea gull wheeled above them, its head arcing back and forth, its wings a steady boomerang curve against the even blue of the sky. "Why Friday?" Max asked.

"I told you about that investment property. Well, the

reason I can't sell it is because Kat and I live there. I mean, she lives there all the time and I stay with her Monday through Thursday. I come back to Sausalito on the weekends for Irene and the kids. Did I tell you I have kids? Lindy's sixteen and Todd's thirteen. Kat and I manage a few weekends together, she goes on business trips with me, and I've taken her on vacation the last two New Years. But I usually go back to Sausalito on Fridays."

"How does your wife feel about this?" Max saw the outline here, as surely as he knew how to shave.

Royce stretched his long legs and locked them at the ankle. "She doesn't know about the divorce yet. We have an agreement. I can have my affair as long as she doesn't have to worry about a divorce. Last Friday morning Kat showed me a passport and told me she was thinking of going to Africa. She wants me to divorce Irene or she'll leave me."

"Africa?" Max saw Katlyn swinging through the jungle on a vine, clad only in a leopard pelt, laughing. He wished Patrice would go to Africa, leave Conrad with him and just disappear into the bush. Patrice and all her boyfriends were no substitute for a father. Sometimes he wondered if Conrad recognized him from one visit to the next.

"Africa. She claims she's going up the Nile and down the Congo. But that's not even the tough part. I mean, if she were really going to Africa, I'd have to live with that. So it's really the divorce I think she wants, and Irene won't divorce me."

Max nodded. The signs and signals of communication. Pat's suit was an equivalent of a letter or phone call to him. Maybe Pat wanted to see him again. What if she wanted him to take more of a hand in raising Conrad? Maybe she wanted to resume their, what, relationship? friendship? What did he and Pat have between them now? Had they ever been friends? Maybe she needed money.

What did the suit mean? Why so much anger and guilt now, six years later? If only there were something Patrice could do besides tying up all her identity in being Conrad's mother and taking those damned endless classes.

"You see, of course, how I couldn't stay."

Max blinked. "You'll have to back up a bit." He hated it when patients caught him when he wasn't paying strict attention. "To why Irene won't divorce you."

Royce looked perplexed for a moment, clearly past that part of his story and not sure where Max lost the thread. "She won't divorce me because we've been married sixteen years. We've got kids, there's her father to deal with, Gerald. Irene's an only child and Gerald's very conservative, protective. Over the years Irene and I have been through everything. She knows about Kat. She won't tell her father if I don't threaten her with divorce. Which is exactly what Kat just asked me to do."

"Why this week? You had no notion she was lobbying for you to get a divorce?"

"I don't know," and Royce truly looked as if he didn't.

Max liked this part of the process, putting a person's history together like pieces of a jigsaw puzzle. Each person was a different kind of picture. Some, a busy scene full of people. Some, a solid object. Some, like the endless flat skies of the Midwest, with only a windmill in the foreground. "Irene doesn't mind your affair but won't give you a divorce. Surely she must have some feelings about Kat."

"Oh, she didn't like it at first. I wasn't around much anyhow, but then I met Kat and I guess I got pretty blatant. I'm sure Irene suspected something, but she didn't make an issue of it and naturally I wasn't going to say anything. The whole thing came to a head one time when I was spending the weekend with Kat, although my excuse was I was working on the house, and Gerald and Margaret came down unexpectedly on Saturday. If Irene had told them I was working on the house, they might want to drive over to the city to see it. So she told them I'd gone fishing in the Sierras with my neighbor Tony.

"About two hours later, Tony drops over. Gerald pieces it together that Irene is covering for me and jumps on her case. They drove over to the house, but fortunately Kat and I were out. But he noticed the curtains, no For Sale sign. I'd been telling Gerald the house was on the market. By then, it was like trying to sneak a horse into a second-story flat. I told Irene about Kat and said I wanted a divorce, because you see, Dr. Bodine, I truly love Kat, whatever that means. I haven't had a strong feeling for Irene, except maybe anger, in years. The kids are almost grown. There was no reason for us to stay married, at least the way I saw it."

"And Irene? She tried to protect you, after all." Max wondered if Irene was one of those housewives who'd let themselves go. Katlyn, with her brightly patterned skirt and the flashing flapper dress, would certainly outdistance a dowdy housewife.

"She wasn't protecting me. She was protecting herself. She doesn't want a divorce. Gerald told her if we didn't make this marriage work, he'd step in." Royce rolled his eyes. "That could mean anything. He set up the family counseling thing. But it really didn't work out."

"Depends on what you expect." Max didn't think Lois Sorenson would be very useful to a man like Royce Chambers. He referred most of the women with what he called The Zelda Syndrome to Lois. She was very good at letting women believe they'd been wronged.

"I don't want to save my marriage, but I found myself in the odd position of wanting to save my business. Irene wanted to solve the problems in our marriage without changing her life-style. I used to be more of a fatalist. I used to believe Irene and Gerald and the kids were my lot in life. It might not sound like I'm much of a father, with my relationship with Kat, but when my kids were younger, there was nothing in the whole world that made me happier than those two. Christmas, Disneyland, even watching them sleep. So I agreed to go to counseling and Irene finally agreed to keep Gerald happy. When Gerald and Margaret came down this last weekend, of course I couldn't take time to talk to Kat about Africa.''

Max felt the chill of the breeze against his ears, the gentle rocking of the boat at its mooring. Every time Royce mentioned Kat his eyes danced, as if he could see her standing against the railing, just suddenly dropped on the boat to surprise him. Marriage and money. Or more precisely, love and marriage, divorce and money. ''How did Katlyn handle all this?''

''Then? Two years ago? That's the difference, you see. I hadn't told her about Irene. So when I did, I expected the same treatment I'd gotten from Irene, hysterical scenes, outrageous demands. If Kat acted the way Irene did, the whole problem would be gone. I don't need two women like Irene in my life. Don't forget, I'd known Kat only about six weeks. I know a lot of things can be said in six weeks, but Kat was a vacation for me. When I went over there I never thought about Irene.''

''But you finally told her?'' Max watched Royce's face closely. This was a man in love. He sparkled every time he mentioned Kat, deflated when he talked about Irene.

''Here's the difference. Kat glosses it over. She says to me: 'Ah, but I am your queen.' I know this all sounds a little weird, but she began to play sex games with me, night after night. We hardly talked about Irene at all. The next night I came over, and she had this brocade costume on, complete with jewels in her hair, and she says she's

Queen Elizabeth. A couple of nights later she's Mata Hari." A ripple passed through Royce's shoulders, as if he felt the physical presence of the memory. "I was going through a lot of shit with Irene and here's this beautiful woman keeping me pleased and diverted throughout the whole thing."

Max tried to picture the scene. It was too perfect in some ways, too easy to see the redheaded woman in costume, saying all the right lines. "You must have talked about it to some degree."

"Not really. Kat rents the house from me, and I pass the money on to Gerald, who now thinks things are square with Irene and me. Irene eventually gave up and accepted it."

Max smiled in sympathy. "You catch more flies with honey." He loved stories like this, people who met their problems with imagination, who took generous risks, all too rare in his line of work. People in love are capable of mysterious, wonderful things. He watched the sun glint off the water, winking back at him the way the sequins caught the light last night. He imagined all these boats filled with women in fur coats and tiaras, sailing away. But he wondered about Kat. "And this is the perfect life you spoke of."

"I don't know what to do. The choices are very clear, but I'm not sure I have the courage to make any choice."

Max heard a sound like muffled bells. He looked around the slip and noticed the other boats were deserted, neatly shrouded in their sail covers. A cluster of people, looking like tourists in a foreign country, peered at them from the end of the dock with their kids and cameras and knapsacks bursting with Sausalito souvenirs. One of the boys looked a little like Conrad. There was probably a divorce or two up there with the cameras and kids. "Are you more afraid of Irene or Gerald?"

"Irene says she's pleased with the way things worked out. She's got her whole life right up there." He pointed to the houses hidden in the trees on the hillside. "There's more to it than that." Royce jammed his fists deep in his pockets and slumped on his spine, his feet reaching across the deck, almost touching Max's. Suddenly, in spite of the graying hair, he looked like an adolescent who had to explain failing a subject in school. "There's the sex. Irene's never cared for sex. I'm not sure she ever cared for me. Our agreement also includes not having sex, and this has worked out real well. We're nicer to each other now, fight less and all of that. I don't think many people in Sausalito know we don't sleep together, don't really live together. She tells them I'm busy. Captain of industry stuff."

"So everyone is happy."

"Except Kat. At thirty-eight I'm having postadolescent rebellion and it's not even my own father." Royce shook his head sadly. "Gerald never would have chosen me for Irene's husband. I met Irene when she was in college. My family was poor, living on Social Security after my dad died. I was in trade school, working in a gas station. I worked on her car. I think when we're young we don't know enough to see the world without the filter of our dreams. I was excited by a rich girl with a fancy car who kept coming around, like I was a real stud. When in truth, she just found me exotic. She'd never dated a real work-ing-class hero before. That was back in the days before they started high school girls on birth control. I got a bit from her and she got pregnant. She was eighteen. That's the curse of my generation: too late for birth control."

Max thought about Patrice, who didn't have the ex-cuse of being surprised by biology. The wind picked up, ruffling the water in the slip, and Max remembered the tattooed shark of the anorexic. He listened to the whine of

97

a motorcycle as it seemed to rise and die on the wind. "That's a long time ago," he said. "You've built a business for yourself in the meantime. If you're thinking of buying this boat, you probably can afford a divorce."

"I was thinking of Gerald buying this boat for me. I've grown used to thinking like that in the last sixteen years. Gerald's the Fig King of the United States, which isn't saying a whole lot because figs aren't in much demand, but it's still pretty lucrative. He's got about three hundred acres, which makes him the largest U.S. producer. I had one stroke of luck. I knocked up a rich, Catholic only child in the days before legal abortions. There was nothing to do but come out here and tell Daddy. I wasn't against it, really. Vietnam was building and I was sure my number would come up. You don't get a deferment to go to trade school part-time. But you do if you've got a kid. I was sure I'd have to become a Fig King too and spend all my time talking to people from Nabisco. But Gerald let me pick what I wanted, and I've always loved printing. Gerald financed the whole shot and we've got a very profitable business." Royce looked to the hills again. "He's not a bad guy, but if I pull out on Irene, Gerald might pull out on me. And I don't have the faintest idea how to start over."

Max looked at the sun hanging above the hills. He'd heard this part over and over again. Every one makes a trade, drives a bargain. They all backfire. "Gerald doesn't know about Katlyn. But you're sure that's how he'd react?"

Royce looked over his shoulder as if he were afraid someone would overhear him. "I'm afraid I'm a coward, that I've never tried to grow up. I've never really taken full responsibility for my life. Until Katlyn, I've been a good husband and father, all that, but to be honest, I feel I was railroaded into it. I loved my kids when they were younger, adored them, spoiled them rotten. But kids grow up, grow away from their parents. At thirteen and sixteen I hardly recognize them from one day to the next. And they act as if I'm invisible. Running a business isn't the same as running your life. A business is steady. Life changes all the time. At the bottom line, I think Kat wants me to make a decision, to start acting like a man, rather than Gerald's surrogate son. In sixteen years I've done everything he's told me to. I'm afraid I don't have the strength of character to act on my own."

Max nodded. "You won't know until you try. If you don't give it a shot you'll always wonder. It's not so much what happens as what you're willing to find out."

"Hey," Royce caught himself before he ran his hands through his hair. "When someone else is calling the shots, it's like losing control of your life."

"Not total control." He thought Royce might jump up and start running in circles, pant like a dog. He smiled. "You just have to test the waters, find out how much power you actually possess. California divorce laws split property fifty-fifty. After sixteen years, you've earned a spot."

Royce brightened at this. "Yeah?" Then his face fell again. "I've never looked into it before. I've rolled over on the whole thing. All I know are the horror stories other men tell about how much their wives soaked them for."

"Let's get back to Katlyn. Is she happy to share you with Irene and your father-in-law?" Perhaps the dress was a present of atonement. Tall women always struck Max as strong, demanding, something in the set of a tall woman's shoulders. She'd want more than exotic dresses.

"That's another thing I felt pretty stupid about. I assumed Kat was happy. I never questioned it. Yet on Friday she called herself a part-time woman."

"Do you think she's jealous? Or maybe there's another man?"

Royce seemed to shrink, hunched into himself, his back bowed like a question mark. "I don't know."

Only the evenings, Monday through Thursday, maybe five or six hours a day. Max realized Royce spent more time with his stony secretary. The weekends belonged to Irene. Even in two years, it wasn't as if they'd spent a lot of time together.

Suddenly Max heard a dog bark, as if it were in the water under the hull of the boat. He looked around and Royce smiled and stood, motioning him to the rail. Below, a seal cruised back and forth, its head and neck arched out of the water, as a dog would circle your feet for scraps. It bobbed up, its flippers breaking the surface of the water, then rolled on its back and continued to lap the end of the boat.

"Beautiful animals," Royce said. "Know what it is?"

"A seal, of course."

"Everyone says that. It's a sea lion. Seals don't have ears."

Max looked. The sleek chocolate-colored animal sported buttons on the sides of its head, ears, which it wiggled as if to prove Royce's point.

"They come in the harbor for handouts, as tame as park pigeons. I wish I had something for him. He probably heard us talking."

Max looked around and realized they were still the only people on the water. Even the crew of tourists had disappeared. Yet the boats made him feel the place was full of people, each ship as distinctive as a person's handwriting.

The sea lion barked again and Max could see the long incisors, the velvety pink tongue. He couldn't believe he was looking at a wild animal, an animal performing tricks for handouts, without the prompting of a trainer, the way the keepers at the zoo made the lions roar at feeding time. The brown eyes were deep pools, intelligent eyes sizing up the two men standing on the aft of a boat in an otherwise deserted harbor.

"Kat always brings scraps for them. They'll do all kinds of leaps and rolls for food." As if the sea lion understood, it gave a flip and rolled away underneath the green water. They watched a long time for it to resurface, Max holding his breath as the sea lion must. They didn't see it break the surface anywhere in the slip.

They returned to their seats. Max noticed the wind pick up and felt the sun dip a notch closer to the tops of the hills. He wrapped a blanket around himself and Royce asked if he wanted to go below. For a moment Max was curious to see the inside of the cabin, but the feeling of being out on the water, if only in the slip, made him think of summer. Spring. Spring fever. He watched a pair of brown pelicans dropping through the sky above him to settle somewhere on the bay, behind the rows of masts. He declined Royce's offer, and prompted them back to the job at hand.

"I'll never be happy with Irene again, not since knowing Kat."

"It's not impossible to divorce her." Max patted the teak deck. "Frank gave up a lot. The last I heard he was in Hong Kong." Any good friend could have told Royce that, yet Max knew people often wanted to spend money to hear the obvious. It made their desires more valid when they paid for them. Psychiatry was the modern form of fortune-telling. The bits and pieces of stories were the cards and tea leaves brought to the psychiatrist. The pattern, or fortune, was usually what the patient already knew and wanted to hear from someone else's lips.

"What if I go through with it, divorce Irene, and Kat just wants out of this?"

"Why do you think she wants out?" Max spoke softly

to counter the panic he could see rising in Royce, the pinching in of the eyes, the nervous motion of his hands running through his hair.

"Because I'm blind to a lot of stuff. Like I said, I never even questioned if she was happy or not. I always thought you just knew things like that, the way you know a storm is coming in. You just know whether a person is happy or not. I thought Kat was happy. But yesterday afternoon I went over there as a surprise. She could have been in bed with another man. Didn't call or anything, as if it were my real home. I walked in there as if she did nothing but sit around buffing her nails waiting for me to show up. It made me think about her position for once."

"What is her position?"

"I guess I don't know." Royce looked as though his face had collapsed. "Just like I didn't know how to describe her as we came across the bridge. She's my Kat."

"Let's start at the beginning," Max said kindly. "How did you meet her? What does she do?" He wanted to see Royce's face light up again, not the sadness.

"I met her in the all-day movies down on Market. I go there when I have a fight with Irene or a particularly knotty problem to work out. I don't care what the movies are, I just like sitting in the dark with all that busyness and light on the screen."

Max nodded. He'd done that himself a time or two. "Some strange characters hang out down there."

"That's the beauty of the place. You never see anyone, just the silhouettes of heads. In the mornings especially, people tend to sit pretty evenly spaced apart. Once in a while a bottle rolls down the aisle, or you can hear someone snoring. There's all this privacy and solitude, yet you don't feel alone."

"Then how did you meet Katlyn?"

"They'd been working in the street outside when I came in."

As Royce talked, Max visualized the story as if it were his own. Max had patronized the three-for-a-dollar movies on Market when he first came to San Francisco. *Downhill Racer, Rosemary's Baby,* and *The Wild Bunch,* all during a Thursday afternoon in February when he couldn't stand another moment of burning sunshine and longed for snow. Those days when California was as unreal to him as Africa. But even after six hours of movies, when he stepped out into the street there was none of the chill of winter, just the mild San Francisco fog and winter rain. He sat in his car watching the rain sliding down the windshield and imagining the long streaks of water were melting snowflakes.

Two years ago Royce had been sitting in the movies about an hour when the lights went out. He told Max what an odd feeling it was: to be in a place that's supposed to be dark when the one thing to depend on, the light in the darkened vault of the theater, fails. The light failed, and he sat there, like the six or seven other people finding refuge in the movies that day. Without light, the illusion of doing something was destroyed. He was alone with his problems in the dark. He found himself drifting through the lobby at ten in the morning as the ticket taker explained that a construction crew accidentally hit a power line under the street. Royce could see them working under a brilliant sun but hesitated to leave the theater and go back to the printing plant. He stood in the lobby, waiting for the light in the darkness to come on once again, when a tall redheaded woman came up and asked if he had a cigarette. Royce never smoked anything but grass, and the woman seemed to know this. Cigarettes weren't the issue. He and the redheaded woman were the only people in the lobby who didn't want to share a pull on the Thunder-bird the other patrons were passing around.

Royce offered to buy the woman a cup of coffee and a pack of cigarettes at a diner up the street. He thought she must be a film student. He thought they would go back to the movies when the power was restored.

She told him she was killing time trying to figure out what to do. She said she didn't have anywhere to go. She'd been burned out in a fire.

Royce had gone to the movies on the heels of a visit to a real estate firm where he'd put his bachelor digs on Elizabeth Street up for sale. He didn't want to sell the small Victorian, but had to pay Gerald back. And now, just like the movies, here comes a damsel in distress. A lady down on her luck. In a sudden burst of generosity he told her she could stay on Elizabeth Street until she made a decision.

Having seen Katlyn and Royce together on Union Street just the night before, Max could stay well ahead of the story. Before long, Katlyn and Royce were wrapped in each other's arms, rolling on the cot Royce slept on when he was too tired to return to Marin. There would be white cartons of take-out food and square boxes of pizza, then some patched together meals in a bachelor's kitchen. And Royce simply not mentioning his wife and other home in Sausalito. A woman burned out in a fire would be travel-ing light and she could camp there for days as their affection deepened, as they explored each other's bodies. Royce took the house off the market, just until she could get something going. He went through his days at the printing plant cutting corners in order to leave early, getting to work late. He quit going home on the weekends and simply dropped by for a few hours to pick up some clean clothes.

Things began to show up, Royce said. A coffee pot.

Drapes. Sheets for the bed. Towels. They went to garage sales and flea markets to patch together enough furnishings to make the place cozier than his working bachelor digs. She had some things in storage, and Royce never questioned why a woman who loved fresh squeezed orange juice for breakfast would keep her juicer in storage. They worked on the house together. She set up a workshop in the spare bedroom and designed clothes for a boutique. She planted a garden, with fresh herbs and vegetables, rosebushes and morning glories. She cooked gourmet dinners for the two of them; and for the first time Royce took delight in food, savoring the spices Irene never used. He learned to enjoy working with her at the stove in the evenings and she taught him to cook as easily as a cat sleeps through the day. When she used his tools to refinish furniture she found at garage sales and flea markets, she took care to keep them clean and oiled. He would come home in the evening and find a hideous green lacquered stand in the middle of the garage and a week later it would be an oak table with the lacquer stripped off and wood putty strategically added to fill deep scratches.

They were Nick and Nora Charles, dressed out in natty clothes on the Dashiell Hammett walking tour. Royce was in love for the first time in his life. Until Gerald and Margaret came down unexpectedly and Tony the neighbor inadvertently destroyed Royce's idyllic affair.

"And now she's talking of leaving," Max said.

"Or divorce Irene." Once again, Max watched as the light went out of his face. Royce rose and began pacing the small deck, causing the boat to tip back and forth with the slow motion of a rocking chair. "I mean, when you think of how she just turned up in my life, I suppose I have to look at the possibility she could vanish just as suddenly."

Max pulled the blanket more tightly around his shoulders. "You know, you might have two very separate problems here. One is your relationship with your wife and family. And one is your relationship with Katlyn. One solution won't necessarily solve all the problems."

"Oh, that's good news," Royce said bitterly. "Then what am I going to do? You asked me before what I was afraid of. I think I'm most afraid of tearing apart the fabric of my life, dissolving everything I've done in the last sixteen years, and Kat still leaving me. Wasn't it Freud who said people must settle for a life of common unhappiness? Before Kat, I was willing to settle for that. But now I've had two years of great happiness, an uncommon thing. It's hard to scale down after that."

"So if Kat weren't pressuring you, you wouldn't divorce Irene?"

"And the other side of this is that if Irene weren't who she is, Kat would have never become so important to me." Royce was lost in his own train of thought, not listening to Max's questions, but using the sound of Max's voice as the signal to say what he was thinking.

Max repeated the question. "Would you divorce Irene if you hadn't met Kat?"

Royce looked up, focusing on Max as if surprised to see him here. "Of course not. I'm thirty-eight. I've been pretty spineless up to now, telling myself I was doing the right thing. What am I supposed to do if Gerald takes that printing plant from me? And he could do it. No matter what the divorce laws say. I'm divorcing Irene, not Gerald."

"I think you're jumping the gun here. There's no reason to believe Gerald is so devoted to his daughter that he would liquidate a profitable business." Max needed to quell the panic rising in Royce again. The afternoon was slipping by, they would have to stop soon, and this man was trying to solve the problems of the last sixteen years in brief therapy. By Friday.

"I don't know what I know right now." Royce ran his hands through his hair again and slumped back into the beanbag chair. "I want you to meet her," he said at last. "I don't know what this Africa thing means. Maybe you can tell if she really wants to leave me or just wants me to get a divorce."

"Is that the issue?" Max asked. "Is it that simple? If Katlyn promises not to leave you, you'll divorce your wife, perhaps have to look for another job? It's that simple?" He watched Royce closely for this answer.

Royce thought about this. "I don't know." And Max saw the panic again.

The sun was now poised on the hilltops to the west, balanced there like a perfect orange in a Magritte painting. In just a few moments the shadows would come gliding across the harbor. Max didn't know what to do. In four hours it was difficult to do more than raise the problems, and Royce seemed to expect to have things settled, to be given a direction which would guide him for the rest of the week as he decided how to handle the women in his life. Still, Max envied him a bit, as he always envied people in love. Great strength and courage could be found through loving someone. Royce didn't need a psychiatrist, he needed only to know his love was returned and then he could act. But Max couldn't supply that reassurance for him. Only Katlyn could.

"I want you to meet her," Royce said again. He, too, looked at the sun beginning to sink behind the hills. "But it looks as if our time is up, doesn't it?"

Their eyes met, and Max knew what he would do, professionalism be damned. He always got involved with his patients too quickly, too personally. Not enough professional distance, his own analyst had told him. This man was trying to rearrange his life in brief therapy, deal with at least sixteen years in the course of a week. It couldn't be done, yet Max knew he would help Royce. "She'd have to want to meet with me," Max said. "She'd have to make another appointment."

Royce gave an embarrassed smile. "I didn't tell her I was seeing a psychiatrist today. That's why I suggested we meet at the plant. I'd have to bring the whole idea up to her." His face fell again and fear flitted through his eyes. "I'm afraid of what will happen if I go home this Friday."

Max reached in his pocket and brought out his business cards. "She has to call me. And I'm afraid the only time I have before Friday is tomorrow afternoon. I usually take Wednesday afternoons off since I see patients on Saturday. I keep hairdresser's hours." He gave a little chuckle and wondered when he would find a more professional metaphor for his schedule.

Royce studied the card. "I'll see what she says. I hate to ask you to give up your free time. But if she won't see you, I'd like to. I'm afraid my problems are bigger than just Africa."

Max unwrapped the blanket from around his shoulders, stalling for time. He pulled the sweater over his head and returned that too. "We'd have to work out a different time. If she calls, you both can have tomorrow afternoon. If she doesn't, then I think you and I should work out something for next week." Max watched Royce's face as the knowledge of what this meant sank in.

Royce's eyes dilated and he pinched them in at the corners. "I see." He nodded absently a few times. "If she doesn't call, we'll set up something for next week."

Royce locked up the boat and they returned to the car for the drive back to the city. They were silent until they passed the Dillingham-Tokala construction crew, responsible for the renovation of the Golden Gate Bridge.

Then, as if Max and Royce had been to lunch, rather than paging through Royce's life for the last four hours, Royce began to talk about the bridge and the ongoing construction work. Max realized how important this bridge was to Royce, a steel link holding the two parts of his life together, at least for now.

"Frank was a wheel in Dillingham-Tokala, you know," Royce said. "This project is a bitch. Heavy fines if they run late, that kind of thing. But the worst, Frank said, is when they find the suicides. Ever notice the concrete moat around the middle pier? That's where the suicides go. They all jump into the moat so their bodies will be found, won't wash away. And they all jump facing the bay, with the lights of Berkeley ahead of them. Only one or two jump facing the ocean. Don't get me wrong," Royce added with a sudden smile. "My problems aren't serious enough for suicide. But I thought, as a psychiatrist, you'd want to know."

"I know," Max said. "If they live they're arrested for disturbing the peace."

Behind the wheel of his Mustang, Max thought of Elaine and the suicides in the moat, floating on the water. Jumpers. He wished Claire had jumped into water. When they called him to identify her, he tried to take her hand, but it felt nothing like a hand, more like a wet towel. What did she think about during those last seconds in the air, falling, falling. How long does it take to fall seventeen stories? Thirty seconds? A minute? More? Did she hear music?

Falling, falling. Claire, all alone on the top of the building, dressed in her tennis whites in the sun. Max had been in a seminar on statistics, his father, at the sporting goods store. Why that Wednesday? Why that building? Why hadn't she talked to him first? The minister at the service had said if God couldn't stop you, He would go with you. This didn't console Max. He would have stopped her if he had known. He would have chained her in her room if nothing else would work. Protect her until the idea passed. Everything passes, eventually. So many people could be saved if they just remembered that.

A black-backed gull soared high above him. Max wondered if jumpers were under the evil influence of birds. Unhappy people with a sincere desire to be anyone except who they are at that moment, or perhaps who they have been for a long time. Seeing a bird mastering the air inspires them. To fly, away from the ground where they've spent their sad lives. To fly, if only for a few seconds. The last graceful act of a long, unhappy life.

Electricity coursed through his body, every cell felt numb. He watched his hands tremble on the steering wheel, felt his heart begin to race.

Jumping. Water. His father died while launching a boat, just slipped away with the tide and washed up three miles down the beach two days later. And his father had been a good swimmer. His father, a fanatic about sports and physical fitness. Perhaps drowning was proper. When his father sold the sporting goods store and retired to St. Petersburg, his favorite site was the bridge that had been hit by a tanker, collapsing the span and sending thirty-some people riding in a bus to their deaths. The one time Max visited his father in St. Petersburg, his father took him to see the broken bridge four times. There always seemed to be a reason to head over in that direction. Max looked at the gap in the bridge, imagined the tanker shearing off the piling, the busload of people falling, the white foam of the sea curling over the debris as guardrails, lights, sections of pavement pitched into the water.

Royce's life depended on bridges, fragile and sturdy, massive and delicate, metal constructions spanning the waters. Connecting the two parts of Royce's life. Royce was perishing by a blessing, the blessing of his father-in-law turned into a curse. The good life gone sour.

He began to whistle, like calling a dog, until he could change his thoughts, put a tune in his mind. He wondered if he would hear from Royce's fanciful Kat, or failing that, if Royce was serious about therapy. Royce was perishing. He hoped Katlyn would call—that choice would tell him a great deal about her feelings for Royce. If she wanted to stay with Royce, she'd call. They could begin a process after that, the logistics of dealing with Royce's family, the complex bonds which grow up between people and become cemented by time. People outgrew their marriages just as they can outgrow their friends or their jobs. He wanted this case to work out. He wanted to be part of a love story with a happy ending.

TUESDAY
EVENING

"We've really gone and done it now," Katlyn told the dog as she dug her espadrilles out of the laundry hamper. "Haven't we, Dagmar?" The dog cocked an ear and sat at attention, as if the clothes hamper would yield some delicious scrap the way the refrigerator often did.

For a man who declared he wanted to spend time with her, Royce was hardly around any more than when he went to work. This morning, it was true, they spent the hours lying in bed, warm in each other's arms, making love twice since sunrise. There was something delicious about wasting away a morning like that, as physical as the taste of sharp blue cheese. While their bodies curled and wove together Katlyn remembered the electricity of their first days, that breathless feeling when she'd become as giddy as a girl of thirteen by simply thinking of him. Wasting a morning like this freed her of the nagging doubt that she and Royce might be slipping into the doldrums of an old married couple, the Sargasso Sea of lives spent together, which must be the impasse he and Irene had reached.

And then, just at the moment when the champagne he'd promised would have tasted as sweet as forbidden fruit, Royce announced he had to leave.

"What?" She'd tried to keep her voice from wailing. Lower your expectations.

"I have to go down to the plant for a while."

"I suppose you're going to work," she'd said with as much sarcasm as she could muster. But it was difficult to be catty with Royce. Only when he was gone could she feel the full power of her anger, her jealousy of Irene. That was the hardest to keep in check, her irrational condemnation of the sixteen years Royce spent with a woman who didn't love him. Being married to Irene tarnished him in her eyes, as if one poor choice had damaged him somehow. Tarnished him the way Alan had tarnished her, damaged her. She could never square herself with the thought Irene didn't love Royce as she did. Yet if Irene loved Royce, Katlyn knew he would never have pursued this affair. If Alan had loved her, she would have never gotten involved. Yet somehow, with Alan dead, the whole charade had to stop. Like a Moebius strip, her thoughts circled back and forth, going nowhere.

Royce stepped into the shower, without answering her. She sat on the end of the bed painting her toenails, wondering where he was going. To work, or home. Or there could be a thousand other possibilities. She carefully layered each nail a deep raspberry color, keeping her hands busy, marshaling her thoughts. Sometimes she felt she had the memory of a forty-year-old, the body of a thirty-year-old, and the emotional development of a twelve-year-old. She wanted him to drive over to Sausalito and end it with Irene, a clean break. Just once, a wish like that had come true, her father showing up when she was twelve, after she'd spent those years dreaming about him.

"I'll be back," Royce said. And then he was gone. Champagne in bed.

Knowing she was pushing him on the one thing he couldn't change frightened her a little. Her mother would tell her the only value in a cardinal rule is what you have left when you break it. She'd broken their cardinal rule. Once a thing like this gets started it becomes impossible to stop, their agreement disappearing in a landslide of ideas they'd never entertained before.

She could work on those new shirts, send a sample batch off to Bendel's. She could call Harris, her feather wholesaler, and start working on the masks. She could change the sheets, wash the walls, any of those domestic chores which are ultimately as important as ironing underwear. The hell with it. Royce would be back, when? This afternoon she'd do something different. She'd make some plans for her trip, because truly, she couldn't face the thought of staying in the city knowing Royce was going about his life, working, living in Sausalito. A small thing, like renting his house, would keep the lines of communication open. It was the same amount of work to move across town as to put everything in storage and travel.

Her linen dress with the epaulets would get her in the mood. Memsahib. Imagine being addressed as Memsahib. She couldn't really imagine it; the whole thing ran like a movie or dream in her head. So, just to cover all the bases, she called Harris and left a message on his machine that she would stop by the next day to see what he had in stock for the masks.

Research. The colors, the fabrics. African masks. Hear

the beat of throbbing drums, not on a record, but close enough to touch. See the vibrant plumage of exotic birds, the sweep of their wings cutting the air. Perhaps a trip to Africa would wash both these men from her mind and give her an experience which would prepare her for getting on with the rest of her life. She could go to that great map store off Market, the one she and Alan discovered when they planned their trip. Spend the whole afternoon in the map store as the special calligraphy of maps dissolved time. Browsing the outlines of foreign countries might focus what she was looking for, offer a clue to her future.

Earth-toned dyes. Ornaments of shell, bone, nuts, stone.

She locked the door and stood in the bright sunshine. The brown humps of Twin Peaks looked like the backs of camels to her today, a caravan heading south. She should take Royce to the map store, give him a sense of her seriousness. She could tell him about Alan. But after two years, her silence was as normal as breathing. The idea leapfrogged—revealing Alan would reveal all that unfinished business, his house, their marriage, his disappearance, his death. Spots of color filled her field of vision. Tell Royce about Alan. Alan hung over her life like a cloud stalled in front of the sun.

The map store calmed her. The same balding clerk who worked there before was still shuffling about, fussing with the maps. The little man was a delight. He'd never been out of California, but was living proof you didn't have to travel to know about foreign places. He once spent the better part of an afternoon showing Katlyn and Alan the virtues of a particular map of the Arctic. What had always been, to them, dead space in the world, came alive as the clerk spoke of lemmings and seals, the great fishing industry that sails the waters north of the Arctic Circle, docking in Honningsvag and Murmansk.

The clerk didn't remember her, and for this Katlyn was grateful. She liked the anonymity, no questions about that trip she never took, no questions about Alan. She would start all over again and organize a journey which wouldn't be tainted with Alan. Sometimes it was better to quit than fail.

"The oldest map in the world was found just east of here," the little clerk told her, pointing to a spot between the Mediterranean and the Persian Gulf. "Iraq, called Mesopotamia then. A clay tablet showing the water course of the Euphrates River in 3800 B.C." He smiled at her with awe and wonder on his face. "Imagine."

He pulled out an armload of maps. There were maps printed in six languages and maps printed only in English, or German, or Japanese. There was a beautiful map printed in the predominant language of each country, and the clerk told her she would have to know twenty-three languages to read every word on it. She thought Royce might enjoy this map, not as a symbol of Africa, but because he could appreciate a splendid printing job like this, the beautiful colors and the way the words were laid out so none of them disappeared into the terrain.

There were maps outlining industry and agriculture and a geological map showing rock strata and minerals. A water map revealed the great blank yellow quarter for the Sahara, the Kalahari spotted across the southern tip.

From a bottom drawer he pulled out the historical maps, countries which no longer exist proclaiming themselves in their national colors. Natal. Bechuanaland. There were maps drawn for different periods in history, back through the seventeenth century when the Dark Continent was pictured with dragons and serpents. Katlyn wanted to take this one home too, to remind Royce the world was larger than the little house on Elizabeth Street. But the timing wasn't right. *This* wasn't a map for just anyone. Katlyn knew she could come back for it another day.

She settled on a Michelin 153, a road map of Africa above the equator and west of the Nile. "This is an interesting section," the clerk told her. "I sold one of these about a year ago, and just the other day the fellow came in to report on his trip. This road here," he pointed to a red line running through the Central African Republic, "the jungle takes this one every once in a while. In the rainy season the only place you'll find this road is right here on this map. About fifteen miles out of Bangui the jungle takes it back. The Mbali Lim and the Mopoko flood over it. Sometimes you have to cross the mountains, go all the way up to Dohoukota before you find this road again. Better to cross here," he drew his nail across the blue line for the river, "over into Zongo. The Oubangi is a lovely river, this fellow said. A floating world of flowers. But be careful through here. They once had a killer hippo in Bangui. He just chomped a guy in the middle of the city square."

Katlyn smiled as she thanked the clerk. For a man who'd never been out of California, the flooding of the Mbali Lim and the Mopoko were as real to him as if they were just this minute stranded in the jungle trying to cut their way through to Bossangoa. He chuckled over the image of the killer hippo as if it were a cartoon he was watching. For him, travel was simply a state of mind.

Boarding the Muni to return to Noe Valley, Katlyn decided the Michelin 153 was completely inadequate. She also should have bought the Michelin east of the Nile and the Michelin south of the equator, the best road maps in the world for touring the Dark Continent. Where in the world are you going to go in Africa? Good question. Everything she knew about Africa was hopelessly out of date, descriptions of the Congo in 1890 from Conrad's *Heart of Darkness,* and photos of diamond miners near Pretoria in the 1920s. Hemingway on a big game safari.

117

Isak Dinesen raising coffee in the highlands of Kenya. Traders bargaining with gold-filled vulture quills in Timbuktu. Books on the White and Blue Niles had been published twenty years ago, before the dams were built. A part of Rhodesia was now Zimbabwe, but were guerrillas still fighting in the mountains? And what ever happened to Idi Amin in Uganda? Gaddafi in Libya. Riots in South Africa. Why would a sane person visit Africa?

Killer hippos in Bangui. In the middle of the city square. What did an African city square look like? Was there an African equivalent of Main Street? Bechtel was said to run the Dark Continent now. What was Bechtel doing about bilharzia and river blindness and leprosy? What do you eat in a country where people are starving?

Men saw the world through wars; Alan had seen Vietnam and the Tet Offensive. Even her father had been in Japan during the occupation under MacArthur. Women traveled the world either on someone's arm or because they were running away from someone, something. A woman's place was in the home, but what passed for a home these days? Where was Royce's home? What kind of home had she ever had? Or rather, how many homes, each place a house for a separate part of her life, each one cut off from all the others.

She didn't want to go home. She didn't want to face Royce, or the emptiness of the house if Royce wasn't there. She could go visit Danny in his apartment above his rep theater. But she already knew what awaited her at Danny's. Danny, his long hair matted, his kimono covered with grease spots, and another lecture on Japanese filmmakers, fueled by puffs on his joint.

She decided to stop into Saving Grace. Charlotte was sure to have something to say about all this. She wondered if he'd ever been out of the country.

Three women were browsing when Katlyn walked in.

Charlotte leafed through a magazine and sipped white wine from a crystal champagne glass. "Care to join me?" He tipped the long-stemmed glass at her. He looked hung over, a bit of unshaven stubble on his cheek, blue bags under his eyes, rumpled khaki fatigues. Even his close-cropped hair looked limp.

"Sure." She and Charlotte could sit here and get quietly drunk for the rest of the afternoon. Smoke dope, snort coke, discuss heartbreak. Katlyn felt as if something was loose in her mind, a whole series of thoughts which might belong to someone else. The mind is a monkey.

"It's just cheap white wine." Charlotte handed her a goblet. "But then, cheap white wine goes with every-thing. Should I offer a toast, a bon voyage?"

"I haven't really decided." But she thought of show-ing him the Michelin map in her purse. She should go to the library, study up. How does a white woman behave in Capetown?

One of the women said "Thank you," and left.

"Oh, too bad." He propped his feet up on the edge of the desk. "I was going to share with you all my sexual fantasies about Africa." He ticked them off on his fingers. "To be shot at by snipers. To be put under house arrest. To feel the air pass around a herd of stampeding ele-phants." He fanned the air in front of him as if doing a breast stroke. "And to be mauled by a lion."

"You call those sexual fantasies? To be mauled by a lion?" Katlyn laughed.

"You never know. I had a friend once who was excited by sharks. He had a whole jaw of a great white shark he kept in his bedroom, right next to the bed. When we had sex, he would put his hand on the jaw, feel the teeth."

"Did you ever keep track of how many lovers you've had, Charlotte?"

"Just the boys? Or boys and girls?"

"Whatever. Did you keep track?" She sipped her wine.

"Back when I was in high school, of course. It's always important then. But once the number of lovers I'd had was more than my age, and I think that was when I was around twenty-four, I quit counting those things. It was too depressing. I could remember some of the faces, and bodies, but hardly any names. So I just quit." He shrugged. "It's depressing to think I couldn't even find them if I wanted to. Just faces and bodies. No names."

She watched the other two women drift out of the store. "I'm afraid Royce will be my last lover."

"Nonsense." Charlotte gave a snicker. "There's never any such thing. After all, anticipation is the most reliable form of pleasure."

"I'd take dead solid certainty over anticipation any day."

"How boring. Besides, nothing is ever dead solid certain."

She drew a cigarette out of her purse, stalling for time, trying to think of one thing which she would call a dead solid certainty. "Here's one. Royce loves World War II movies. He gets as intent as a kid on a video game, watching all those blasting bullets. He knows the end. We won the War. I don't know what he sees in them, but they're dead solid certain pleasures for him." The thought of Royce, making love to him this morning, gave her a rush. In their early days these rushes would come over her in the damnedest places, waiting in line for a movie, in the laundromat. Once, in a grocery store, she'd wanted him so badly she couldn't concentrate. Forget the strawberries. She wanted to get on her back in the vegetable bin, roll around on the lettuce and tomatoes. Charlotte was right, anticipation.

"I suppose a World War II fixation is a dead solid certainty. But still boring. How about a lovely black African? A biddy little Bantu or a giant Masai? I wouldn't mind anticipating one of those fellows. Of course, you could probably come close, down in the Fillmore. No need to go to Africa, really."

"I haven't a single sexual thought about Africa. Is that strange?" She felt hollow, as if her spirit had left her. She could see herself on a bed, as big as an ocean, all alone.

"You don't have to have sexual thoughts about everything. But I'd say the notion of a last lover is a sexual thought." He eyed her thoughtfully. "But that's more like a marriage."

"It's funny," she said, "but when I was married to Alan, I never thought of him as my last lover. I sort of knew I'd have other lovers after Alan, as if I knew all along the marriage wouldn't last. But the thought of leaving Royce made me think of him as my last lover. Maybe I've gotten too old for sexual sports." She looked out the door of the shop, trying to see through the bullet holes. She felt as if that door surrounded her, like a phone booth, and all she could do was look out. No one could get in. She wondered if someone had been standing inside when the shots were first fired.

"Anyone would think that about Alan. He was gay. I'll never believe you didn't know that when you married him."

Katlyn shook her head sadly. "Nope. It really never crossed my mind. I thought he might be having an affair, but I never guessed it would be with a man." She wondered if leaving your wife for a man could be considered a crime of passion. Was leaving your wife legally a crime, or did it just feel like one?

"Well, I never thought he'd marry. Or marry a woman at any rate. But then people do the most unpredictable things. My mother told me a story about a movie star, I forget who now, but she was a big star back in the forties. She had her career, owned her own home, was loved by millions, had famous affairs. When she was fifty she married her bridge partner. She said they'd always have something to do.''

''Was he her last lover?''

Charlotte opened his hands, shot up an eyebrow. ''How should I know?''

''Royce isn't exactly my bridge partner.''

''Well, you're no movie star either. Why so maudlin this afternoon? Last week you were in love with Royce. Yesterday you were going to go to Africa. Today you're talking about last lovers. Did Royce tell you to go ahead and get lost?''

''We sort of left things up in the air. He's going to think it over this week.''

''Well, I think you've made a huge mistake here. You're going to shoot to hell a lovely affair with a beautiful man. I mean, even I get the hots for Royce when you bring him in here.''

She seemed to be the only one plagued with memory. The hollow spot in her chest expanded and she felt as if someone were telling her she didn't have any clothes on, or that she'd been robbed. ''Charlotte, have you heard from Guerrero?''

''I wish.'' He drained his glass and reached under the desk for the wine bottle. ''I've called, but all I get is his damn machine. And it's spooky because the message is Alan's voice. He could at least have changed the message. Guerrero could be in the Caribbean for all I know. If you ask me, he owes it to Alan's friends to tell us what happened.'' He lowered his feet from the desk and stretched, his arms spread-eagled as if he were making a snow angel. ''I've been having the most awful time, as

real as acid flashbacks. Can't eat. Can't sleep. So I drink."
He toasted her with his wine glass. "I keep seeing Alan
being hit by a cab, crashing through the windshield. I see
him with those horrible purple Kaposi spots." He swirled
the wine in his glass. "Ah well. Life is tough and then you
die, but you don't have to be a wimp about it. Did I tell
you I called that guy and he gave me five hundred and
fifty beautiful green bills for your lion?"

"That's nice." She could only vaguely remember making the lion this weekend. Her thoughts were loose again,
rolling around in her mind with no more pattern or logic
than leaves in the wind. Flashes of Alan came back to
her, reading in bed with him, playing 'The Perfect' game,
sitting beside him in the MG as they followed the coast to
Monterey. The way he whistled when he shaved.

"So do me a favor," Charlotte was saying, "no more
lions. I promised this guy he'd have a one-of-a-kind."

"Okay." Katlyn sipped her wine. She wondered if
Royce was home yet and if she should stay here with
Charlotte, just to make him wonder. That was the kind of
game Alan used to play: Katlyn was the Perfect Fool, the
Perfect Foil, the Perfect Scapegoat. "With Alan, it never
was a question of love, was it?" She gave a hollow
chuckle. "A marriage of convenience, isn't that what they
call it?"

Charlotte looked helpless, his eyes wide and plead-
ing. "How would I know? You married him."

"Love isn't something you're born with, Charlotte.
You either earn it or people give it to you unexpectedly.
But you're not born with it, like ears."

Charlotte rose and headed for the back office. His
hand parted the beaded curtain, then he turned to address
her. "None of this blather will bring Alan back. He loved
you in one way, he loved Guerrero in another. There are
as many types of love in this world as there are pieces of
money."

A man stepped into the shop. Katlyn rose and walked over to Charlotte, kissed him lightly on the cheek. "I'm going. Forget it. Don't worry, I'm just in a strange mood today."

The afternoon was warm and the sun shone summery as June. All these questions. How did Alan die? Where was he buried? Where was Guerrero? How hot does it get in Africa? Was it true you could fry an egg on a rock at noon? As she turned into Elizabeth Street, Katlyn saw Elaine Lifton basking on the Liftons' front porch.

This was the first time Katlyn had seen her since she watched the ambulance pull away in January. Katlyn stared. Elaine's arms rested in her lap, red mittens covering her hands. Katlyn couldn't keep her eyes off the red mittens, which looked like deflated balloons.

"Hello," Elaine said. "You don't happen to have a smoke do you?" Her smile was quite pretty and lit up her whole face.

"Sure." Katlyn felt all her weight sink to the soles of her feet. How do you smoke a cigarette without hands? She reached into her purse.

"Menthol?" Elaine's eyes widened, a hunger for pleasure.

"Sorry." Katlyn stepped toward the porch. She felt her heart quicken, sweat on her palms. But she knew what she was being asked to do. "How you doing?"

"I've had an accident," Elaine said. "But I guess you know that. Would you mind holding it for me?" Nervousness crept into the corners of her eyes and the color rose in her cheeks.

"Not at all." She placed the cigarette in Elaine's lips and snapped flame to her lighter. Elaine took a deep drag, nodded her head, a sign to remove the cigarette.

"I enjoy a cigarette every once in a while."

"I've been smoking since I was twelve," Katlyn said.

Her thoughts whirled, what could she say? She thought the ultimate pleasure, aside from sex, would be to smoke and swim. But one needed hands to smoke, one needed hands to swim. One needed hands to get dressed, to touch your lover.

Katlyn sat next to her on the porch and placed the cigarette between Elaine's lips, watching as she inhaled. When Katlyn removed the cigarette a great plume of smoke rose from her mouth.

Clouds tumbled across the sky. Katlyn could only think of her own hands, guiding the cigarette into Elaine's mouth. The Koran punished thieves by cutting off the right hand, forcing them to eat and clean themselves with the one remaining hand. But Elaine didn't have either of her hands. Just the empty red mittens. Sioux warriors were said to cut off the hands and cut out the tongue of cowardly men who weren't worth scalping.

"I'm trying to learn how to predict the weather," Elaine said. "There was a man who lived in China who could predict when ships would dock by studying the clouds, even though he was miles from the ocean."

"You could make a fortune," Katlyn said. "I had a friend, Alan, who used to bet on TV weathermen, see which one of them actually came up with the weather for the following day. I lost a lot of money that way."

Elaine scanned the clouds. "I'm surprised there was a right answer."

"Every day has some kind of weather."

"Life's a bitch, isn't it," Elaine said. "I've got to think of something to do for the next thirty or forty years. Like this." She lifted her arms and the mittens flopped at her wrists. She laughed and flopped the mittens again. "So I settled on the weather. I was never very good in school, so I don't figure I'm going to come up with any new developments in quantum physics."

Katlyn wanted to ask Why? Why? but she reached the cigarette over to Elaine's lips for another drag.

"You're very kind," Elaine said.

"No problem. Is there anything else you're interested in besides the weather?"

"That's what made me do this." She gestured with the mittens again. "When my father died, I lost interest in everything. It was like my brain short-circuited, blew a fuse. Now I can't even remember anything I thought about in all that time, before my accident. I don't even remember planning to do it. I have a psychiatrist who says the brain is a very delicate organ. Delicate things are easily broken."

The cigarette burned down to the filter and Katlyn stubbed it out against the sole of her shoe and threw the butt into the street. She tried to think of other things besides the weather to keep Elaine interested in life, so she wouldn't short-circuit again. "Do you like birds?"

Elaine shrugged. "It's hard to dislike them."

"I had a friend once who was very sick, in much worse shape than you." Her hand trembled, perhaps she shouldn't have said that. "Anyhow, she was in a lot of pain and to keep her mind off it, she learned birdcalls."

Elaine's eyes brightened. "Like she whistled them?"

"Yep. For a while she had a job, at home, whistling birdcalls for the Library of Congress, for records." Dorre was small as a bird at that time, sitting in the big double bed, whistling while Warren tiptoed around the apartment.

"Oh yeah?" There was interest in Elaine's eyes. "What happened to her?"

Dorre was dead, but she couldn't tell that to Elaine. "Well, you know." How lame. No tact at all. Dorre was dead. Elaine was alive.

The light went out of Elaine's eyes. "You think I should take up whistling for the next fifty years? Boy. Last year I auditioned for a band, as a singer. I really thought I was strutting my stuff. When it was over, the leader kind of shook his head and said, 'Honey, you ever had anything which might pass for experience?' I was so humiliated, I just left. I think that was probably the end of my musical career."

Katlyn felt helpless. She knew how painful it was to give something your best shot and fall miserably short of the mark. "The reason I told you about my friend is because I thought you might want to know, to know." She couldn't go on. It sounded too patronizing.

"I know why you told me. I'm getting a big dose of that stuff these days. Reasons to live. One of the nurses in the hospital wanted to try to teach me to write with my toes."

"Sometimes we all need a little help." More lameness, but it was true. Could she have helped Dorre and Warren?

Elaine closed her eyes. "I'll have to think about that." She slumped down in the chair as if going to sleep.

"Is there anything else I can do for you?" Katlyn asked.

Elaine smiled, her eyes still closed. "No. I'm fine. Thanks again, thanks so much."

"I just live down the street," Katlyn pointed to the house, hands again, and fingers. "If you need anything, just let me know."

"I know. You have a brown dog and you walk her without a leash," Elaine said. "I think I'll just take a nap. In my dreams I still have my hands. I've been having a lot of dreams about building things. Cars. Metronomes. This morning I dreamed I was building a ship out of pencils. Yellow pencils." She scooted farther down in the chair.

As she walked back to her own house Katlyn felt as if she were inside a deep tunnel, a mine shaft, and even though she could see the late afternoon sun, the day felt dark. Dorre. Dorre. Dorre. And now Elaine. In a hospital bed in D.C., Warren slept endlessly. No one to look in on him. No one to hold his hand, brush the hair off his forehead. No one to care.

Dagmar greeted her happily when she unlocked the door; it didn't look as if Royce had been here since this morning. Where could he have gone? She stared at her hands, at the knuckles and nails, the veins under the skin. The empty red mittens hanging from the stumps of wrists.

But there was the evening to come. She couldn't dwell on Elaine. Or Warren and Dorre. She had her own problems to solve. Maybe some grand fantasy. Those costumes, their games, the one thing which set her apart in the constellation of his life.

Elaine's red mittens troubled her deeply. They say the feet are the most important part of the body, a few inches of skin and bone to carry the whole weight of a person through life. But without hands, without hands. Without hands a person was totally dependent on others. One could think and walk, but that was the extent of it. The full horror of punishing thieves by cutting off their hands came to her. Elaine would live the rest of her life at the whim of the kindness or cruelty of others. She'd tried to kill herself, a pretty young woman with her future before her. Now her future was as thin as a dime.

Wisps of fog trailed over Twin Peaks like steam rising off dry ice. It was after six o'clock and still light, the days lengthening toward summer. Dagmar curled up on the couch, her nose under her tail. To calm herself, Katlyn kept busy while she waited, creating the harem costume, winding the glittering gold cloth around her breasts, cupping each one individually for lift. Sex, like anything else, was mostly illusion. Winding the cloth around her body wasn't the least bit sensual, more like layering her chest with bandages. She kept watching her hands, all the things they could do. The swirly harem skirt, flags of acetate and silk hanging from a sequined bikini bottom. Royce's eyes danced with pleasure when he saw the sequins winking in the evening light.

Irene was in Sausalito, making dinner for her children, perhaps even for Royce. I'll be back, he said. When? As Katlyn tied up her hair in an intricate knot, she wondered about Royce's marriage. What was a real marriage? Certainly nothing she'd experienced. Like mother, like daughter. Opal's marriage lasted only long enough to conceive her daughter. Her own marriage to Alan had been a fraud. Honesty night. She would be Scheherazade and tell him about Alan.

She topped the knot of hair with a string of old pearls and the ostrich tiara. Drawing thick lines of kohl, she created sloe eyes. She tied a gold chain around her waist. Like all her costumes, this illusion had an eclectic flair. She decided she looked like a cross between a belly dancer and a Paris designer's idea of what a shipwrecked castaway would be wearing this season.

The dog barked. The garage door rumbled. Royce was home.

"That's okay, Dagmar. It's only Royce." Katlyn moved into the living room and tossed all the pillows on the floor. She arranged the flags of silk around her legs and thighs. The dog came over to lick her face. Dagmar. What would she do about Dagmar if she went to Africa? Dagmar was better than a friend or lover. She would never run off with a travel agent, never leave each weekend for Marin. A dog would never drive you to cut off your hands. Could you take a dog to Africa?

The first thing she spotted when Royce walked in was the fisherman's knit sweater he kept on the *Singing Stars*.

129

"Well, let's see." Royce looked as happy as a child discovering a present. "Ah, ha." He walked around her as Katlyn lay back on the pillows, her arm over Dagmar's neck.

"Imagine the bells," she said, "tiny, tinkling, Arabian bells. Reedy flute music. In the marketplace below us," she waved an arm covered with bracelets toward the window, "camels are marching, hundreds of camels with the dust of days upon their backs. They carry cobras coiled in wicker baskets. Monkeys squeal. Parrots chatter. The caravan is loaded with ivory, cloves, and gold. Come," she patted the pillow beside her, "I'll tell you all about it." She'd tell him about Alan. Maybe in the third person. *She once married a gay guy, although she didn't know it at the time.* Someone told her only criminals and schizophrenics refer to themselves in the third person. She felt a little bit of both at the moment.

Royce eased himself down on the pillow, his hand reaching under the scarves and up her leg. He squeezed her thigh. "Sorry, sweetheart. No games tonight."

This surprised her. He'd never turned down one of these games before. She felt cold inside, the bird of fear beating in her breast. Fear drilled through her veins, scouring away little bits of her with each heartbeat. He'd gone sailing. He had a look in his eye she'd never seen before. "Lie down," she said. "You've got a lot of sun on your face, and as your slave girl, I will bathe your forehead in oils." She needed to collect herself. There was something very wrong here.

He grabbed her hand before she could rise. "No you won't. I appreciate all the trouble you've gone to, all this," he indicated the costume, "but I want to have a serious talk with you."

"I thought we were going to give it until the end of the week." She stared at his strong hands. She shouldn't have dressed up in this elaborate costume. It gave him the advantage and made her look silly. The look in his eyes told her tonight would hold as much passion and imagination as a banker negotiating a mortgage.

Royce picked up one of the silk scarves. "Is this what you call a subtle hint?"

She pulled away and stood, the bells and trinkets of her costume rattling and tinkling as she moved. "I'll change. It will only take a moment."

Royce was on his feet, blocking her way to the bathroom. "No you won't. Changing clothes will just give you time to boogie into another persona. I don't want to talk to another persona. We ducked everything last time. Maybe we were too easy on ourselves. But we're not going to slide out of it this time. I want to talk to you, not Hedy Lamarr or Catherine the Great."

She would never have the nerve to tell him about Alan now. "We agreed not to talk about it this week." This was madness. She wanted to talk to him, yet she could feel her fear like sweat running off her skin.

"I'm not sure we necessarily agreed to anything like that. It's time to put all our cards on the table." He seated himself on the couch, his back straight, his feet neatly paired.

"What if I'm not ready?"

"You might not have to say anything. You might just want to listen to what I have to say."

There was nothing to do but play it his way. She took the chair opposite, feeling ridiculous in the fake silk and sequins. Irene probably went around the house looking like Donna Reed or Beaver Cleaver's mother. That would be the right kind of outfit for a confrontation like this. Or perhaps a black suit, something she would wear to a business meeting or a funeral. What had Alan's funeral been like? Katlyn removed her bracelets and tiara and placed them on the end table. "So talk."

"I spoke to a psychiatrist this afternoon, and I'd like to have you talk to him too. We need to get some things straight around here."

She looked at him as if he'd told her he was pregnant. "Now who's playing dress-up? Do you know women have a much more acute sense of smell than men? Women can smell when their men are fooling around. You say you went to see a psychiatrist and I can smell the fact you went sailing. As if your sweater didn't give it away."

"We sat out on Frank's boat all afternoon. It's part of the way he operates."

"He only does therapy on boats?" She smiled. "And you think I'm bizarre."

He held his hand, palm up, to stop her. "I don't know exactly what you call his kind of therapy, but he likes to meet people where they feel comfortable. I took him out to the boat. Tomorrow, I hope, if you'll talk to him, he'll come over here."

"What for? I don't have a problem."

"Well, I have a problem with you and maybe Dr. Bodine can help me figure it out."

She stiffened, her fears confirmed. Like riding a bicycle, there was no way she could backpedal, no way to reverse the direction she'd chosen. The best she could hope for would be to steer around the obstacles and pray this wasn't going too fast to control. "Let's slow down a moment," she said. "You don't have a problem with me. My position's pretty clear in all this. There are some things you and Irene have to work out. Maybe you should take him over there, if that's the way you want to play it. But you don't have to work out anything with me."

"Maybe you don't see it the way I do, but if you're interested in keeping this relationship going, you're going to have to stretch yourself a bit. Try to see things through my eyes for a change. Put yourself in my shoes."

What did he mean by keep this relationship going? Did he mean as it had been for the last two years? The way she wanted things to go? Or the way he wanted his perfect life?

"If you want to talk about point of view, it's about time we took it from my point of view," she said. "We've been living this situation to suit you for two years now." But suddenly she felt it was all a masquerade, as silly as her costume. There were people with real problems, like Elaine.

Royce's tone went cold. "I didn't realize it was such a burden to you."

"I'm not saying it was. But we can't go on like that." She wished she didn't have the heavy makeup on. Her face would be more mobile without it. She could tell him things with her eyes if they weren't all gunked up with kohl.

"What exactly do you want to do, Katlyn?"

"I'd like you to divorce Irene."

"And if I don't?"

"I won't wait for you any more." She watched his eyes and felt the pulsing of her blood echoing in her ears. Why couldn't she let things alone?

"And if I do?"

She smiled and felt her whole heart settle into her face. "We could have a life together. That's what I want."

He stood and paced the living room, stretching his arms and shoulders. He parted the curtain and stared at the bright globes of the streetlights. She didn't know if he believed her or not. She wanted to pour out hyperbole and far-flung metaphors. But there needed to be some dignity in all this. She'd made her statement. Now it was his turn. Luck changes with every turn of the wheel.

He continued to look out into the street, his back to her. "I have all kinds of funny thoughts these days." His voice was very mild. "I thought of taking you over there, to meet her. It would be perfect in that costume." He dropped the curtain and turned to look at her. "Just so you know what you're asking me to do. And if I do this, what are you going to do for me?"

"We're not dealing favors here, Royce. But if you divorce Irene, I won't leave." She found her temper rising. "If you're so sure this is all make-believe on my part, have her over for dinner." Meeting Irene in Sausalito was unthinkable. Irene might poison her, shoot her. But here, in her own home, their house, Katlyn knew she could handle it. If Royce wanted her to meet Irene, she'd rather make a stand on her own ground.

Royce gave a hollow laugh. "That would be some dinner."

Her heart went cold. The blood pounded in her ears like surf striking the beach. Meet Irene. Meet Irene. Meet Irene.

"Well, let's see." Royce strolled across the room, ending up behind her chair. "First I want you to meet Dr. Bodine. Then we'll see about dealing with my wife."

My wife. That possessive. He never referred to Irene as his wife. Irene was an entity, not a possession. Irene commanded power and presence. My wife implied all the connections she was asking him to sever.

If she could satisfy him by talking to a psychiatrist, that would be a small chore compared to confronting Irene, his wife. She rose and slid her arms around his neck. "Sure thing." Sometimes the safest place is closest to the gun. Maybe this psychiatrist could get them back on track, unblock this Mexican standoff. She couldn't back down and he couldn't change. Perhaps his Dr. Bodine might tip the balance, like shaking loose a clogged salt-cellar. But as they kissed she knew, beneath it all, she'd committed herself to a process she had no way of completing. Perhaps this was how Alan felt when he left her, unable to stop a rapidly spreading fire, a fire started with the simple flick of a match and now beyond control. As surprising as a firecracker.

"So, you'll do it," Royce said, and the happiness in his voice thrilled her.

"Of course." She pulled away from him and began taking down her hair. "You're missing one essential element in all this. I might not want to go to Africa. But I don't want to go on sharing you with Irene." She pulled the pearls out of the knot. "I'd be very happy to continue living with you here. If you don't love Irene, if you mean that, it's all very simple."

"Then what's Africa got to do with it in the first place?"

"When I say it, it sounds so awful, but Africa is really a test. The object is to see where we finally stop, what will happen after that." The light in his eyes faded to the color of smoke. "Maybe I'm making a mistake. But there are only two kinds of mistakes a person commits. Ultimate mistakes and accumulated mistakes. You and Irene might have drifted on for years, accumulating little mistakes until you're sick of each other. Going to Africa is an ultimate mistake, one big grand notion that might be absolutely wrong-headed, or just the right thing for me at this moment. Ultimate mistakes are tests. You either win or lose, fly or die. Things change, just as completely as a butterfly comes out of a cocoon." The red mittens. Which type of mistake had Elaine made? There was more to it. Elaine must go on every day. Predicting the weather. Building imaginary ships. What would the future be like for Elaine? "We've got no future this way. I've got no future. We're at a standstill, the eternal present. Time goes on, but we don't. That's entropy. Love isn't a perpetual motion machine." This, she knew, was the truth.

He placed his hands on her shoulders, reached up and stroked her hair. "You don't understand the difficulties. You've painted this only in black and white. There's always a middle course. Not everything has to be viewed as a mistake."

She moved away from him, saddened at how desperate he looked. "It doesn't matter. We all do what we want to do, no matter how difficult or impossible it might seem. There's no reason to be chained to the past. You can make the world over every day if you want to. If you want to stay with Irene, you will."

He slumped back into the couch, curled in on himself. "Will you talk to Dr. Bodine with me?"

"Of course." She unclipped the gold chain and placed it on the end table with the rest of the jewelry. "I want you. That's the point here. If I can't have you, I'll have to go on to something else. So I'll do anything to make this work."

"Will you call him up and tell him that?"

"Sure. What's the number?" She didn't know what she was letting herself in for, but it didn't matter. She would ride the whole thing out now, no matter where the trip ended. Talking to a psychiatrist would be an act of good faith. Unless Royce wanted to call in a third party to explain why he couldn't leave Irene. In that case, she'd use the same third party to explain to Royce she had no choice but to leave him. Two could play this game.

Royce pulled a business card from his wallet and raised it the way he would hold out a candle in the dark. She went to the phone and dialed, a piece of theater on her part. No office would be open at this hour of the evening, either it would ring or she would get a recording. It was a recording, with just the faintest trace of an eastern accent in the voice. And no music.

Katlyn had grown to prefer talking to recordings rather

than total strangers on the other end of the line. No visual image of the person, the phone held to the ear like a monstrous flower. But a machine, carefully rehearsed and recorded, gave her time to rehearse too. She spent those seconds inventing her own statement, which she delivered when the tone sounded. "This is Katlyn Whiston. I'm a friend of Royce Chambers, and he suggested we all get together and talk. I think that's a wonderful idea and look forward to meeting you." Let Royce and the good doctor work out the details.

She handed back the business card, hoping to see some animation in his face. "It was a machine," she said, "so I couldn't set up a time."

"One o'clock tomorrow. He's coming over here. If you didn't want to meet him, we'd have done something else."

"Isn't that a rather weird setup?"

"I kind of like it. I like him. You'll see."

She felt safe, at least for the moment. Surely by tomorrow she would think of something, Royce would give her some clue as to what was really going on. She still must tell him about Alan. The harem costume hadn't worked. Nothing left but cold turkey. "Let's go for a walk on the beach," she said. "Run the dog."

"You're just full of ideas tonight, aren't you?" Royce gestured at the costume. "This whole business makes me feel as if my brain were bleeding. This house, you, Irene." He rubbed his neck as if it were stiff and sore. "Go change." He looked sad and lonely. "If we live together, it's going to be on the up-and-up. We'll have to be real people, not the ones we've been pretending to be."

She suggested the Taraval Street entrance to the beach, near the house where she and Alan used to live. Unlike Ocean Beach, with the lights of the Cliff House shining down upon it and bums and tailgate parties wandering around, the beach near the Taraval Street entrance was dark and deserted.

They were silent during the ride across town. At least for tonight Katlyn knew he would be with her. She'd taken a terrible chance asking him to divorce Irene. What if he wouldn't? Charlotte was right. Africa wouldn't solve what she would feel if Royce decided to go live on the other side of the bridge.

The moon was a shining fingernail. Overhead, Orion with his glittering belt faced the red-eyed bull, the horns reaching through the heavens. Sirius, the Dog Star, leapt at Orion's heels and the sky surged with movement, Orion, the bull, the dog, and the setting moon. She tasted the salt spray on her lips, a little kissing motion.

Royce took her hand. "I had a wonderful fantasy the other day, a real escapist indulgence. We'd steal Frank's boat and sail out under the Gate. We'd just keep going. I'd chart a southwesterly course so the land would drop away from us slowly. It would just fade away, like when the sun goes down and you can't name the moment when the sky turns completely dark."

"Where would we go?"

"Clear across the Pacific. You want to go to Africa? We could sail all the way to Madagascar. Up the coast. Through the Canal."

"I'd like that," Katlyn said sincerely. "I really would." She could see them sailing the seas forever, docking in ports where they didn't speak the language, eating strange food. The *Singing Stars* would be surrounded by schools of porpoise, trailed by big oceangoing birds. At night the water would turn luminescent with phosphorescent diatoms, sparklers shooting from the prow.

Ahead of them a flock of willets walked the edge of the water, sand birds ghostly as shadows, mirages imitating the white and dark patterns of the surf meeting the sand. The willets followed the ebb and flow of the waves, their feet in the last inches of the tide, drilling with their long bills into the sand for tiny morsels of food. Dagmar raced up the beach behind the birds, hard sand spitting from underneath her paws, her tags jingling. Katlyn always expected to see sparks fly when she heard them ring. The willets rose as one, revealing the dramatic flash of their wings and underbellies. They wheeled away over the water, only to settle farther up the beach, along the last inches of the ocean.

The sea was high, whipped into lines, with waves breaking far out against the horizon. Plumes of spray shot up into the inky night like fireworks seen from far away. It was as if a great storm were coming, yet there was no wind and the air felt close and warm. Katlyn watched the breaking of the long swells, leaving foam rolling in the wash, white upon the black sea like swirls in Italian marble.

By the light of the quarter moon they could see white sand dollars left behind by the outgoing tide. Katlyn searched for an unbroken one. Alan had called them Holy Ghost Shells and said his grandmother saw the pattern in the shell as the symbol for Christ's crucifixion. But when Katlyn looked at the shell, all she could see was money. She believed if she could find a perfect one, it would bring her luck. The thought of the sand dollars lying deep on the ocean floor, torn from their moorings by the action of the tides and tossed through the surf to lie stranded on the beach like this, must surely be a sign of luck, if one could survive without being chipped or smashed. The chalky sand dollars when moist could be scored with a thumbnail. When they dried they hardened to the consistency of limestone.

If she found one, she'd give it to Elaine.

Katlyn said, "You know what I wanted to do a couple of years ago? I wanted to walk the beach from San Diego to Vancouver. I'd start in San Diego on April Fools' Day, appropriate don't you think? It would take six months, all summer long, and I'd wind up in Vancouver as the leaves start to change on the first of October. I'd sleep on the beach. I'd eat all my food roasted over a bonfire. I worked out mail drops to add clothes, change books, replace worn-out shoes. One night every couple of weeks, I'd check into a motel so I could have a hot shower, watch TV, and sleep in a bed. To remind myself of the things I was abandoning on this hike. In those days I figured six months would cost me one thousand dollars for food and gear, and my motel stops."

Royce laughed. "Motel stops. I'll have to remember that if we ever run off to the South Seas together. There's a Hilton in Bora Bora, you know."

"I just wanted to keep reminded. You know how it is when you get into something. You forget what everything else is. There are whole days, a couple in a row, when I can forget who I was before I met you. I don't remember what I did with my time, what I felt about things. Then I remember, but it's as if it happened to someone else. On my hike I didn't want to get lost like that. Just as soon as I started to feel comfortable marching along, I'd stop." The motel stops had been Alan's idea, he was the one afraid of getting lost in an adventure. He'd convinced her of the importance of keeping in touch and she could no longer remember what she thought the trip might have been without them.

"What made you want to walk the beach like that?"

"I had a friend who turned thirty-five." Why couldn't she just say Alan? Just say his name. "All of a sudden he gave up smoking and drinking and sex and meat. Talk about limiting your life! Bang! Maybe he was trying to save himself by denying the things he took pleasure in. I thought at the time it might be traumatic, to turn thirty-five I mean. If something like that was going to happen to me, I wanted a real solid experience behind me. Something I would never forget and would never go fuzzy in my mind."

"And now you're thirty-five and want to go to Africa." Royce sounded hurt.

"There are all those different countries in Africa, each so distinct one from another. If I walked the beach I'd just touch my toe in a foreign country after six months." Up the Nile and down the Congo. The little man in the map store thought it would be an excellent trip. She wondered if he'd seen the pictures of the starving Ethiopian children on TV. Lake Tana, the headwaters for the Blue Nile, was in the Ethiopian highlands.

"Going to Africa." Royce said it as if pronouncing words in a foreign language.

"It has a nice ring to it, don't you think? Go to Africa. Of course," she squeezed his hand, "it's very different than actually getting there." If she went, it would be alone. Thinking about being alone was very different than actually being alone. Was she really ready to actually be alone?

Royce stopped walking and took her other hand, holding her away from him as if he were going to start to dance and would swing her in a huge circle on the sand. "Katlyn, you're talking about a major change here, like the difference between dying and death. If for some reason I can't divorce Irene, are you seriously thinking of going to Africa? I mean in the sense of being there, not just planning to go."

"I don't know," she answered honestly. "You see, if for whatever reasons you can't or won't divorce Irene, I thought Africa would be a wonderful place to heal a broken heart. I'm hoping the things I'd see in Africa would make a broken heart very minor."

"I don't want to break your heart."

"You already have. I let you." She dropped her hands from his. "Lucky in cards, unlucky in love. We just can't go on like this forever."

"What do you intend to do?" His voice was sharp. "Bounce around from man to man?"

"Isn't that what you did? Only you didn't bother to extract yourself from your marriage. I should have left you when I found out you were married. But I thought there wouldn't be anything safer than a married man. You couldn't promise me anything. There wouldn't be any future to worry about. You couldn't break my heart. But you did. I let you."

"I didn't, I mean," Royce seemed unable to put his thoughts into words. Then suddenly he smiled, his white teeth a flashing bar in the darkness. "Lesson One in How To Pick Up Sexy Girls says never tell them you're married. I thought we were talking a week or so, until you got yourself together. And then, I didn't think I could hold on to you if you knew I was married. And when you knew, and you still stayed, I couldn't have been happier. I thought if you could get over that, nothing could stop us. Besides," his tone dropped an octave, "it's not just Irene. Her father helped me put that business together."

"No one on their deathbed wishes they'd spent more time with their business." But as she said this she realized what he was telling her. What's a man without a business? Relationships come and go, but there was always work to do.

Quickly, before he had time to challenge her, she pulled her woolen poncho over her head and spread it on the sand. She placed her hands on his waist and guided him to the poncho, seating him in the middle of it, facing the ocean. Her fingers worked quickly as she shucked out of her jeans. She lowered his zipper and her cold hands on his skin made him laugh.

Her tongue and lips coaxed him up, stiff and throbbing. How well we learn to read each other's bodies. First, his breathing deepened, then he sighed rhythmically, a hoarse, throaty sound. His cold hands moved under her sweater and cupped her breasts. The sound of the water beating against the beach timed their movements, the long swells breaking, reaching up the wet sand only to be pulled back to the deeper water. Smells of salt and seaweed in the close air, the ripe aroma of sex.

His hand moved down to the tender spot on her belly, his cold palm pressing beneath her navel as the muscles deep in her body tightened, lurched. The small of her back contracted and a silver shiver passed down her spine. Slowly, she slipped her mouth up the length of his cock, nipping the tip with her teeth, and arced her body up the length of his, closing on his mouth.

As he entered her the tightness in the backs of her thighs and across the width of her ass crystalized, sharp as a stone on tender flesh. They rocked, her knees grinding in the sand, twin declivities at his sides. She listened to his heart knocking in his chest and realized she couldn't hear her own heart, a ghostly feeling she'd never experienced before.

The cold salt air, the sand. She felt dangerous, alive, electric. Somewhere down the beach she heard the two-note cry of a foghorn, then the joyous sound of a woman's laugh. A wave exploded against the sand; it sounded like gunfire. Charlotte's friend with his hand in the mouth of a shark.

When they came, Katlyn felt a whirlpool drawing her down the way a ship sinks in the sea, swirling in its own power and weight, a vortex, the center, a vacuum. Sand scudded up her nose, the waves boomed and rocked the coast. Royce cried out, his breath a whistle.

Later she watched him walk away from her, down to

the edge of the ocean. He stood at the waterline, like the willets, and seemed determined to keep the tips of his shoes on the ever-changing border between land and sea. As the waves came slowly up the shelf he backed up, his hands stuffed deep in his pockets, his head down as if studying the pattern of the water as it died at his feet. He met the waves with the concentration of a tightrope walker.

At first she imagined he was lost in deep thought, following the ebb and flow of the water automatically, blindly, his mind exploring complex ideas. But as she stood there watching him, she realized it could be the absence of thought, absolutely nothing more complicated than the placement of one foot in front of the other, his mind shut and sealed. Once or twice before she'd seen him like this, a couple of evenings after he'd told Irene about their affair, the time his head pressman was busted for dealing cocaine. He lost all animation and followed a machinelike routine. He might be in a pure void, a state of nonthought, while his body moved to the rhythm of the dying tide to keep his spirit from failing altogether.

Dagmar bounded up to her, as excited as if she were going to tell Katlyn something bright and wonderful. Sometimes Katlyn was convinced Dagmar was on the verge of speaking in full English sentences and was trying to teach her the army alphabet. "Able, Baker, Charlie, Dog." Dagmar barked, her only trick. The dog leapt up against her jeans, rubbed her long nose against her knees, and trotted off up the beach again. Royce continued to follow the waves, in and out, in and out.

Katlyn looked toward the Marin headlands and saw the film of fog coming off the ocean in parfaited layers, separate wisps playing against each other. She must fill those stories of walks on the beach with the person who belonged to them. Alan. Alan vanished from each story by the time her words cleared her mouth. It wasn't even

144

that what she had to say was so unique. Everyone suffered a desertion or two. Except perhaps Royce. In her mind Royce came into her life with his childhood spent in Boston, and then his adult life with Irene in California. There was nothing in between, as if Irene were the inevitable result of gaining his full height. His teenaged pimples disappeared and Irene, the kids, his knowledge of printing, all happened on the same day. Royce talked about his life the way Carl Sagan explained evolution, squeezing all known history into the last thirty seconds of December 31.

She cupped her hands around her mouth megaphone-style, and hollered at Royce's back. "I'm married! My husband left me! He ran off with our travel agent! And now he's dead! I don't want to die without having lived my life!" Her voice echoed slightly in the quiet night, bouncing back from the dunes by the highway.

Royce continued his steady advance and retreat with the ebb and flow of the waves. At least she'd said it, screamed it across the beach. Her one big secret. The one thing she was ashamed of, hurt by, deceived about. He paid no more attention than one does to traffic noises outside the house.

TUESDAY
NIGHT

Royce couldn't sleep. Not even encircling Kat in his arms and feeling the rhythmic pulse of her heart helped. When he dozed, his dreams were neon flashes of trouble. Kat laughing at him over the shoulder of another man, an invisible man Royce could only sense, and that bothered him as much as the fact Kat was laughing. The two of them parked in a car, looking out over a neighborhood he knew as intimately as his childhood, but couldn't name.

He finally got up and went into the kitchen to mix a stiff bourbon and water. In the dark of the living room he tossed Dagmar off the couch, but she only looked at him from the corners of her eyes and crawled back up on the other end. It was 4:27 in the morning. His head hurt. But worse than the headache was the fact he knew exactly what was the matter. He felt as if he were about to be caught in a blinding blizzard after the winter warmth of a chinook wind.

The last two years sparkled as the best of his life, as if he'd been given the opportunity to explore an exciting and unknown land. But playing at Nick and Nora Charles was a more sinister hobby than fishing or bowling. William Powell wasn't Nick Charles any more than Dashiell Hammett was, or he was. He and Kat had been acting as if they believed they lived in a land they merely visited on a vacation. They'd distanced themselves so nothing could be put on the line. What he loved about Kat was not who she was, as he once thought even a few days ago, but the fact he didn't know who she was. And she didn't know who he was. They'd loved the image of each other as strangers.

So how do you start over? Should they sit down in front of Dr. Bodine with little résumés for each other? A list of all the mundane experiences that add up to form a person. He remembered the cartoon of the old man who comes home to his dog in the evening and says: *And then a grape rolled down the aisle of the bus and stopped right at the tip of my shoe. It was of the seedless variety, I believe.*

The seedless variety, such attention to detail. Did he really need to know anything at all about this husband of hers?

The facts: Her childhood in Reno with Opal. The couple of times he'd met Opal she'd been cold and distant, a brittleness she tried to hide behind snappy cracks and indifference. His mother had always been warm, humorous, at least until near the end. The death of his father brought them closer. But Kat and her mother seemed to share no secrets. They didn't even seem to share the same past.

Kat didn't have a father. She'd told him about inventing fathers, sometimes three or four a day, when she was a little girl. She said she'd liked having so many fathers, each one giving her something different. Opal's friends, movie stars. How important was a father, really? What had he given Lindy and Todd besides the money to make their lives comfortable? Too comfortable maybe. Kat started working at fifteen, he'd started working at fourteen. Yet Lindy, at sixteen, had her own credit cards, and the only job she'd ever held was babysitting for the neighbors.

Working against the war. He'd been fascinated by her stories of forging IDs for deserters leaving for Canada, building a bomb. For him, Vietnam occurred on TV, while Kat had been fighting a war on the homefront. Then suddenly she dropped out of the movement because none of it made any sense to her.

The years traveling, dotted with men's names. Tending bar and skiing at Sun Valley. A Manpower job in Kansas City where she'd met a Hell's Angel. Chicago: she'd sketched models for the Marshall Field's catalogue. Pittsburgh: doing layout work in the ad department of the *Press*. Working on a farm in West Virginia. But he could never picture any of the men, didn't want to. Dorre and Warren in D.C. But never any mention of a husband who ran away with a travel agent.

What did he need to know about Kat he didn't know already? Royce pushed his fingertips deep into his eye sockets. What if the marriage to the man who ran away with the travel agent was as invented as any of the roles they'd played? Why did she tell him tonight, when she'd never mentioned being married before? What did his death have to do with things? *I don't want to die without having lived my life.* Yet her life seemed so full, touching down like a tornado in places all across the country.

Not knowing about that husband left them free to enjoy every day as it happened, no husband, no Irene, no hangovers from the past. But it wasn't something to build a future on. Sand castles wash away with the tide. He had a business, children, a wife to support. The consequences of trying to divorce Irene would cloud every day. Kat might be able to keep moving her sand castle from spot to spot but Royce's was too big, too anchored in responsibilities to others.

So what was he afraid of? Another good question from Dr. Bodine. The fact she'd been married to another man? Who hadn't been married by this stage in life? There was no way to avoid that mistake, if it hadn't been Irene it would have been some other woman just like her. She and the children would be with him for the rest of his life in the same way he would continue to drive a car. Marriage and children separated the boy from the man. Why couldn't he show Kat the same generosity she'd shown him, be able to see her trapped in a youthful mistake. Her husband ran off with a travel agent. His greatest dream was to run off with her. This was deep and disturbing and not nearly as simple as he wanted to believe.

Water will eventually smooth a stone, round off the rough edges until it's reduced to a grain of sand. At the heart of his fears and worries was his gratitude that her love hadn't been returned, that her husband had left her for him to find. He didn't like that idea, the notion that unhappiness brought her to him and bound them together. If her husband hadn't left her. If Irene hadn't been so cold. Loneliness so powerful it can turn to love, which is simply craziness directed at the nearest available object. He hated that idea, yet he knew it was true. All those negatives were the basis of the good things that became their life together.

The dog let out a whimper and sculled her legs across the couch. Dog dreaming, chasing rabbits. To leave

Irene would cause even more unhappiness. Lindy and Todd. Yet Lindy would go off to college next year. And Todd, in his mind, would always be the little boy who believed the fog curling over the hills above Sausalito went the same place as the stairs in an escalator, not the sullen adolescent who drifted through the house with his Walkman stuffed in his ears. The end of childhood. The treehouse he'd built for them was now rotting, dangerous. A few weeks ago, drunk in the middle of a Saturday night, he'd climbed up to the platform, felt the nails work loose under his weight.

He would see them less than he saw them now, which was hardly at all. They would grow up strangers.

Christ. He might as well move to Africa or Hong Kong.

If he left Irene they would turn a corner as swift and unpredictable as a car wreck. If Kat left him he would be forced to return to the desert of his home. He felt as though he had been told he would never walk again, or that Europe didn't exist and he would never be able to visit the cathedrals. He stretched his legs, placed them on the glass coffee table. He couldn't remember ever thinking of his life in such black and white terms, using words like *never* so freely. Could they really never enjoy each other with the privileges this arrangement guaranteed? Would Irene never change her mind about their marriage?

He was a prisoner of his own indecision, by his own definitions. Kat was free to do as she pleased. Irene had a right to his loyalty and support. Separate worlds. Different languages. There was no solid bridge between them.

He felt her, more than saw her, in the blue predawn light. She was standing in the doorway to the living room, watching him, as still as any of the furniture, yet he felt her presence and knew she'd been standing there for some time. He wanted to invite her over to the couch, to hold her on his lap. But he was unable to address her, just as he hadn't been able to mention her husband after she shouted the news across the beach.

He focused his eyes on the glass in the front window, past the lace curtains, and could see her reflection as a shadow. She was leaning against the doorjamb, her arms folded, the silk of her kimono following her body in graceful curves. He thought he could hold her eyes in the wall of the dark glass.

Suddenly, from her dreams, Dagmar barked. They both jumped, startled by the sound in the quiet of night. He heard her laugh and turned to face her. The dog twitched and followed her rabbit.

"I missed you," she said. "It gets cold without you in bed."

He patted the couch beside him and she crossed the room to nestle in between him and the sleeping dog. "It's a good thing you're not a burglar." She looked at Dagmar, deep in dog dreams. "I'm afraid she's not much of a protector."

Royce put his arm around her shoulders. "When I have nights like this, I always fall asleep at dawn. I've never understood why, except maybe, once you pass through the night, your soul knows you're safe and can sleep again."

"You can sleep in tomorrow. Today. Or we can party until the good doctor shows up."

"I've been thinking about the way we party. How all of that will change."

"It doesn't have to. It's like going sailing, when the weather is right."

"Do you realize," Royce said, "I don't know a damn thing about you. That husband you mentioned is just the fin of the shark, isn't it? We're practically perfect strangers."

She laughed and ran her hand along his cheek. "How about that? A fresh start, just like winning a lottery."

"You haven't squared off against me in a vicious temper. You've never nursed me with the flu. You've never done my laundry and I've never seen you drive a car." His examples were ridiculous. Did it matter if she couldn't drive?

"That's your definition of living together? That's what you and Irene have been sharing for sixteen years?" She chuckled with pleasure. "Boy, are you in for a surprise."

"There are going to be problems and laundry, Katlyn. You seem to lead some kind of charmed life. You never ruffle. You handle all your problems, whatever they are, behind my back, when I'm not here. That doesn't mean they don't exist. The fairy tale is over. I know I'm going to have problems. And I wonder how you'll handle them."

"Did you enter into your relationship with Irene based on the way she handled problems?"

"No, of course not. But those problems became the relationship, the rock of our marriage. Divorcing her isn't going to change my responsibilities." But he wondered about that, tempted to believe he could leave those sixteen years behind as cleanly as Frank had, that the years were already irrevocably gone.

"That's not for me," Kat said. "I don't believe it has to be that way at all. I'm anyone I want to be. You can be too. All it takes is a little imagination. There's nothing to say you're stuck for your whole life with who you are, with the things you've done. Quit when things get stale. Otherwise the circle of your life becomes a treadmill."

He looked at her sadly. "Maybe you can. My wife and kids aren't going to be too happy if I turn into Tarzan and traipse through Africa with you."

She draped her long legs over his lap and nestled her

head into the wing of his arm. "Opal told me there was only one lesson in life I had to master. I had to find a man to love me, to take care of me. But when we moved out here I suddenly saw the big world. I tried to make up for all that lost time in the desert."

"I know all that," he said. "But I didn't know about your husband. We've been together two years and I've heard stories about men from here to the Atlantic, but not a goddamned one of them was ever identified as your husband. Marriage is a serious commitment. I suppose I preferred to think of all these guys as just people you knew. Not someone you planned to spend your life with."

"They were people I knew. I never told you about Alan," she drew a breath and cut her eyes to the windows, "because of Irene. You might value marriage, but I don't. I didn't want our relationship to have anything to do with marriage." She turned her head and looked him squarely in the eye. "It would have been too easy to fall into basing our time together on what had happened in our marriages."

"Well if you don't value marriage, why did you marry this guy?"

"I don't value marriage *because* I married him. You see, I wasn't locked into anything. I kept drifting around until one day nothing looked clear. I felt dizzy, the way you do on a roller coaster or a merry-go-round. Opal's life is no prize and I didn't trust her view of the world, but then, I don't know, I decided I should give it a try. So I married Alan. Charlotte calls it the emotional flu. It was like picking a name out of the phone book. Then things just stopped." She studied her hands for a moment, her head bent, hiding her face. "As a little girl all I wanted to be was grown-up. So there I was, a grown-up. I'd found a man who supposedly loved me. And I was all hollow."

"Not everyone feels that way." Royce remembered how happy Irene had been during her pregnancies. How the world opened up for her and how sweet the future seemed. Irene took each day as her own, as careful of her time and what she did with it as she was selecting apples, only the best apples, at the market. Irene never drifted, she moved forward as smoothly and steadily as time itself.

"So what do you do if you're all hollow like that?" She passed her hand to the silk of her kimono, the terry cloth of his bathrobe, the fur of the dog, as if testing to make sure the pieces of her world were still in place.

"Children." His favorite memory was of Lindy at ten, Todd at seven, dancing on the lawn in a sudden summer shower. They were playing Indians, or witches, he forgot now what, but they were absorbed and happy, dancing with the rain.

She shook her head. "I never wanted children and neither did Alan. My childhood was a disaster and I saw no reason to pass that on to anyone. I wasn't about to turn back to all those miserable years I'd left behind."

Royce's mind felt suddenly blank, a blackboard with no chalk marks.

"You don't have to follow in lockstep what's given to you. When Alan left, I thought I'd have to go back to square one, to find a man to love me. But that seemed like such an empty victory, if you can call being abandoned by a husband a victory at all. I didn't want to face that hollow spot. I decided there were other things I could do, other people I could be, besides simply a woman who'd been left by a man. I realized between Opal, various guys, jobs I hated, Alan, I'd always been someone else's creation. I kept making stuff for Charlotte, doing my own work instead of someone else's. I quit going to the bars, needy and desperate for a man to notice me. I was figuring out my life for myself for the first time, not letting someone else tell me who I was. Suddenly I had a life of my own, as soon as I turned that corner where I wasn't looking at my life through someone else's eyes."

And there was the problem, Royce realized, as clear and round as the hole in a donut. He was someone else's creation. Irene's. Gerald's. He'd handed his future over to them as casually as he would hand Donna Moon the keys to the shop.

"I was free then, don't you see. I didn't have to keep living out someone else's idea of my life. Now I'm ready to take the next step. Take some risks."

"Not everyone is free," he said. "So unanchored." Certainly Irene couldn't take off for Africa, or become Lady Brett Ashley for an evening. "Some people have very strong anchors holding them in place. They don't drift, the way you have. They have responsibilities, people depend on them. I'm not sure I can up and change my life just like that." He snapped his fingers, surprised at how loudly the sound echoed in the darkened house. The dog snorted, looked at the two of them sleepily, and buried her nose under her tail.

"Everyone changes," she said. "It's just a matter of quality and style. I'm not proposing anything radical here. This isn't exactly a new idea. Irene's already done it to you. She's not the woman you married, I'll bet. And children, well, that's all they do. They start out babies, and pretty soon they're strangers in your own house. Ask Opal. She'll tell you I'm not the daughter she thought I'd be. Everyone does it, you see. I just believe in it a little more strongly than most."

He felt the heat of her breath and the blood pulsing through her body, the softness of her hair against his fingers. "I'm afraid I don't have the style you do. I'm a little more hung up on the real world."

"Like hell. You'd never have gotten in this far with me if you were."

He thought she might have a point, but like every other point he'd reached in the last day or so, none of them formed a pattern. They couldn't go back to the old ways and he wasn't sure he had the courage to invent a new one. None of this addressed the question of how he would handle his responsibilities. Frank had simply thrown in the towel, left Nancy with a hunk of money and disappeared. Much as he was attracted to the idea, Royce knew he couldn't just disappear. He would still be responsible for Irene's future, for Lindy and Todd. "I don't know," he said. "There are plenty of movies about true love between starving people, but they always end up rich and famous. You know that's going to happen when you walk into the film. What's going on here isn't scripted. There's not going to be any flowery type rolling up on the screen with a swell of music to say THE END and everyone filing out of the theater feeling justice was done. It might be all downhill from this moment. Would you stand for that?" Or was this just his cowardice speaking, his fear?

"Shhhhhh." She ran her fingertips around his lips. "There's no given it goes downhill if you make some changes. You have to choose what you make of your life. It's your decision, not what someone else makes of it. If you stay with Irene you've lost nothing but me. You'll be willing to do that, you'll want that."

"It might be too late," he said. "Some things only come around once. I'm too old to play pro basketball. No matter how much I'd like to play pro ball, I can't do it now." It was fear, the fear of running his life.

"We're not talking about something you've never done before. We're talking about something you're already doing. Living with me."

"It's like pro ball in the sense I might have to come up with a whole new career. Half of that printing plant belongs to Irene's father. You can believe he's not going to be very happy if I divorce his daughter." Fear of poverty.

"If you stay with me," Kat continued, "I'm pretty sure we don't have to go to the poorhouse because of it. Some interesting things might turn up."

"She'll take everything. You know that, don't you?"

"So what? Let her have it. I don't love you for your stock in figs. Even if we lost this house, I know we could manage."

He looked into her face and watched the lights in her eyes. She was telling him something she wasn't saying, promising something she would only reveal when he took enough steps in her direction. Her sense of timing was theatrical, withholding her information until the crucial moment. She could bluff clear through to next Tuesday. Perhaps she had money of her own, money from her mysterious husband. But why should the thought of loving Kat have to do with money? Why should his desire to live with her have to do with their finances? Money. Her money, his money, her husband's money, Gerald's money. What did that have to do with the way he felt for her? Everything. Without money feelings didn't matter much. Being without money was an existence in itself, a former life of his he had no wish to return to.

Money. Fear. Cowardice.

Then again, perhaps her meaning was simply what she said, something would turn up, and that was all she needed to stay with him, that faith. "Do me a favor," he said. "Just be yourself tomorrow."

"Today," she said. "This afternoon."

"Okay. Today. Just be yourself. No Myrna Loy, Rita Hayworth. Just you."

Gently she removed his arm from her shoulder and reseated herself, cross-legged on the couch beside him, facing him with a seriousness he rarely saw in her. "You know how it is when you're learning something new? A new recipe or how to ski. Did it ever happen you forget the same thing over and over again? Always forgetting the eggs or to shift your weight ahead of the turn? Like the way you always forget to turn the light off in the bathroom. You're like that, you know. You keep forgetting I am Rita Hayworth. I am truly whoever I want to be. I'm a new world every morning, for you, for your psychiatrist. For myself."

"Then what's all this?" He swept his hand in front of him, to indicate the room now brightening with the rose and gold of dawn. "Who's talking to me right now? There's no movie for this one, Kat. It's just you and me talking about our problems."

"And so it might be this afternoon. We'll see when we get there. If I were fat you couldn't tell me to be thin for this afternoon. Just a different groove in the record, a different part of the song." She ran her fingers through his hair, pulled on the lobe of his ear, her blue and green eyes looking deeply into his, searching back and forth, one to the other. "My mother had a friend in Reno, a really sad guy. She always wrote him off with the line: 'Just like he had always hoped, nothing ever happened.' But things happen to most people. Great, wonderful, unexpected things. No one knows how to react to the unexpected. Whole new worlds open up, worlds you might be afraid of, or thrilled by. There are no guidelines to tell you how to react. It's *Queen For A Day*, but in real life there's no applause meter. You do the best you can, hit a different groove in the record. You make new plans."

His headache was returning, his thoughts fragmenting into chips and shards, bouncing back from each other to lodge in isolated corners of his mind. "It starts out as a simple choice: you or Irene. Then suddenly it looks more like dropping a stone into a well, those little circles of waves that roll out so nicely, evenly spaced, and then bang against the wall of the well and come tumbling back on each other. Those nice evenly spaced rings get all choppy and bumpy. All that water colliding together. And then, you see, you've lost the stone."

"The stone isn't important." She placed her hand on his shoulder as if trying to give him power and strength. "It's how to quiet the waters."

"How am I supposed to make a decision when I haven't the goddamnedest notion who you are?"

"You aren't any more handicapped than I am." She tossed her hair back out of her eyes, but he thought there was defiance in the shake of her head. "You lied to me too. Your wife and kids."

"But at least I told you the truth, eventually. And I'm trying to tell you the truth now, for the future. What's the truth about you?"

"I'm five foot eight, have red hair and hazel eyes. I can't change any of that. The rest I can. I'm not stuck with anything past that."

Royce left her to go to the window and watch the light of the rising sun. God, if only it were that simple. If only there weren't consequences for every action, as well as every action one didn't take. He hadn't made decisions about his life in sixteen years, his options had always been handed to him by someone else. He wished he'd been in the military. Marines Build Men. He'd avoided Vietnam, not by his own choice but through Irene's pregnancy. He wondered if the army would have taught him how to think through his options, how to make a decision. For the first time he felt robbed by the way Irene and her family took over his life. Kat could make decisions. She wanted this or that. She had no responsibilities and therefore no consequences for her actions. His responsibilities were second-hand, as if he'd been given a script to follow, a part to play. He couldn't make his family disappear by writing them out of the script. But they could make him disappear, by taking away his means of making a living, the foundation for the way he thought of himself after sixteen years.

"Okay," he said. "I'm tired of this." It was dawn now and he felt he might fall asleep on his feet. "Be whoever you want to be. Dress up in your Mae West. Sit around in your bathrobe and tell him you've got amnesia. I don't care."

He watched her in the window as she glided up to him and put her arms around his waist. "You care. That's the real problem here." She rubbed his shoulders to ease the tension in his back. "Either come to bed or come out into the kitchen with me. We could make a Dawn Pizza: english muffins, bacon, tomato sauce, cheese. Olives. Anchovies!" She started to sing: "Start your day a little bit better. The breakfast pizza way!"

"Breakfast pizza." The whole idea made him smile. "Anchovies. For breakfast."

She kissed the tip of his nose. "Either that or bed."

He let her lead him back to the bedroom and curled up, lying across her breasts. Frank set off for something more unknown than life with a woman like Katlyn. She made him happier than any other person in the world. In her own way she was working with this problem, even if it wasn't his way.

Her hands stroked through his hair and she began to talk softly, as if telling him a story. "Today I spoke to

Elaine, you know, the woman down the street. She wore red mittens. I gave her a cigarette and had to put it in her mouth for her. I keep trying to imagine what her life will be like, her future."

Royce thought of the young woman, only a couple of years older than Lindy. All he could visualize was a pretty California blonde. He could see her in a sweater, in a bikini, but he couldn't see her without hands. He could see the red mittens, but couldn't imagine them empty.

"The head of maintenance in the casino where Opal worked was a one-handed man. He'd been a butcher and lost all the fingers of his right hand above the palm in an accident. A slicing machine." Her fingers circled her own palm to show him. "Even his thumb. But his hand wasn't flat, it was smooth and round as a doorknob. It was a mysterious, wonderful hand to me, and I used to like to hold on to it, to feel the skin, which was tough as the sole of an Indian's foot. He could do everything, run machinery, thread electrical wires, everything but hammer a nail. But what he wanted to do was deal blackjack. He used to show me how he dealt cards, the stump on the deck, the left hand whipping out the cards as quick as a two-handed dealer. The management wouldn't let him deal, said it would upset the customers."

Royce tried to imagine running a saw, one-handed, threading electrical wires. "He still had the other hand."

"Yeah. And it was an accident. He wasn't trying to kill himself. That's what they say she tried to do. He spent his life overcompensating for that accident. Because he believed in himself. I'll probably never know why she did that, but I keep thinking if she believed in herself or believed someone loved her, she wouldn't have. Maybe she was all hollow, like I was, when she did it. Maybe in her heart there was no one home. Living without love is like cutting out little pieces of your heart. Maybe you can't truly love someone if you don't love yourself. I didn't always believe this. I think I've learned it from living with you."

"Can't you let me love you in my own way?"

He felt a deep sigh through her breasts. "I'm trying. But it's hard to switch it on and off. You're here and then you're gone, off to a whole other life, as if you're a different person. I feel like you've disappeared, like maybe I made the whole thing up, when you go back to Marin."

"I don't feel that way," he said. "You're with me even when I'm in Sausalito, or at work. I feel you're with me all the time." His hands became cold, numb. If she left him. If she left him. At least, if she left him, he would have had this time with her. Maybe that was all one could ask of life.

"I'm a slow learner. I never learned about love until I met you. Opal saw me as a nuisance. I never cared about the men I lived with the way I care for you. I needed them to know I was alive. Alan married me for his own reasons, and when those reasons stopped working, he left. Maybe I'm emotionally retarded. Maybe most women feel this at eighteen or twenty. But when Alan left, that was the first time I could really say 'I don't deserve this.' At least I haven't missed it altogether. I'm afraid Elaine might miss it, no matter how old she becomes."

"Maybe not," Royce said. "You're the one who believes it's a new world every morning." Suddenly his problems felt very small compared to the woman with the red mittens. He felt ashamed, carrying on like a child who can't have his way.

"Do you think she would have done that if she had a sense of herself? Or if she felt loved?"

"Love doesn't solve everything, Kat. We're always alone, even when we're loved." And he knew what had been the central problem for him, his denial of this simple fact. Irene, his family, Gerald, the business, had kept him occupied and he'd forgotten this. He'd been so busy for the last sixteen years, as if being busy were a form of sleep, that he hadn't noticed. With Kat, when all the drapery of his family fell away, he was himself, alone, but no longer quite so afraid.

He looked up into her eyes, and stared into her the way people gaze at the stars. She smiled and stroked his head. Sleep was coming on. He took her hands between his palms, holding them until the cold tips of his fingers grew warm.

APRIL 9
DAWN

His deep, rhythmic breathing told her he was sleeping but she continued to stroke her hands through his hair. She imagined mothers must soothe children like this. She only remembered the boardlike feel of Opal's hand slapped across her face. And the sting of the wire hairbrush across her butt. That hairbrush, the small nails driven through the rubber pad, the wooden handle. Once, when Opal was spanking her, Katlyn kicked and the brush came down on her heel. For days afterward Katlyn would look at her heel, the pattern of small holes, as even as the mesh in a window screen.

It was almost full day, six in the morning, and the birds sang a chorus in the trees. From the bed Katlyn couldn't see any birds, any trees, only the band of daylight on the building next door. But she was glad she could hear them. She loved birds, but only if they were free. Years ago, on a farm in West Virginia, her lover Bill had found a fledgling crow fallen from its nest and decided to raise it as a pet. He tried to teach it to talk and the crow adopted Bill as its mother or mate. Who knows what crows think about. The crow would groom Bill's beard, standing on Bill's shoulder while combing through the whiskers. Like a dog, the crow would follow Bill around the house, hopping and jumping to keep up with Bill's long strides, the iridescent blue-black wings fanned out to his sides like sails. One fall day the crow disappeared. Katlyn was secretly happy. She knew it was flying south for the winter.

Heading south. A new world every morning. If only that could be true. Ever since she entered Berkeley, over twenty years ago, she'd been trying to be someone other than who she really was. Somehow she'd never outgrown Opal's opinion of her. A nuisance, a problem, a pain in the ass. Surely other people outgrew their parents' opinions. The best she could say for herself was that she'd tried to hide her true self, to never let it show.

If she were to leave for Kenya or Victoria Falls, the trip would be just another way of hiding. Royce, sweet Royce. She looked at his sleeping face, eyelashes as long as a girl's. His feet were the most beautiful feet she'd ever seen, kissable feet, strong and symmetrical. You could walk on water with those feet.

There was no way she could talk to his psychiatrist, it was all too tawdry, too bleak. What could she say? My mother resented me, my father never acknowledged me. Every friend I've ever had has disappeared.

The men, all those men, most of them found another woman, a woman who could do things right. When she was younger it didn't matter so much. There were always plenty of men in those days. The country was full of men on any given evening. For a while, she'd simply accompanied the men and they led her further and further east. It felt like hitchhiking. She could name the moment when the trip started, an Art Appreciation class with Rob. High Gothic art was being discussed at eight on a late January morning. St. Francis of Assisi and how various painters depicted him, romanticized him. Rob passed her a note: Let's go skiing. They left Berkeley late that afternoon and drove to Sun Valley where she tended bar and took up skiing with a passion. What was that girl's name, the one he ran off with? She had eyes as hard as emeralds.

Each man going further and further east until, after D.C., there was only the Atlantic to cross. She worked in D.C. with Dorre, and that whole year there wasn't one single man. But there was Dorre and Warren. For a while.

"California," Dorre had said that first day at lunch. "I'm going to get to California some day. I've never been west of the Mississippi, but one of these days Warren and I are going to get a van and just travel. I know exactly how it will happen. We'll be sitting at dinner, me complaining about this dipshit job, Warren complaining about his dipshit job, and we'll just look at each other and toss the whole mess." There was light in her eyes, a peach-rose blush in her cheeks. Katlyn's first impression of her office mate was that she looked like Mary Martin in *Peter Pan*. A pixie.

She and Dorre worked together in the secretarial pool, mindless work, everything in quadruplicate. The highlight of each day was lunch hour, snickering about government mismanagement. But suddenly Dorre began to feel plagued by strange aches in the deep recesses of her body.

"If I'm pregnant, Warren wouldn't stand for an abortion," Dorre said sadly. "But I just don't feel ready to have a kid. There's so much I want to do before getting tied down like that." She dropped her half-eaten sandwich into the paper bag and tossed it, like a basketball, at the trash bin. She missed, and the bag skidded across the floor. "And we can't afford it."

"Do you want me to go with you?" Katlyn was worried. Small and delicate Dorre had been losing weight until it seemed her skin was draped over her bones. The luster had gone out of her blonde hair and it looked like a thatch of straw, so dry Katlyn could imagine it catching fire.

The first appointment was inconclusive and the doctor ordered a series of tests. Much as she wanted to, Katlyn couldn't go with Dorre to every appointment. They both couldn't miss that much work. And then she didn't hear from Dorre for over a week. She called, but always got a busy signal. Katlyn knew they'd taken the phone off the hook.

One Saturday morning at seven Katlyn banged on the door of their apartment until she heard Warren cursing as he undid the chain. "You're my friends," she said. "I want to know what's going on."

Warren rubbed the sleep from his eyes, soft eyes like a teddy bear. Katlyn always thought of him as the cuddly type, a perfect companion for a cold winter night. She envied Dorre. Warren was devoted to her. Nothing in this world made Warren happier than being with his wife.

In the bedroom Dorre managed to sit up against the pillows, looking lost in the double bed, tiny as a child. Katlyn sat at the foot of the bed and heard Warren making coffee in the kitchen. "They think it's cancer," Dorre said.

Cancer. Inoperable cancer. The more she learned about her disease, the less hope, less spark. Each time Katlyn visited, Dorre seemed closer and closer to disappearing. Katlyn kept imagining talking to Dorre and how her voice would go on as Dorre faded from sight. Chemotherapy didn't slow the spreading metastasis and, after long weeks in the hospital, Dorre insisted on going home to spend a few days with Warren.

Driving home from work one night, Katlyn realized she'd never known anyone who was dying before. In high school back in Reno, two football players had died when their car clipped a telephone pole out in the desert. They were drunk and doing 110. A few weeks before Opal and Katlyn moved to California, a man down the street shot his son in the face. The boy had sneaked out for the night and was climbing up the trellis when his father thought he heard a burglar and loaded his shotgun. The closed caskets from Vietnam. In her mind's eye, the faces and bodies were as clear and whole as the day they left. Death was sudden, not the slow process she watched in Dorre.

For several weeks the three of them spent the evenings in the bedroom listening to music, Dorre propped up in the big bed, a small bird under a floppy forties-style hat to hide the loss of her hair. Katlyn cruised the second-hand stores for hats, the only present she could bring for Dorre. Turbans, straw sun hats, cowboy Stetsons. She laughed about hats on a bed, bad luck. "When your luck is bad to begin with, the only thing a hat can do is change it."

Dorre wanted to hear harmonies and melodies from all over the world. Folk songs, piano concertos, African drums, bagpipes, Andean flutes. The music muffling Dorre's thoughts, Warren's panic, Katlyn's sadness.

"Music is the only thing you don't have to think about," Dorre told her. "Even when you read, you're thinking. You think in your sleep. There's always something in your mind, unless you're listening to music. Then it's like the thinking is outside of you. Do you ever wonder what really primitive people thought about? Did they have music? When did we learn how to hum?"

Six years ago, on the first hot night of summer. The cherry blossoms and dogwoods had been gorgeous that year.

Katlyn heard about it on the morning news while getting ready for work, but the name of the couple was withheld. Later that day, two officials came asking questions. Her name had been found in the note detailing how Dorre and Warren wanted their possessions distributed. They didn't have much, a young couple with a used car, living in a rented flat. They left Katlyn their lovebird, Andros, and instructions on how to care for him written in Warren's neat hand.

Although he'd been a conscientious objector during the Vietnam War, Warren had purchased a gun. Edvard Grieg's suite of Ibsen's *Peer Gynt* was playing on their stereo when Warren fired the shot into Dorre's brain. The downstairs neighbors heard it, an explosion above their heads. But when he tried to take his own life, his hand shook and the bullet rattled around his skull, destroying his intelligence and senses, but not his life. A vegetable, that was the only prognosis. Katlyn hoped Warren wouldn't be able to think or dream. She tried to imagine the dreams Warren might have, why Dorre had chosen *Peer Gynt*, what movement was playing when Warren fired the shot.

She visited Warren in the hospital, held his hand and watched him breathe, in, out, in, out. Sometimes she could feel the muscles clench, as if he might be trying to return her grasp. But the most painful was to watch his eyelids twitch. Warren's dreams troubled her. The odds were against him. If only she could be sure he dreamed of Dorre before she got sick. If only she could be sure he wouldn't dream of Dorre's death.

"Andros," she would say to the bird, "don't they piss you off? Leaving you like this." She studied the lovebird as he tipped his head back and forth, looking at her. "So violent. So stupid. I could go down the street and pick up the paper, and there are as many chances as not that the headline would announce a cure for cancer." Andros ruffled his bright blue wings for her.

Sometimes the little things are the hardest to bear. The morning she woke up to find Andros lying on the bottom of his cage, she called work and quit, packed her car and headed back across the country. Five days later she was in San Francisco and still didn't know what to do. But she recognized what she'd done. She'd abandoned Warren, left him with no one to care for him, no one to care about him. The one gift she could have given Dorre— look after Warren until his body died. If she had stayed, she would have buried him next to Dorre. But she left, turned her back on him.

And that is where it all began. All the pieces of the puzzle which led her to Alan. Another job, another anonymous flat, countless nights in the bars until she met Alan. Why had he died? Why had he married her? She would never know the answers now. That first night in Lord Jim's it was as if they looked at each other across their drinks and silently said, *Me too. I'm alone. This is unbearable. Help me.*

Things moved so quickly after that, she had no time to think of Warren and Dorre. Two days before the ceremony, they put Alan's father in a nursing home and they spent their first night together as man and wife in Alan's parents' bed. The marriage was a sham, but Katlyn never questioned that things could be better. Look at Opal, no husband at all. Anything is better than nothing. What she didn't understand was why it couldn't have continued, why Alan couldn't have let her ignore the situation. We do things we can't explain as easily as we do things we don't understand.

"Being married isn't the same as being Siamese twins,"

Alan said while he was getting dressed to go out one night. "You have your life and I have mine."

She studied him, his preppy good looks, the neat symmetry of his body. This is my husband, she thought. And he's not a bit like Warren. She dreamed about Warren, the way he'd been with Dorre. One night she awoke with the distinct feeling she'd been dancing with Warren, Dorre, propped up in bed, applauding.

By the end of the first year Alan slept in the room he'd lived in as a child, she slept in his parents' bedroom. Once a week they both visited his father in the nursing home, but his father kept mixing Katlyn up with Alan's mother and Alan would scream "I did this for you!" as if by sheer willpower he could make his father understand.

But she couldn't say she was unhappy. She'd met Charlotte who wanted more and more things for his boutique. For the first time she was her own boss, organizing her time and her talents as she pleased. Alan came and went. At night, if she couldn't sleep, she would wander through the house and touch Alan's father's furniture. This is mine, she would think. This table is mine.

After his father died, Alan stopped going out in the evenings. But he seemed restless, pacing through the house like a caged animal. "You know," Alan said one night, "we never had a proper honeymoon."

Katlyn shrugged. The civil service in City Hall didn't seem like a proper wedding either. Alan threw a party for his friends at the house. Katlyn's few friends who were still around Berkeley left early. Opal refused to attend. That was all there was to it.

The trip to Portugal promised to be a new start. "We'll make it work," Alan said. But by sheer accident they walked into Guerrero's travel agency. Was there really such a thing as love at first sight? What was the difference between being in love and being afraid to be alone? Day by day, week by week, the trip to Portugal was postponed. She didn't mind. The future lay ahead of her like the horizon. She continued working for Charlotte, making plans for the trip, indulging in mild flirtations. She'd never been unfaithful to Alan, but that wasn't the same as being faithful. A smile from a man would do, could even excite her. But things never went further than that. The doctor who gave them their shots, the florist who gave her plants, the checkout clerk at the supermarket. She felt as if she'd retired and could start enjoying her life.

Alan disappeared for a week. On Thursday night, as she was washing the dishes from her dinner she heard his key in the door. He was wearing camouflage fatigues, lace-up army boots, a black beret. Guerrero was dressed the same way.

"Let's not have any trouble here," Alan told her. "I want to get a few things, and I don't want to have a scene."

She looked him over, but the army outfit didn't seem threatening, more like a costume for Halloween. "What's going on here? Are we about to become terrorists or hijackers or celebrate Bastille Day?"

"I'll let you have three months to get reorganized. Then I might sell the house. I don't know yet. But I've got to get out of here. Try to understand." He turned his back on her and headed up the stairs.

"I have a knife," Guerrero said. "But I don't want to hurt you. Just leave him alone and you'll be all right." He went into the living room and turned on the TV. "Why don't you just come sit down. This won't take long."

So they sat there with the television on, while Alan lugged suitcases and trunks across the bedroom floors. She wondered about the knife as she listened to closet doors opening, drawers being pulled out. Why a knife?

What did they think she would do? She inventoried his clothes, the gray suit, the blue suit, the brown suit. His leather jacket. Three cashmere sweaters. How many pairs of shoes did he own?

He came downstairs lugging two suitcases which he set by the door. Guerrero rose and went upstairs for the trunks. For a long moment Alan stared into her face while she felt her mind as empty as air.

"This isn't anything personal," Alan said. "I want you to know that. It's nothing you've done. It's just something I have to do for myself."

"That's worse," she said. "If all this were personal, I might understand it better."

"It has nothing to do with you."

"That makes me feel invisible."

Royce let out a snore and Katlyn cuddled down, feeling the warmth of his body. Ah, Royce. She could never tell Royce this story. As she folded him into her arms she tried to imagine being alone again. Those nights when she would stroke Alan's father's furniture with the tips of her fingers. All the hours drifting through the bars, across the country. She tried to imagine wandering a continent she had no clear notion about. But he wouldn't leave his wife, she knew that. And she couldn't go on like this. What else was there to do? How many more poor choices could she make? Luck changes with every turn of the wheel. And if your luck keeps running badly, you try a new table.

WEDNESDAY
MORNING

Royce was still asleep, burrowed deep in his dreams like a fox in a den, when Katlyn awoke after only a few hours sleep. He curled around himself, snoring and purring voluminously. Few things were worse than lying awake next to a gusty snorer. Crackers in bed, maybe, or whistlers, like Alan. Since he didn't stir when she slipped out from under the covers, she decided to go to the pool. She needed to think out how to approach Dr. Bodine.

Jody was sitting on the steps in front of the pool in the clear cold sun, her elbows resting on her knees, folded over like a collapsed A. "Hey! Where were you yesterday? I waited the whole hour."

Jody wanted to talk. She hadn't brought her swim gear, and Katlyn sensed there wouldn't be enough time for both of their troubles this morning. "Things with Royce suddenly picked up a head of steam. Know what we're going to do this afternoon?"

"Let's go over to the park." Jody nodded toward the

swings under a grove of eucalyptus and rose slowly, as if all her weight had settled in her feet. Jody's life seemed so orderly to Katlyn, her problems as hard to picture as the taste of a chocolate hamburger.

Jody slipped onto a swing and pushed off, the wind catching her short blonde hair. With her legs stretched out in front, her head back, Katlyn thought of magician's assistants, ladies who were willing to be sawed in half, women who rose inches above tables while hoops passed beneath them. The magic of illusion.

Katlyn sat on a swing, idly twirling left and right, her feet dragging in the dust. She lit a cigarette, waiting for Jody to get on with it. But Jody seemed content to swing out into the air, arcing back and forth, gaining speed. "Royce and I are going to talk to a psychiatrist this afternoon," Katlyn said.

"We didn't have anything to say," Jody replied.

Katlyn was relieved. For a moment she'd thought there might be trouble with Bruce. Whether Jody acknowledged it or not, Katlyn believed Jody's lovers were what Charlotte would call the emotional flu, but that Bruce was the solid center of her life, the true home of her heart. "You must have said something."

"Not really." The swing began to lose momentum. Jody tucked her legs under the seat and let herself drift to a stop. "He looks just the same, still wears his hair a bit longish, stylish but nothing controversial. I sat in this lovely Spanish stucco hall and floated off into a dream. I saw the places we'd been, the dinners we ate together, the sunrises we saw when we'd spent the whole night screwing. I saw us dancing. But I couldn't feel any of the energy I always remembered being so much a part of Eric."

"People change." Katlyn wondered how she would feel if she ran into Royce ten years from now. She used to imagine meeting Alan again, what they would say. She would ask him if Guerrero really had a knife that night.

Jody pulled on a strand of her hair, a nervous gesture. "One of my favorite memories is of a summer afternoon playing Frisbee. He'd taken off his shirt and his big, tanned shoulders looked like a pair of coiled bronze springs. But I didn't see any of that at Stanford. Until Monday, that memory was always one of motion, his arm coming back to snap the Frisbee off his wrist. While I watched him from my seat in the back of the auditorium, that memory became more like a still picture. I tried to make the arm and shoulder move, to throw that Frisbee, but I couldn't."

"So what happened when he got done reading his paper?"

Jody dug the toe of her running shoe in the dirt, carved a series of lines, then smudged them out with her other foot. "Like I said, nothing. He asked about Spike Africa, a great old guy who used to hang out at the No Name Bar in Sausalito. One Christmas Eve, Eric and I were there when Spike came in wearing open galoshes, a trenchcoat, an aviator's cap and carrying his new Christmas chain saw. He tried it out right there in the bar, cutting off the legs of the tables in the back. 'Have you seen Spike?' he says. 'No,' I say, 'he died. He claimed it took a real man to smoke two packs of Camels a day in the face of lung cancer.' Eric says 'I quit smoking four years ago.' And what am I supposed to say to that?" Jody threw her hands open. "Flat. The whole afternoon went like that. I asked him, as a joke, if he owned a chain saw, and he asked me what would he need a chain saw for in London."

Katlyn felt a tingling in her toes, as if her circulation had been cut off. "You've got to expect things to be a little awkward at first."

Jody laughed. "You'd be amazed what I expected."
She shook her head. "I expected passion, that we wouldn't
be able to keep our hands off each other and would head
straight for his room. But we walked and walked. By then,
we'd ticked off everyone we knew, and he'd told me
about this woman in London he's been living with for the
last ten years. Ten years. I told him how Bruce was, but
we both knew he wasn't going to see Bruce, even though
they've known each other forever." She ground her toe
into the sandy earth. "I told him about the gallery, but
somehow I managed to make it sound as complicated as
biochemistry. By then we were in some tacky little shopping mall and I couldn't stand it anymore. It reminded me
more of a blind date than being with a person I'd loved
for a long time. I suggested we get a drink or a cup of
coffee. But he looked at me, and I could see I wasn't the
person he'd called up and expected to meet Monday
afternoon at Stanford. And you know, I felt the same way
too. This wasn't the Eric I'd loved. I'm sure he's a very
nice person, whoever he's become. But he wasn't the
man who'd filled my dreams for so many years."

"There was no spark? Nothing? Really nothing?" Katlyn
pictured Jody in one of her gallery outfits, a sleek, colorful
dress and spike heels, dropping down on the pavement in
Palo Alto for a quick set of twenty-five push-ups, working
out the tension. Whoever Eric was, she could imagine the
look on his face.

Jody shook her head, her eyes down as she watched
the lines and squiggles her feet were making in the dust.
She looked up and followed the flight of a sparrow until it
disappeared into the lace of the leaves. "We did the
whole thing about getting together again. But you know
how it is when someone suggests getting together like
that. There's a tone of voice or the way the words are

phrased that lets you know you've officially been written off."

"I don't believe it," Katlyn said. "He's still at Stanford? Call him up and try it again. Find out what went wrong."

"No," Jody said. "I don't think I will. If I had any idea what was missing Monday afternoon, maybe I'd call. But I don't want another Monday afternoon. We both grew up, grew into our own lives. The best I can say is perhaps our lives, who we are now, leaves no room for who we were. To tell you the truth," she gave a weak smile, "I think I'm saddest about losing the motion in my memories of him. I still want to see him fling that Frisbee, but all I can see now is the sun on his shoulders."

"That's not like you," Katlyn said. "I don't believe it." Eric's rejection of Jody frightened her, a premonition of what might happen with Royce. "Aren't you the lady who covers the subway walls with the lipstick motto: Open Cans of Worms?"

Jody smiled warmly for the first time. "I wish I knew who that lady was. I'd make her eat those worms."

Katlyn gazed across the park to the powder blue sky, a perfect blue for sky writing dotted with clouds which looked like loaves of french bread. "That is absolutely the last thing I need to hear this morning."

"I'm an art dealer now, not a pregnant hippie. I wanted him to know that."

"I can't believe you just let it go like that."

"There wasn't much choice. We never even had a drink together. He never even asked about Ricky. Oh well." She locked her knees, her legs sticking out in front of her.

"Ricky?" But Katlyn was beginning to understand why Jody was so upset.

"He's never known for sure he's Ricky's father."

"Why? Why wouldn't he know?"

"Because I never told him. Just like I never tell anyone. I think he suspects, but I never told him for sure." She stared at the toes of her shoes. "How's Royce? Where were you yesterday?" Jody tried to look interested, but Katlyn felt her heart wasn't in it. She was still mourning her missed opportunities on Monday afternoon. *I want these thighs to glow.*

"We're going to talk to a psychiatrist this afternoon."

"A psychiatrist?" There was light in Jody's eyes, her attention now focused on Katlyn as if she'd walked through a door into a new room.

"You betcha. Those types terrify me."

"Why?" Jody spun her swing in a circle, forcing the chains to tighten in an hourglass which raised her several inches above the ground. When her toes could no longer push her into the circle, the swing spun loose, revolving, dizzying.

"You tell them all this stuff, and they twist it around until you're convinced things are worse than they are. What am I going to say to this dude?" How could things be worse than they already were? Perhaps there was no bottom to hit, no solid ground. She watched as the swing towed Jody into another circle, going the other direction. "I told Royce I was married. I don't think he liked that."

Jody tipped back and forth in the swing until there was no more momentum to move her. Her feet rested on the ground and she looked out across the patchy grass. "I wonder if I can still do a cartwheel. Were you ever a cheerleader? Can you do a cartwheel?"

Katlyn stood and ran her hands along the smooth, peeling bark of the eucalyptus. "I'm doing nothing but cartwheels these days. What am I going to say to this damn psychiatrist?'' She could hear herself, possibly speaking in the third person. *She married a gay guy who just died. She's not proud of why she married him and she doesn't know why he's dead.* That ought to spark some analysis.

Jody slipped off her swing and launched herself as if she would spin away like a pinwheel. But in the twenty years since Jody last attempted a cartwheel some fine points of balance had been lost. She ended up spraddled in a heap in the dirt. After studying her position, she dusted off her hands. "For my next act," she said, "I'll show you how to fly."

Katlyn gathered up her gear. "You're no help." If Jody wanted to break her neck or snap her spine over her lost lover, she'd have to do it on her own time.

"Psychiatrists deal in lies and dreams. You can tell them anything and they'll make something of it. They love craziness. They study craziness. It's their sacred business." Jody rose and brushed off her jeans. "Come on, let's go for a walk. I promise I won't mention Eric again. It's a dead issue. We'll come up with something interesting to tell your psychiatrist this afternoon."

"He's not *my* psychiatrist." She felt as if all the molecules of energy holding her together were about to fly apart, each whirling off in a separate direction. Fight or flight. She wasn't sure if either would be appropriate. She couldn't face telling the truth about Alan, she couldn't face the fact he was dead. Opal used to say unalterable facts were the hardest to bear since they offered no options.

They headed off through the quiet residential streets crowded with houses the color of cupcakes. "What's a psychiatrist got to do with all this anyhow, I mean as far as you're concerned? People need psychiatrists when they fall out of love, not when they're in love."

"Royce says he doesn't know anything about me. Maybe he wants his psychiatrist to find out. But, Jesus, that means going back to all the trash of my life which I've been trying to put behind me for years."

"So tell him about someone else's life. He won't know the difference." Jody kicked a stone on the sidewalk, like punting a football.

"Should I tell him my mother and father were happily married and we all lived together in a house with a Maytag washer?" This was her favorite childhood lie, the one she recited on the first day of school each year when they had to stand and introduce themselves to their new teacher.

"A Maytag washer?" Jody laughed. "What's that got to do with it? A Maytag washer."

"It was the one thing my mother really craved when I was a kid. A Maytag washer was her symbol for everything we never had. As good as a first class train ride to heaven."

"Well, that ought to eat up a chunk of time. Maytag washers. Don't forget, Katlyn, we're only talking an hour here. You can say anything for an hour. Think of filibusters in Congress."

"Oh no," Katlyn said. "This dude's strange. We're going to be at it the whole afternoon. Royce didn't just call up any old shrink. He's got this progressive dude who only does therapy on boats or something. He's coming over to the house."

"He's coming to your house?" Jody gave her the same look Katlyn had given Royce last night.

Katlyn nodded. "You see, here it all is, like those Chinese mystery boxes where you open one box only to find another inside, then another inside that. I was running away when I met Royce, trying to run away from my feelings." She reached down and picked up a red plastic eagle lying on the sidewalk. One wing was broken away. "I pretended I was someone else when I met Royce."

"That's no great crime. You think I told Bruce Eric was in town? I told Bruce I was checking out a new artist. I've never even mentioned Eric to Ricky."

Katlyn launched the plastic eagle into the air as if setting it in flight. It fell quickly, heavily, like a plane dropping out of the sky, and landed on the hood of a silver Porsche. It bounced once and flipped over, resting on its wings. Katlyn went to see if she'd scratched the paint. She ran her hands along the silver hood of the car, her palms picking up the warmth of the metal. "Well," Katlyn's fist closed around the aerial, as long and slim as a fencing foil, "last week Charlotte told me Alan was dead."

"Okay. He's dead. People die. But, look here, Katlyn. Lots of women are left by men. That's just about all some men do. Brigham Young had twenty-seven wives. Artie Shaw was married eight times. He left Lana Turner and Ava Gardner. So Alan left you and you never got around to telling Royce about it. Now he's dead. Big deal. Let it go."

Katlyn clutched the antenna and gazed at the white clapboard house across the street. It was the kind of place her mother had always wanted, a picture-book house with flowers in the yard, similar to the cottage Opal now shared with her seven cats. We do things we can't explain. "Alan left me for a man." It sounded so flat when she said it, none of the curves and depths her thoughts of him held.

A sudden snap! as fresh as a surprise, and the feeling her hands were floating in the air. Katlyn looked at her hands, still clutching the aerial, broken off at the base. "Oh God, look what I've done!" She flourished the aerial like a wand. "I hope this guy's got insurance."

Jody looked nervously up and down the street. "I hope he's not sitting in his living room watching." She studied the clean break in the metal.

Katlyn tried setting the thin aerial back in its socket, but it fell against the windshield, dropping and clattering against the car as soon as she let go. She'd broken off an antenna, a Porsche's no less. Grabbing the plastic eagle and the aerial she followed Jody down the street. "If he can afford a Porsche, he can afford to get his antenna fixed. But I can't afford to tell him, at least not today."

They rounded the corner, casting quick glances back over their shoulders. No one followed them, no one shouted. "Maybe I'll leave him a note," Katlyn said. "Maybe tomorrow." The aerial whistled in the air, cutting figure eights in front of her. As a kid, she'd snapped a lot of aerials one summer, a collection of them hidden under her bed, all those slim metal rods that seemed mysterious and powerful to her then.

Jody scuffed her foot against a Big Wheel lying wrecked on the sidewalk. "Yeah, leave a note. Sign it Godzilla." She reached out and took the antenna from Katlyn. "How'd you do that?"

"It's all in the wrist. I made a career out of it one summer when I was a kid. Later I found out other girls had sex, or shoplifted, but I snapped aerials."

Jody tried to twirl the antenna through her fingers like a baton, but it was too thin, too light, and flipped out of her hand. "Why?"

"They fascinated me. Lightning rods for music. Conductors of invisible airwaves. That summer, when I wasn't popping aerials, I'd ride my bike out to the desert. I had a little transistor radio and I'd practice dancing to the music, all by myself out in the desert."

"I watched *American Bandstand*. I spent years of my

life in love with Dick Clark.'' Jody assumed a fencing stand, arm back, feet splayed, the antenna ahead of her like a weapon. She advanced a few steps down the sidewalk, lunged at a fireplug. "A man. Alan left you for a man.'' She danced back from the fireplug, lunged again. "You didn't know?''

Katlyn shook her head. "I waited around for him to come back, for a visit, a phone call, a letter. Nothing. I called all his friends, but everyone except Charlotte just said: *Can't help you, Katlyn. Nice talking to you.* Just like your promises from Eric to get together again. A write-off. I mean, this was a man I'd slept with, made love to, planned my future with.'' The sun suddenly seemed too bright, the houses washed in white light. "When I met Royce I wanted to put it all behind me, forget about it for a while. I thought the best thing for a woman who'd been left, left for a man no less, would be to have an affair with a man who couldn't hurt me, couldn't promise me anything.''

"I suppose that's one advantage to having an affair with a married man, if you want to call that an advantage.''

"I fell for Royce and did everything I could to make him fall for me, to soothe my wounded vanity I suppose. A married man would patch up my ego without screwing around with my future. I mean, anyone would understand if Alan left me for Lana Turner. But I didn't know how to think about myself, as a woman, when he left me for Guerrero. I picked what I thought was a surefire situation. A man who could make me feel like a woman, who'd proven himself with another woman. I thought there was no risk. Everyone knows they never leave their wives.'' She took the aerial from Jody and whipped it in a tight circle in front of her, a hum in the air. "I'm afraid if I say anything this afternoon, everything will come down like a row of dominoes. We don't know why Alan died. What if it was AIDS?"

"Oh God." Jody rolled her eyes. "Right. Yeah. There's a real problem explaining that one." She seemed to be putting this together like repiecing a broken vase. "Stories like that make you want to drink in the morning."

Katlyn sat down on the steps of the nearest house, suddenly too tired to continue walking. The houses and cars and trees across the street were so bright and vibrant they left no room for thought. The colors spilled together like mixing paint in a bucket. "I can't go into that this afternoon. Eventually Charlotte will find Guerrero and we'll know. I don't want to play emotional uproar until I'm sure. Royce has a decision to make. He's the one who feels he needs to see a psychiatrist. It'll throw the whole thing off track, to go into all that about Alan."

Jody sat down beside her and put her arm over Katlyn's shoulder. "I wouldn't go into all that, not this afternoon. It would be like a crash diet, too much too fast. Lie. Say he left you to become an international terrorist. Nobody even tries to understand terrorists. They're beyond baroque, and even Royce would understand why you didn't say anything about him."

"Emotional terrorism. That's exactly the way I feel."

"But I'll tell you one thing," Jody said. "This might not be the time to force an issue with Royce."

"It's too late now. Sure, it's been over three years since I slept with Alan. I took the antibody test when the AIDS thing first hit. I'm clean, healthy as a horse. But that doesn't mean I didn't have to do some serious thinking. Like what my life was about, or rather, the things it's not about."

"You could tell that psychiatrist about your trip to Africa. Make it up. Use the *National Geographic*."

185

"But I've never been to Africa. I've never been out of the country. When you never go anywhere you're left with nothing but wishes and dreams."

Jody bit her thumb. "You going to bluff your way through the whole afternoon?"

"I just don't think this is the time to deal with my feelings about Alan and Guerrero. Or Africa. I'd rather just leave it on Royce to decide what he's going to do." Was that making a decision, she wondered, by letting Royce decide?

Jody stood up. "If I were you, I'd look stunning. I'd spend a lot of time making coffee and such. I'd let Royce do the talking. If they ask you about Alan, just dog it off. I mean, you don't have to tell him the truth. Just sort of flutter around in the background, play hostess. Royce is the one who has to make a decision, not you. You've made yours."

Katlyn gave an embarrassed grin as she dusted off the seat of her jeans. "Yeah, but I keep waffling. Know what I was going to do this afternoon, if I didn't have to entertain this damn shrink? I was going to visit my feather wholesaler, see what kind of stuff he's got for the Halloween masks. Last year he had some wonderful Chinese chicken feathers, with lovely ebony spots. I'm thinking of taking a trip, and I'm also designing new masks for Charlotte for Halloween. Schitzy, huh?"

"Halloween is months away."

"They take a lot of time, getting the feathers in a smooth pattern, the glitter to swirl right. Last year Charlotte sold out, over one hundred and fifty masks. And twenty-five headdresses. And we've got that New York account this year, maybe even one in LA, if Charlotte gets on the stick."

Jody twirled in a wobbly pirouette. "Open cans of

worms. Let's go see your feather wholesaler then. Keep you from going nuts until the shrink shows up."

Katlyn's feather wholesaler, Harris, lived on Potero Hill, not far from Noe Valley. When Harris opened the door, after Katlyn rang several times, she was surprised to see him, unshaven, in a pair of dirty running shorts and a wrinkled silk shirt. "Ah, business, business," he said. "Just when you think you can't handle any more, something more comes along to be dealt with."

"We can come back some other time, Harris," Katlyn said, making no attempt to hide her concern. "What's wrong? I thought I had an appointment today." Usually Harris, even though he did business out of his home, looked like a sales representative for a large corporation. He'd turned his living room into a very formal office where he displayed samples protected in Plexiglas and cellophane envelopes. Harris dealt in feathers, precious stones, exotic hides and skins, and any other ornamentation that pleased him.

"Come in, come in." He picked up a vodka bottle from his desk. "Mona left me." He waved his arm to indicate the room. "What you see is what I got. She took the truck, cleaned out the bank account, and turned off the phone and water."

Katlyn had never met Mona, but she'd heard noises from the other parts of the house when she visited Harris, domestic sounds she assumed represented Mona. "But why? I thought you two were pretty tight."

"I don't know." Harris shook his head sadly. "The other day I flew to Phoenix for some turquoise. Mona dropped me off at the airport as if everything was fine. But when I came back late last night, she didn't pick me up. I called, and found the phone disconnected. I got a cab, and when I walked in, I knew she was gone, her and about every valuable thing we own."

"She turned off the water and the phone?"

"I think she wanted to inconvenience me. Or maybe she was afraid I wouldn't notice." Harris let out a nasty laugh. "The place is gutted. How could I not notice? The only decent thing she did was she left all this alone." He waved his hand at the office. "Let me pull myself together here and we'll do some business. You want feathers today? I wish I could interest you in stones. I have some lovely carnelians and amethysts I'd like to turn."

"Just feathers today. Got anything interesting?" Katlyn wanted to look around the rest of the house and see exactly what he meant by gutted. But she'd never been invited into any of the other rooms, only this office, which looked the same as always. The big desk, plush black leather chairs, displays of his samples, and a bookcase full of ring binders.

Harris pulled a large loose-leaf notebook from a shelf. "Your best bet here will be the Russian pheasant feathers. A beautiful deep rust color. Page seventeen. I'll be right back." He scooped up the vodka bottle and disappeared into another room.

"He always like this?" Jody asked.

"I've never seen him like this in the four or five years I've been buying from him. He's Charlotte's connection."

Jody raised an eyebrow. "Just goes to show you what love, or the lack of it, can do to you. I mean, imagine how Royce will feel if you leave him."

Katlyn felt a wave of anger so strong and bitter she thought she might spit nails. "I'm here, aren't I? I'm picking out the materials for Halloween masks. I am not buying luggage or airplane tickets."

Jody put her hands up as a sign of surrender. "Okay. Okay."

Katlyn browsed through the sample book until Harris returned, dressed this time in his usual business suit.

Except for the fact he hadn't shaved, and the glass of vodka in his hand, he looked quite steady. Business as usual.

"Please excuse my appearance but the water won't be turned on until some time this afternoon." He rubbed his hand along his jaw. "I can't offer you coffee because of the water. Amazing, isn't it, how you never think about something like the water until you don't have it. I've got vodka, though. Want a drink?"

"No thanks. You look as if you've been up all night." Harris's face was usually clear as glass, but today there were deep circles under his eyes, stubble of his whiskers.

Harris shrugged and took a sip of his drink. "I was. I spent the night making an inventory of what she took. If nothing else, I might report it to my insurance company. Tell them a burglar broke in. That is, if I don't hear from her. But I should have remembered you were coming. How's business?"

"We all have our ups and downs. I'm actually early." Katlyn gave a shrug. "I have another appointment this afternoon. Surprises happen in my life too."

"This one caught me quite unaware. Mona and I have been together now almost nine years. Certainly, we've had our share of problems, but the last thing I expected was this little number."

"We do things we can't explain as easily as we do things we don't understand. My mother's phrase. I'm thinking of having it engraved on her tombstone."

"Now, now, Katlyn," Harris said. "Let's not be bitter. Let's spend some money, buy some feathers. Consumer therapy. How did you like the Russian pheasant feathers? Beautiful, aren't they?"

Katlyn nodded her agreement. "I'll take two pounds."

"You buy feathers by the pound?" Jody asked. "How many feathers in a pound?"

"It's tricky," Harris said. "But that would be approximately five hundred." He smiled at Jody. "Are you interested in stones? They're much more substantial than feathers."

"Do you sell those by the pound too?"

"Per stone. And I'm getting into fur. Squirrel and raccoon tails."

"Disgusting," Jody said.

Katlyn placed her order. Two pounds of pheasant tails, a pound of peacock feathers, three dozen speckled pigeon wings, sixteen bantam rooster collars, three pounds of blackbird feathers, six lyrebird tails, and four bird of paradise crests. She decided to try a couple of squirrel tails, even though she had no designs in mind.

"You go shoot these creatures?" Jody asked Harris. "How do you get all this stuff?"

"Oh no," Harris said. "I've never even touched a gun. I deal with an Indian tribe up in Lake County. The kids shoot squirrel and raccoon and eat them. I buy the tails from them. As for the feathers, except for the Australian stuff, mostly I collect them from restaurants. Oriental restaurants especially. Next time you order any kind of fowl in an Asian restaurant, remember the bird you're eating once wore feathers." He waved at his sample books. "This is the ultimate in recycling. Much better to sell them to Katlyn and turn them into masks or whatever than to throw them away." He turned to Katlyn. "That it for today? Visa, MasterCard, or would you like me to put it on your bill?"

"Put in on the bill. Do you have all this in stock?"

Harris gave her his salesman's smile. "I can let you have the peacock feathers, the lyretails, and the bird of paradise. I'll have to check on the others. The tails are up in Lake County still. I'll have to get another truck. Mona's a greedy bitch. She took the antiques with her, the Tiffany lamps, that sort of stuff." Harris's face crested, fell. "I have a feeling she ran off with our drug dealer. Which means all that stuff will end up hocked, gone. You spend almost a decade with someone, building a home, sharing the little joys like the light from a lamp, and then—" He shrugged. "The grass is always greener."

"I know, Harris." Katlyn felt the hollow spot again, like a rash spreading inside her chest. "Your drug dealer, huh? Do you have any idea whether being in love is different from not wanting to be alone?"

"My, my, you split hairs, don't you, Katlyn. You're the only person I know who would even ask the question." Harris opened a cabinet and weighed out the peacock feathers on a baby scale. "Mona wasn't alone. She had me. But love? Love is for the young. Or the foolish." He rolled the feathers into a cone of white wrapping paper, like a bouquet. "He'll leave her. I just know it. Then what will she do? Then she'll really be alone."

Back at the house Katlyn let herself in quietly in case Royce was still asleep. She left the antenna, plastic eagle and the paper cones of feathers in the hall and was surprised to discover how late it was. Dr. Bodine would be here in less than an hour. Dagmar frolicked against her leg, and except for the noise of the dog's excitement, the house was silent. There was a note on the kitchen table.

I'm sorry, Sweetheart,

There's been an accident at the plant. Donna Moon called and I have to go down there. I called Dr. Bodine, but only got his machine. I'll try to be back as soon as I can. I'm sure you and he will have plenty to discuss until I get home.

Love - yr Capt. of Industry

"Oh, terrific." Katlyn looked around the kitchen in despair. Just the thing she didn't need, fielding Dr. Bodine until Royce returned. It blew all to hell Jody's advice, difficult to flutter about in the background when there was no one in the foreground. She was tempted to have some kind of accident too, to call up Jody and hide out with her all afternoon. They could go to the races or shoot pool in a bar. But although the idea was attractive, the motivation was cowardly. And perhaps Royce would be back, but she doubted this. When one of the presswomen broke her arm at work, Royce spent the afternoon and a good chunk of the evening at the hospital with her. He'd bailed the cameraman out of jail when he was picked up for parking tickets, fronting the three hundred sixty-five dollars for bail. He was probably a good boss to work for and undoubtedly would see this accident through, whatever it was, before he returned. That left her to deal with Dr. Bodine, who would ring the doorbell in about forty minutes. She felt much the same as falling on skis, the ground slipping out from under her feet and those few airborne seconds knowing she would hit the ground, knowing the fall hadn't completed itself yet.

Unsure what one wore to entertain a psychiatrist all afternoon, she pulled out a taupe and black forties-style with padded shoulders and a plunging neckline, which suggested much more than it showed, one of Royce's favorites. She put on stockings and heels, brushed on a quick gloss of makeup, and rolled her long hair into a Joan Crawford style, in keeping with the dress. If nothing else, the dress would tell Royce she was trying to please him, to accommodate him and his psychiatrist.

What do you do with someone else's psychiatrist for the afternoon? A small tic jumped at the corner of her eye as she put on mascara. The dog barked, the doorbell rang. Dr. Bodine was here.

She was ready for anything. After all, this was a man who did therapy on boats. She was glad to see he wasn't a hairy-chested, tanned type with gold chains hanging to his navel. Nothing faddish or trendy. Shorter and younger than she expected, no Santa Claus in a business suit towering down at her like an omnipotent father. He was dressed like a banker and she warmed to his smile.

Dagmar sniffed his shoes and looked up at him with her ears cocked for danger. Dr. Bodine touched her head cautiously, the way he might handle a loaded gun. This man was no animal lover.

"Easy, Dagmar," Katlyn said. "She won't hurt you. Please come in, I'm Katlyn Whiston."

Dagmar followed them into the living room and hopped up on the opposite end of the couch. Katlyn smiled. "I'd tell her to get down but she'd jump right back up. Territory, you know. I hope you don't mind dogs. If you do I could put her out."

Dr. Bodine looked at Dagmar. "She doesn't look all that dangerous. Sort of reminds me of the dog on the old RCA records, same ears." He reached out tentatively, and Dagmar licked his fingers. "She sounds as big as a wolf-hound. What kind of dog is she?"

"Old brown dog. I found her at the pound. The SPCA people told me she'd been brought in because some couple divorced and neither of them could keep her. They thought she was a German shepherd and they thought Dagmar meant bitch in German. But as you can see," she leaned over and ran her hand along the dog's neck, "she's not a German shepherd, and I don't think Dagmar means bitch in German." Dagmar, the result of a day aimlessly riding the buses after Alan left. On a whim she'd stopped into the SPCA, came out with Dagmar, hoping the dog would fill the hollow spot Alan had created.

"Wasn't there a famous transvestite from Cleveland named Dagmar?" Dr. Bodine smiled, his face relaxing a bit. He scanned the room, obviously looking for Royce.

"I'm not really up on famous transvestites." She fondled Dagmar's ear, then decided to let the afternoon begin to unfold. Damn whatever happened at the printing plant this morning. "I'm terribly sorry about this, but Royce isn't here. There's been some kind of accident at the plant. But I'm sure he'll be back soon. Would you like some coffee?" She handed him the note so he would have it in Royce's own words.

He glanced at it briefly. "Sure," he said. "Some coffee would be fine." He rose to trail after her into the kitchen.

"No, no. I'll get it." She wanted him to sit quietly on the couch until Royce could arrive. She wished she could offer him a book to read or could interest him in a soap opera or MTV. That would be something, spending the afternoon with Royce's shrink discussing rock and roll and punk styles. She hoped Royce would get his ass back here soon.

"I like to look around," he said from behind her. "That's part of the point of working the way I do."

She might as well find out just how weird this guy was. "Royce said you spent the afternoon on Frank's boat."

"I don't like to work in an office. I'd rather let the client decide where we meet. It's more comfortable that way."

"How did you come up with that idea? I mean, most psychiatrists use offices, don't they?" She blushed at how rude she sounded, how mocking.

"Did you know," his tone was conversational, "in the very early days, psychiatry was referred to as alienism.

Nothing to do with UFOs or men on Mars. People with problems were thought of as alienated from their society. We're talking a hundred years ago. All that Victorian blindness and hypocrisy." He gave her a friendly smile. "Psychiatrists were called alienists. But I don't like to think of myself as an alienist."

"Alienism," she repeated. "It does sound like someone from Mars, *Invasion of the Body Snatchers*."

"I don't use an office because I believe we all have problems, they're part of our lives. A person's house says a lot about who lives there, the kind of problems they might have, or might think they have. Now, this is a great kitchen. I always think the kitchen should be the best room in the house. I had a kitchen once that was big enough to put a couch in."

"A couch, how cozy."

"I like a nice, warm room like this. Lots of space." She watched him as he opened the door to the refrigerator and peered inside. He closed the door and examined the breakfast nook. "You could have a party in here. My kitchen's about as bleak as arctic light. About the only thing my kitchen's good for is a hangover."

While she scooped fresh coffee into the filter, Dr. Bodine strolled through the rooms as if he were a realtor, noticing Royce's parquet floors and her refinished furniture. Under his eye, this house, which she and Royce had worked so hard on, seemed to grow smaller. Would he peek in her workroom, the bedroom, the garage? Katlyn was afraid the house looked less than refinished and more like the best of a Salvation Army store.

"Royce said you helped him restore this place." He smiled again and Katlyn was struck by the friendliness in his face. "It's lovely. Very tasteful."

"Thank you." He seemed to really like the place, his face open and appreciative. "When I moved in, Royce had most of the heavy structural work done. But I helped sand the floors, hang shutters. Then he helped me decorate, the painting and wallpapering. I'd never done anything like that before. It was kind of exciting." She wondered how long they could talk about the house. "I think Royce secretly wanted to be a carpenter. He's got some before-and-after photos. Would you like to see them?" Not exactly MTV, but it would eat up the time. Maybe he would tell her more about alienism.

"Not now, thanks. That's really not why I came over." He drifted back toward the living room.

While the coffee brewed, Katlyn busied herself with the peacock feathers, unrolling them from Harris's paper cone. She took out a Chinese vase she'd found at a garage sale. There was a crack on one side but she would turn that to the wall. She felt Dr. Bodine watching her as she arranged the peacock feathers in the vase. She fluffed them and moved the eyes so they formed a fan sweeping the vase from side to side. Something told her she might have to entertain this man most of the afternoon.

She tucked the Chinese vase with the peacock feathers in a corner and got out the cups for coffee. She wished there were some Danish in the house, croissants. She should have cleaned the house for this visit. Would he notice dustballs and see that as part of Royce's problems?

"Are you from San Francisco?" He was suddenly behind her again. "A native, as they say?"

"No." She listened, hoping Royce's car would sail into the driveway.

"San Francisco people fascinate me," he said. "The natives and seminatives. Maybe it's the fact there's no real winter, no time when you're forced to sit inside and worry about the weather. They always have projects, like this house." He swept his hand to indicate the rooms. He fingered the buttons on the blender, ran his hand along the side of the juicer. "Maybe it's because we all come from somewhere else. Where are you from?"

He sounded as if he were making small talk at a cocktail party. "Reno," she said. "When Opal, my mother, and I moved out here she called it the land at the end of the rainbow. She said it was against the law to be unhappy in California."

"I have a lot of clients who believe that, mostly the ones from somewhere else. It's not exactly true." His hand trailed along the top of a mission library table Katlyn had recently refinished. "Did you salvage this? My mother used to have a table similar to this."

Katlyn nodded, smiled her thanks for his appreciation of her work. As she handed him a cup and saucer she wondered how long they could talk about furniture. "Cream of sugar?" Maybe she could show him her workroom, offer to whip up a set of Hawaiian pillowcases for him. Would a psychiatrist read anything into a set of pillowcases?

"No thanks." Dr. Bodine's tone turned serious. She knew what was coming. "Why don't you and I talk a little while we're waiting for Royce. No sense wasting the time." He smiled again and returned to the living room and indicated a chair for her.

Dagmar took her position on the other end of the couch. If only Royce would show up they could get on with things, whatever that would be.

Tell him about someone else's life, Jody had said. Make it up. He'll never know the difference. But without Royce, this was an opportunity to talk about Alan. She must eat up the time until Royce returned. Dr. Bodine didn't want to talk about their furniture. He wanted her to talk about herself. She'd tell him a story, tell it as if she were Jody, that would take the sting out. If she told the truth, Royce would undoubtedly walk in and she would be left hanging in the middle of more unfinished business than part of an afternoon could contain. And his ethics might dictate telling Royce everything she said. He was, after all, Royce's psychiatrist. She watched the way he looked at her, as if he were searching for something in her face. He studied her in the same way people stare when they are trying to remember a name.

WEDNESDAY
AFTERNOON

Later Max remembered Katlyn's story as a mixture of lies and dreams and hocus-pocus with some fair portion of truth shaded by deep hurt. He believed truth often wasn't as illuminating as lies. The truth can be facts improperly understood.

He was struck by the color and intensity of her eyes, each a slightly different shade, like water in a quickly moving stream. Her outfit reminded him of the old *LIFE* photographs, British women during the War keeping a stiff upper lip. As she spoke he imagined them dancing to Erroll Garner's slow, cool piano. "Misty." "Stella By Starlight."

"It's a recurring dream, Dr. Bodine, maybe once a month for the past two years." She stands on the veld, staring out across the windless savanna. In the distance, a long, golden seahorse rockets over the prairie. As it approaches, it gains legs and spots and transforms into a giraffe which trots up beside her and begins to eat her hair. The more he eats, the longer and thicker her hair grows, and the sound of his square teeth nipping through her curls reminds her of biting into a crisp apple. The muzzle, warm and soft as a horse's, whispers in her ear in a musical language she can't understand.

She told her husband, Alan, about this dream and he suggested they visit Africa, a land of purple skies and burnt white grasses. Africa. Imagine seeing a giraffe loping across the land.

As they studied French and Swahili she realized the true purpose of the trip. After three years of marriage, Alan was becoming a stranger, a man who drifted through their house, as if she, the walls, the meals they ate together, were blocked from his consciousness the way people on a bus will accept the speed and movement but never acknowledge it. Alan became deeper, moved farther away. At night he smelled drier, darker, the scent of an animal denned in a deep cave.

Alan's father had died, and with his inheritance they decided to book first-class seats for the flight from San Francisco to Cairo, stopping in New York and London. As their departure neared, she found herself less and less able to feel a part of this trip, and more like a camera recording her journey. Nothing fancy like a Hollywood film, more like old home movies from the fifties, bad lighting, no sound. She could visualize them together, not from her own point of view, the limits of her field of vision, but as if she were part of the picture. As she sat talking to Alan, she would sometimes glimpse her entire body, dressed in a different, more dramatic outfit, as if she were looking over her own shoulder.

Max watched her talk, his eyes following her legs as she crossed them. He visualized her breasts beneath the black dress, remembering the way the shimmering sheath sent the light swirling along her body. She spoke calmly, stretching out her story. But her eyes gave her away. Passing cars caught her attention and she would cut her eyes to the windows.

On the plane, she and Alan sat across from an African businessman who imported leather from Morocco and exported perfume to Nairobi. He'd been to Madagascar, the land at the end of the earth, and he told them that in Malagasy, God is referred to as the man who sits on top of your head.

Max wondered if they'd met a spy. Perfume to Nairobi, only the CIA would think of something as silly as that.

Over brandies they practiced their Swahili with the African businessman. They knew only a handful of phrases.

Do you take American Express?
I do not wish to buy.
I will give you nothing.
I am catching a cold on the brain.
Burn the politeness.
Which way to the British Embassy?

They all laughed and thought it quite funny, the phrases you need to travel in Africa these days. Alan was convinced they could tour the world if they could call for a waiter in the local language and give him the equivalent of the local dollar to find someone who spoke English. The African businessman agreed with Alan and even told him what bank in Cairo gave the best rate of exchange.

The African businessman reminded her of Humphrey Bogart in *Casablanca*, not that he looked anything like Bogart, just the same weary air of a man who's seen too much, loved too deeply. The strains of "As Time Goes By" drifted through her thoughts and she wished she spoke with a cluttered European accent and possessed a mysterious past. He had a mole, a little triangle near his left eye, and she experienced the sudden desire to run her tongue around it. She studied his strong hands and knew their exact feel on her shoulder blades if he were to kiss her. He told them about the desert, mountains of sand-blasted rock reaching eleven thousand feet into the air, and the vast, stony hummadas that lie in between. He described nautilus shells embedded in the coral reef high in the desert near Tangier. He'd seen footprints of dinosaurs three feet in diameter, over one hundred million years old.

When it got late they tried to sleep, but she never slept well on planes. Flying east into the rosy light of dawn she watched three businessmen get up and go off to the little bathrooms, carrying their briefcases. When they returned, they were wearing splotched-khaki jungle fatigues and black ski masks which only showed their eyes. Looking around, she knew one of them was the African businessman they'd been talking to about their trip. She discovered he was holding the first-class section at bay, the triangular mole peeking through the ski mask.

Using the stewardess's intercom, he explained that they were being hijacked. He carried a syringe full of chemicals, a seventeen-syllable amber fluid which sounded strong enough to kill sharks. He held the stewardess locked to his chest like a wrestler. Any trouble, and he would inject a small amount. A scratch could kill her.

The hijackers had dressed up like businessmen, and businessmen are just like waves on the ocean, indistinguishable one from another. They'd passed through the metal detectors with plastic syringes in their briefcases, as if they were all of them diabetic and needed insulin shots. They demanded money, and she wondered if that made them robbers or hijackers, and explained their politics, but Katlyn couldn't follow. Her attention was on the man with the sexy mole, and he seemed to hold her eyes too. Her heart knocked around her rib cage and she wondered if the pulsing in her pelvis and the silver shivers shaking down her spine were fear or desire. The hijacker with the triangular mole held the key to everything Alan denied her.

Max felt she could follow the hijacker off to Casablanca, make love to him with the smooth sandy tones of the desert beyond the windows of a North African villa. Moorish arches would shelter them from the searing sun, and in the cool of a moonlit night, the hijacker would show her the Devonian coral reef. Africa, she wanted to go to Africa, a continent of deserts and hijackers as well as Archbishop Desmond Tutu and loping giraffes.

As Katlyn explained it, a hijacking isn't very eventful. They sat passively in their seats as the plane droned on toward Heathrow. In the silence of the captured jet, soaring high above the clouds, she held Alan's hand but felt nothing pass between them, as if Alan were absorbed by his own thoughts. She knew her life was in danger, giving her the fullest sense of being alive.

Max couldn't recall a hijacking quite like the one Katlyn described, but he encouraged her with a few nods when her story seemed to falter. He could see her passion for the hijacker, feel Alan's remote coldness as if her husband were an Alpine mountain rather than flesh and blood.

Katlyn pronounced this a successful hijacking. The ransom was paid, then the passengers released, and the plane lifted off the tarmac at Heathrow and disappeared into the drizzling sky. Watching the contrails evaporate in the rain, she felt laid open to their hijacker like a vast tumbledown house whose owner had gone away, leaving the place to sink into ruin.

Without discussing it, they booked passage back to San Francisco. With the hijacking, Africa was out of the question.

Max wondered about this. He'd never worked with a patient who'd been hijacked or kidnapped. What do those people feel, so helpless facing a gun or a madman.

Two nights after their return to San Francisco, Alan came to bed with a black ski mask on. They laughed, hysterical laughter like champagne for the spirit, releasing all the tension of the last few days and the previous months of their marriage. For the first time in almost a year, they made passionate love, sweating through the sheets, tumbling onto the floor, locked together as if in combat. She kept her eyes open, imagining the mole.

They began following the news, searching for their hijacker. They studied embassy takeovers, assassination attempts, bank robberies. Alan became interested in medicine and kept vials of murky-colored liquids in the bathroom. She discovered a collection of syringes hidden in the kitchen. When they made love, she would create a triangular mole with her makeup pencil, high on his cheekbone, just peeking through the wool of the ski mask. Later, for her birthday, he had it tattooed, a dark smoked-blue, like the color of a charred log.

They discussed a trip to Morocco. Africa, Alan said, was the last great theater where power and passion can be played out against the sky. Africa and the Arctic, myth and dream, strongholds where a man could test himself to discover what he was made of.

She longed to ride camels over oceans of dunes.

Max wondered if she'd seen this story in a movie or read it in a book. He puzzled over how one rode a camel, western-style or sidesaddle.

Alan believed their hijacker would surface in San

Francisco and he began to scout strange corners of the city, looking for him. Alan disappeared for days on end. When he returned, he brought presents. Sten guns. Machetes. Hand grenades. One evening they sat in chairs facing each other, their syringes balanced dangerously in their palms. Nerves, Alan said, needed exercise like any other muscle.

The weapons fascinated Katlyn. She recalled her father's collection of Nazi memorabilia, everything from a porcelain coffee cup with a swastika on it to a picture of Hitler practicing on a target range. During World War II her father, a doctor, was stationed at Walter Reed for the duration. He despised home duty. He knew aneurysms and shell shock and the best possible way to amputate any part of the body. But he felt left out of the entire affair. To make the war real, he collected the detritus. When she was a small girl, his collection was merely some boxes in the basement and attic. When she left home to take part in the resistance against Vietnam, her father turned her room into his museum. Where her dresser used to sit, a frilly heart-shaped thing, her father placed a bookcase full of helmets, with skulls under some of them. Where her bed used to be, he positioned a .37 mm. antitank cannon, the bore in line with the second-story window, aimed above the tops of the trees.

Alan's guns and machetes made their hijacker as real to her as her father's helmets and skulls. She and Alan began to study the war of nerves that has replaced Vietnam. They laughed about detente and marveled at the erratic economics of banana republics. Alan began teaching her terrorist tactics, the psychology of mass, random destruction. They studied desert warfare. Rommel's campaign left Alan breathless.

And then, one evening shortly before she met Royce,

Katlyn came home and they were both there. Except for the fact Alan was shorter and slighter, they were identical. The splotched jungle fatigues, the knives strapped into their combat boots. The tattooed mole peeking through the ski mask. They drank brandies to celebrate their reunion. She felt as if she'd been waiting for this moment all her life. This was what they headed off to Africa to discover. The evening, as it unfolded before them, would explain all the secrets Alan had been harboring.

Max saw them as three soldiers of fortune stumbling through the desert beneath a blazing sun. They would be silhouetted in moonlight, setting out plastique explosives. Afterward, they would share a jug of warm wine while watching fires flare on the horizon. He envisioned her role in their lives as Etta Place, mistress to Butch Cassidy and the Sundance Kid. Belle Starr, Alexandra Kollontai, Bernadette Devlin, Patty Hearst. Only a handful of women had experienced what was about to happen now that her hijacker had returned.

She said they exchanged looks, the kind of look only one man can give another. A look which dismisses a woman so completely her very breath becomes irrelevant. A look bred in the secret circle of men no woman can enter.

Their hijacker rose and kissed her hand. "Vous êtes mon bijou," he told her. He saluted Alan, and closed the door quietly as he left.

Max watched her stiffen in the armchair as she described her last evening with Alan. Her voice lost its cadence and rhythm, the breezy tone. Her pitch dropped as if this part of the story had fallen into a sinkhole. Her heart's desire. How can you tell your wife you're leaving her for a man? she wanted to know. How can you tell her that her life, real and imagined, will now be irrevocably changed?

Max couldn't answer these questions. Her heart's desire. Irrevocably changed. She read his look, and with disturbing calmness continued, daring him to stop her.

That last night together she and Alan behaved like children fighting over a favorite toy. She told Max about home movies her father had taken in the fifties. Her favorite was a Christmas movie of her sister, a dazzling towhead at that age, and herself, opening the presents Santa brought them. This movie has been staged. Her mother has curled and fluffed their hair, and the indoor lighting for the movie camera casts a halo all around her sister's head. But near the end, Katlyn opens one of her sister's presents and her sister becomes angry. They push and shove each other, each clutching opposite legs of a stuffed pinto pony. Her sister, with her halo, grabs Katlyn's bangs and gives a pull. She winces in pain and raised a fist to strike. The film ended at this point and she couldn't remember what happened to the pinto pony afterward.

Max noticed her sister didn't have a name.

Katlyn said she always remembered that movie when she thought about the last time she saw Alan. She'd been sitting in an armchair, just like this one, she said as she patted the upholstery, and their hijacker had given her a beret which capped her hair. She saw the scene from over her shoulder and remembered Alan with the same kind of old-fashioned, harsh lighting as her father's home movies. Although she could see they were talking, the memory was without sound. Alan paced the room, explaining his decision, swearing she wasn't the reason he was leaving her. At one point Alan beat his chest like King Kong, then dropped his face into his hands and cried, his narrow back beating against the jungle fatigues.

Max phrased a look to let Katlyn know he doubted the extent of her story. He believed lies were built on the emotional punch of an important experience. Perhaps there hadn't been a hijacking, but metaphorically she was telling the truth about her feelings for her husband.

He checked his watch. Quarter to three. He knew she could sit here for the rest of the afternoon fabricating stories for him. He hadn't expected the session to work out like this, and felt he'd heard enough. She offered him more coffee, which he accepted to provide a break. He began to formulate the questions he would ask when the dog barked and hopped off the couch, ran for the front door. A car pulled into the driveway.

Royce looked flustered, harried, compared to the calm Katlyn. He greeted Max breathlessly, as if he'd run over to Noe Valley rather than driven there. "I'm really sorry about this." He collapsed back against the couch, his long legs angled in a V, his feet turned out at the ankle. "You never know whether things begin to roll because you set them in motion, or whether they're already rolling and sweeping you along."

Katlyn entered the living room with the pot of coffee. "What's going on at the plant?"

"Donna Moon called to say she quit and that there'd been a fire in the camera room."

Max watched Royce as the explanation unfolded. The strain on his face convinced Max Royce's problems were escalating.

"Quit?" The surprise showed clearly on Katlyn's face. "Donna Moon can't quit. What would she do?"

"She can always get another job, that's what. She's a wonder of a secretary. That place will fall apart without her." He looked at Max. "I had to go down there and try to talk her out of it and check on the damage. Chemical fire, happens sometimes when someone's careless."

Max sipped his coffee and cut his eyes back and forth between Katlyn and Royce. The timing was all off on this. They'd wasted two hours with the hijacker nonsense.

They should've discussed Royce, not Alan. He possessed no more information about their problems than when he walked in at one o'clock. He'd been given only a hint into Katlyn's world, and no idea how to apply what he'd learned to her feelings.

"Why would Donna Moon quit?" Katlyn looked as if she wanted to sit next to Royce, to touch him, but she remained in the easy chair, leaning forward on her elbows. "Irene?"

"You got it. I'll have go over and talk to Irene. She and the kids showed up at the plant. On a Wednesday morning. They should've been in school." He ran his hands through his hair and sighed deeply. "Donna Moon told Norton and the others I was sick with the flu to explain why I wasn't going to be in this week. Irene and the kids came down to the plant, why I have no idea yet, and ran into one of the pressmen who asks if I'm feeling better. Irene loses her cookies, which is too bad because Aurelio, the pressman, doesn't speak English very well and he was just trying to be polite to the boss's wife. Irene's standing in the hall, babbling away, too fast for Aurelio to follow and making a hell of a racket. Donna Moon comes out of the office and Irene lights into her."

"What for?" Katlyn's look revealed anger or fear, Max wasn't sure which.

Royce straightened a bit on the couch. "I don't know what started it. But Irene has a real wicked mouth. No one has to put up with that kind of personal abuse. Donna Moon's the rock of that business. She's real stoic about her feelings and not impulsive in the least. Then right after Irene left, the fire broke out. The cameraman must have been watching the cat fight and not paying attention to his work."

"Have you talked to Irene today?" Max asked.

Royce looked bewildered. He waved his hand vaguely in the air. "I was supposed to be talking to you."

"Frankly," Max said, "this puts a whole new type of English on the problem." He wondered how the three of them could discuss this. Royce's problems weren't one umbrella. To Max, they looked more like a basket of spilled peaches, bruised and rolling away crookedly across the floor.

"I'm lost," Katlyn said. "Does this have anything to do with a divorce, or is there some other reason for Irene to go on the warpath?"

Royce looked ashen, exhausted and embarrassed, as if he were guilty of an endless list of sins of omission. "Irene's parents were down this weekend. It was Todd's birthday. You and I didn't really talk about divorce until Monday. She doesn't even know yet. How was I supposed to tell her?"

"You haven't been around here, even with taking time off, much more than when you go to work. I don't know if you've seen Irene or not. Was she at the plant?" Her eyes snapped with anger, her eyebrows knitted close.

"Time out," Max signaled with a referee's T. "I don't feel up to a confrontation between you two, not at this stage."

Royce's attention was still on Katlyn. "No, she wasn't at the plant. She reamed Donna Moon and huffed out of there, the kids in tow. That's what I can't figure out, why the kids were with her. So I haven't seen her, but I called and told her I'd be over there this evening. Divorce or not, she can't get away with treating my employees the way she treated Donna Moon." He looked at Max. "Irene has nothing to do with the business whatsoever. I think the last time she even set foot in the place was our Christmas party. I can't let her bully my people."

"Agreed." Max turned to Katlyn. "When Royce and I

were talking yesterday we decided that Irene, divorce or no, is really a separate problem from his relationship with you. Maybe it would be a good idea if we worked on that for a bit." He glanced at his watch, a little past three. Setting his coffee cup down carefully, he rose and stretched. "How about a walk, Royce. A little fresh air to clear your head." He looked at Katlyn. "You don't mind, do you?"

He could read in her face fear and anger mixed together, a confusion of emotions difficult to keep in check. The story of the hijacker made more sense now. This was a woman who didn't know the extent of the process she'd set in motion and was now beginning to fear the consequences. The story of her husband and the hijacker was designed to divert them from the real work at hand because she didn't know how to frame her feelings. Irene's appearance at the plant had been a wild card she wasn't expecting. And a walk would give her some time to think too.

"Of course not." But there was a trace of sarcasm in her voice. "I hadn't really planned to spend the afternoon this way anyhow, you know. I've got work to do. Actually, if you want, you could stay right here. I've got to go down the street and pick up some things." She rose and moved with that sexy stride Max had watched Monday night, yet before Royce arrived, her walk had been neutral, nonarousing.

Royce rose from the couch and caught her by the elbow. He looked into her eyes, then kissed her lightly on the cheek. "I didn't expect Irene to show up today." He gave a snort, neither a laugh nor a sigh. "I was hoping we could get this all worked out, then just present Irene with the facts. Nothing's ever as neat as we'd like it to be. Something else is going on and I have to find out what."

Max watched her face soften, and thought for a moment he should just leave the two of them. *Present Irene*

211

with the facts told him Royce had made his decision, even if Royce didn't know it yet. Katlyn had called, and from the look in her eyes when she watched Royce, her decision was also clear. This really wasn't a psychiatric problem, in the old Freudian sense of the term, but then not all of his patients needed the years of technical training he could offer them. Some of his patients, like Royce and Katlyn, were people forced into a situation which frightened and confused them. Lonely people with nowhere else to turn and enough money to buy an ear for an afternoon. American loneliness. Brief therapy sometimes made him feel he was a friend for hire or a specialist in loneliness, and this thought always saddened him. The world had lost a valuable resource, as vanished from the lives of the people he treated as the passenger pigeon was gone from the skies.

Would Royce see it as one simple decision? Everything in the present has a counterpoint or shadow in the past. Was Royce ready to tackle that?

Katlyn left, promising to be back shortly, and they could hear her whistling a show tune as she sauntered down the street. Royce led Max to the backyard under a sun hanging over the rooftops like a melon of butter. They sat on the pantry stoop, looking out over the rosebushes which were just beginning to bud and the newly spaded garden primed with fertilizer. The dog stretched out in the sun, shook her shoulders loose, and promptly went to sleep.

"I'm glad you suggested this," Royce said. "Irene isn't the only problem I have today, as if that's not enough, but I want to talk it over with you before I broach the matter with Kat." Royce looked exhausted. "At the rate things are going, I probably won't get all the facts straight. Driving over here this afternoon, I wished you and I could take a train to New York, the *Silver Streak* or something.

Just get the hell out. Maybe by the time we pulled into Grand Central Station you'd know everything."

Max wondered what more could have happened in one short morning. But he knew events snowballed, an electricity in the air catapulting sleeping forces into action simultaneously.

Royce's hands strayed over packets of seeds, shuffling their paper wrappers like a deck of cards. "I couldn't sleep last night, and this morning when I woke up, Kat was gone. She goes swimming in the mornings, and I did something I've never done before." He shifted the seeds to his other hand, apparently enjoying the sounds as they tumbled and rattled inside their envelopes. "Last night I was thinking about the fact that Kat and I really don't know much about each other. When I woke up this morning and she was gone, and I knew she'd be gone for another hour or so, I started going through her things." He shot Max a guilty look, hoping to be reassured it was all right, knowing it wasn't. "The idea came to me as if I'd drawn it on a Monopoly card. Look Through Her Things. I could see it in that spare sans serif type, complete with the little man and his top hat. I mean she lives here all the time. Women display themselves in their houses. Women are all the same. Our house in Sausalito is a display of Irene's personality. Her chairs, her china. The whole chintzy place."

"What did you find?"

"I don't know what to make of it. I don't even know why I did it. Normally I respect other people's property, but there I was, rifling the drawers, reading her mail, searching for her bankbook. I felt like a thief, checking the windows to see if she was coming down the street, trying to put everything back just the way I'd found it. My impersonation of a cat burglar."

"What did you find?" Max repeated.

"Some things made sense. Some didn't." He walked out to the small brick patio and unfolded two director's chairs, indicating one for Max.

Max settled his chair so the sun wasn't in his eyes. The high fences around the backyard cut the wind and made the patio as warm as a summer afternoon. "Have you ever looked through her things before?"

Royce shook his head. "I knew where to look, of course, just from living with her, knowing her habits. There's a desk in her workroom. It's not that the workroom is off limits or anything, but I've never had any reason to go in there. I can run a four-color press, but I wouldn't know how to turn on a sewing machine. I went through her desk. She pays her bills promptly and keeps all her receipts. I looked at her tax returns, and she makes good money with the stuff she designs. I found an African road map and wanted to hang it upside down on the wall. But I didn't."

Max wondered if there were newspaper clippings of the hijacking, pictures of a man with a triangular mole. "Pretty understandable so far."

"She owns a house out in the Sunset district. There was a bill of sale for one dollar from Alan Quales, her husband, I suppose, dated about two years ago, right before I met her. It used to be women were given dowries in order to make them attractive for marriage. The modern way seems to be to give the dowry with the divorce. That commercial on TV, 'She got the house, but I got the Sony.' So much for your fifty-fifty property split." He shifted in the chair, winding his long legs one around the other. "I couldn't find her checkbook, and I couldn't find any property tax receipts, although she keeps receipts for everything else."

"That would seem to explain where a lot of her things came from," Max said. "All those mysterious juicers and sewing machines which you said just showed up after she'd been here for a while."

Royce nodded. "I never thought it so simple. When I met her at the movies she had one of those big forty-pound shoulder bags women tote around. And that's the extent of the luggage I've seen her bring in here. Yet when we went to Mexico, she had suitcases. And that doesn't explain all the stuff in there."

"No," Max agreed. "It doesn't. But I don't think it's terribly mystifying." He remembered the gradual way his flat on Parnassus Street filled with books and clothes and pots and pans after he married Patrice. He could recall a day when the place surprised him, when he looked up and realized the spartan furnishings he'd gathered in that flat as a medical student suddenly were relegated to corners, almost hidden from view, by what Patrice had moved in.

"Well, besides being surprised I guess it isn't mystifying. I just wish she'd told me."

"But it seems to distress you. The fact you didn't know."

Royce shifted again, nervously recrossing his legs, one ankle hooked over a knee, making a figure four. "Yeah."

"There's still nothing criminal about it. If you and Katlyn are going to live together there'll be a lot of little surprises you'll have to work out."

"Well, the house, maybe I could understand that. But there was some stuff I couldn't figure out at all."

"Like what?" Max imagined Royce turning up a sten gun or a syringe.

Royce leaned forward, his elbows on his knees. "I read her mail too, or what there was of it. I couldn't find any letters from Alan Quales, just some stuff from Opal, that's her mother. Opal hates to talk on the phone so she

sends postcards, even though she only lives in Berkeley."
Royce rose and headed toward the house. "Come on. I'll
show you."

The spare bedroom was obviously organized for professional efficiency. Nothing like the scraps and patterns
Patrice used to leave lying around on the kitchen floor
when she wanted to make something. Bolts of cloth stood
in a row like pickets in a fence. A riot of colors and
fabrics festooned the room, but on closer examination,
Max could tell this was an organization which placed
everything at fingertips when viewed from the wheeled
office chair placed in the center of the room. There was a
wooden spool cabinet, each drawer filled with buttons or
lace or snaps or facings, all the small components for
clothes that are taken for granted. Max tried to imagine
how the fabrics and zippers would come together, but
had the same feeling as visiting a lumberyard. All that
wood never translated into tables, walls, or bookcases,
just rows of lumber stacked like kindling waiting for a
match. He searched for something finished, an example
of what she made, so he would have an idea of how it all
came together. He noticed a dress fitter's mannequin standing by the window, like a sentry guarding the room with
its shadow stretching across the floor. Two sewing machines dominated the room, a big industrial-looking black
beast and a blue portable like Patrice's, each on its own
worktable. Charts on the walls listed sizes and patterns. An
ironing board, a cutting table. For a moment Max felt he'd
wandered into a small shop in the garment district in New
York.

Royce handed him an envelope, addressed to Katlyn
Whiston. He felt a small thrill as he opened the flap and
three cardboard rectangles, the size of a pack of promo-
tional matches, fell into his palm.

The first card was the ideograph for SU:

rusu - absence
suna - sand
asu - tomorrow

Max turned the card over and saw the painted character on the back, inky flourishes from the Orient, a looped line crossed in the middle like the top of a T.

The second card was JU:

jusho - address, living place
manju - bean-jam bun
judia - important

They looked at each other and shrugged, equally at a loss to explain the cards. "She's learning Japanese?" Max asked, but felt the cards were too random for any kind of systematic study. Her workroom told him this woman was well organized. A bilingual dictionary would be more appropriate than these mysterious cards. The back of the JU card looked like an abstract of a kamikaze Zero plummeting into the sea.

Royce tapped the envelope, indicating there was no return address. "Somebody mails these to her. Absence, sand, tomorrow." He ran his hand through his hair. "I'm sure it's perfectly innocent, but it looks like some kind of code. Normal people don't communicate in code."

Max studied the third card O:

onna - woman
aoi - blue
otoko - man

The back of this card looked like a chicken track in the mud.

"She said she wanted to go to Africa, not Japan," Royce said. "There are dozens of these, no notes, just envelopes with these little flashcards. Absence, sand, blue, tomorrow. What can you make out of that?"

Max handed the envelope and the flashcards back, feeling as uneasy with them as Royce must have early this morning. Secretly reading other people's mail was like spying on them as they undressed. The flashcards felt very intimate. "First these, then Irene." Carnival. Crazy Monday. Crazy Wednesday. Crazy spring. It was still spring. Two months until June when San Francisco would look like autumn to him.

Royce slipped them back into the desk drawer, checking to be sure he placed them in the right order. "A week ago, I thought I lived a perfect life." He fussed with the envelopes one more time, then slid the drawer back into place. "I never thought the other shoe would drop. Today I don't have any more idea about what's going on than a dog trying to drive a car."

Lying on the worktable was a piece of green cloth much like Max's favorite Hawaiian shirt, the torn remnants Pat delivered to him. Maybe, when this was all over, he'd ask Katlyn to make another Hawaiian shirt for him, patch up some of the damage Patrice had inflicted. If she didn't go to Africa. "You're going to see Irene this evening?" Casablanca. Moorish arches.

Royce moved to the window and looked out to the garden, idly placing his hand on the mannequin's expandable breast. "I didn't feel I had much choice. I had to call her from the office, so Donna Moon could hear, to let her know Irene couldn't march into her office and give her shit. So now I'll have to go over there and confront her with two problems, or maybe three, depending on what she thought she was going to do with the kids down at the plant this morning."

218

"What do you think brought her down there?" A flash of disasters went through Max's mind. Suicide, cancer, fire, burglary, death. American loneliness.

"Beats me. It could be anything." Royce fiddled with the left breastplate, cranking it out at a ridiculous angle. "If one of them were in trouble in school, or something, I could see Irene bringing them down to the plant. But both kids couldn't be in trouble."

"How does Irene usually handle problems?"

Royce cranked the other breastplate out, Mae West in black. "She doesn't. Irene believes men are born to take care of women. Men handle problems." He cupped his hands on the black breasts. "Here's an example. When Lindy was about eight I asked her what she wanted to be when she grew up. She said she wanted to be a dilettante."

"A dilettante?" Max laughed.

"Yep. Irene's legacy. I explained to her what a dilettante meant. What she meant, what Irene had taught her, was that she wanted to have fun and be taken care of, without having to do anything for it. A dilettante has no special talents and expects someone else to pay for the drinks. That's the way Irene looks at life. When I thought about it, I couldn't think of anything comparable from a man's point of view. Boys always want to be someone who does something. A fireman, an astronaut, that kind of thing. But a girl, and Irene in particular, just wants to be taken care of for who she is, not what she does."

Max knew the type, all too common. "Doesn't she have any goals?"

"No. A couple of years after we were married, I asked her if she was going to finish school. She was a sophomore at Wellesley when I met her. She told me she'd been sent off to college to get married. Studying was simply a way of passing the time until the right fellow came along. She hadn't anticipated getting knocked up, but as far as she was concerned, that was as good a way as any to get a man. She would eventually have kids anyhow. That's all college ever meant to her. She's passed that on to Lindy. And whatever brought her down to the plant this morning she was going to pass on to me."

Max now regretted asking Katlyn to leave. Maybe she should hear this and get some feeling for the scope of the task she'd set up. "How serious is Katlyn about her deadline?"

"I don't know, but I'll tell you one thing. The house, which means money, and those flashcards scared me. She can afford to go to Africa, and whoever sends her those flashcards might go with her. Although I can't figure the Japanese aspect at all." His hands went back to caressing the black body of the mannequin.

Max tried out the wheeled office chair in the middle of the room. The deadline was the problem here. Given enough time, Royce could sort out his troubles with Irene and discover what took her to his office this morning. Given enough time, he could figure out what the flash-cards meant. As he swiveled back and forth in the leather chair, touching fabrics and fringe lying on the workbenches, he tried to pull together a picture of Katlyn from the jigsaw pieces of information he possessed. Sometimes he saw himself as a psychic detective, pulling the clues from the past into the light of the present. A Colombo of the spirits. She'd set up a game of Come And Get Me and games like that follow strict and unbending rules. Katlyn was capable of leaving Royce, by the end of the week no doubt, if Royce didn't pass this test. There's no compromise in a game of Come And Get Me.

"Maybe I should blow up the bridge," Royce said suddenly. "You and I and Kat will all drive over to Sausalito and present Irene with a lecture on decency and notice of divorce."

"Count me out on that," Max said. "I'm not a fighter on the lines. I work the fringe areas, the prep work and the aftershocks." He checked his watch. Katlyn should be back. He wondered if Royce was lingering in her workroom deliberately, hoping Katlyn would return and ask what he was doing. Unlike the rest of the rooms, this room was Katlyn's alone. There were no traces of Royce in here, and he felt they were as out of place in this room as they would be in Omaha dressed in pearls and heels. "You need to talk to Irene. I'm not sure about bringing Katlyn along. Like I said, these are separate problems."

"I know," Royce said. "I don't think I want her to be involved at this point either. It was just a thought, trying to find the easy way out."

"I doubt a meeting between Katlyn and Irene will be easy."

"You're the psychiatrist here. You're supposed to find out about people's past, what makes them tick, all their deep dark secrets. What did you find out about Kat this afternoon that'll throw some light on this mess?" Royce's eyes flickered with uneasiness.

Max had been waiting for this question and wasn't sure, until he spoke, exactly how he would answer. "She's quite imaginative and she's been hurt deeply." He was stalling and Royce knew it.

The mind seeks to organize, even under stress. There's a logic, even with pathological patients. The trick to psychiatry was discovering what the logic was, to follow the patient through with it. Max didn't know exactly what the hijacker story meant, but felt it would give Royce even more to worry about in the short time between now and Friday. Royce was ready to believe she'd leave for Africa with whoever sent the flashcards. If Katlyn wanted Royce to hear about the hijacking, she'd have to tell him herself.

"Settle things with Irene. That's first on the agenda, don't you agree?"

"You're not telling me much." Royce looked out the window and Max could judge by the shadow of the mannequin their time was almost up. Katlyn might purposefully not return until after Max had gone. "I have to go over to Sausalito soon. What am I going to say?"

"What do you want to say?"

"I want to tell Irene she's a bitch and I'm divorcing her."

"Why don't you do that then. Work things out with Katlyn when things are clearer between you and Irene."

"But what if she just simply wants to leave me? Who sends her the flashcards? What's she doing with the money from that house? She's got to do something. You let money like that sit in the bank and they'll take everything in taxes."

Royce's mind circled all this information and stopped right back where it began. He needed jogging onto another track. "For the moment," Max said calmly, "that's her problem. I think you better find out what the trouble is at home. If it's something serious, illness or an accident, divorcing Irene isn't really the issue here. She didn't give you any clue when you called her?"

"Well," Royce ducked his head sheepishly. "I didn't really talk to Irene. I called home, to let Donna Moon know I wasn't going to let Irene get away with such rudeness. But Lindy answered the phone, and I told her to tell Irene I'd be there this evening."

"Lindy didn't say what was wrong?"

Royce shook his head. He turned his back to Max and stared out the window.

Max stood and stretched. Katlyn could be sitting on the corner waiting for him to pull away in his car. It was past five now, and Max had one more stop to make and a dinner invitation for seven-thirty. Overtime wouldn't help Royce at this stage. Max thought perhaps Royce was stalling, not quite ready to begin his drive over the bridge. "It doesn't look as if Katlyn's going to be back."

"Didn't you find out anything from Kat about what she really wants?"

"You have to work this out yourself. I can't do the work for you. I can only help you put together what you discover and help you make sense of it, sense to you. If you want to know about the flashcards, you'll have to admit you looked at them and ask her what they mean. If you want to know about Alan Quales, you'll have to find out yourself. I didn't come over here this afternoon to listen to Katlyn's life story. I had in mind a counseling session between the two of you. But," Max rolled the chair back to where he found it, "things didn't work out the way any of us expected. Your job for this evening is Irene. Then you'll know more about what you need to do as far as Katlyn's concerned." Panic like Royce's reduced people to children. They must be told the same things over and over again.

"How am I going to find out about Alan Quales? She never even mentioned him until last night. Two years I've lived with that woman and I never heard a word about him until last night." Royce's voice was bitter. "If it takes two years to get his name out of her, how long do you think it will take to learn anything about him?"

"Have you tried the phone book? If he's around he probably has a phone. If you want to find out about him, and don't trust what Katlyn has to say, why not try to locate him?" Max was pleased with this idea. If Royce had the nerve to look through Katlyn's drawers, he might be willing to find Alan Quales.

Royce considered this. "The guy would think I'm

nuts if I called him up and asked to discuss his ex-wife. Besides, she said he's dead.''

"Then ask her." Max was ready to go. "One thing I learned about Katlyn, she says a lot of things. But don't forget, that's really not necessary this evening. You have to think about Irene.''

Royce walked him to the door and they both glanced up and down the street, looking for Katlyn. Children skipped along the sidewalk, played chicken with the passing cars, arced a soccer ball over the traffic.

Max held out his hand. "Let me know what happens. Feel free to call." And then he noticed it, a tiny triangular mole by Royce's left eye. Hijackers indeed. The little mole was the color of a charred log, blue-black. No wonder she worked up such feeling when describing her hijacker.

"What about Friday?" Royce looked nervously into Max's eyes, hanging on to his hand as if afraid to let go.

"Give me a call," Max said again and withdrew his hand from Royce's grasp. "We'll see what we can work out when we know more." The look in Royce's eyes saddened him. He clapped Royce on the shoulder, football-style. "You can't go anywhere from this point until you know what's happening at home.''

Katlyn appeared on the sidewalk a few doors down, her arms full of grocery sacks. She waved at them and began to hurry, running with that tottering stride necessary to hold her balance against the high heels and the packages. Max watched her awkward approach, the way her hips moved and how her copper hair caught the light.

"I'm sorry." She handed one of the grocery sacks to Royce and swept her hand past her hair and along the lines of her dress, composing herself after her run. "There's a handicapped woman up the street, and I stopped to give her a cigarette." She looked at Royce and an understanding passed between them.

"I was just leaving," Max said. "I have a dinner engagement."

"Well." Her eyes searched his eyes, left and right, left and right, as if one would tell her what she wanted to know, but which eye she wasn't sure. "I don't want to keep you. But," she shot a quick glance at Royce, who was also waiting for what she would say, "but, I wanted you to know everything I said this afternoon was made up. I've never been out of the country except to go to Mexico and Canada."

Max nodded, then gave her a wink. "I guessed as much."

"There's a lot of truth in it, though." Her look was serious and convincing.

"If you throw out the details."

She smiled, as if she was now sure he understood her. "Right. I lied about the details. But the rest is the truth. Maybe I'll tell you about it some day."

"Tell me one thing," Max said. "Did you get that whole scenario from a book or a movie?"

She smiled. "I used to play 'The Perfect' game. The Perfect Hijacking, The Perfect Killing, The Perfect Bank Robbery."

Max was interested. "What's the Perfect Bank Robbery?"

"Naked women. No one can describe a naked woman."

"What?" Max and Royce both laughed.

"Noon on a payday Friday. Women in big forties-style hats," she circled her head with her hands to demonstrate, "sunglasses and trenchcoats. The hats and glasses would hide their faces and hair. They walk in, pull their guns and take off their coats. They stand there buck

225

naked. No one can describe a naked woman, what could you say? She had big tits? A nice ass? When they have all the money they put the coats back on, step out of the bank, take off the hats and sunglasses and melt into the lunchtime crowd. It would work, don't you think?''

SUNSET

As a matter of policy Max tried to keep his patients as separate as possible. Of course, occasionally a Tuesday patient would run into him with a Thursday patient. Wandering about the city the way he did, that was bound to happen. But the idea of people passing in a waiting room, eyeing each other, always troubled him. That was part of the reason he worked the way he did, so his practice didn't look like an assembly line. People waiting in line to have their problems tuned up. He could picture his patients wondering about each other: Am I better off than he is? After he said good-bye to Katlyn and Royce he got in his car and drove around the block.

One short stop before his date with Teresa. He thought it an unfortunate coincidence that Elaine Lifton lived on the same street as Katlyn and Royce. When Katlyn said she'd stopped to talk to a handicapped woman, Max knew exactly who she meant. But he wanted to keep their problems separate, and so he parked two blocks away, and after retrieving the grocery sack from the trunk, walked back without passing Katlyn and Royce's house. He hoped this would work.

Mrs. Lifton answered the door, a small woman in her forties who seemed to be aging more quickly from week to week. For the last month Janet Lifton had been living in the nursing home with Elaine, learning how to take care of her. They'd come home last week. Suicide is a vicious form of control, and a failed suicide, like Elaine's, creates an ultimate situation. Max still didn't know who Elaine was trying to punish. Her father? Her mother? Herself? Elaine now depended on her mother for everything and until he could convince her to try the prosthesis, Janet Lifton would have to manage an unbearable burden. A baby was less trouble than Elaine in her present situation. A baby doesn't complain about being bored.

Mrs. Lifton smiled, but it was the smile of a sleep-walker. "Come in," she said. "We weren't expecting you this afternoon."

"I was in the neighborhood," Max said. "I just wanted to drop this off." He held up the grocery sack. "It's for Elaine. I'd like her to start using it before we meet again next week."

Janet Lifton's look told him she didn't expect Elaine would bother. So far Elaine had been completely passive, not even experimenting with her limited abilities. He was determined to reverse that attitude. She was still falling, hadn't yet hit the ground, like Claire. He would stop that fall. He would help her fly back to life.

Elaine appeared in the doorway and Max wasn't sure he could read her look. "I told you I didn't want the hooks." Her arms hung at her sides, red mittens covering the stumps of her wrists.

"Did I say these were hooks?" He thrust the sack

228

toward her. "I thought of an answer to that problem we talked about on Monday."

"That's prompt."

She turned into the living room as if dismissing Max, but he suspected it wasn't dismissal as much as an act to cover her fear. Attitude. Elaine possessed a lot of attitude. She'd scared herself with her knowledge of the power she now held, power she didn't trust, power she didn't know how to use. He would teach her.

From the back, she looked like any young woman ushering a visitor into her home. She wore jeans and a sweatshirt, easy clothes to put on. Last fall, when they walked along the beach, she'd worn boots and jackets with lots of zippers and buckles. Max imagined a closet full of shoes with straps, pants with zippers, blouses with buttons, all useless.

Max placed his package on the coffee table. "This isn't a favor," he said, "I've put this stuff on your bill."

"Open it." She looked at Max, then at the grocery sack, keen and intent.

"No," Max said. "You open it."

"I'll do it." Mrs. Lifton moved toward the coffee table.

Max waved her off. "No. If Elaine wants this, she'll have to open it herself." He'd made the package purposefully easy, even practiced all the operations with his hands fisted inside a pair of socks.

Elaine stood up to leave. "I can't." She headed toward the hall.

"Then it will stay here until you can." He watched as she paused in the doorway, torn between her own idea of helplessness and curiosity as to what the package might contain. Max seated himself in a chair and folded his arms across his chest. "I've got all the time in the world."

He watched as her eyes narrowed, as she tried to gauge his bluff.

"I could just go to my room." Her voice bordered on arrogance. "You can sit here all night."

"If I get tired of sitting here, I could go sit in your room with you." He watched as the new knowledge of her situation flashed across her face. Old habits are hard to break. Sitting in her room meant closing the door, locking it, two very minor motions Elaine could no longer perform.

"Okay. I'll try." But her voice was sullen.

Slowly she returned to the living room and stood before the package on the coffee table, eyeing it. With a cutting glance at Max, she sighed deeply and sat back on the couch. The first step was to take the package out of the grocery sack, and as Elaine passed her arm over the lip of the bag, it unfurled enough for her to reach inside. She stuck her arms in the sack and came up with a tissue-covered object pinioned between her wrists. "Will it break?"

Max shook his head no.

She dropped it on the coffee table and the tissue paper fluttered open. Using her wrists, she levered the paper off the baseball cap. San Francisco Giants.

"That's just a present," Max said. "Try it on."

The soft form of the baseball cap made it easy to trap between her wrists. She lifted it over her head and managed to set it, slightly askew, onto her hair. A smile played around the corners of her lips. She looked at Max. Her hostility was gone. "How am I doing?" She worked the cap around and went out to the hall to look at herself in the mirror. Max was pretty sure this was the first item of clothing she'd put on her body, by herself, since her attempt. A small start.

The Romans cut off the hands of suicides and buried

them separately from the body. Japanese honor suicide with ceremony and would never try to save a suicide's life. Elderly Eskimos walk out into the tundra to meet Sila, the goddess of natural order, and wait for death in the snow when they feel they are a burden to their tribe. Mark Rothko's suicide had been a gesture of triumph, inserting razor blades in the arteries of his armpits, then throwing his arms into the air, welcoming death. Max wondered if pronouncing suicide a sin and a tragedy was a particularly Western notion. He believed a successful suicide should be mourned for the pain that drove them into arms of death. Claire, the pain she'd felt before she jumped. The true tragedies were the unsuccessful suicides, like Elaine.

Max had worked with other handicapped people, Vietnam vets mostly, but they all possessed one trait, the will to live, which he still questioned in Elaine. *If I had the hooks I might try it again.* They had a long way to go before Max could be sure that wouldn't happen. He wished he could find the connection between Elaine's attempt and the death of her father. Perhaps her boyfriend, the veteran, would know.

When she returned to the living room, the cap was set at a slightly rakish angle, flattering to her face. She touched the brim with her wrist, as if tipping it to Max. "Thanks."

"Now the next one." He hoped the success of the cap would give her enough confidence to try the more difficult package. In their discussions on Monday afternoons at the nursing home, Elaine complained of her dependence on her mother, of how they didn't share the same tastes. They didn't like the same books, music, or movies. *I'm turning into an old lady,* Elaine wailed. *All she wants to listen to is bubble music. Flowerchild stuff. Judy Collins and Joan Baez. Antiques.* Max had purchased a cassette player, with oversized buttons. He'd found it in a children's department, a cassette player toy actually. But the big buttons meant Elaine could operate it with the stumps of her wrists. He'd brought along some tapes: Madonna and "Miami Vice" for music, John Le Carré's *The Quest for Karla* and Maxine Hong Kingston's *The Woman Warrior*, books on tape.

She stared into the grocery sack for long moments, trying to guess what might be in the package, wondering if she could ever get it out. If Max could convince her to learn to wear the prosthesis, she might begin to have a life again, be able to feed and dress herself, the ordinary motions of daily life. His hand strayed to the crease in his new suit, straightening it. The fabric felt good against his palm. He'd been doing some research on a new development, the Seattle hand. He hadn't told Elaine about it yet; she still thought in terms of hooks at the ends of her arms. But the Seattle hand would be a tremendous improvement. Made of plastics and electronic wiring, the hand looked like a replica of a human hand, a dead-looking thing, to be sure, but with all the fingers, nails. The appearance of a hand. Simple finger movements and clutching motions were operated electronically by brain impulses. Learning to use it would take training and concentration. Max wanted to be sure she wasn't thinking in terms of trying it again before he offered her this hope.

Using her wrists like tongs, she pulled the cassette player from the grocery sack. Max had wrapped it, but there was only one piece of tape. Elaine eyed it, turned the package over and found the tape. "What am I supposed to do? Bite it off?"

"That might work," Max agreed. "Whatever works."

Again she stared at the box on the coffee table for long moments. Then she began wrestling with the paper, flipping the box over and over. Max was glad this was a toy, could take abuse. She kept flipping the box over, slamming it against the coffee table until the tape popped loose. She spread open the wrapping. "I already have a tape player."

"But can you use it?" Max nodded his head to indicate the mittens hanging from her wrists.

Studying the cassette player, she discovered his intention. Tentatively she pressed a button with the edge of her wrist. The machine whirred. The light in her face was truly lovely. If she had only talked to him during those walks along the beach. If she had only been able to say what was on her mind. Now she'd traded muteness for dependence. Had he failed her or was she past helping? Had she truly wanted to die, or was she counting on the postman, or her mother, to stop her? He wasn't sure even Elaine knew the answers to these questions.

Once more, her arms went into the grocery sack, lifting out the tapes. "Hey! *Miami Vice*. I figured you for a *Masterpiece Theatre* type."

Max gave her a smile. "You never know." She was just a girl really, eighteen years old but still a child. The happiness on her face could have been that of a six-year-old. Yet minutes ago she'd been hostile, haughty. Her moods were as quick and fleeting as the wind. The tantrums and smiles of preschoolers. The quick shifts Conrad performed on those rare times Patrice let him spend an afternoon with his son. Children have no patience. Without patience, the world becomes a strange and confusing place, a place where everything becomes flat, weighs equally. Elaine would have to learn patience.

Mrs. Lifton smiled when Elaine lifted out the earphones. "That was thoughtful," she said to Max.

Max rose to go. "I want you to start one of those books," he said. "I don't care which one, but when we meet on Monday, I want you to tell me some plot line." Elaine nodded her agreement, too busy trying to work the tape into the machine to notice he was leaving. That was good, Max decided. She could prove to herself there were things she could do.

"I appreciate it," Janet Lifton said as she saw him to the door. "You didn't have to do this."

"I know," Max said. "I wanted to."

But once back in the Mustang as he headed off to pick up Teresa, he felt as if a weight had settled on his heart. Elaine's lovely smile should have buoyed him, yet, as he drove closer and closer to Teresa's apartment on Nob Hill, the evening began to feel more like a chore than a pleasant experience. Teresa reminded him too much of Patrice, that's why he'd begun dating her in the first place. Maybe all the women he would ever meet would remind him of Patrice.

At that party, over ten years ago, Patrice had arrived with another woman, yet abandoned her almost immediately and circulated among the men until she finally settled on Max. He'd relived this memory many times, always puzzled as to why he hadn't spotted the essential Patrice that first night. But that night his thoughts had been full of Claire. The toss of her blonde hair as she laughed at a joke. The way her strong hands would hold a wine glass. "So you're going to be a doctor," Patrice had said. "Psychiatrist," Max replied. He was testing that notion, a new decision since Claire's death.

During their relationship Patrice proved to have no real interests, therefore she was interested in everything. Her attention span was as flexible as a cat's. She took gourmet cooking lessons and tried the overly spicy dishes out on Max. She talked of taking flying lessons, although she was afraid of heights. She joined a Great Books reading circle, but dropped out when she found the books boring, not enough romance in them to suit her. T'ai Chi interested her for about three lessons, even though she liked the austere Asian uniform.

Max encouraged her in all these activities, hoping he could help her find herself. Perhaps even Conrad was just another of her whims, a dangerous one, since Conrad would require her attention for a lifetime.

He saw a parking place ahead and nipped into it. He rested his head on the steering wheel. Teresa was cut from the same mold as Patrice—rootless, centerless, empty. And she, too, thought marriage would solve her problems, even though her two previous marriages should have disproved her of that notion. Tonight she wanted to see a French film, although her eyesight was poor and she couldn't read the subtitles. Dating Teresa was like going to a different theme park each time. Max could picture her dressed in some vaguely Frenchified outfit, wanting to go out to an expensive French restaurant afterwards.

In his pocket he found some change and spotted a phone booth up the block. One good thing about being a psychiatrist: there was always some emergency he could manufacture. As he strolled toward the phone he knew this would be the last time he would call Teresa.

But back at his apartment, he realized how empty the evening would be. A few dirty dishes, some laundry. He thought of Janet Lifton and all the work caring for Elaine required. He mixed a Scotch and water and sat in the chair facing the window, looking for the mysterious bird that sang at night. Mothers and daughters. Mothers and sons. He tried to remember the feel of his mother's hand cupping the back of his head. But except for brief flashes that remained as still as photographs, Claire's face always replaced his mother's. In the few pictures Max kept of his mother and sister, they looked very different, his mother dark and small, Claire blonde and tall, even as a child.

Max was ten when his mother died and Claire, thirteen, was the first to recognize what this would mean to their family.

The third Sunday after their mother's funeral, Max and Claire sprawled across the living room floor pretending an interest in Scrabble. Last week they'd played Parcheesi, the week before, checkers. It was as if they were both waiting for something and wanted to be quiet, invisible, until that something happened.

Their father spent all his hours at the sporting goods store now, even Sundays. He seemed to have disappeared along with their mother. A hired housekeeper, Mrs. Rose, came twice a week. But she was much like their father, cold, distant. "I have work to do," she would tell them when they wanted to ask questions. "I don't have time for children." Max sometimes wondered if she said that because she didn't have the answers to his questions. But he couldn't form his questions. He only knew something was wrong.

Claire picked a handful of wooden tiles from the bag and spread them in front of her.

"You can't do that," Max said. "It's not even your turn. And you can't take a whole handful." But Max wasn't really angry. He knew her moods. Claire sat across from him, her blonde hair in uneven braids, her eyes focused out the window where thunderheads gathered on the horizon. She moved the tiles under her palm, swirling them over the carpet with a clockwise motion.

"Mrs. Rose told me Daddy thinks we're grown-up now that Mommy's not here." She kept her eyes on the clouds.

Max felt a chill behind his ears, although the air was moist and humid. He looked at the clouds too, wondering when the storm would break. "Are we grown-up?"

Claire picked up the board and tipped it, spilling all

the tiles back into the box. Max held his breath. Claire picked up one tile from the rug and dropped it, watching it flip over. F, worth four. She picked up another and dropped it too. S, worth one. "I guess so. If Daddy thinks so."

"What are we supposed to do, if we're grown-up?" Max associated grown-up with height. At ten, he was still too short to reach the cookies his mother always kept on the second shelf above the counter without the aid of a chair. How could he be grown-up if he couldn't even reach the second shelf? Claire could reach the cookies. Perhaps Claire was grown-up. Maybe that's why she didn't want to play Scrabble with him.

"We'll do what Mrs. Rose does." She boxed up the Scrabble set. The room darkened as the first of the thunderheads passed by. "She's the only grown-up around."

After school on Mondays and Thursdays Claire would dash home and follow Mrs. Rose as she vacuumed, or did laundry, or ordered the groceries. Max would follow Claire, and by dark the two of them would stand in the kitchen watching Mrs. Rose cook dinner. Max couldn't see the dials on the washer, dryer, or stove, and took to hauling a wooden stool around so he could get a better view.

Mrs. Rose would squint down her long nose at them. "Why are you children always underfoot?"

"It's a project for school," Claire said. "We have to describe work. This is work, isn't it?"

To Max's mind grown-up now meant work as well as height. He despaired of ever mastering either of them. Claire was his only guide and if she thought he could manage, he was determined to not let her down.

Tuesdays, Wednesdays, and Fridays, Claire and Max would repeat what Mrs. Rose did. If Mrs. Rose was dusting and waxing on Monday when Claire and Max got home, Claire and Max would dust and wax on Tuesday and Wednesday. Max polished the legs of chairs and tables while Claire waxed the tops. But dinner was the most difficult. Mrs. Rose made her own favorites at first, chicken and dumplings, lasagna, pot roast with carrots, potatoes, and onions, explaining that this family should have at least two good meals a week. "He feeds you TV dinners," she would say with disgust. "That's no food for children." The next night, Claire and Max, standing on his stool, would attempt chicken and dumplings. Their father, always indifferent to food, would stick the TV dinners in the oven or order out for Chinese or pizza if the meal was too burned or cold or just plain awful.

One Wednesday night Max set part of the kitchen on fire. Grease from a pan of pork chops caught fire, and when he tried to douse it with water, the flames spread across the wooden cutting board near the stove, to the dishtowels, and up the curtains. Claire called the fire department, and the two of them stood in the dining room watching the kitchen burn and listening to the approaching sirens. Firemen in hats and boots stormed through the house with their hoses, but put the fire out with a hand-held extinguisher. When their father got home, he beat Max and Claire twenty times each with his belt.

On Thursday morning Max and Claire left for school, but circled back to the house once they saw their father pull away in the car. Claire explained to Mrs. Rose what had happened.

"So that's what you've been doing, under my feet all the time." Mrs. Rose looked at the charred kitchen. "Children don't start learning to cook with pork chops." When Claire and Max returned from school that afternoon, Mrs. Rose was waiting for them. "We'll start with defrosting and reheating and work up to cooking pork chops." She opened the freezer door and showed them labeled packages of chicken and dumplings, lasagna, and pot roast.

They began with simple meals, soup from a can, eggs, hamburgers. They graduated to spaghetti and tuna noodle casserole. They learned how to order groceries, Max's favorite chore, since the meat came packed in dry ice and Max loved to watch the ice steam in the grass in the backyard. By the time Mrs. Rose left them two years later, Claire was in a Home Ec class and Max had mastered pork roast with apples and onions. He was especially proud of his City Chicken and potatoes au gratin.

It was full dark now and Max rose to put on a light. He'd cooked all those meals for Claire. He'd cooked for Patrice. But although he was hungry, he had no desire to cook a meal for himself. Perhaps he should go down to Perry's and see if there was someone there who would go out to dinner with him. Perhaps he would just get drunk, alone in his apartment. Maybe he shouldn't have canceled on Teresa. At least she was someone to share a meal with. He went into his small kitchen to empty the ice cubes from his glass. Opening the cabinets he looked at his roasters, pots, skillets. All useless. One egg for breakfast and a piece of toast was the extent of his cooking these days. He knew the refrigerator held only eggs, and cheese, and juice.

This was depressing. He had to get out of the apartment. Donning his coat, he headed for the door. Why had Claire left him? Who would ever take her place?

WEDNESDAY
EVENING

B uddy Holly and the Crickets. As Royce took the
Sausalito exit off the bridge, he clucked his tongue in
rhythm, thumb pounding on the steering wheel, echoing
Holly's near yodel, a joyous joke. Holly broke into "That'll
Be the Day." That'll be the day. That will be this evening.
Say good-bye. Kat would love the irony; Irene wouldn't
see the humor. Those two women were the same age, yet
their lives were as separate and different as sides of a
coin.

Or perhaps he was different with them.

Last year, after Irene claimed to be adjusted to his
affair, they'd been invited to a reception in Sausalito.
Royce looked forward to the evening, a chance to show
Irene this arrangement would work out well for both of
them. They'd been sitting in her bedroom, a briefing on
the neighbors since Royce spent most of his time in the
city now, when Irene realized they were running late.

While she was in the bathroom Royce opened her jewel box, searching for a necklace he'd given her that he wanted her to wear. At first he didn't know what he was looking at, the tiny silver spoon, the burnished steel straw, the small vial of white powder, right there in her jewel box, a gram of coke next to her diamond rings. He heard the rushing water of the shower, and his first thought was that he'd found the coke like a fifty-dollar bill lying on the street. Of course, it really couldn't belong to Irene. He would take it over to Kat's and they would have an evening with it. But the coke was Irene's, as much as the rings and necklaces that flanked the vial. He couldn't get over the idea of Irene buying coke, even harder was trying to imagine someone giving it to her.

He tried it. It was good. He was still exploring the first rush when Irene, wrapped in a towel, stepped out of the bathroom. "You could have asked first," she said. "I would ask, if it were yours."

"What is this?" he demanded, although he knew perfectly well what it was.

She tried to make a joke of it. "And laying a finger by the side of her nose, giving a nod, up the chimney she rose." And then she did something Royce had never seen before. Her left nostril collapsed like an apostrophe, the skin sucked in tight to the cartilage.

During their argument he knew he didn't care about the coke. What bothered him was how casually she hid it among her things. And that collapsing nostril trick. That couldn't be healthy. While the reception went on without them, he rummaged through all her drawers and closets, all her cosmetics in the bathroom, the backs of the cupboards in the kitchen. He found more coke, not a lot like a dealer, but certainly a good stash for a housewife. He found hundred-dollar bills secreted away between folds of scarves and silk underwear. He found a vibrator and a dildo. Hidden behind a can of cashews in the kitchen were the pink slips to both cars, taken from his desk.

Insurance, she called it. In case he left her for his beloved Kat. She wanted some insurance against that disaster. He felt the gesture was pathetic, a few hundred-dollar bills and the pink slips for the cars. And yet, only hours ago, he'd been rummaging through Katlyn's drawers, looking for some insurance of his own.

Surprise was perhaps more useful for women, a tool they knew how to manipulate and control. Kat's ownership of that house bothered him more than the fact Irene snorted coke. He wished he could have looked in Kat's purse. The whole woman is there, in her purse.

He pulled up the shallow drive and cut the engine. If this were some detective movie, the kind Kat loved, he would park down the street and give no warning. He hoped Irene was in the bathroom. She hated to be disturbed while on the john, as if her bodily functions were a terrible secret, a growth or blemish.

At the front door he was tempted to ring the bell, to prolong these moments of wonder. But the bell implied he was a stranger in this house. Not tonight, at least for tonight. He stuck his key in the lock and walked in.

The house was still, light from the street lamps playing over the perfect arrangements of chairs and tables and lamps. Although it was after sundown, no one seemed to be home. No lights were on. In the dusk the place looked better, as if someone might really live here. He'd never liked this house; the place smelled too new. They'd lived here over ten years and Royce still felt as if the price tags were on the furniture, a showroom with all the items on sale. The house spelled Irene, from the moldings to the linoleum. If Irene needed a totem, it wouldn't be an animal or bird. Irene's totem would be a door. Separate bedrooms, with doors. Separate bathrooms, with doors. A separate wing for the children, with double doors.

Perhaps she'd taken the kids and hit the highway up to Sacramento. Driving back to Daddy would be Irene's idea of retaliation. She'd refused to talk on the phone and would expect him to drive up there if he wanted an explanation of why she badgered Donna Moon. The quiet and darkness of the house made him feel as if he'd gained safe harbor for a moment before the fireworks began. Listening closely, he couldn't hear the murmur of the TV, or the beat of the stereo, or clanging in the kitchen, or the giggles of girls talking on the telephone. He couldn't remember the house ever being this still. For a moment he wondered if he were in someone else's home.

That stillness made it just possible to hear the faint echoes coming from the patio back of the garage. Tap, tap, tap, taptap. He walked cautiously through the house, leaving the lights off, dimly aware of the furniture as he passed it, the hollow silence of the kitchen.

Full night now, with stars winking through the clouds. Royce felt the wind rising. He located the sounds behind the garage and stopped to pick up a heavy-duty flashlight he kept by the back door. Of all the noises he associated with this house, he couldn't identify what was making the tapping sound. As he got closer he could hear scraping and shuffling, as well as the tapping, but although the sound was familiar, he couldn't place it. Burglars. Punk kids playing pranks. He moved around the side of the garage, the flashlight pointed ahead of him, and flicked on the beam. "What's going on here?"

"Shit!" Todd dropped the basketball and covered his eyes with his hands. "Get that out of my eyes, will you?"

Royce flicked the beam to low and pointed the light to the ground. "What are you doing? Shooting baskets in the dark?" It astonished him he couldn't identify the sound of a basketball. Dribbling a ball. He knew the rhythms and feel of that sound more intimately than knowledge of more practical noises, like the ringing of a telephone. Imagine not knowing what it meant when the phone rang.

Todd registered equal surprise. "What are you doing here? It's only Wednesday."

Royce placed the flashlight so a cone of light pointed at the sky. He walked across the concrete and picked the basketball out of the dewy grass. "Sorry I scared you. Where is everyone?" As his eyes adjusted to the darkness he shot for the basket, but missed, the ball echoing in the night against the backboard.

"Lindy's gone out with John because Mom's at her therapist."

"I thought Lindy wasn't supposed to be seeing John any more." Royce caught the ball and dribbled it across the small court.

"That's why she's seeing him when Mom's at her therapist."

"That's clever enough." Royce shot another basket, making a clean pass this time, the ball rolling away toward his son. He watched Todd dribble and shoot. To Royce, shooting baskets alone in the dark looked as sad as decorations the morning after a party. "What are you doing out here?"

"Shooting baskets."

Royce was tempted to snap at him, but held his tongue. Lately Todd had mastered the art of empty conversation. *What did you do today?* Royce would ask and feel the immensity of the hours of the day, all the things which could occur. *Nothing,* Todd would answer. *Where are you going? Nowhere.*

There would be no lecture tonight. What would he say? As he watched Todd dribble and shoot, pointedly not passing the ball to his father, Royce felt disappointed

Irene was gone. He'd envisioned this evening beginning with Irene, ending with Todd and Lindy, not the other way around. But Todd was the only one here tonight, right now. Royce must start somewhere. He watched the ball carom around the rim and fall out of the basket on his side of the court. He stepped over quickly and snatched the ball, tucking it under his arm. Todd stood mutely across the court.

"We have to have a talk," Royce said.

Todd stuck his thumbs in the belt loops of his jeans. His hair hung in his eyes and Royce noticed he wasn't wearing his Walkman. Todd shrugged his shoulders, shifted his weight from foot to foot. His T-shirt sparkled in the dark. IRON MAIDEN.

Royce juggled the ball from hand to hand. "You want to talk out here or go in the house?"

Todd looked up at the stars, as bright as new pins tonight, and Royce took that as his answer. Talk in the yard. Royce bounced the basketball a couple of times, his fingertips tingling when he snapped them against the rubber. He wanted to talk to Irene first, have some concrete plan to announce, instead of telling Todd what he undoubtedly knew. "Your mother and I aren't getting along, son." Even the dog Wichita knew that.

Royce plunged ahead. "How would you feel if your mother and I divorced?"

"Better."

In the dark, Royce could detect no motion or look to qualify Todd's answer. Better. He'd been expecting an *I don't know* kind of response, probably Todd's favorite phrase these days. "Better," Royce repeated.

"When?" Todd asked.

"Well, I'll have to talk to your mother about that. But pretty soon."

"Good." There was a lightness to his voice now. "How about the ball?"

Royce shot the ball across the small court to him. "What's good about it?" Perhaps they could have a regular conversation here.

Todd fired, the ball bouncing off the backboard. "This is the pits."

"Yeah," Royce agreed. "In some ways you're right."

Todd arced the ball, stretching on his toes, but not jumping. The ball swished through the net, right on target. "Do we get to pick sides?"

"What do you mean, pick sides?" But Royce knew what he meant, and felt himself go cold all over. He hadn't thought of Todd or Lindy living with him, living with Kat. Just in the same way he'd assumed Kat's happiness, he assumed Lindy and Todd would remain with Irene.

Todd executed a jump shot, and as Royce watched his body rise in the air and land lightly on his toes, he saw Todd when he'd been a Little League shortstop, the huge glove and cap on a small boy, lunging for the white ball. "I'd only pick you if you go away like Gary's dad. But if you're going to hang around, I'll stay here until I get my weekends. But then we'd do something, go somewhere."

It took Royce a moment to think this all through and process what his son was saying. The length of the speech itself was surprising. Gary was Frank Hennessey's son. What boy wouldn't want to go to Hong Kong, to explore the world with his father? My weekends. Royce slowly began to realize there was an etiquette involved in divorce. Visiting rights. He wondered how many of Todd's friends were children of a divorced couple, how much he knew about what would be in store for him.

"I'm not going away like Gary's dad. But if I hang

around, where would you like to go?" Hang around. He'd never thought of himself as hanging around.

"Fishing."

"Fishing," Royce repeated. Todd was right. Things were the pits this way. He'd taken his family fishing once, a camping trip into the Sierras. It rained, Irene complained there was no way to put her makeup on, and Lindy didn't like the smell of frying fish. But maybe Todd had enjoyed that weekend. Outside of that one weekend, Royce had never taken his son fishing. "I didn't know you liked to fish."

"I go with Graham and his dad. Mono Lake and the Forks of the Salmon."

"And you liked that." Royce vaguely remembered these trips. He'd used them as an excuse to spend the weekend with Kat.

"Sure." Todd fired off another shot, showing off a bit this time, his body looser, the shot a bit trickier. "Graham says his father's really a good guy when he's not around his mom."

The kid has a point, Royce decided. What sense of security and love can children receive from parents who bicker and quarrel? He and Irene were guilty of that. His mother would have called this a broken home, but perhaps some relationships could be improved by the separation. Todd was thirteen and he'd never gone fishing with his father. When he spent time with Todd, he demonstrated how to tune the car, or repair a leaky faucet. Maybe a divorce would change that. Todd would have the opportunity to see him at his best, rather than always at his worst, which is the way he invariably was with Irene. He could teach Todd to sail, just the two of them.

"Have you talked this over with your mother?" Royce asked.

"Yeah. Sort of." Todd dribbled the ball under his leg,

then collapsed on his haunches, trapping the ball beneath him. "She said no."

"No to what?"

"I asked her if I could go live in the city with you. Or even just go visit you over there. She said she'd cut off my allowance if I asked you."

Royce wanted to spit. This was the first he'd heard of any plan like this. It might have been a good idea for Todd to meet Kat, to work his family and Kat into the weave of his life, rather than this all-or-nothing split. "I didn't know," Royce said. "I know that sounds lame, but I truly didn't know."

"That's okay. I didn't lose my allowance."

"Maybe we can work something out. On your weekends as you say."

"I want separate weekends from Lindy. I see her all the time. Graham's dad does separate weekends."

"You know a lot of kids whose parents are divorced?" Todd's knowledge of what would happen, his calm assurance about what the future would bring, surprised Royce.

"Sure. Lots. There's a guy in my class who has three fathers. But he only likes one of them."

They heard the purr of the Lincoln engine as Irene drove up. Royce remembered his car was parked in the drive, so there'd be no surprise now. Irene cut the engine, but it was a moment before they heard the sigh of the heavy car door.

Todd rose and tucked the ball under his arm. He looked at his father for a moment, then held out his hand in a slap-five. Royce smiled and slapped his palm, turned his hand over and they slapped again. "Take care, man," Todd whispered.

"I'll be seeing you," Royce whispered back, and watched as Todd disappeared into the darkness of the yard, the ball abandoned in the dewy grass.

Royce picked up the ball and cradled it in his palms. He looked up at the indigo sky, cherishing this moment of peace between one encounter and the next. He imagined Irene taking a quick hit from the liquor cabinet, or a fast snort on her coke. Todd might be halfway down the block by now. There was no sound at all except the crickets and night bugs and the singing of the wind in the trees. Royce stood motionless, holding his breath, his eyes locked on the onyx of the sky. Something was missing, some noise he was used to as an integral part of his home. It took him a moment to place it. He hadn't heard or seen Wichita. He picked up the flashlight and walked over to the dog kennel in the back of the yard. He cast the light all over the pen, but it was empty save the blue water dish, the yellow food dish, and a well-gnawed bone the size of a child's thigh.

He continued staring into the empty pen, the flashlight and basketball in his hands. There was nothing to look at, the dog was gone. Irene waited for him in the house. Spider and the fly. He turned to look back at the house now, and the lights were on in the kitchen. Silhouetted in the doorway he saw Irene, as featureless as a paper cutout, leaning against the doorjamb with the light spilling out into the yard all around her. As he approached across the lawn he saw her turn, and there was some movement, a shrug of her shoulder, or a swivel of her hip, which reminded him of the woman, girl, he'd met so many years ago in Boston. She looked like a perfect English schoolgirl to him then, and he was sure she spent her evenings playing Mozart on the piano. Her smile was shy, none of the hardness which dominated her face these days. It amazed him to remember he used to think of her as fragile, vulnerable, that he must protect her, care for her. He couldn't remember the last time they'd kissed, even a social peck on the cheek. He couldn't remember the last time they made love.

He followed her into the kitchen.

Her back was to him, standing in front of the sink, and he admired the fine shape of her ass, neatly concealed in designer jeans with an eye-catching white tag on the hip pocket. Calvin Klein. Her dark hair, cropped close to the shape of her skull, picked up highlights from her blue cashmere sweater. "Here," she said as she turned and handed him a Bloody Mary complete with celery stalk.

He let the basketball fall to the floor and watched it roll into a corner while he returned the flashlight to a shelf by the door. He accepted the cold glass from her hand, his eyes searched deeply into hers. Her face was as fine and calm and still as a porcelain figurine. "You usually drink these in the morning," he said. The clock read twenty past eight.

"This day has been nothing but morning." She moved to the glass kitchen table and Royce noticed for the first time the cereal bowls, soggy clumps of cornflakes staring up at him like pale yellow eyes.

He watched her clear the table, pour the milk down the drain, stack the bowls in the dishwasher. She reached under the sink, the beautiful lines of her legs snug in her jeans, and brought out the Windex. The room smelled of ammonia with the first squirt. "I've always hated that smell. I wish just once you wouldn't do that."

She finished wiping the table slowly and deliberately, squirting more Windex until the ammonia made his eyes sting. He watched her breasts moving above the glass, the fine bones in her hands as she worked the paper towel across the surface. Then she seated herself behind the Bloody Mary and the Windex bottle and looked up at him with clear eyes. He had no idea what she was thinking.

He took the chair opposite and sipped his drink. "You always made a good drink."

"We probably should have champagne, but we're out at the moment. Cheers." She cocked her glass at him.

He couldn't take his eyes off her lips, outlined in glistening red lipstick. "Where's the dog?" Not that he cared, but he had to start somewhere.

"Dead."

Royce felt his ears ring, a humming or buzzing in his brain. Perhaps the dog had been dead for weeks and he'd never noticed, in just the same distracted way which kept him from recognizing the sound of a basketball drumming on the pavement. He couldn't remember the last time he'd seen Wichita, whether it had been alive this weekend, on Todd's birthday when Irene's parents had been down. "Dead," he said. "What happened to Wichita?"

"I told you. She's dead. Hit by a truck."

"When?" He was afraid she would say last week, last month, last year. Wichita, her flashing white ruff. He thought of Dagmar curled up sleeping on the end of the couch. He hoped he wouldn't get them confused.

"This morning." She licked her lips, her tongue darting out of her mouth for just an instant. "Todd left the pen unlocked when he went out to feed her, and while we were eating breakfast Lindy noticed her slip out of the yard." She pointed to the glass doors in the dining room, and Royce could see the dog heading for the road in the morning sun. "We jumped up to catch her, but I guess she thought it was a game. We'd whistle, and she'd turn around and look at us and then shoot ahead as if she were chasing a stick. We followed her all the way down to Sweetbriar, cutting through the yards. We didn't see it but we could hear it. She went across Sweetbriar right at the turn there and a Parcel Post truck hit her."

"Christ." Todd hadn't said a word about the dog, as if nothing out of the ordinary had happened.

She toyed with the celery in her glass. "Hell of a way to start your day."

"Your day, from what I hear, went on from there."

Irene nodded silently and swirled the celery stick.

Royce felt the blood drumming in his veins, heard the tick of his teeth as he ground them together, waiting for her to continue. Her silence could be as formidable as a weapon and she could stare at her drink with all the concentration she might show a strangely beautiful bug. "You going to tell me about it?" he finally asked.

Her eyes were hard, chips of light which radiated her hostility. "What for?"

"You didn't have to treat Donna Moon the way you did."

She settled back in the chair, her arm draped over the top rung so her breasts were a soft blue expanse under the cashmere. "Well, now you try it some time. You take two teenagers and let them witness their dog being hit by a Parcel Post truck. It was like you could hear the muscles tearing, the snap of her bones. *Kathunk*. Her screams sounded human, like an injured baby. The truck driver helped us pick her up and she bit him. You try handling two teenagers and a full-grown Afghan with blood streaming out of her mouth."

Royce could feel it, like the sudden rush of pain when an ankle breaks, that popping sound as the bones come free from their mooring of muscle and tendon. He wanted her to stop, but knew she wouldn't, not until she could make him squirm. Revenge. Irene's ideas about men and fathers were very fixed. Men and fathers took out the trash. Men and fathers made sure the car ran and that there was gas in the tank. Men and fathers were responsible for paying the bills and handling dying dogs.

"So there we are. Lindy's crying. Todd stood around as if he were stoned. The truck driver put her in the Parcel Post truck and we went to the animal hospital, making a lovely sight I'm sure, with blood and dog vomit everywhere, her howls echoing in the truck. Dr. Stewart put her down right away. Lindy got sick. The truck driver had to go to the clinic for stitches and shots. Then Dr. Stewart asks if we want to bury her, or have her disposed of."

He rose and made himself another Bloody Mary, nothing fancy, just a solid shot of vodka and a splash of tomato juice. Poor Wichita, who followed Todd around. "What does that have to do with Donna Moon?"

"Well, if you'd think about it, you'd see. Lindy wanted to bury her, have a little service. We walked home and decided you should know, be there. It's still only about nine-thirty in the morning, and I didn't feel the kids were in any shape to go to school. So we got in the car and drove over to the city to tell you and see if you could come home and we would make sort of a family thing out of it. There was no point in calling. Donna Moon never puts me through."

Royce could see the rest of it, and felt his breath coming in short, quick puffs. First would be the surprise of finding him not at work, Aurelio asking after his health, the knowing looks in Lindy's and Todd's eyes as they understood why their father wasn't around to help them bury their dog. Then Irene, after handling a fatally injured dog, suddenly snapping like a rubber band under too much stress. Placid, quiet Donna Moon receiving the first sting, then Irene, forgetting the dog completely, continuing to take out years of feelings on the closest substitute, his secretary.

"You know the rest," but her voice had lost its edge, was quieter, humbler. "Tell Donna Moon I'm sorry about the way I behaved this morning."

"Donna Moon threatened to quit."

"We all have our problems."

"What did you do with Wichita?" He was still surprised Todd had never mentioned any of this when they were shooting baskets behind the garage.

"Well, then I had to tell the children why you weren't at home in bed with the flu. I told them you were having a tacky affair. Then they just drifted off," she gave a helpless gesture, "you know how they do. One minute I looked around and they were gone. I called Dr. Stewart and told him to dispose of her. I didn't want to have a service by myself."

"I think you better apologize to Donna Moon."

Irene nodded and drained her drink, carefully timing her movements so Royce was reseated at the table when she got up to refill her glass. "I'll send her a note and some present. Does she like plants? An African violet, maybe."

He could tell by the way her body relaxed and the slow, methodical way she prepared her drink that she believed the situation was solved. Wichita was dead, Donna Moon would receive an apology. He'd come home to shoulder his share of the responsibility. She probably was truly sorry she'd yelled at Donna Moon. Todd had said she had a session with Dr. Sorenson. The modern family. His and her shrinks. The kids drifting off into the night, melting into the darkness like nocturnal cats.

"Well, let's see," Royce said, and then stopped because he could not imagine what he would say next. He hadn't come here to talk about dead dogs.

Irene sprinkled salt and pepper in her drink, added a shot of Worcestershire, and went to the refrigerator for a slice of lemon and a celery stalk. "Are you going to stay here tonight?" she asked, "Or go back to the city?"

"Does it matter?"

"Yes." She closed the refrigerator and moved slowly back to the counter. Royce thought he was going to scream; he'd never seen anyone take so long to mix a simple drink. "Lindy's gone out with John, I'll bet. And we agreed she wouldn't see him again. He's a hoodlum. If you stay here tonight, I'll let you talk to her when she comes in. I'm really too tired to try and outwait her."

From the dark shadows under her eyes, he believed she was tired. Her face lost the energy of her anger and looked soft, exhausted, as if she would drift off to sleep in her kitchen chair. He thought about waiting until morning, but he'd postponed this moment for over two years. If he waited until tomorrow, as he'd done several times before, he might never have the courage. It wasn't exactly like kicking her when she was down. There would never be a good time for this kind of news, dead dogs or not.

"Irene. Irene," he said her name as if calling her back from some secret place. "Irene, I didn't come over here just to find out the dog died."

She took a deep breath, getting ready for a new attack. "Then maybe you should start by explaining why you aren't going to work any more."

"I think we should talk about getting a divorce."

"Nothing's changed, Royce. The dog died, that's all. I'm sorry about Donna Moon. You can't divorce me for what I said to Donna Moon."

"That's not the point. We can't go on like this. It's too bad about Wichita, but don't you see what it means to us as a family? I wasn't there. Donna Moon has nothing to do with it. You needed me for something and I wasn't there. I haven't been there for a long time. So why do you persist in hanging on to me when I can't help you the way I should?"

"I don't see any point in going through all this now.

255

This isn't the Russian Revolution where everything has to happen in ten days. I've had enough for today." She reached over and flipped the switch on the dishwasher, the sound roaring through the room like a crescendo as she marched out as if exiting a stage.

Watching her walk away gave Royce a chill. There was authority in her step, possession, command. She looked as if her whole life had been designed to show her off for this one moment, a natural birthright. Irene was the one with the perfect life, everything she ever wanted, including a husband who came around every couple of weeks to find out the dog died.

Royce snapped the dishwasher off and followed her into the living room. "You better get straight what you need from me. If I have to go off to Mexico, or off to Hong Kong like Frank, I'll do it. But we're going to get a divorce and we might as well get on with it right now."

She was curled up on the end of the couch, leafing through a magazine as if they were talking about the neighbors or the weather. "You make it sound like buying a car. We're not getting divorced. If you want something to talk about we should talk about what we're going to do about Lindy's attachment to John. That kid's going to get in trouble, I can just feel it."

"I can't go on like this, Irene. And I don't see how you can either."

"Is that why you haven't gone to work this week? Is this some kind of weird strike?" She ruffled through the magazine as if she were fanning a roll of bank notes. "Refusing to go to work isn't going to make me divorce you."

"What would?"

"Nothing. You're not working for me, you know. You're working to keep your precious Kat."

His face flushed and he felt his scalp tingle. If he

wasn't careful, Irene could turn the hours between now and dawn into a fight over Kat. But he believed Dr. Bodine. Kat was a problem he would settle tomorrow. Tonight he must reason with Irene, somehow get free of her so he could get on with his life. "It's better for the kids if they know the truth. God, I love those kids. I don't like lying to them. They're old enough to understand what's going on here. There's no reason to deceive them. I understand why you came down there today, but don't you see all the damage you've done? How you hurt Donna Moon? How the kids must've felt?"

"It's interesting to see you worrying about the kids." She took a sip of her drink and replaced it carefully on the coaster. "They don't count on you anyhow."

"And you want me to wait up for Lindy and give her hell about dating John?"

"Don't bother. I can handle it. I have to handle everything else around here." She opened the magazine to a page splashed with ads and pretended great interest in the fine print.

"This is going to stop, Irene." He snatched the magazine out of her hands. "*Bon Appetit*. What do you read this crap for? Truth is you can't boil water. You keep it lying around on your coffee table because it's got a pretty cover." He threw it toward the window where it rattled against a potted plant.

Her eyes grew sharp again, all trace of exhaustion vanished from her face. "You're trying to start something you won't be able to finish."

"It would be good for you. You wouldn't have to put up with me. You'd never have to see me unless you wanted to, then maybe the next time you have to deal with a dead dog or the punk your daughter's dating, I'd be able to help you, support you. That's better than all the lying and subterfuge we go through now."

"Oh, you think it's that simple. You don't understand. It's not that I don't want you. I don't want anyone. I want to be left alone, to run my life. I don't want to complicate it by splitting up our responsibilities to the kids, having my well-meaning friends find dinner partners for me, by having to look for another father for my children. As long as we're married I don't have to face the problems of being a divorcee, of having to go back to the sexual free-for-all single people wade through. It would be just like college again, every man looking at me as if I'm a new car. What would it be like to drive me? Can he afford me? What's the upkeep on a model like me?"

"This is such utter bullshit. I can't believe you're telling me this with a straight face. You're not afraid of men, Irene. Your great talent is in organizing your life so men take all the responsibility while you reap all the pleasure. You glory in it. Gerald and I have set you up so the only thing you have to do in this world is breathe. You're not afraid of me, or Gerald, or any other moonstruck yokel who'll find you attractive."

"Dr. Sorenson says I am."

"I don't give a flying fuck what Dr. Sorenson says." Although her mention of Dr. Sorenson made him question anything Dr. Bodine had been saying. The truth was that Dr. Bodine hadn't really told him anything; he'd been doing all the talking. It was probably the same for Irene, mute approval for whatever fantasies she entertained at the time. The modern family, his and her shrinks, the only people they could talk to.

"I don't care what you think, Royce." Her eyes narrowed to slits as if she were squinting into a strong sun. "I'm in no mood to be a single woman. I don't want to have to explain this to Daddy. This is the best possible solution for both of us. You can have your precious Kat and I can have my sham of a marriage. I think you ought to count yourself lucky. You're getting away with quite a lot."

"This isn't exactly what I'd call luck. What do you think, I'm going to outgrow Kat the way the kids outgrow shoes? If anyone's been outgrown, Irene, it's you. As you said, this is a sham of a marriage. Why go on with it?"

"You don't have a choice. There are the children. There's your business. You can't keep a woman without money." She gave him a faint, wicked smile.

Royce worked his hand over his face and thought about tying her up and setting the house on fire. He wanted to kick the ottoman, punch out the plate glass window facing the street. But he calmly walked over to lean against the fireplace mantel. Lost among all the bric-a-brac was an agate Irene bought when they drove out here from Boston sixteen years ago. She was four months pregnant and they were on their way to California to explain to her father. Irene found the agate in a truck stop in Wyoming, deciding on it because she said the mauves and swirl of silver reminded her of the depths of his eyes. She thought the agate might bring the three of them luck. Within the month, they were quietly married, Gerald and Margaret, the only witnesses. Now, sixteen years later, the agate was just another object to dust. Until he laid his hands on it, he'd forgotten its existence. He turned the agate over and over in his palm, a thunder egg.

He returned the agate to the mantel. Any decision would be the wrong one, but any decision would be better than this limbo. "I'm going to pack my stuff."

She sat with her legs curled under her at one end of the couch and seemed to be studying the polish on her nails. After a long moment she said, "What are you going to take?" She still didn't look at him.

Royce gave a vague gesture. He had no idea.

She looked up at him now, a full steady stare. "You

259

don't have anything." Her voice held all the warmth of a polar sea. She reached for her half-finished Bloody Mary and gestured with it to take in the whole room. "All this," she said, holding up the glass, "is mine. You're no one. You don't own anything. If I could, I'd make you give back your college education, the money, the time. Nothing is yours. You should have stayed in that filthy gas station. That's about all you're good for. Grease. When I was in high school we called people like you greasers. You've been living off my father, but underneath it all, you are still pumping gas in a lousy gas station." With the same motion as shifting gears in a car, she tossed her Bloody Mary glass. They watched as it arced across the small space between them and shattered against the stone of the fireplace, the shards and smithereens of the tumbler raining onto the tops of Royce's shoes.

He watched the tomato juice sliding down the stone facade, too thin and pale to be blood, too thick for water. The rough surface of the stone divided the liquid into separate trails that ran across the face like the paths of bugs fleeing a light.

"You can't divorce me because you'd be left with nothing. What can you do, for God's sake, without my father to prop you up? Tell me, Royce, tell me one thing you can do on your own. My family pulled you out of a gas station and you're too old now to go back to being a grease monkey."

The toes of his shoes shone with the sparkling glass. Calmly, which surprised him, he tapped his shoes against the fireplace apron to remove the slivers.

He took a deep breath and picked up the agate. "Remember this?" He held the eye of the thunder egg toward her. He steadied himself by placing his palm against the stone fireplace and felt the difference in the quality of the two rocks, the sandstone fireplace against his left palm, the quartz of the agate in his right. In her eyes he saw defiance. He knew she was expecting him to strike her with the agate, but instead he pitched it through the front window. His windup was perfect, the arm carrying through smoothly. He winced when he heard the agate strike metal, the hood of the Toyota parked in the driveway. The echoing waterfall of glass.

"Lovely," Irene said. "Just lovely." She stood. "Do you think that matters? Does that solve anything?" In the corner was a vase of purple daisies, and she darted toward them as quickly as if she'd been on skates. She picked the vase up and slammed it to the floor in front of her, water and daisies and a shower of glass scattering at her feet. She grabbed a glass ashtray and hurled it against the fireplace, aiming for the spot where she'd thrown her tumbler. All the time her voice was very quiet and calm. "I can break this and replace it. I can smash this, get another tomorrow. I can even hire someone to clean this all up in the morning." Another ashtray shattered against the fireplace, quite close to his hand. "None of this," his Bloody Mary met its fate against the floor, "none of this matters in the least. You simply pay for things like this. You buy more. But you can't pay for anything, not without my father. And on your own? No, Royce, you can't make it on your own." She stepped into the dining room.

He could see the wheel of her anger engaging, the motor turning over and propelling her energy. "You going to break all the dishes?"

"I might." A plate shattered, then another. "It makes no difference, you see. If I break every glass and plate in this house it makes no damn difference. It has nothing to do with getting divorced. We can replace every fucking bit of this. But you can't replace a marriage."

He thought a war zone might sound like this, the loud splatter and explosion of the guns and dishes, the anxious whispers of the combatants. "You can stop now," he said. "I get your point." She stood in the dining room, a dinner plate in her hand, ready to add it to the pile of shards at her feet. "I'm going to pack my stuff."

The plate hit the floor with a resounding smash. He was afraid she would be cut by the flying splinters of glass. As he took the first step toward the stairs, glass crunched under his feet.

"And you know who's going to pay for this?" Her tone was still quiet, as normal as if she were talking on the phone. "You are. You're going to pay for every new dish." Another plate hit the floor. "Think you can afford that?"

"I suppose I'll have to." He turned to look at her, standing in an island of brightly colored chips, slices of plates. "But I wouldn't break all of that if I were you, Irene. Sure I'll replace it, but I might have to replace it at Woolworth's, not Williams-Sonoma."

"You wouldn't even know about Williams-Sonoma if I hadn't taught you. When I met you, your idea of a good restaurant was Howard Johnson's. You thought a Seven and Seven was a fancy drink. But you know better now, Royce. You wouldn't eat at Howard Johnson's now on a bet."

"I'm leaving you, Irene."

The last plate simply dropped from her hand, as if her fingers were too weak to hold it. They stared at each other for a long moment.

Royce said, "Sorenson's right, you know. Divorce is financial. Even divorced we'll be tied in some ways, especially financially. So I'd think about it if I were you. I'd think about how tough I'd make things. Because if you make it tough for me, it'll be tough for me to support you.''

He turned his back on her and headed up the stairs.

His room was as cold and anonymous as a motel room. Everything had been picked with an eye to decor. The long white curtains matched the ones in Irene's bedroom next door. The bedspread matched the curtains and Royce always had the feeling the room was designed for female visitors, maiden aunts. What man kept pastel throw pillows on his bed?

One corner looked like an office with a desk, bookcases, and a massive filing cabinet. But the desk needed dusting, the filing cabinet was mostly empty, and the bookcase held back issues of *National Geographic* and *Bon Appetit*. Royce knew he could empty this room of his things and Irene would never notice.

Five hundred thousand men were in Vietnam the year he and Irene drove out to California to meet Gerald, to get married, to await Lindy's birth. The time between then and now was difficult to define, shifting the way a dream changes when you try to recall it later. His children had grown, his business prospered. His marriage had vanished.

As he drew his suitcases out of the closet and began stuffing them with his clothes, he realized he'd already left. His departure had been slow and symbolic. Three years ago he'd taken his tools over to the house on Elizabeth Street and as he worked on the house he'd borrowed the portable TV to watch the World Series, the tape player to listen to music while he worked. When Kat moved in, he began bringing his books over, some favorite things he wanted to share with her. His bedroom was now a repository for old tax forms, medical receipts, and loan applications. After he'd found the pink slips for the cars behind the cashew can, he'd removed everything of importance from his desk and stored them in the safe at the plant.

It surprised him how little there would be to move. He wanted to hire a truck to prove he'd lived here over twelve years, but he would have nothing to put in it. He didn't want Irene's tables and chairs. The desk, maybe, although Kat had refinished a library table which he'd been using for some time. He didn't want to take all those old tax forms stored in the cabinet. There was a footlocker which he'd brought with him when he moved out here from Boston, but when he opened it, he found an old address book filled with girls' names and an intricate code of stars and triangles which made no sense to him. There were snapshots of drinking parties, many of the faces a mystery to Royce now. He hadn't looked in this trunk in several years, and as he closed the lid he felt he'd been prying into someone else's life.

One drawer of the desk was filled with kids' artwork, Father's Day and Christmas presents. Crayoned bookmarks, ashtrays made out of hardened dough. He wondered if other fathers used their bakery boxes covered with Con-Tact paper to store their cuff links and tie pins.

He kept shuffling papers and mementos across his knees, stuffing some in the suitcases and some in the wastebasket. The top of the desk filled with papers to be saved, but never read, and the obvious data Irene would need, the mortgage for the house, the insurance on her car. He tried to keep from glancing at the doorway, knowing she would appear sooner or later, wondering if she would be armed with more glasses to smash. He heard her on the stairs, very softly, but mounting the stairs nevertheless. He kept his eyes down and tried to appear as busy as he could for as long as he could, but was finally forced to reach for another stack of papers. She stood in the doorway. "You were always good at sneaking up on people," he said. "That, and remembering drinks."

"I think you're being hasty."

"Hasty? You call this hasty? I haven't even lived here for two years. A week's worth of groceries would fill my car more than the stuff I'm taking out of here. I bought that house as a sanctuary, some place to go away from here. You and I've slept in separate bedrooms for thirteen years. You call that hasty? If that's hasty, I suppose you'd call splitting an atom slow."

"We can get on as we've been doing. There's no need for you to move out."

He went over to sit on the bed, propped back on his hands on the quilted comforter. The stitching tingled his palms and he moved his fingers up and down on the cloth as if he were playing a piano. He couldn't believe she wanted him to stay. "I wouldn't worry about it if I were you. You won't lose anything except the one thing you don't want. Me."

"The children should have a father."

"I'll still be their father."

"I told you. I don't want to be a single woman."

"That's tough titty, Irene. Actions speak louder than words. You've shown you don't want to be a married woman either."

"So you're going to marry her? Let me tell you something, Royce. That's a cunt game, one of the oldest in the world. If she really loved you, she'd have some respect for you, for your life and your family."

"I'm not going to marry her, Irene," and he felt empty when he thought of the flashcards, Africa. "I'm simply leaving *you*."

"What's the point of a divorce?" She looked truly bewildered. "If you're not going to marry her?"

"I want to be in charge of my own life for a change. I don't want you and Gerald calling all the shots all the time." And as he said it, he knew it was true.

"It's just the sex? Is that it?" She hesitated for a moment, and looked like she might have a bad taste in her mouth, something stuck on her tongue. Then, with her shoulders thrown back she began to take off her sweater. She crossed her arms in front of her breasts and pulled the blue cashmere over her head. Her white, lacy bra stood out against the remnants of her tan, the strap marks of her bathing suit still faintly visible. She glanced at him, then swiftly cut her eyes to a corner of the room as she began to lower the zipper on her jeans. "If it's just the sex."

He watched as the white of her panties flashed at him, her eyes still anchored in the corner. She pulled the jeans down so he could see her dark pubic hair curling around the elastic encircling her crotch. Her body was as smooth and hard, curved and attractive, as a woman ten years younger. In some ways her body was better than Kat's, perfectly proportioned. Kat's three-mile thighs which made her look a bit short-waisted. Irene stepped out of her jeans and reached behind to unclasp her bra. He saw her small breasts with the deep, dark nipples hang free of the white cloth. The beautiful matching hollows beneath her shoulder bones, the V-shaped hollow of her pelvis. Yet for all this classic form there was a coldness as if he were staring at a statue. Irene refused to look at him as she worked her panties down her sleek thighs. He stared at her flat, hard belly, remembering when she'd been truly beautiful, not angular and sculpted like this, but with her breasts full of milk and her belly swelling with a baby. That memory took his breath away, the fullness and warmth of her when she'd been pregnant.

He blinked his eyes and shook his head slightly. This was no time to get sentimental. This body she was presenting to him was the product of years of attention. Exercising, dieting, tanning, moisturizing. She cared for her body the way he cared for Kat's house, each blemish smoothed and worked on, perfected. Another man might have found this show arousing. "Don't embarrass yourself, Irene. I've had sex with you. I know what I'm missing."

She turned coy, crossing the space between them to place her hands on his crotch. "You haven't given me much chance in the last couple of years." Her hands were cold, even through his clothes, ten dead twigs brushing mechanically over his body. He willed himself to not respond. Think baseball, multiplication tables. Change the oil in the Toyota.

Placing her mouth on his, she kissed him, not passionately, but tentatively, waiting for him to take the lead. She'd never been aggressive in sex, not like Kat. He wished they could have a friendly, good-bye fuck, old buddies enjoying each other for the last time. But Irene would never see it that way. If he accepted, she'd take it as a sign of commitment.

The lovely light which came into her face when she smiled, the attention she'd showered on their children as babies, none of that could make up for the lack of feeling in sex. Every time he approached her, he felt he carried his cock in his hands like a toy. Her response to him was the same as if he'd held her at gunpoint.

He placed his hands on either side of her head and pulled her face away from his, gently, trying to show her he meant her no harm. He looked into her eyes, her hands stopped moving over his groin. "You don't want to do this, Irene. You don't have to. You shouldn't cheapen yourself."

They searched each other's eyes, trying to find the
window to the soul. As he looked at her he knew they
were as different as dogs and cats, birds and fish. The sun
and the moon.

She moved away from him, reaching for her underwear. He felt the knot in his groin dissolve as she stepped
back into her panties, snatched up her bra and locked it
behind her back. He watched her twisting her hips as she
pulled up her jeans, reaching for the sweater dropped
onto the floor. She jammed it down over her hair. She
tucked the ends into the waist of her jeans, dressing as
hurriedly as she would to escape a fire. "You don't even
want to try with me?"

"We've been together sixteen years. Don't you think
I've tried in all that time?" His chest tightened. What had
happened to them?

"You're not really going through with this."

"Oh yes, I am. Don't worry. It won't happen over-
night. I don't know the first thing about getting a divorce.
Honest Injun," he held up his hand in a scout's salute,
"in all these years I've never looked into it. We're both
amateurs in that respect. You could either make it harder
or easier for us. We could try for a no-fault divorce. But if
you fight this, I'll fight back."

"With what?" Her haughty manner was back. "Have
you even talked to a lawyer, Royce? When you do, you'll
find out you have nothing to reproach me with. I've been
loyal to you. I've given the kids a good home. I'm not the
one who's out there playing around. I believe legally
that's called adultery. Infidelity. Desertion."

He wished now he'd forced her to stand before him
naked and try to get away with the same speech. She was
never haughty when unclothed. For a panicky moment he
thought he would tear her clothes off her body, keep her

naked until she agreed to the divorce. He unlocked his elbows and fell back on the bed, his hands sculling across the covers. "The fact you're not having an affair isn't exactly the same as loyalty. There's such a thing as alienation of affection. Do you remember the last time we slept together?"

"That's a crime? Like adultery?"

He would have to see a lawyer, a different lawyer, not the firm he and Gerald used for business. Maybe Dr. Bodine knew a good divorce lawyer. Maybe Kat did. "Irene, you never developed that itch you couldn't scratch. That goes some distance in holding a marriage together. I would think your mother could have told you that."

She crossed her arms under her breasts. "What are you going to do?"

"Live on talent and love." He clasped his hands behind his head, a parody of a man in a centerfold of a woman's sex magazine. He thought of flexing his muscles at her, unbuttoning his shirt, unzipping his pants. He could take her dog-style right there on the cream-colored carpet. He could make her cry.

"But what am I supposed to do?" She wasn't sniveling, merely assessing her situation.

"You don't have to do anything. You've got the whole setup right here. Gerald's not going to let anything happen to you. We could do this no-fault, you know."

The air seemed to go out of her body, and Royce felt she might truly be considering what a divorce could mean. "Don't tell me you never thought it might come to this. You've been seeing Sorenson for two years now, just to get ready for this."

"Oh, sure. We've talked about it, about the difference between marriage and divorce. Dr. Sorenson says marriage is emotional and divorce is financial. But I'll never get it through my head. Getting divorced is very emotional."

"I'll still see Lindy and Todd. I'll even see your dad, if he's willing. We're just going to make legal what's been a fact for a long time now." Royce felt very clear about this. Living with Irene had been like living alone. If Kat left him, he would survive it. Todd was all for it. Lindy would either go live with her punk boyfriend or go off to college. The only thing Royce regretted was that this fine, dispassionate discussion would have to be repeated for Gerald and Margaret.

She walked over to the windowsill and leaned against it, her hands cocked next to her thighs, her elbows locked. For a moment or two she breathed deeply and slowly, her nostrils flaring with each breath. "How are we going to tell my parents?"

"We could have a party. You're good at throwing parties. I'll never forget that guy from Crown-Zellerbach. We saw him once at dinner in a restaurant, and two years later when he showed up here for a party, you remembered he drank White Russians."

"Maybe I should divorce you for mental cruelty."

"Now you're talking."

"I mean it, Royce." She seemed to be giving this her full attention, studying the situation the way she would have dealt with Wichita this morning. "How are we going to tell Mother and Father? Don't you realize what this will mean to them?"

"As my mother used to say: You've got the emphasis on the wrong sylLAble. A couple of years ago I probably wouldn't have done this. Obviously, I didn't. But remember when we lived over in North Beach, when we first came out here? I'd fly back east and see some of my old buddies, my mother. In those days I'd crash on someone's floor for the week or two I'd be gone. I go back east now and check into a hotel. I don't sleep on floors anymore." He turned on his side to face her across the bed, his head propped on his fist supported by the triangle of his arm. "Every winter has a spring. Things change in the spring."

"Don't do it. Please."

"I'll handle it however you want. I'll call Gerald, if you like. Or you can call him and break the news. We could drive up there if that's what you think is right. I've already told Todd. I could wait up for Lindy tonight." He wanted her to believe he wasn't her enemy. At this moment he felt nothing but concern and kindness toward her, as if she were a little girl he was forced to disappoint.

She passed her hand over her face, held it cupped over her mouth. "I'm going to have to talk to Dr. Sorenson about this."

"Sure," he said. "Anything you want."

She rose and steadied a potted plant on the windowsill, adjusting it in the dark of night so the leaves would catch the morning light from a different angle. "You've talked to Todd."

"Yeah. Before you came home."

She straightened some issues of *National Geographic* as she moved toward the door. "I'd better clean up that glass," she said softly, as if speaking to herself. "Will you stay tonight?" She turned now to look at him, but there were no tears in her eyes, no hardness, simply a sad and confused look on her face as if she were trying to understand an important message in a foreign language. "We could talk more in the morning."

"Sure," he said. "I'll help you clean up."

He watched her drift out of the room and down the stairs, pausing to touch little knickknacks and potted plants arranged along the hall. Her hand trailed along the bannister as she descended, and he thought he could hear her humming to herself.

He would call Kat and tell her he wouldn't be home tonight as he'd promised. He might even have to spend a day up in Sacramento. But now that he was headed on this course, he wasn't worried about what Kat would think. This was what she'd asked for. She'd have to wait out the time it took to get everything arranged. Unlike her husband, who sounded as if he just vanished, Royce would take the time to insure no one was unnecessarily hurt. He wondered if Kat and Irene should meet, how he would introduce her to Todd and Lindy.

He went to the phone and dialed their number in the city. He listened to the empty tone, a faint static like the subtle clicking of a clock keeping slow time. And then he remembered. He remembered he'd unplugged the phone after Donna Moon called. Twelve hours ago he was afraid Irene would call him, that the phone would ring while Dr. Bodine was there. Everything had turned around since then. He wondered how long it would take her to notice he hadn't called as promised, couldn't call because he'd tried to protect them by unplugging the phone.

APRIL 10
THURSDAY MORNING

A bird sang outside Max's windows at the oddest times, day and night. It lived in the little courtyard in the dense shrubbery overgrowing the tiny lawn. Max thought birds slept at night and the singing in the darkness intrigued him. No other bird answered the song. Last night Max had opened the window and played some trills on his electric piano, warbles and quick-fingered runs up and down the keyboard, hoping the bird would answer him. It didn't.

It sang this morning, though, while Max was getting dressed. He looked out the window but couldn't spot it, a drab brown bird he usually detected only as movement in the leaves. This morning reminded him of the clear, light air of a Virginia summer dawn, before the day turned hot and humid. As a boy, Tidewater weather puzzled him. Those light, comfortable mornings inevitably gave way to days of insufferable heat where the air was as close and thick as a coat of paint. In San Francisco he could have

Virginia morning weather without suffering through the afternoons, and Max appreciated this much the same way he could appreciate a fine example of gingerbread on a Victorian house.

This afternoon he would meet Ivy Ingram, who'd recently moved to the city on the heels of her divorce. But the morning was all his own, his Saturday. He thought of practicing his piano, but since the day was clear and bright as an eye, he decided to drive over to Oakland and stop in Leo's to look at new pianos. His little electric piano made his fingers feel as if they were lying on top of each other when he tried playing two-handed chords. He might trade this one in on a larger model, one that didn't feel like such a toy under his hands.

Today he would just window-shop, see what was out there. But as he drove across the Bay Bridge he admitted there were other reasons for going to the East Bay this morning. Hijackers, a powerful image for surprise. People make up stories in the same spirit as a child invents an imaginary friend. It fills a void. Hijackers, like skateboarders, tended to be a male-dominated activity. He'd looked in the phone book last night for Alan Quales, but found no listing. Katlyn's lie about the hijackers still puzzled him. Her mother, Opal, lived in Berkeley.

Max was an early riser, something he'd have to change if he ever abandoned psychiatry and took up a musician's life, a new fantasy which gained ground daily. Musicians were men of the night. Musicians don't deal with words. Musicians don't work alone. Musicians create the music of darkness.

It didn't surprise him when he parked in front of Leo's and found them closed. Hours: 10:30–6:00. He would get a cup of coffee while he waited. And as he sipped his coffee he knew what this trip to the East Bay was really about. As strange and unorthodox as it seemed, he wanted to meet Katlyn's mother. He wanted to call her up and talk to her about her daughter. He realized it was none of his business, she wasn't even his patient, but somehow he felt he needed to know more about her if he was to help Royce. Or maybe the question really wasn't even helping Royce. Katlyn was a craving he had to satisfy like the need for sex. He kept seeing her in the shimmery flapper dress.

She reminded him of Patrice, not in any physical way, just in the sense he couldn't predict what she would say or do. Those surprising turns their marriage had taken. After Conrad was born, Max had come home one night to find the lock on the apartment door changed. At first he wasn't concerned, thought perhaps the landlord changed it for some reason and he would get his key from Pat. When she didn't answer his ring he went around to the little courtyard in back, thinking he would climb the back stairs and let himself in through the kitchen door and wait until she came home. In the little yard, four stories below their flat, lay a heap of rubble. Medical books, clothes, records, shaving gear, his alarm clock, papers, broken glasses, his turntable, portable TV. Everything Max owned had been dropped from the fourth-story porch. As if the impact upon hitting the ground hadn't been enough, hadn't already destroyed the spines of his books and smashed his records, popped tubes and transistors, Pat had set up the sprinkler on top of the pile. Max watched the water wave back and forth over his belongings. In the dusk, rainbows of light played over the shards.

There'd been no explanation for her action. Later, she told him she thought her meaning was clear enough. Although Katlyn admitted she'd lied about the hijackers, she hadn't explained what the hijacking meant or why she made up the story. Max sensed some connection as he found himself paging through the phone book. No Quales in the East Bay. But there was an Opal Whiston in Berkeley. Address. Phone number.

He hesitated before dialing. Royce said she didn't like to talk on the phone.

He dialed. A woman answered.

"Hello. Opal Whiston? I'm Dr. Max Bodine. I'm hoping you can help me with a patient. Do you know Katlyn Whiston or Royce Chambers?"

"Oh God, what's happened?"

"Nothing's happened. They're both fine." She probably thought he was calling from an emergency ward. "I'm a psychiatrist. Royce is my client."

"What kind of trouble is he in?"

"He's not really in any trouble. There's a technique we use called networking, talking to people who know the patient, trying to shed a different light on the problem. I was wondering if I could talk to you."

"You're sure they're not hurt?"

"I just saw them yesterday. They both are in very good health."

"Are you selling anything?"

"No. I'm not selling anything. I'd just like to talk to you about the relationship between Royce and Katlyn. I was wondering if I could come over and just take a few minutes of your time." He sounded like a cop, asking a question that couldn't be refused. One part of him didn't believe he was doing this. Not just calling the woman up, but asking to visit her. Snooping around like a detective.

"I can't help you," she said. "Kathy's problems are of her own making. I've only met Royce a few times."

But he couldn't back away. He had to see the woman behind the voice. "It would just take a moment and help me considerably. A psychiatrist works in the dark. Any information you could give me would be useful."

"I have work to do," she said. "I'm too busy to chatter on the phone."

"Please," Max said. "Don't hang up." He sounded like a salesman down on his luck, desperate to unload his Bibles, encyclopedias, insurance. "I could come over. It would only take a few minutes."

There was a longish pause, almost a sigh. "When would you like to come?"

Max looked at his watch. Leo's would be open soon, and if he browsed the pianos, that would give Opal Whiston a chance to get ready, organize herself for his visit. "Would an hour be convenient? This really won't take much time."

"You got the address?"

"I'm sure I can find it."

"I'll see you then." She hung up.

Max looked at the phone in wonder, amazed he'd done such a thing. His stomach fluttered at the bottom of his rib cage. What the hell was he doing, calling the woman up like this? Insisting on visiting her. He'd really gone too far this time. Networking, indeed. Just plain snooping was more like it. He had no business bothering this woman. He should tend to his own affairs. If he was going to bother anyone it should be Patrice, that's what he should be doing on his day off. Find out how she was raising Conrad. See if she'd found any meaning in her life. But no. Instead, here he was about to intrude on a perfect stranger, Katlyn's mother. As if that was really going to do Royce any good.

Families. Mothers and fathers. We never really escape them. Kat, with all her imagination and flights of fancy, was linked to this woman. Max wished he knew more about his own mother, but neither Claire nor his father talked much about her after she died. As a child, Max's strongest impression of death was as a form of disappearing, a very serious game of hide and seek. Until he was in his teens he kept expecting to run into his mother, find her hiding in some remote corner of the house. She would be the same, never aging. She would be wearing her white dotted swiss sun dress, one of Max's favorites.

Perhaps, if his mother hadn't died, he would have understood his father better. Maybe his mother could have explained that cold, remote man. His father had played pro ball, served as a paratrooper in the war, and later opened a sporting goods store that became a chain. As a boy, small for his age, the arsenal of sporting stuff never interested Max. He liked archery and shooting pool, but he couldn't win, couldn't live up to his father's ambitions for a son who would use his body to prove his worth. Books were his territory, as useless to his father as ownership of the moon would have been.

Claire was the athlete his father desired, a tennis pro making her name on the regional circuit. In the days before her death she spent her time sitting in the sunshine high above the city, staring down at the street. Max always imagined her in her tennis whites, the clouds floating in the blue sky above her head. Then the leap into the air, falling, falling. It took her death for their father to notice his children, grown now, their childhood not even a memory, more like a long remembered dream. Max turned his back on his father, unable to comprehend what drove him so unmercifully. And then his father drowned and Max was cut adrift from his family forever.

And now he'd bullied Katlyn's mother into letting him talk to her. Talk about insanity. He'd never understood his own parents, what was he trying to prove? Networking, ha! Perhaps this was even faintly illegal. Certainly it was unethical.

He entered Leo's, whistling a jazzy Jelly Roll Morton

tune to try to raise his spirits. Inside he strolled among the pianos, organs, keyboards, Moogs, synthesizers, running his hands on the keys but asking no questions. "Just browsing" he told the salesgirl, who looked at him as if she thought he was a shoplifter, a piano booster. He fiddled with a synthesizer, creating an eerie whistle like a train, a clacking which reminded him of horses on cobblestones. What was he going to say to this woman? What did he really want to know? He bent and sustained a high E until it sounded as taut as a bowstring. He could start with the story of the Nazi mementos, her father the doctor, which he suspected might be as invented as the hijacking story. He wondered if Katlyn had a sister.

The side streets of Berkeley always reminded Max of summer in a midwestern town. The only detail that gave away California was the fact the curbs were so low, no height needed for the snowplows to run against when clearing the snow. No snow. The big leafy trees, the warmth of the sunshine, the small houses set uniformly back from the streets seemed ironically stable in contrast with the local history of riots and demonstrations. Once off Telegraph, the whole town could have been in Ohio in May.

Opal Whiston's house sat on one of these quiet streets, an overgrown yard with an ancient palm in front of a one-story house shuttered against the morning light. He rang the bell beside the screen door.

"It slides," a woman's voice called out from the dim rooms, and Max's stomach took another roll. His throat felt dry.

He put his hand to the doorknob, found a handle instead, and realized this was a sliding screen door, battered around the frame where many people had tried to pull it open. The door moved easily on a track into the wall. He walked in, like stepping into a closet, adjusting his eyes to the dim light. A calico cat nosed his shoe while two others eyed him from their perch on the mantel.

"In the back," the voice called.

Max moved through the house, noting the bamboo and wicker furniture covered with Mexican blankets. Another cat, a black one, skittered across his path as he worked his way toward the voice. He passed under an arch and found a woman sitting in the middle of a sunroom, light falling across her shoulders and a worktable strewn with spools of ribbon, boxes of buttons, and pieces of fabric. With a blink of the eye, Max saw Katlyn's workroom in the city.

In the corner stood a man-sized green satin alligator, rearing back on long hind legs, propped up by a stiff tail. Shark's teeth fanned a red felt tongue. The eyes were brown agate marbles. The woman didn't turn to greet him. "I'm Opal. Take a seat." She indicated the chair across from her. "My hands are full."

As Max walked around to the chair opposite he noticed a head sitting in her lap. It lay staring with one blue glass eye on the ceiling, the other under the skillful hands of Opal Whiston, who stitched on eyelashes.

"I'm not normally this rude." She looked up at him for the first time. Her eyes were extraordinarily clear. "This is a rush job, and you rather surprised me on the phone. But hell, they're all rush jobs. Just move whatever's in your way. Watch out for pins. Plenty of pins in this stuff."

"I'm Dr. Max Bodine." He felt silly saying this, so obvious, yet someplace to begin. "I'm sorry if I'm intruding on your work."

"I'm not Spiro Agnew. I can work and talk at the same time. Do you follow politics? The only thing I can remember about Spiro Agnew is that crack about not being able to walk down the street and chew gum at the same time. But I don't remember who said it. Do you know?"

"Sorry. Afraid I don't." Max moved a bolt of bright lime fabric off the chair and found another cat nestled in the cushion. The cat regarded him slowly, then hopped off and disappeared under the table, waving a tail as wide as a baseball bat.

Opal Whiston didn't look any particular age, not a middle-aged woman and not an old woman. Her skin was wrinkled and tan, but without the liver-colored spots so common to elderly women. Her hands, covered with ropy blue veins, worked surely and quickly fastening the eyelashes in place. Her hair gave her age away, not gray or red or blonde or brown, just some indefinite lack of color, a lack of care, Max often noted about women Opal's age. She was big-boned, like her daughter, with even features and large, searching gray eyes. Max thought if she dyed her hair, she might pass for Katlyn's older sister. This was a woman who had aged gracefully.

"You're not selling anything, right? And no one's sick or in trouble, right?" She tipped her head toward him, looking out under the arch of her eyebrows. "Could I see some identification?"

Max handed her his driver's license and a business card, wondering if she planned to call the police. He took a deep breath and plunged ahead. "Let me explain. Royce is my patient in brief therapy. I'm trying to help him sort out some problems with your daughter Katlyn."

"Oh, so Kathy's in trouble."

"Kathy?"

"Katharine Lynn. She's been Kathy and Lynn. For a while she called herself Roxie. Kay. Rene. Lydia. As if changing her name would change her personality. Maybe it did. I just call her Kathy, no matter what she's calling herself. I'm used to her as Kathy." She handed back his license and card. "I'll never understand these women who try to live with all their names strung together. They're trying to hold on to something that's gone. It must be very confusing." She held the doll out to him, the blue glass eyes sparkling in the light. The nose hooked like a shepherd's staff. "Are the eyes straight? She's for a leukemia fund-raiser. The Wicked Witch of the West. They're doing *The Wizard of Oz* with puppets and actors. The real people are played by the actors, the supernatural ones are puppets. Afterwards they'll auction the puppets."

"Beautiful work," Max said. "There's evil in those eyes. True evil."

"Thank you. We're both just here doing our jobs, is that it? What do you want?" She set the face aside and picked up a length of black felt.

Max felt himself blush. Her tone put him on the defensive. "Psychiatry is often a study of a person's history. You can help me understand Katlyn's past."

"You want to know about Kathy, you ask her yourself. But if you want my advice, you'll throw out everything she says. What you'll have left will be the truth."

He nodded. "That's what I'm trying to do. That's why I called you."

Opal gave him a level look. "I see." She studied the cloth in her hands. "She was always a troublemaker. She was born with it, caused problems before she was born." Opal looked up and smiled. "But then, that's a perfect thing to tell you, isn't it? Psychiatrists specialize in troublesome people."

Max shifted in his chair. "We both know Katlyn won't tell me. Will you tell me some things about her?" And then it struck him. Families. Mothers and daughters. Why should this woman tell him the truth? How would he know if she was lying? He was making a perfect ass of himself. He could picture Katlyn and this woman laughing at him.

Opal folded the felt evenly, several turns, as if to make an origami. She picked up a pair of long scissors and clipped two arcs through the black felt. "She was always like a handful of air. You could never get a hold on that girl."

"That's a pretty accurate description," he agreed. "I'd like to know a little more about her father and sister." A place to begin. So far they were on the same track.

"Her sister?" She smiled and began folding another piece of felt. "Kathy doesn't have a sister. She didn't really even have a father to speak of."

The origami unfolded, a black cone. "She said her father was a doctor."

"A doctor?" Opal laughed. "I wonder who she took that from. I think Louis eventually became an electrician. He was living on his army mustering-out pay when I knew him. Just back from occupied Japan."

"Japan." Max thought of the flashcards. Sand, address, bean-jam bun.

"And she doesn't have a sister. There was only just Kathy and me." She began to fit the felt around a flat cardboard donut.

He began to relax and propped his elbows on the table, leaning toward Opal. He wanted her full attention. "Listen to this for a minute. Yesterday she told me her father was a doctor at Walter Reed during the war and collected Nazi helmets and human skulls. She said he installed a cannon of some type in her bedroom."

"You want me to verify the fact she lies?" She placed the cardboard donut on the table and looked up at him. "She lies. Anything else?"

"Have any idea where she'd get a story like that?"

Opal bit her lip for a moment. "When she was a kid I

283

knew a man, a black, who'd served in the European theater. His name was also Max, like you, but we called him Black Max because there weren't many Negroes in Reno in those days. Black Max had a collection. He'd lost a lung in some bombing attack. That's why he lived in Reno, the dry air. Ever live in the West, the wild part?"

Max shook his head.

"There's something about all that space that lets you believe in your fantasies. Black Max ran a casino, but what he really wanted was to open a World War II museum. Lots of people get that idea out there, rattlesnake museums, Indian museums, old car museums. As if anyone would come clear across the country to look at that."

"Did he have a cannon?" She nodded. "A sten gun?"

"I don't know what that is, but he had guns and all that stuff. I don't remember any skulls. Kathy used to play in his museum when I'd go over there. Reno's no place for children. There wasn't much else for her to do."

"Did you make puppets then?" But Max couldn't imagine the world needing that many puppets to support them for all those years.

"No. I made costumes then. I didn't start dolls until we moved here, so Kathy could go to college. Before that I was a dancer, a chorus girl. When I got pregnant I switched to making costumes. It's rather ungainly to be a pregnant chorus girl. Plays hell with the symmetry of the line." She uncorked a tube of glue and applied it to the cardboard crown. "You want to hear all that about me?"

"Sure," Max said. "If you don't mind." He watched as she placed the black cone onto the crown. Presto! A witch's hat. "I need background if I'm to make any sense of what she said. Like what you just told me about Black Max."

"Maybe she felt Black Max was like a father to her.

He and I kept pretty steady company for a number of years."

"What about you? Are you from Reno?"

"You want to hear all that?" She gave a little laugh. "It's a wicked, tawdry tale. It might cost you."

"Hey," Max said, "that's my business. Personal history. How people get where they are from where they began." But he wondered what she meant by cost. Opal's blunt manner was easy, but Max still felt he had stepped over the line. That could cost him.

"Well, you asked for it." She looked him over, cocking her head to see beneath the table, as if she were looking at his legs. She stood and walked around the table, sizing up Max. "Okay. One good thing about getting old, it's easier to see the story of your life. I would have had a very different life if my mother hadn't contracted tuberculosis when I was fifteen. But then, we'll never know what that life would have been, would we?" She waved the witch's hat at him as if it were a baton. "You sure you want to hear all this?"

"Yes. Of course." And he did want to hear, everything. "You never know what's going to be important. Tuberculosis."

She began tacking the loose ends of the hat down. "She just began to fade away. By the time I was seventeen, I knew she was dying. I hated myself for just sitting there watching her as if she were something in a bottle in a sideshow. I had some kind of breakdown, or maybe you'd call it a crisis, you supply the proper psychological term." She held the hat out in front of her, admiring it before tossing it on the table. "I took off. I ran away with a cowboy."

"I thought you said he was an electrician."

"Maybe you don't want to hear this part. It has nothing to do with Kathy."

Max gave her one of his most winning smiles. "All of this might be useful. You never know. The smallest detail can unlock a dream."

"Okay. Hand me that ruffle, would you?"

Max picked up a white ruffle lying in front of him and passed it across the table. Tuberculosis. Cowboy. Berkeley.

"Do you think ruffles are appropriate for a witch?" She experimented with the lace around the doll's neck. "Ruffles are okay for witches, don't you think?"

"Sure," Max said. "Gives her a bit of class."

"You betcha. A witch needs some class. Where was I?"

"You ran away with a cowboy."

"Winnemuca." It could have been a curse the way she said it. "Has all the charm of a car wreck. I thought I'd start my life all over. Instead I sat out there on the high desert for three years. I couldn't go back and I couldn't go forward. I was what they called ruined. I don't think that term exists anymore, but back then it was very important. Men and women didn't just *live* together, like Kathy and Royce. But no one cares on the high desert. Then, in late '40 we started to gear up for the war. We'd been what they call paper millionaires, not a penny in our pocket but plenty of money on the hoof. With that government contract we had a little money for a change, and I took a hundred dollars and left a note saying I was going to San Francisco."

Max gave her a knowing look. He could see the pattern and was sure Opal saw it too. This was a woman who turned her back on her problems. A heritage she knew she'd passed on to Katlyn. That's what she was really saying.

Opal stitched the ruffle to the tiny black bodice, carefully holding the yarn hair up in the back, like dressing a child. "I got as far as Reno. I was out of money, never mind how that happened, and got a job in one of those casinos as a chorus girl. I danced my ass off for years, all through the war. You'd think I was born with electric tap shoes on. All those soldiers spending money like the first night after Prohibition. With all the excitement of the war, time seemed to go so fast. All those years just became the same nightly show." She fluffed out the gray yarn hair over the ruffle. "Still evil?" She held the puppet out for Max's approval.

Max took it in his hands, turning the face in his palms and watching the light glint off the glass eyes. They followed him like a cat's eyes as he moved the witch around in the light.

"Try her on," Opal said.

Max stuck his hand up underneath the black bodice and the puppet twitched. He felt he was doing something slightly obscene. The Wicked Witch of the West twisted and bowed from the end of his hand, a small person scolding him. Max took it off. "She's wonderful." The face made him uneasy, a combination of soft feminine features with a hard masculine slant, accentuated by the hooked nose. He supposed a witch should look like that, dark forces more than sex. His eye caught the alligator again, tall and green against the far wall. "Is the alligator going to be in the show too?" He placed the puppet on the table and she tipped over as if dead.

Opal laughed. "There's no alligator in *The Wizard of Oz*. He's my Halloween costume. He's a bitch to wear, though. You have to look out of his mouth. I wear him to the Hookers' Ball." She picked up the Witch and examined her from all angles, adjusting the hang of the skirt, fluffing at the yarn hair. Then she placed it like a child in a chair next to her. "Where was I?"

"Reno." Max watched as she got up and moved to a large cabinet next to the alligator. She still had a dancer's movements. He thought he could see through her age, back to the days when she danced in Reno.

"A lot of girls just like me ended up in Reno. All of us were on our way to San Francisco or Hollywood and got sidetracked. You're probably too young to remember the war, but it was a different atmosphere then. There was so much excitement in the air it was like your life was on hold until it was all over."

"My father always talked about it like that too," Max said. His father's favorite stories were about parachuting behind the German lines, drifting through the air, listening for the whine of bullets. Families. What kind of stories would he have to tell Conrad? Elaine and her father's saw. Claire falling.

Opal pulled a bolt of iridescent material out of the cabinet and returned to her seat. "After the war everybody got married. I mean everybody. All us ruined girls were finding soldiers who were so glad to be back alive they didn't care if we were damaged goods or not. There was even some kind of cachet in being a performer, even if it was only Reno. Now it makes as much sense as the hula hoop fad, but I had to get married. I had to have a baby. I felt as if all those years took up no more space than a dress that had gone out of fashion. I found myself a husband, Louis Whiston, straight out of occupied Japan. I wanted to settle down and read Betty Crocker cookbooks cover to cover."

She began to clear the table, handing Max buttons, boxes of stuffing, ribbons, bolts of cloth. "Now for Oz himself."

Max put the stuff on the floor to either side of him. "Louis Whiston." Occupied Japan. Address, important.

"He was a bastard. Spoiled by those geishas, I'm sure. He married me, and within two months I was expecting. I'd held out all those years for a legal father for

288

this baby. And that," she flourished the long shears, "brought Louis Whiston to his senses. He felt he hadn't survived the war and a foreign country to come home and tie himself down to a child. He wanted his massages, and his food brought to him on a tray, and his bath drawn before I made passionate love to him every night. You'll have to help me now. Nothing in this world comes for free."

"What do you want me to do?" Max cast his eyes anxiously around the room.

"Oz. The actors play the real characters and Oz was a real man stranded without his balloon. The girl who plays Oz is about your height. Stand up."

"Oz is a girl?" He rose slowly from the chair.

"For the voice. Remember Oz's funny voice? This girl can do it perfectly. Would you mind taking your clothes off, just down to the essentials."

"What?" A wild image she was about to seduce him, and then that seemed awfully silly. She was old enough to be his mother.

"I'll do a refitting later in the week, but this will save time. You want something from me, and I'm giving it to you. I'd appreciate something in return. I'd like to measure your body, that's all. You're about Oz's size. It certainly won't hurt. Where was I?"

"You were pregnant." Max felt a bit foolish as he stepped out of his shoes. He shucked off his bulky sweater and jeans, folding them carefully over the arm of the chair. Opal ran the tape around his chest, down his legs, around his waist, along the length of his outstretched arms, all the while jotting down numbers in a fine hand. He wished he was covered with startling tattoos, birds taking flight off his shoulder blades, snakes slithering up his legs, sharks swimming beneath his ears. Her hands were the texture of soft kid gloves and as they glided over his body he stood stiffly, holding his breath, to see if she would measure his crotch. Her hands didn't feel like a woman's as she touched him, colder, smoother, professional.

"I should have known something was wrong even before the ceremony. All those other girls were getting married and whisked off to New Jersey to meet Mummy. But Louis was satisfied to stay in my little apartment in Reno. He had no plans to take me anywhere. He lived off his mustering-out pay and I kept dancing, for a couple of months at any rate. But of course, you know that couldn't last. He left me during a New Year's Eve party, just walked out into the night about eleven o'clock, took the car, and I didn't see him again for a number of years." She ran the tape across his shoulders one more time. "You can sit down now."

As he stepped back into his clothes, Opal took a quick look at her figures and began arranging the iridescent cloth on the table. "I was in a real jam, seven months pregnant wandering around like I had a medicine ball in my belly. He left me no money, and I'd never had any job but on the chorus line in the casino Black Max managed. Men are just like the seasons, when they leave you they're gone. There's no snow in the summer. When I finally realized Louis wasn't coming back, I went to Black Max. The rent was due. I walked in on my swollen ankles, so big I couldn't sit in a booth in a cafeteria. Kathy was a big baby, almost eight pounds. Black Max set me to work making costumes, sewing sequins on those skimpy bathing suits we wore. Setting feathers in caps, gluing rhinestones on gloves. I sat there and cried and sewed."

She gave him a quick look. "You're a psychiatrist. You know all this. Why do we rent the rooms in our heads to our enemies? I had to turn Louis out of my head like I would a bunco artist out of a hotel."

But Max didn't know, just in the same way he didn't

know why Patrice forced him out after Conrad was born. He could patch you up after a divorce, comfort you after a suicide attempt. But he didn't know what to do for himself, Patrice, Conrad. Claire. The more they improve telescopes, the more stars appear. But looking at the stars isn't the same as studying the planet you're standing on.

She unboxed a square of chalk and began drawing lines freehand on the shimmery cloth. "That's all I did for years. There's nothing like a pregnancy to flat-out ruin a dancer's body. And I think it must have done something to my mind as well. It's not like there weren't plenty of men in Reno, but I just wasn't interested in them anymore. I never rented Louis's room in my head to anyone else. I'd go down in the morning with the baby and repair the rips and tears in the costumes, make rhinestone capes. I did some designing, fountains of feathers in skullcaps, ropes of pearls, gauzy silks and netting. I became the costume crone. I started to gamble, something I'd never done as a dancer. I was as bad as an opium addict, a junkie. Black Max kept me staked, but if my luck got bad, he'd take us to the movies until it changed."

"You must have been very close." Max could see the backstage of the casino with early morning light glittering off the rhinestones and sequins, drafts of air tossing the ethereal feather boas. A fairyland for a little girl to play in. Opal had taken ordinary women and dressed them up like frosting on a cake. She was a magician, creating sexy princesses before her daughter's eyes.

Opal frowned. "I was working. There was nothing else to do with her until she was old enough for school."

"Is that why you came out here?"

"A child grows up." She reached for the shears and began cutting along the chalk outlines. "When Kathy was about fifteen, she started talking about joining the chorus line. That shook me out of my lethargy. For the first time I realized I had some responsibility other than to just keep her fed and dressed. And about that time Black Max moved away too, said he was going to Hollywood, but I've never seen him in any films. I couldn't see myself making costumes for my daughter, see her strutting on that stage, ending up the way I did. It seemed time to pass on through. The sand had run out of the hourglass."

Max watched as the arms and legs of the Oz suit emerged from the cloth and how the piece caught the light like soap bubbles as the shears moved through it. He thought of the arms and legs of the suit Pat sent back to him, the ripped-up hearts. "So you came to Berkeley." He wondered if Patrice would ever see the sand running out of her hourglass.

"I'd never even been to San Francisco, my original destination when I left Winnemuca. I suddenly realized just how much time had passed. Even the girls were different, not us tramps passing through hooking a quick and easy job. These girls had gone to school, were trained dancers. I didn't want Kathy to be a dancer, all that concentration and devotion to your body only to have the whole thing betrayed by a roll in the hay. I wanted Kathy to go to college. We moved out here, and I got a job with Theater Arts. They do a lot of costumes for stage productions. Kathy enrolled at Berkeley, and then the sixties took hold and ruined everything."

Max watched the growing pile of pieces for legs and arms. "What do you mean, ruined everything?"

"She went radical. We both just fell apart. It turned out I didn't like living in San Francisco, all boxed up like that after all the open space of Nevada. We moved over here where things felt more open. Kathy got involved in politics. I suppose she couldn't help it. It was in the air. She dropped out, disappeared for a couple of years. When she finally came back, she wasn't the little girl I raised. She was someone else, like she'd gone out and auditioned for a part and got it. She sheds her past like a snake sheds its skin. The difference between Kathy and a snake is that when the snake grows a new skin, you still have a snake. With Kathy you've got someone quite different. I'm not telling you much about your patient, am I?'' She flashed him a quick smile.

"No, really,'' Max said. "I want to know all of this. To help Royce I need to know more about Katlyn. This is exactly what I'd hoped to hear, things she won't tell me herself.'' He returned her smile. "What happened to her father?''

"Louis? Oh, it's hard to say about Louis. He just drifted through my life like a bad smell. When he left I felt like that woman who'd been beaten and raped and left for dead. When the police asked her to cooperate in catching the guy, she refused. She said, 'That man gave me the worst hour of my life. I'll be damned if I'll give him another minute.' Just like that.''

"Did she ever meet her father?''

"He popped in for a visit sometime in '59. Reno's biggest industry is divorce, but we never got around to it. One afternoon, it was real hot, he called from a gas station down the street. I had on some skimpy halter top and shorts. I said he could come over, and he was there before I had a chance to change. The surprise on his face was as fresh as if I'd opened the door with a gun in my hand. He kept staring at me, probably expecting me to look the same as I did on New Year's Eve when he left me, with my belly all billowed out like a wind-filled sail. Then Kathy came up behind me, and he kept staring at us as if he was having trouble with his vision.''

Max felt close to something now. "That was the first time she'd seen him?''

"Oh yes.'' Opal seemed very busy with the pieces of

cloth. "She asked about him from time to time, but I don't remember what I told her."

"Did you tell her he fought in the war?"

"Probably. I don't remember. I do know it was a mistake to let him come to the apartment. It was just a small place, and Kathy heard the whole thing. He wanted a divorce so he could marry some woman in Oregon. He could care less about Kathy. As far as he was concerned, she was my mistake. I wanted to get some settlement from Louis in exchange for his divorce." She sighed and rested her hands on the table as she looked up at Max with her clear, deep eyes. "We do things we can't explain as easily as we do things we don't understand. We'd been managing all right and I was throwing a fit to get my hands on Louis's money. I didn't need the money. I needed to throw a fit."

Her eyes reminded Max of the anorexic with the shark, the blues and greens of the swimming tattoo moving beneath her hair when she spoke about her mother. Mothers and daughters, fathers and sons. Men and women. American loneliness.

"It got very ugly." Opal picked up a spool of blue thread and reeled off a piece the length of her outstretched arms. She bit off the end. "For years Kathy kept picking up things from that fight and using them out of context." She threaded the needle. "One of her favorite sayings which she got stuck on, like when a baby is two or three and all they can say is 'no,' was: 'You're a big disappointment to me, Opal. You were never who I thought you should be.' "

Max could feel the pain of that line come right across the table at him. Opal looked into his eyes for a moment, then began basting two pieces of the suit together with the bright blue thread. Max wanted to say something to her, to ease the pain, when the phone rang and Opal excused herself.

Now the pieces began to fit together. Katlyn would remember that hot summer afternoon, maybe not as it really happened, but as a fulfillment of her dreams and curiosity. A fatherless girl would be fascinated by an encounter like that. Royce said she was a new movie every night, like the women in the Reno stage shows, while her mother continued the same year after year. Katlyn grew up watching the way fantasy and illusion worked, and her one encounter with her father confirmed what would happen when the magic failed.

He'd seen this story before. At some point, Opal and Katlyn imploded. No one can be everyone for someone else. Opal and Katlyn discovered that years ago, perhaps when Katlyn dropped out of Berkeley and disappeared. Although they lived across the bay from each other, there was no reason to believe they depended on each other anymore. The moon does more than provide the night with light. He could follow the logic now, everything but the flashcards.

Sofia's story about the Roms perishing by a blessing. A blessing turned into a curse. Katlyn's blessing was her imagination and independence. But that could become a curse if she wasn't sure she could ever be close to anyone. Africa was half a world away.

Opal stepped back into the room and remained standing in the archway. "I'm sorry," she said, "but I have to ask you to leave. I'm going to do a fitting in a few minutes and I really don't have anything else to say. I have to get back to work."

Max stood and extended his hand. "Thank you so much. You've been very helpful, truly. I think I've figured out something."

Opal gave him a wry smile. "So it all doesn't come from books, huh? You got what you came for?"

"Only the bare bones." He waved his hand at the worktable. "Sort of like the pieces for the Oz suit." He wished he could stay and see it finished.

"She's going to break up Royce's marriage, isn't she?"

"I don't know," he said. "That's for Royce to decide."

"The world's changed a lot in my lifetime," she said. "My parents were married, even after my mother died. Marriage got a little shaky in my day. Now I guess the term is serial monogamy. Not one marriage, but several, one right after the other."

"Do you think Katlyn wants to marry Royce?"

"Who can tell about that girl? After her husband left her, and I knew that wouldn't work out, you could just smell it on that boy, she said she preferred her affair with this married man. No futures. Just today. When you're young the future seems as far away as the stars." Opal shrugged. "But maybe she's changed her mind."

"That's what it's all about, I guess. What happens when we change our minds."

Her eyes became distant, thoughtful. Max knew she was reviewing her memories. "You know why I told you all this, don't you?"

"I think it's more than the fact that I'm Oz's size."

"Kathy and I are too far down the line for it to make any difference now. You can't put a scrambled egg back in its shell. But I wanted someone to know I'm sorry I didn't see things better back then." Her eyes swept the neighborhood. "I don't think anyone over here even knows I have a daughter. When she left, I tried to erase her from my mind, like Reno, Winnemuca, my parents. But you know, one is either haunted by history, or cast off from it. When you cut yourself off from your personal past and have no passion for the present, time stops."

A cinnamon cat nosed his shoe, a new cat Max hadn't seen before. He reached down and scratched its ears. Much as he wanted to stay, he knew he couldn't. He would return Opal's favor. He'd take her message with him back across the bridge.

"They're a new discovery for me," Opal said. "When I moved here, the place sort of came with a cat. Then more showed up." She began leading Max toward the living room. "I like them. Unlike children, cats reach a certain personality very quickly. And they stay that way. You can count on them to do the same thing over and over again." She smiled as she slid the door open for him. "It's the difference between cats and people."

Max thanked her once again as he crossed the porch and headed toward his car. He glanced at his watch, hoping there was time before his appointment with Ivy Ingram to check the messages on his machine. On with the day, onward through the fog, from one set of problems to the next, switching off and on like a stoplight. The past was a mysterious memory, changeable every day. The future was built on this shifting sand, hopes and dreams rooted only in memory. The present was the only thing anyone could control.

NOON

Katlyn once browsed a self-help manual entitled *Dress for Success* but abandoned it because she didn't feel the somber blue-gray business suits were her style. Dress For Stress became her motto. Since Royce hadn't come home last night, hadn't called this morning, she decided on her English riding habit to go to the pool. Beige jodhpurs, black waistcoat, a bright blue ascot, and her black derby. It might be just silly enough to raise her spirits. Even in San Francisco the outfit drew some looks. This made her feel better. When Royce was gone she often felt invisible. Why is it we can never really believe ourselves? Why must we always have someone tell us we are valuable?

Jody loved it, posing in the derby as Katlyn wriggled the long black boots with the delicate silver spurs off her feet. "Now this is a hat! You never see hats on women anymore. Berets, baseball caps. Never any real hats." Jody eyed herself in the mirror. "Thing is, I look great in hats."

"Let's start a fashion revolution. Wear hats to the market, hats to bed." Katlyn still kept the hats she'd given Dorre stored in various boxes in Royce's garage. But she never seemed to have the occasion, or perhaps the nerve, to wear them.

As she stroked sluggishly through her laps her mind felt loose again, flitting from idea to worry, worry to memory. What made her think, after all these years, she was ready to see the world? Alan. She'd had plenty of chances and never made it out of the country before. Why now? And alone? Alan. In some ways she'd always been alone, she knew that now. Having another person next to you while locked in your own thoughts only gave the illusion of safety. No one knows you're crazy unless you advertise it. Elaine.

Back in the locker room while they were dressing Jody said, "I have an idea I think you'll like."

"I'll go for any idea this morning." She straightened the cuffs on her white oxford shirt and picked up the ascot. Africa. Cairo. Kenya. Tanganyika. Victoria Falls. Madagascar. Had Alan ever gone to Portugal?

"I have to admit," Jody said, "there's plenty of selfish motivation behind this. But I was thinking we could mount a show of your work. Fabric sculpture and costuming."

"My work?" Katlyn turned to face her, the ascot dangling from her hand.

"It would be fun. It could even be a kind of comic, you know, Wardrobe for the Well Dressed Woman. We'll get some mannequins and dress them in your costumes and place them in the gallery like they're at a cocktail party. Or better yet," Jody gave a little skip, "just position them as if they're looking at the stuff in the gallery. What do you think?" Excitement played over her face.

"A show of my work in your gallery?" She was flattered. "God, Charlotte would die for that idea."

"So let's do it. Why not? I'm so sick of that overly subtle gray and mauve stuff I've been showing. Too trendy. This would be different."

Katlyn sat down on a bench. "What if I take that trip? You know, I haven't heard from Royce since he left yesterday. God knows what he and old Irene are up to. What he and his shrink talked about. I think he's trying to call my bluff."

"Like I said, selfish motivation. I don't see how you could mount a show of your work and go to Africa at the same time."

"You've been to Europe. Don't you think I should see a little of the world too?"

"Maybe it would do you good to take a trip, but I know Africa isn't the place. I told you, I think you should go to Paris. You could do that easily." Jody sat down next to her. "I can see the whole thing now. I even know some people you could get in contact with. A stopover in New York, then Paris. I bet even Charlotte would help with that. But I think this show could be a lot of fun. If Royce stays with Irene, all you really want is to do something different for a while, right? Why not do the show?"

Katlyn drew the ascot through her fingers, the silk caressing her skin. "But all those costumes are clichés."

"That's the beauty of the whole idea. You have dozens of those things. We'll set them up like George Segal's plaster people." Jody paced, working out her idea. "We'll get some Plexiglas cases, like Harris has, and put the masks and other stuff inside them like paintings. Here." She moved to the wall and described a square with her hands. "In this case is that fox-looking mask you did last year. And here," grabbed Katlyn by the shoulders, standing her up and positioning her in front of the imaginary box, "is a mannequin in your riding outfit. Some of them would make literal connections and some of them would be incongruous. Like it?" Jody perched on her toes, her hands together as if she were about to applaud.

Katlyn looked at the locker room wall, over to Jody, and down at her riding habit. "It might work. We could paint the mannequins' faces, streaks of blue, green, gold. War paint."

"Great!" Jody clapped her hands. "What are you doing right now? We could go to your house and see just what you've got. I can't really do anything until one anyhow. I had to take the Triumph in for a tune-up and it won't be ready until then."

"Nothing," Katlyn said. "I've spent this whole week doing nothing. Maybe I've got mental illness. You can't believe how much time I've wasted this week." If Royce wasn't home, at least Jody could keep her company. For a while. The hollow spot was back, spreading inside her chest. She was headed for a fall. She'd thought she was strong enough to accept Royce's decision, one way or the other. But it wasn't really Royce. This morning, waking up in the empty bed, she realized she missed Alan, not like Royce, a companion, but the knowledge he was out there in the world. She missed him the way she missed Dorre and Warren, the sound of their voices still echoing in her ears.

They gathered their gear and headed up Twenty-fourth Street. As they approached Charlotte's shop Katlyn said, "Let's not say anything to Charlotte just yet. He'll want to take the whole thing over." She wasn't convinced she would do the show for Jody, and Charlotte would put that much more pressure on her. To be shot at by snipers, mauled by a lion. At least Jody entertained the possibility of a trip. Paris. Charlotte got nervous when she went out of town with Royce.

Jody nodded. "Right. Charlotte will be great for the

finishing touches. But I'd like us to put the body of it together."

They turned into Elizabeth Street and Katlyn spotted Elaine sitting on her porch, a cassette player on her lap and "Miami Vice" blaring into the street.

"Hey!" Elaine used her arms like tongs to remove the cassette from her lap and place it on the porch. She skipped down the steps. "Major outfit! That's just great." And then she noticed Jody. She looked at Jody a long time while she slowly moved her arms with the red mittens behind her back. She smiled nervously. "Someone once said that if you stayed on your front porch long enough, everything in the world would pass by. So today I get Lady Di home from the hunt."

Katlyn smiled and waltzed through a modeling routine, tapping her foot to make the silver spurs jingle. "I forgot my riding whip, though."

"And your horse." Elaine backed up toward the porch stairs.

"I actually saw a woman in an outfit like that riding in Golden Gate Park once." Jody gave Elaine a warm, friendly smile.

"This is my friend Jody," Katlyn said. "She runs an art gallery and she wants to look at some of my stuff. Want to come along?"

"No." Elaine said. "I've got a lot of work to do." Her heel rested against the last stair, poised for flight.

"Come on." Jody said. "We need an outside opinion. All this art stuff can be pretty subjective."

Elaine shook her head and looked back to Katlyn again. "Remember I told you I was trying to learn to predict the weather? Well, it's supposed to rain this afternoon. A drop in barometric pressure. They say when the barometric pressure drops, it affects you. Some people get depressed. I'm going to kind of monitor that, see if they're right." She cut her eyes quickly from Katlyn to Jody. "Bye," she said. "See you." Then she turned, moving her arms in front of her, ran up the stairs and disappeared into the house. "Miami Vice" continued echoing down the street.

"God," Jody said as they entered Katlyn's house. "And she's so pretty. Such lovely long hair."

"Yeah." Katlyn sighed. "I've been talking to her some since she's been home. I give her cigarettes. But I guess we spooked her this morning."

"What happened?"

Katlyn looked for Royce or any sign he'd been there. As she put coffee on, she told Jody everything she knew about Elaine Lifton, and was surprised at how little there was to say. Her father died of a heart attack. She'd tried to kill herself by placing her hands on a table saw. The postman found her.

Jody cringed. A shiver went through her shoulders. "How gruesome. How painful. Why couldn't she just OD on pills like other people?"

"I don't know. I keep wanting to do something for her, but I don't know what to do." She'd wanted to do something for Dorre, for Warren. What could she have done for Alan?

Jody picked up her coffee mug and went into the bedroom. She started pulling out the costumes. "Oh, men's stuff too. That's great." She caressed Royce's leather jacket. "This will definitely add balance."

Katlyn sat on the edge of the bed. "How old is Ricky now?"

"Almost fifteen." Jody threw Royce's tuxedo and zoot suit on the bed. "I say we pick a dozen of the most colorful ones."

Katlyn knew very little about teenagers these days.

Ricky seemed to be about Elaine's age. "What's he interested in?"

"Who?" Jody inspected a midnight-blue velvet opera dress, scooped neck, muttonchop sleeves, and two-foot train.

"Ricky."

"I don't know. Girls. He wants a motorcycle." She held the dress against her body, posing in the mirror. "Could you do something with those lyretail feathers for this? Something across the shoulders and neck?"

"Girls. Motorcycles. What else?"

"What are you getting at, Katlyn? Come on. You're not paying attention here. It's your work, after all."

"I'd like to do something for that girl, but I don't know what people her age are interested in."

"Listen here. You don't want to get involved in something like that. You can't do anything for her. People have to do for themselves." She stroked the velvet like a kitten. "I'll tell you a story. My very wealthy great-aunt had advanced rheumatoid arthritis. She was a widow in her eighties, no kids. She set all her affairs in order, made visits to her friends, although she didn't tell anyone what she had in mind. Then she took a handful of sleeping pills. My uncle was passing through town and wanted to see her. When she didn't answer the bell, which he thought odd at her age and in her condition, he checked with the neighbors and they hadn't seen her for a couple of days either. So he broke down the door and finds her in bed, but still breathing. He has her rushed to the hospital and put in intensive care. And he keeps her like that until all the money is gone, and I'm talking a couple of years here. Finally they pull the plug and within a few hours she dies. She never regained consciousness. And that's what became of the family fortune."

"It's not the same," Katlyn said. "Your aunt probably

had a very full life behind her. Elaine has her whole life ahead of her. And if we only think about ourselves all the time, that gets either boring or depressing."

Jody tossed the velvet dress on the bed. "Don't go bleeding-heart on me. We've all got to save ourselves. Sure, that girl's a sad case, but you can't take away her pain. Why don't we think about mounting a show? If I can't light a fire under you, I'm going to tell Charlotte."

"I'd still like to try to do something for her."

Jody stuck an armful of clothes at her. "Fine. But today we're going to start to doxie these up and make them art."

As Katlyn paged through the clothes, combinations came to mind, colors for the war paint, arrangements of feathers and scarves. Maybe Jody was right. She was having enough trouble getting on with her own life. Alan. Royce. Elaine could figure out what she would do on her own time.

THURSDAY
AFTERNOON

Late Wednesday night Irene and Royce cleaned up the broken glass. As he picked through the rubble the objects in his house became familiar again. "Where'd this come from?" he'd ask, and she would tell him that ashtray had been a Christmas present from some friends they no longer saw, the vase was a souvenir from a trip they took ten years ago. Once identified, Royce could remember clearly and the years came flooding back to him. The Millers, who moved to Texas. The trip to Washington where they'd stopped to see glassblowers.

As he taped newspapers over the broken window he recognized one of the things he would miss, that sense of someone being beside him throughout those years. Someone to verify his history. *Remember when we . . .* Someone to fill in the blanks in his memory. *Where were we when . . .* Kat couldn't replace that.

The dishes were the biggest loss. She'd smashed half the dinner plates, a set they'd put together one cup, saucer, plate at a time, when Royce first opened the printing plant. Each job that made a profit over the initial estimate bought one piece. In the course of several months, Irene had assembled a matching dinner set for ten, soup bowls, serving platters, dessert dishes, the works. The broken plates now scattered across the floor, the refuse of their marriage.

As Royce washed the tomato juice from the fireplace he offered to replace the plates. Irene, sweeping the glass into a dustpan, didn't think the pattern was still available, wasn't sure she really wanted to keep the set if Royce wasn't going to be around. They discussed this as dispassionately as if they'd been talking about what they would eat for dinner. And then they heard Lindy's key in the front door.

Irene straightened, the broom in one hand, the dustpan in the other. A look swept across her face Royce couldn't read. But then Lindy stepped into the living room, her eyes going wild at the sight of the broken glittering glass.

Handing the broom and dustpan to Royce, Irene said to Lindy, "Your father wants to talk to you. I'm going to bed." She turned her back on them, ascending the stairs.

Royce stared at his daughter, the dark hair dyed orange at the tips, standing up on her head like the plates of a stegosaurus. She wore the uniform of the eighties: leather jacket, lacy hose under a frothy skirt, delicate loops of chains. At her age, Royce had worn blue jeans and madras shirts, his hair just beginning to flow over his collar. He kept trying to see Irene's features in his daughter's face, looking into her sulky eyes. He always thought his children much younger than they actually were. The roundness and firmness of Lindy's breasts startled him.

Lindy eyed the room. "Want some help?"

"Sure." Royce handed her the broom and dustpan.

"Was it fun, or simply destructive?"

"Think of it as therapeutic for your mother."

While they worked Royce told her about his decision, about Kat, about Irene's reaction. Lindy took the news in much the same manner as Todd. "No problem," she said. "Mom'll get over it. Will I get to meet your new lady?"

As Royce looked at his daughter he felt himself drifting far away, seeing Lindy as a stranger, and then with the blink of an eye seeing her as a baby, a child. But he couldn't seem to pinpoint who she was in that outfit, sweeping up the glass in the room. "We could have lunch," Lindy said, with the same authority as a businessman. And yet this was the same girl who wanted to hold a family service for their dog.

When Royce awoke on Thursday morning, Lindy and Todd had already left for school and Irene sat at the kitchen table nursing a cup of coffee. "I've called Daddy. He wants you to come up for dinner."

"What about you?"

"He wants to talk to you," she said. "If you go through with this, he'll have plenty of time to talk to me." And then she rose and picked up her purse and left the house. He heard her start the Lincoln and drive away.

He packed boxes, sorted papers, folded clothes into his suitcases. The clocks ticked loudly in his ears. Turning on the radio, he felt as if he were taking a long drive through the desert, from one coast to another. Whenever he glanced out the window, the neighborhood looked like a photograph, nothing moved except the wind in the trees and a few birds flitting through the hedgerows. What was a grown man doing in a suburban home in the middle of the day?

Leaving his family.

Absence, sand, blue, tomorrow.

His mind seemed unable to go any farther than that. He couldn't picture what would happen to him ten minutes from now. He couldn't imagine what Gerald would say, where Irene had gone, if his children would ever return from school. He had no idea where Kat was, what jobs they might be running on the presses at the plant. The sound of the clocks became the ticking of his heart. Radio music punctuated his thoughts with random words which held no meaning. Bangkok. Walking in the dark. Dance, dance, dance. Money changes everything. Come on, Come on.

He picked up a box and headed down the stairs, out to the Toyota. He couldn't stay in that house any longer. He felt displaced, like a button popped off a shirt, a sock lost in the laundry. Dance, dance, dance. Heart and soul. He began loading up the car to take his things to the city on his way up to Sacramento. The lyrics to the songs became jumbled. Nairobi Rodeo. Hit me with your best dance.

There was a dent the size of a tennis ball in the hood of the Toyota. He searched the driveway, the lawn, in the gutter of the street, but couldn't find the agate.

By two o'clock, the trunk and back seat of the car were filled with boxes and suitcases which meant nothing to him. He might have packed his car full of bricks for all he knew. But he felt better when he turned the engine over and pulled away from the house.

Don'tcha know destruction. Do you really wanna jump.

Driving across the bridge he watched the dirty pearl color of the fog bank hanging over the ocean. The wind was up and he wondered if it might rain. Songs rang with bells and synthesizer sounds, a pop choir. So Long. Dance the night away.

As he headed toward Noe Valley he rehearsed what

309

he would say to Kat, how he could explain unplugging the phone, what his plans might be. He thought of taking her up to Sacramento to meet Gerald and Margaret but knew his courage would fail him at the last minute, and he'd drop her in a bar or motel before he got anywhere near the house. She'd love that, dropped off as if she were an embarrassment. *We could have lunch*, Lindy'd said. Sure, in Cairo or Capetown.

Absence, sand, blue, tomorrow.

On Twenty-fourth Street he passed Saving Grace and pulled into the first parking spot he could find. He couldn't face Kat just yet, but perhaps Charlotte could tell him something, give him some piece of advice. He'd never understood it, but somehow, if anyone knew what Kat was thinking, Charlotte would. And who knows, she might even be at the boutique. It might be easier to talk to her with Charlotte around. He was surprised at how much he suddenly feared her.

The first drops of rain began to fall as Royce stepped into the shop. "Ah, my man, my man," Charlotte said when he looked up from a basket of beads he was sorting. "What have we here?"

"Got a minute, Charlotte?" Today Charlotte sported evening clothes, a black bow tie, white dinner jacket the color of eggshells and black trousers with the shine of ribbon up the side. A red carnation sat on his lapel. Charlotte's smile was reassuring.

With persuasive charm Charlotte bustled the customers out of the store, ringing up a sale for one hundred fifty-nine dollars in the process. Royce idly inventoried the merchandise while he waited, a lot of the stuff familiar, Kat's work. Charlotte stepped briskly behind him and flipped the Closed sign over the door. "We've got to talk," he said.

Royce looked through the glass door at the rain pelting the street. He wondered if it would hail.

"I don't want us to be disturbed. I think we have a few things we need to discuss, n'est-ce pas?" He motioned Royce through the beaded curtain into the back of the shop. "Refreshments? Champagne? Irish whiskey? Columbian gold? Coke? What's your pleasure Royce?"

"How about a new life?" He slumped down into a deco wing chair. "Do you know what's going on these days?"

"Champagne. It'll raise your spirits. Even the Perrier boys will take a little champagne. Not that this is a festive occasion." Pulling a bottle from the small refrigerator, he worked the cork out slowly and aimed it at the ceiling. With a shot the cork blew off and Charlotte brought the bottle to his lips, pursed like a kiss, and whistled across the open neck. Foam billowed up and frothed around the lip of the bottle, then receded. "Cordon Negro. Good afternoon champagne." He reached long-stemmed goblets from a shelf and blew dust out of the bowls.

Champagne in the afternoon. Why not. "Seen Kat today?" Perhaps he would drive back from Sacramento and find her already gone. Africa.

Charlotte shook his head. "You've got to do something with her. You can't let her take off for Africa or God knows where she thinks she's going. She could get in a lot of trouble. I mean, if she wanted to go someplace civilized, that's another question. But this is insane." Charlotte flourished his glass. "Africa. Take her to London. But Africa? Do you watch TV? It's a mess over there." He reached out and cupped Royce's chin in his palm. "You don't really want her to leave you, do you?"

"No," Royce said. "But maybe she wants to leave me."

Charlotte sighed and settled himself back into a matching wing chair. "I don't understand you two. What's the problem here?"

"Love and money."

"That's no problem. That's paradise. I just can't stand to watch two people I care about make jackasses out of themselves."

"You think I like it? It's not exactly my notion of a good time."

"Well," Charlotte sipped slowly from his glass. "What are we going to do about it? Hum? Just sit here and toast the finish of a fine relationship? Is this the way you want it to end? In the back room of a second-hand shop?" He cast his eyes around the clutter of his office.

Royce felt as if his spirit were bundled around his ankles like hobbles for a horse. "That's not why I came over here. Not to toast the end. I've got half my life packed in my car parked up the street. I'm on my way to Sacramento to tell my father-in-law I'm divorcing his daughter. I'm likely to find out by the end of the evening that I no longer have a marriage, a job, an income, or a lover. That's not exactly playing with the cards stacked in my favor."

Charlotte fingered his pencil-thin mustache. "My interest in this isn't all just personal feeling, you know. I think the world of Katlyn and would truly lose a good friend and companion if she were to leave. And, if the truth be known, I'd probably also lose this shop. All that out there," he pointed to the beaded curtain separating the back office from the display area, "all that is really Katlyn's doing more than mine. She has taste, talent. I can pretty much count on selling everything she makes. The rest of it's pretty sketchy. Come here." He rose and parted the beaded curtain and ushered Royce back into the main room.

"Now this is lovely," Charlotte said as he held up a

perfect miniature tin soldier. Royce examined the figure, a Confederate private, complete with the cap angled forward, crossed belts for powder horn and shot bag, single-loading rifle held cautiously to the side, almost as if the little tin man were leaning on it. The paint was carefully applied to give the uniform a worn air, the face a tired expression. The whole thing was less than three inches high.

"I have forty of these little beauties. Look here, Sherman, Grant, Robert E. Lee. A wonderful set, perfect in every detail. And one of these days I'll make a lot of money on them. Just the right person will come along and see them and be able to pay the price to appreciate them indefinitely."

Royce gave him a quizzical look. "So?"

"So, until that person comes along, I pay a lot of the bills with the sale of the stuff Katlyn makes for me. And do you know how I came upon these?" He picked up the figure of Grant, the hat cocked rakishly over one eye, seated astride a dappled horse complete with tiny saddlebags. "While you're at home being the dutiful husband and father, Katlyn and I go to garage sales. She's got an eye, no doubt. She found these at the bottom of a trunk filled with baby clothes. Who would suspect these darlings would be under baby clothes?"

Royce looked into Charlotte's eyes, then cast his glance around the shop.

"That's right," Charlotte said. "Oh, we started this long before she met you. When she was married to Alan, whom I liked, don't get me wrong, I'd call her up sometimes to see if she'd go with me. I felt sorry for her, the way Alan ignored her. I asked her if she'd like to go shopping, and you know all women love to shop. I'd take her around with me on Saturday and Sunday mornings and she'd spot the damnedest things. So," he returned

Grant to his place in the display, fussing with the little tin figures until he felt they were positioned just right. "So, you might say I have a vested interest in seeing her happy." He looked Royce directly in the eye. "And she's happy with you."

Royce handed back the Confederate private and ran his hand through his hair. "I'll tell you what, Charlotte. Anything you can work out would be fine with me."

Charlotte's eyes went wild. "There's nothing I can do! You're the one. I mean, if she were in love with me, well, I'd consider it. But she's not. I just want you to know I'll help any way I can."

Royce took another sip on his champagne and felt the bubbles rushing up into the dome of his brain, bathing his mind. Charlotte motioned him back through the beaded curtain and poured more champagne. Royce smiled when he thought of Gerald and Margaret and Charlotte and himself all sitting down to dinner together. He imagined Irene and Kat bustling back and forth from the kitchen with plates of potatoes and roast, each wearing a little black-and-white French maid's outfit. Margaret discussing the roast, Charlotte appraising the stemware.

"Would you believe this, Charlotte," he settled himself back in the wing chair, "I didn't even know about her husband, Alan, until the other night. Never even heard of him before."

"One thing you can say about Katlyn: she's either very private or very stupid. She claims she didn't know a thing, not until everything was all over. Can you imagine?" Charlotte snorted incredulously.

"What do you mean? What didn't she know?"

"Alan was gay." Charlotte looked at him sharply. "It's not that unusual, you know. There are gay men who are married."

"Alan was gay," Royce repeated. "He ran away with a travel agent."

"Guerrero," Charlotte said. "I finally, just last night, got a hold of Guerrero. I'd been frantic, you know, with the AIDS thing and all that. Poor Alan. He was stabbed, a street mugger. That's New York for you. John Lennon shot in front of The Dakota. Now Alan, on his way back home from a party. But please don't tell Katlyn. I'd rather do that myself."

Absence, sand, blue, tomorrow. Man, woman, bean-jam bun. Bean-jam bun. That sounded lewd to Royce, sticky sweet like a woman. Alan moved to New York, but someone in the city mailed her messages about absence, and bean-jam buns. He realized he'd been hoping Alan sent the flashcards, some piece of intimacy left over from their marriage. His hands felt numb and useless, and for a moment he was afraid he would drop and break Charlotte's antique goblet. The thought of more shattered glass nauseated him. "New York. Gay. She just said he was dead. Not that he was gay." He was lost. "Why all the secrets?"

Charlotte flourished the goblet again. "Tell me, if your wife were going to leave you for a woman, would you want the world to know? Would you tell me all about it? Or would you try to just block it out, and go on like nothing ever happened?"

Royce laughed. "Maybe you're the only person I'd tell."

Charlotte smiled. "Well, yes, maybe you would tell me. But you know what I mean. Ego damage and all that."

Royce thought this over. On one hand what Charlotte was saying was perfectly plausible, and yet at the same time ridiculously impossible. All those private, intimate details couples know about each other. The way Irene

315

hated to be seen seated on the toilet. The electric, tender spot on Kat's belly. "She must've known."

"Not every gay man is as obvious as I am. Many are very discreet about their affairs. And some, like Alan, are a little confused as to what they want in the world. If you want my opinion, I don't think there was much love lost between Katlyn and Alan. I think they both got exactly what they were looking for at the time. Some part of Alan wanted a straight life and I think Katlyn wanted to get out of the singles bars for a while. So they met, and both felt the time was right for them to get married. A simple situation of two people wanting the same thing at the same time, but not necessarily wanting each other."

"Jesus." His thinking was at least ten steps behind. Not the thought of Kat and the unimaginable Alan, but reflecting on his life with Irene. Irene's belief she'd gone to college to get married. His use of her as a way out of Vietnam and a ticket to a new life. People wanting something at the same time, but not necessarily each other.

"More champagne?"

Royce held out his glass, but he was sure he would no longer savor the stuff. A thick taste enveloped his tongue. He looked at Charlotte, who opened his hands and shrugged his shoulders as a sign of the incomprehensibility of the world and its desires. "You talk about love and money," Charlotte said, "but there's also need."

"Need," Royce repeated. The Rolling Stones: "Satisfaction." You can't always get it. What did he need? What did he want?

"Of course," Charlotte said. "Need. Alan was a very strange guy. I think he needed to feel guilty about being gay, at least for a while. I know he felt guilty after he married Katlyn, and when he left her he felt even more guilty, the way he deceived her."

"Guilt." Royce seemed to have lost the power of

speech, reduced to a word or two as Charlotte chattered away. He wondered what Alan had looked like: tall, short, thin, husky, dark, light.

"Did Katlyn ever mention the Quintessential Last Remark? It's a joke with us."

"What?" The run of all those syllables seemed impossible to comprehend. "The what?" He felt as if there were marbles in his mouth, bubble gum stuffed in his ears.

"The Quintessential Last Remark. There was an exposé on TV a couple of years ago. A reporter was sent to a nursing home to file a story on the care and treatment of the elderly. He found this old woman wandering in circles," he waved his hand, describing an oval in the air ahead of his wrist, "repeating over and over again 'How much do I owe you? How much do I owe you? How much do I owe you?' She was reduced to her quintessential phrase, the last thing she had to say to the world. Katlyn and I wondered what our last phrase to the world would be. There are lots of them." Charlotte let out a laugh. "Everyone has one. 'It's on the list.' 'I'll do it tomorrow.' 'It's not my fault.' 'Everything's going to be all right.' If Alan had a quintessential last remark it would be 'It's all my fault, I'm sorry. It's all my fault, I'm sorry.' " Charlotte laughed again. " 'I didn't know the gun was loaded.' 'The check is in the mail.' 'I won't come in your mouth.' 'Not my wife.' What would yours be?"

"Help." It was the first word which flashed through his mind.

"Help? Okay, 'Help.' But I must admit, you don't strike me as that type at all."

Royce shook himself out of his confusion. "Well, maybe not 'Help.' It was just all I could think of. What's yours?"

"Mine changes. I haven't hit the bottom line yet.

Probably 'Sex, Drugs, and Rock and Roll.' I know a guy who's convinced his will be 'The one with the most toys wins.' He's very materialistic. Then there's 'Health foods and heroin forever' and 'Quiche goes better with coke.' "

"What's Kat's?" He knew what Irene's would be: "But what about me? What about me? What about me?"

"I'd guess 'A New World Every Morning.' She likes the idea you can start over. But I don't think she's hit the bottom line yet either."

Royce helped himself to more champagne, puzzling over what Charlotte had been saying. "So Alan left her because he was gay and his marriage to Kat was a mistake, right?" New York, bean-jam bun. Kat was a widow. Kat was a homeowner.

"Something like that. But, my, he was dramatic about it. Walked in one night all rigged out like he was headed for the jungles of Vietnam. Guerrero plays the tough guy and threatens Katlyn with a knife. Isn't that ironic? He should have used that knife to save Alan. No point in threatening Katlyn with a knife. Anyhow Alan laid the news on our lady and packed a couple of bags, and by morning he and Guerrero were on their way to the Big Apple. You said love and money before. Well, money is very necessary to some love affairs. Alan's father had just died. Guerrero's got an inheritance. They both took off to start again."

"What kind of money did Alan have?" Money again. Why was he so obsessed with money? His money, her money, Gerald's money, Alan's money. Money changes everything. Maybe that would be his last remark.

"Nothing much. He sold real estate. He put together the deal for this shop." Charlotte gave a wave of his hand, indicating the store as the boundaries of his world. "Alan's father was old San Francisco. His mother divorced him and split when Alan was young, just walked out and Alan never saw her again. His father never remarried and finally contracted Parkinson's disease. Alan put him in one of those nursing homes when he married Katlyn. He was always pretty much under his father's thumb. He decided to get married about the same time he decided taking care of his father was too much for him and he would have to commit the old bastard. This was before he even met Katlyn. It was one of those whirlwind courtships, they were married less than six months after they met. Maybe an attempt to please his father. Then, when his father died, he walked in and told Katlyn he was leaving. Without his father I guess he felt he could get on with his life, the way he wanted to lead it, not the way his father wanted him to be."

"What about the house? Did you know Alan Quales sold Kat a house in the Sunset for a dollar?" He wondered what Alan had looked like, why there was no picture of him in Kat's desk. That bill of sale for one dollar was two years old.

"It's the AIDS thing again. A lot of my friends have made their wills, even if they're perfectly healthy. Sales tax is less expensive than an inheritance tax. I'm thinking of doing it myself, writing up sales slips to all my friends," he waved his arm to indicate the shop, "for all that."

"So she didn't know he wanted her to have the house?"

"Of course not. I think she should invest that money, not blow it on some ridiculous trip to Africa." Charlotte reached for an inlaid box and drew out a lid of dope and some papers and began to roll a joint. "It had been paid for years ago, and Alan was sure he'd never return to San Francisco. He'd spent his whole life here and he wanted a new life with Guerrero."

"I see." Royce felt the whole image come clear, like focusing a projector. Of course. Kat never expected anything of Alan, she just wasn't that type. Without any more warning than an earthquake, her life changed. Her husband leaves her, then dies and gives his house to her, and what's she supposed to do with her life? That's what she'd been saying the other morning at dawn. The surprise of being cut loose from the life she thought she'd been living. "Money" would never be Kat's quintessential last remark, although money changes everything. So she comes up with this plan to go to Africa. A new world every morning. It was all really very straightforward, once you knew all the background. She wasn't playing games here. She just hadn't given him all the information. Except for the flashcards. "I see," Royce said again, nodding his head.

"What *I* see is some fast thinking going on over there, my man. Like those movies of flowers blooming shot with time-exposure film. What do you see?" Charlotte looked truly concerned.

"I, I just see." And he could see it, but he wasn't sure he could explain it to Charlotte. "Until now I've felt as if I've been dancing in the dark, not knowing what the hell's been going on. I mean, she told me, sort of, but I didn't understand what she was talking about." Charlotte must know about the flashcards, maybe Charlotte even sent them. That thought flipped like a coin back and forth in his mind, one side consoling him, one side bothering him. He could see Charlotte and Kat touring Japan, and that was preferable to worrying about some new, strange man, a man Royce couldn't imagine. It was better than imagining Kat alone in a foreign country. But the image troubled him. He looked closely at Charlotte for a moment. Charles Lawrence, not Charlotte. Charles Lawrence, a man close to his Kat. For a moment he tried to drop all the campy gay trappings and see Charlotte as a man, as Kat's best friend. Why would Kat choose a gay man to confide in? Man, Charles Lawrence. Perhaps he was staring at the unimaginable man he'd feared for two years now, the other man in Kat's life.

Charlotte fired up the joint then straightened in his chair, fingering his mustache again. "I have to tell you something, Royce. Something between the two of us. You mustn't tell Katlyn."

Royce accepted the joint and watched as a sad and serious expression came over Charlotte's face. "Agreed." Charles Lawrence. His scalp began to tingle.

Charlotte stood and walked over to his desk, his fingers straying over the papers and pens lying about. He picked up a pencil and began rolling it between his fingers, the bright yellow, a twitching flash. "I feel responsible," he said at last. "I suppose that's why I'm so worked up about this Africa idea. You do something, you have some fun, and then suddenly a world of shit hits you." He turned to look at Royce. "Ever play with firecrackers when you were a kid?"

"Sure." But he didn't know what firecrackers had to do with it. The tingling of his scalp was now an itch. He took a leisurely drag, more like inhaling a cigarette.

"One time, I was about twelve, this other kid and I set off this M-80 on the sidewalk. They make a hell of a bang and we thought we'd get a big kick out of it. I set the fuse and backed off, but this kid wanted to see it blow a hole in the sidewalk, or something. It went off in his face. He lost an eye." He turned to face Royce. "Maybe my line should be 'It's all my fault, I'm sorry.' I'm sorry for what I did to that kid. I'm sorry for what I did to Katlyn and Alan."

His hands were going numb again. "What you did?"

Charlotte straightened the carnation in his lapel and rocked up on the balls of his feet. "I brought Alan out of the closet. It was when he was putting the deal together for this shop. It was right here in this room. I seduced him. I was mad for him, couldn't contain myself at all. He was nice enough, but I guess I wasn't his type. But I was the first, I know that. He'd hovered around the edges of the gay community for years but never took the plunge before. His life might have been different if I hadn't pursued him so." His feet tapped restlessly through the motions of a dance step. "Monday morning quarterbacking. I opened a door in Alan. I ruined his marriage with Katlyn. She didn't suspect a thing, and when they planned that trip Alan met Guerrero. That was it. Within a couple of weeks Alan threw over Katlyn, quit his job, rented his father's house, and went to live with Guerrero in New York. So you see," he looked levelly at Royce. "You might never have met Katlyn if I hadn't, hadn't." His voice trailed off.

"It's okay." Royce passed back the joint and reached for the champagne, but the bottle was empty.

Charlotte pulled another bottle out of the refrigerator and went through the ritual of opening it. The pop of the cork reminded Royce of the explosion of an M-80. When Charlotte filled his goblet the foam bubbled over and down his hand, splashing on his pants like drops of rain.

Royce tried to imagine it, two men making love in this room. With no image of Alan he could only concentrate on Charlotte, Charles Lawrence, whom he'd known for two years now. He'd been over to the house for dinner, the three of them had gone to plays together, openings at Jody's gallery, a couple of parties. Yet in all that time, although he knew Charlotte was gay, he'd never given a thought to Charlotte's sex life. Somehow that had escaped him. Gay was a fashionable life-style, and even with the AIDS articles in the paper, he'd never considered Charlotte in a sexual context. They fuck like bunnies, the libertine image of gays in this city. Yet he'd never thought about Charlotte fucking, Charlotte kissing, Charlotte holding someone in his arms. Charlotte in love.

He imagined a nude male bent over the arm of the wing chair, the smooth marble of his ass and upper thighs, the developed muscles of his back and shoulders. And Charlotte, in his tuxedo, bending over that nude body, desiring the man, making love to the man, screwing. He tried to reverse the image, Charlotte bending over the arm of the wing chair, Charlotte's shoulders, dimples in Charlotte's ass, with some well-built boy standing behind him. The pit of his stomach tightened. What if Charlotte had loved Alan with the intensity he felt for Kat? What if Charlotte had lost a chunk of himself when Alan left for New York with Guerrero?

His groin tightened, the small of his back became electric. Imagining Charlotte screwing gave him an erection. He could see the rough hands of a man against the flat nipples of Charlotte's chest, muscle on muscle. He could feel the heft of Kat's breast in his palms, feel the heat of her heart beneath them. Velvet, smooth and elastic. His lips surrounding her nipple, his tongue ticking the hard bud against his teeth.

He sipped off the top of the champagne and felt the bubbles burning his brain. He shifted in his seat, recrossing his legs, his erection pulsing. Charlotte seemed lost in the drifting smoke of the joint. Charlotte's body, Charles Lawrence, the muscles hard and sculpted from hours at the gym. Charlotte wasn't the other man. Charlotte would want boys, pretty boys for an aging queen. Charlotte screwing a boy. Kat's tall and mannish body might be attractive to gays, not petite and delicate like Irene. But Kat was still a woman, not a pretty boy. And that was the reason her marriage to Alan failed. He was glad he didn't have to feel competitive with Charlotte. "You might feel you ruined their marriage, but if Alan was happy with

Guerrero, he should have thanked you. As you said, if it weren't for you, I might not have met Kat. So I thank you. If Kat doesn't know, she can't hold it against you."

"I don't think she knows. And I've tried to take care of her, make sure she's getting along okay in the world." He laughed. "Of course, it helps that she's talented. But even if she couldn't sew on a button, I'd have still tried to take care of her, given her a job here in the shop or something."

"I know," Royce said. "You've been a good friend to her. That's why I came in here this afternoon. She trusts you."

"Isn't that an irony." Charlotte straightened a crease in his trousers as he sat back in his chair. "She just sort of floated for a while after Alan left, waiting. But she's stopped floating now, stopped waiting for the other shoe to drop."

Royce stood and stretched his back. He kept trying to imagine the scene of the unimaginable Alan walking in and leaving that same night. Actually, it wasn't much different than what he'd done last night with Irene. The unimaginable Alan, tall, short, dark, light. Alan and Charlotte. Alan and Kat.

He checked his watch. Jesus, he should have started for Sacramento an hour ago. There was no time now to drop his things at the house. It was going to be difficult enough with Gerald, who was as punctual as a machine, let alone what would happen if he was an hour or more late for dinner. Gerald would expect him at six—sharp. He still feared Gerald, not exactly the best attitude for this evening.

"Charlotte," he said. "Listen, I've got to go to Sacramento and deal with my father-in-law." It was still possible Charlotte sent the flashcards, or knew who did. "Tell me something, ever think of going to Japan?"

"Japan?" Charlotte looked confused. "Hell no. What would I do in Japan?"

"China?" But the printing looked Japanese to him.

Charlotte shook his head. "I thought we were worried about her running off to Africa."

"Absence, sand, blue, tomorrow. Bean-jam bun?"

Charlotte made a face. "Pistachio. What the fuck?"

"Right, never mind. Some other time." He ran his hand through his hair and could hear Gerald's voice echoing in the back of his mind. There was no way to tie up everything at once. He'd ask Kat about Japan, there was no other way to do it. He felt like a definition he'd once seen for a net. "Net: a collection of holes tied together with string." It was a suitable definition for this week, at any rate. "Charlotte, can you do me a favor?"

Charlotte looked up at him, waiting instructions.

"I really should talk to Kat, but I've got to get my marriage straightened out. Or rather, I'm getting out of my marriage and I have to face the music on that one. I unplugged the phone the other day and I don't know if she's discovered it or not. Can you go up there for me and tell her I'll be back tonight? Tell her not to worry. Tell her I'm going to be there through Friday." He ran his hands down the beads of the curtain. "Be sure to tell her Friday. That's important to her."

Charlotte drained his goblet. "What's the old Puritan saying? Speak for yourself, Miles Standish? Or is it John Aldrich? Fred Schwartz. I don't know."

"Come on, Charlotte. 'Help.' Remember?"

"May I remind you she wants to settle things with you. It's all this by proxy stuff she wants to get shuck of. I think she'd stay if she knew you'd be here for her. Don't forget, she's not going to Africa, she's merely threatening to go. Sometimes that girl's a lot of bluff." He helped himself to more champagne. "Or at least, I hope that's the way it plays."

"It's going to be all worked out tonight. It's just that I unplugged the damned phone. I can work this out, I know I can." But he felt his scalp itching again, his hands beginning to sweat. Gerald and Margaret. He could see them sitting in their living room, as formidable as the gigantic statues on Easter Island. "Just help me out until I get back from Sacramento. Okay?"

"Sure," Charlotte said. "I love patching together my friend's love affairs. It's almost as good as being in love myself."

"You're her friend. She trusts you."

Charlotte gave a sharklike smile. "Some friend I am. You might be better off asking me to meet your wife. I seem to be real good at busting up marriages." The smile vanished. "Sure, I'll go up there. Who knows? If you two work it out, I might have to find something else to feel guilty about."

Royce touched his shoulder, a thank you. Charlotte stood and hugged Royce, a warm, friendly embrace. "Yeah. Okay. I'll tell her."

THURSDAY
EVENING

After Jody left around one o'clock, Katlyn lost all sense of purpose. She stripped out of the riding habit and threw it on the bed with the rest of the costumes but couldn't decide what to do with the rest of the day. Still waiting. Always waiting. Jody's enthusiasm for the show had buoyed her spirits; but when Jody left, the day dissolved. Katlyn pulled on her bathrobe, more for the comfort of the thing than warmth. Paris. Tsavo Wildlife Park. A show of her costumes and designs. Wandering through the house she picked up the Michelin map, books on Africa, her passport, a world atlas, Hemingway novels set in Paris. All these things ended up on the bed amidst the costumes, and she found herself curled up with Dagmar looking at a heap of unrelated objects.

"There is the future," she told the dog. "All on top of the bed Royce and I sleep in. Correction: Slept in." Her eyes swept the room. "Pick an object, Dagmar, any one of those things and that's what we'll do. Maybe." The dog looked at her, then laid her head across Katlyn's lap.

Elaine had been right. The rain began about three in the afternoon, a drizzle at first, then steady sheets of water flowing down the windowpanes. Sharp gusts of wind rocked the house, moving through the walls like minor earthquakes. Dorothy and Toto had been swept off to Oz in a storm like this. She was sure she and Dagmar wouldn't be so lucky. As she lay on the bed, she felt her soul darken when the sun and sky disappeared behind the storm clouds. A drop in barometric pressure. Some people get depressed. The wind picked up around four, tossing the branches of the trees like a handful of snakes. At five she thought she heard thunder. By six she was sure the best she could expect from Royce would be a letter mailed a few days from now telling her where to send the rent check.

A tattoo rang out on the buzzer. Royce would never ring the bell, and as she lay on the bed listening to a rough version of what she thought must be either Morse code or "Camptown Races," she knew only Jody or Charlotte would stand in a rainstorm beating a song on her doorbell. The erratic buzzing sent Dagmar into wolflike howls, so Katlyn swung her feet off the bed and went to the front door. Charlotte stood there under a yellow slicker with a wicker picnic hamper and his shoes filled with water.

"The year I was born they organized the CIA, so don't try to pretend you're not home." Charlotte moved past her, splattering water in his wake. "You'd think if someone were to take the trouble to bail you out of bed," he cast a glance at her hair, snarled and ratted, and the bathrobe, "the least you could do would be to open the door. One more verse and I would have had no choice but to break in."

He shoved the wicker picnic hamper at her, stepped out of the slicker and his shoes, and walked into the bedroom. "I'm going to borrow some dry clothes," he called back through the rooms.

Katlyn followed and took the tuxedo jacket and the black trousers from him and hung them to dry in the shower while he rummaged in her closet. "You know," she said, "I might not have been home."

Charlotte shot her a look. "Dressed like that? I bet you haven't even brushed your teeth today."

She snapped at him, "I've been out. I've been busy."

"I'll bet," Charlotte retorted. "You've certainly been busy making a mess of this room."

She fiddled with the sash on her robe. "Charlotte, you ever have days with holes in them?"

"Like holes in your socks or underwear?"

"Exactly like that. There's the entire sock, the entire day, and right down the middle of the big toe is this big rip, a hole. Kind of ruins the sock, don't you think?"

Wrapped in the silk kimono Royce had given her for her birthday, Charlotte peered around the room. "Where do you keep your socks? On the bed perhaps?"

Katlyn pointed to the dresser and he slid out a drawer and picked a pair of red thermal socks which he pulled over his pale feet like gloves. He groomed his mustache with his fingers and patted at his hair. "I could catch pneumonia," he said. "You'd feel very badly if I caught pneumonia because you wouldn't get out of bed. Got any vitamin C?"

She reached for a bottle from the medicine cabinet, and he washed down a handful of pills with water. "How about a fire? Get the damp off." He walked briskly back to the living room and began crumpling newspapers and tossing them on the grate.

329

"What are you doing here?" She felt completely useless in her own home, watching Charlotte busily making himself cozy. Something was afoot. Charlotte generally could be counted on to stir soup if there was a comfortable chair next to the stove, a glass of wine, and the flame was low enough so he wouldn't have to think about the soup boiling away.

Charlotte continued to fuss with the fire, keeping his back to her. "This might be superfluous," he said. "I was once described as the kind of fellow who brings wild flowers to cheer up a person having an allergy attack." He looked over his shoulder at her. "But judging by your outfit, you're getting a slow start on the day."

"So what? That hole in the day I was talking about. So I took a little mental health time. You're the one who called it the emotional flu. You got the flu, you go to bed." But that wasn't the truth. Time in bed was stopped time, the night of the soul never ending even as the sun rose and set. The world went on without you.

Charlotte laid some kindling on the newspaper and struck a match, catching the corners of the paper. "That's sheer self-indulgence. One is not allowed to go to bed with the emotional flu, dear heart. The only cure for the emotional flu is work."

"Ever hear the old saw 'All work and no play'? I can't work. I don't know what I'm doing. After Royce left last night I was going to go down to Danny's theater. Since he got back, he's on this big Japanese filmmaker trip. He's showing *Woman in the Dunes* this week. I thought Danny and I could fool away the evening while Royce handled things in Marin. But somehow I ended up just sitting on the couch petting Dagmar. Thank God for dogs. Dogs impose structure. Dogs need to be let out, let in, fed. In return a dog will curl up next to you, look soulfully into your eyes, keep the loneliness at bay. A dog is better than a lover, more reliable. Dagmar is always here when I need her.''

"Dagmar doesn't pay the bills.''

She wandered off to the bathroom to curb the temptation to tell Charlotte about Jody's plans. If Jody wanted to do a show, she didn't want Charlotte trying to take it away from her. Charlotte was a kleptomaniac, stealing other people's ideas and plans and convincing himself they were originally his.

She combed her hair. She tightened the sash on her robe. If Charlotte was going to parade around in her kimono, there didn't seem much point in getting dressed.

When she returned to the living room Charlotte had a good blaze going in the fireplace and was setting out the contents of the wicker picnic hamper on the coffee table. Apples, three types of cheese, crackers, Norwegian bread, smoked ham, grapes, pâté, the first strawberries of the season, and several bottles of wine. "Bet you haven't eaten today either. We could use the corkscrew, some glasses, a couple of knives. Go on, make yourself useful. Bring those lovely placemats you bought in Mexico. And the hot mustard.''

Dear old Charlotte. After Alan left he'd stopped by one evening and found her just like this, in bed with no reason to get up, no firm handle on what laid her so low. That evening they'd ordered a pizza, but not until she'd spent almost an hour crying, and then a vomiting jag, dry heaves, as if her emotions made her physically ill. Charlotte's arm around her shoulders, his voice murmuring in her ear. That was one thing she truly cherished about Royce. In the two years they'd lived together, she hadn't spent a weekday in bed, until today. With Royce she wanted to get up. Energy, ideas, curiosity. Without Royce,

331

without Royce. She'd spent the afternoon going back over the years, counting all the days in bed. So many of them, each signaling a major change in her life. A lost job, a lost home, a lost piece of herself. Dead friends, ruined expectations, vanished ideas. The more she thought about it, the more she was sure she'd spent at least a full 365 days of her thirty-five years lying in bed mourning.

And here was Charlotte, once again, pulling her out of bed, a picnic lunch, bottles of wine. It could mean only one thing: Royce would stay in Marin. She'd gambled and lost. And Charlotte knew it.

"I'm playing with fire," she said as she handed him the corkscrew. "Or maybe I played with fire and now the blaze is out."

"Let's hope you only got properly singed. Still got a passion for hot spots?" He ticked off on his fingers. "Africa: run the risk of hijacking, famine, riots. Wars. Central America: there's a war going on down there too. South America: I suppose Tierra del Fuego is quiet this time of year. Not much news since the Falklands conflict. Anywhere else there's always the possibility of a coup. Ireland: now that's taking your life in your hands. Hell, Europe. Terrorists and extremists wage war in airports. Some fun there." He continued counting on his other hand. "Southeast Asia's not such a good bet. Things are pretty hot in Afghanistan. India's unsettled. Russia, but they don't encourage tourism. China, maybe, but they say it takes a year to get a visa."

She sprawled out on the sofa. "I get the point: Stay home and get to work."

"What about Japan?" Charlotte asked. "Ever think of going to Japan?"

"Japan? I don't know. Danny visited Japan, said it was fabulous, so weird." She commanded Dagmar to sit, beg, then she rewarded her with a slice of ham. "You're never alone over there. Danny said the people have developed tunnel vision so no one looks into anyone else's eyes. Imagine that, all those millions of people staring straight ahead, not seeing anything. He said all they do is eat."

"Royce asked me about Japan this afternoon. I reminded him you were thinking of going to Africa, not Japan."

Her heart quickened. "You saw Royce this afternoon?"

"Look at me." Charlotte spread his arms, the wings of the kimono flapping like sails at his sides. "Today I'm a singing telegram." And he broke into an old Beatles tune, "He loves you. Yeah, yeah, yeah."

She smiled and felt as if she'd been holding her breath underwater all day. "He could have called."

"Which reminds me." He went over to the phone and picked up the connecting cord, waving the unattached end in the air at her. "Not only am I a singing telegram, I'm a telephone repairman. Repair person." He snapped the plastic cord back in the jack. "Apparently you two had a lot of fun yesterday and he unplugged the phone. He's gone to Sacramento tonight to announce to his father-in-law that he's getting divorced. He stopped by the store and asked me to come up here and see if you'd noticed."

A weight lifted, her body light and airy. She felt she could fly, soar through the room. "The phone didn't ring."

"Undoubtedly." He picked up the receiver, listened for the dial tone, returned it to the cradle.

The light feeling spread to her bones. Her body felt warm, wonderful, the food in the firelight looked delicious. The mood lasted only a moment. The light feeling turned to giddiness, hysteria. Nothing was solved. His father-in-law in Sacramento. A new problem to face.

"He said he'd be back tonight. And to tell you he'll be here through Friday."

"He said that? Through Friday?"

Charlotte nodded. "He told me that would be important to you. The Friday business. Oh, I've had quite a day." Charlotte flopped back in the chair. "I finally got a hold of Guerrero last night."

"Guerrero." She sat up on the couch.

"He'd gone to his parents, said he was sorry he was so cryptic."

She watched Charlotte's face, how sad and lonely he looked. Where does sadness hide in a face? A moment ago he'd been so bright and cheerful, and now he looked like another person altogether. "Well?"

"This week has been hell for me, thanks to Guerrero. I imagined a million ways Alan could have died. AIDS. Heart attack. Hit by a cab. I started dreaming about him, Alan dying over and over again, like running the same sequence in a film. True nightmare stuff. And then I'd get angry at Guerrero. Where was he when Alan died? Why didn't he do anything to save him? But then, if it was AIDS or a heart attack, I'd feel sorry for Guerrero, having to watch Alan slip away. Hell on wheels, I'll tell you. You know, sometimes hell on wheels can be a car wreck."

She'd had similar moments during the week, playing Alan's death scene in as many variations as she could imagine. "Charlotte, so how did he die?"

"He was stabbed. For forty-seven bucks. Imagine being dead because of forty-seven dollars."

"Stabbed." *I have a knife,* Guerrero said, *but I don't want to hurt you.* Had she really believed Guerrero had a knife? That last evening, the three of them, but she hadn't thought much about Guerrero's knife. Her attention was focused on the sound of Alan as he lugged suitcases and trunks overhead. She'd felt as if she were in the room with him, watching him empty the drawers, pull clothes from the closets. When they left she'd gone upstairs to find Alan's refuse scattered in all the rooms. The shirts he didn't want, the shoes he didn't take.

Would Guerrero stab Alan? For forty-seven bucks? A lover's quarrel? Was Guerrero in jail, was that why Charlotte couldn't get a hold of him? No, visiting his parents. She wrapped her arms around her breasts, rubbed her elbows. "For forty-seven dollars?"

"He and Guerrero had gone to a party." Charlotte swirled the last of the wine in his glass. "They were both pretty drunk and got into a stupid argument on the way home. Something about a pretty boy at the party. Guerrero stormed off to a bar, leaving Alan to go on home alone. When Guerrero got back, the police were there. Someone heard the fight. Alan was already dead."

"Jesus." She could see Alan throwing a drunken punch. Was it like the movies? The surprise in the eyes as the knife goes into the heart? Did the eyelids flutter? Had he bled to death in the street? Would he still be alive if Guerrero hadn't left him?

"Of course, Guerrero feels guilty. They probably won't even catch the guy." Charlotte poured himself more wine.

Alan's beautiful blue eyes, the taper of his back to his narrow waist, the freckles on his shoulders. She always thought of his desertion as something temporary, that some day she would run into him and he would be able to explain everything. They'd shake hands, have a drink, talk about the old days. She could ask him if Guerrero really had a knife that night.

Charlotte stood and went over to poke the fire. "He

always wanted you to have the house. He thought he owed it to you. I promised him when he left I'd keep my eye on you, see that you were okay.''

"What if I'd moved away? How could you keep your eye on me then?''

"I can keep track when I want to. That's why the Africa thing freaks me so. I'm not sure I can keep track of you in Africa, for God's sakes.''

"Well, maybe I won't go to Africa.'' But she couldn't bring herself to mention Paris.

"So glad to hear you've regained your senses. Down the road someplace, love, we're going to laugh at how ridiculous the whole idea was. Africa.'' He snorted. "So now let's dispose of this Africa nonsense and everything will be back on track. We can worry about my problems for a change. My problems are truly more interesting than your soap opera.'' He gave her a faked smile, a smile that said: Let's get on with things.

Dear, sweet Charlotte. She'd never considered him when she thought about going to Africa, if what she'd been doing these last few days could even be called thinking. Africa. She'd been thinking about running away. "Know what I realized today? There's no percentage in anguishing over something you can't change or comprehend. I don't want to see modern Africa. Too much is going on over there. I can only imagine Africa as if it were a movie. A high-class thrill. An exotic shot of adrenaline. I don't want to think of myself as someone who would watch people starving as if I were strolling through a sideshow. I don't,'' she studied her hands, not sure she should say this. "I don't want to be one of those people who heard that fight and didn't call the police.''

Today, lying on the bed, she had the feeling she'd turned off a switch in her mind some years ago. She was afraid it might be too late to turn that switch back on. "I want to see the Africa I've read about in books. Isn't that strange?" She helped herself to a glass of wine. "I want to see vast savannas with elephants giving each other dust baths, native dances by firelight, the mirage of an oasis becoming real palm trees. I'd like to watch a giraffe run, see how much ground he can cover in a stride. I might see some of that in Africa but it would be only a tiny corner of the picture. Like coming to America to see the Empire State Building. You'd have to see New York City to get to the Empire State Building. New York I could handle. But I'm not sure I can handle civil wars, terrorists, and starvation."

"Go to the zoo," Charlotte said. "An afternoon at the zoo and you'll see all the Africa you need. Save you running halfway around the world."

She filled a glass for Charlotte and looked out at the spring storm. Across the street the houses sat like dumb animals, their windows dead eyes, silver sheets of wind-blown rain striping the gray dusk. "The zoo." Charlotte was right. Royce would be here through Friday. What did that really mean?

Charlotte narrowed his eyes. "Now listen up. This is serious shit. You've really put his ass in a sling. I mean, imagine the man right now, talking to his father-in-law, explaining all this because *you* want him to. That's power tripping. You should have heard him this afternoon, poor confused bastard. You ran a nice little game on him. You set yourself up as one woman and in the stroke of an evening, blasted it to pieces." He took a hungry swallow of his wine. "Frankly, I wouldn't blame Royce if he let you leave. You're jacking him around, leaving the man no place to stand, no dignity." He tossed off the rest of the wine and Katlyn noticed his movements were loose, on the verge of drunkenness. "I hear another word about this damned trip and I'll walk out of your life too."

"Calm yourself." She poured him more wine. Another one of Opal's observations: Drunks don't lie, they exaggerate. If Charlotte felt this strongly, he would unravel bits of Royce's conversation as he worked his way down the bottle. Among Charlotte's grand passions, good gossip and good liquor were high on the list.

"You can't be trusted, you know that?" He took the glass she held out to him. "When Alan left, I thought you were a brave, strong lady. A really admirable type. It's not easy to have your lover, your husband no less, walk out of your life like that. I was impressed with how you picked yourself up, no matter about this," he waved his hand to indicate her bathrobe, her afternoon in bed. "But that's not the same lady who's power tripping a man who's been a prince to her for the past two years. And if it is the same lady, then she can't be trusted. You can't count on her. She'll deceive you. Once you break a trust like that, it's like getting back yesterday. It can't be done."

"That's unfair, Charlotte. What a bitch you are." But she knew her anger stemmed from the fact he might be right. "There's a difference between power tripping and trying to manage your own life."

"Not if managing your life involves making, forcing, someone else to change theirs. And especially," his voice rising, spitting out the words like bullets, "when you set it up so he's forced to lose something! A new world every morning, my ass! You want *your* world every morning. You think that's not power tripping?"

"Stop screaming at me! What's the point of yelling about it?"

"How can I know what I'm thinking if I'm not yelling at you?"

She began to laugh. She couldn't help herself. "How can you know what you're thinking if you're not yelling?"

Charlotte looked at her blankly for a moment, the anger draining out of his face. He sipped his wine, and she could see a smile creep into the corners of his eyes. "Well, it's a new therapy," he said at last. "Intellectual Scream. You're cured when you've rendered yourself permanently hoarse."

"I'm not going to Africa. I just told you that. When Royce comes home tonight I'll tell him too." She waved her hands helplessly in the air. "A crazy idea, a feather up my ass. Loneliness." Her brows knit together as she tried to make Charlotte understand. A feeling coloring her whole life and yet she'd never been able to describe it accurately. It was solid and constant, a black hole which swallowed her up. "This whole Africa thing just kind of rolled off my tongue. A panicky idea. It was thoughtless, but I was afraid. Afraid of that hollow spot. With Alan dead I thought of all the things I've missed. I guess a death does that to you, reminds you of life. What it's really all about. Royce fills that spot for me, but I can't keep on in this piecemeal fashion." And yet she knew that wasn't quite it either. "I'm getting older and doing less and less with my life."

Charlotte swirled the wine in his glass. "I certainly hope Royce will understand all that. You might find things were better off the way they were. We're all getting older. This isn't the kind of world where you can give in to loneliness and fear and survive it unscathed. And the older you get, the longer you take to heal."

"Well, I'd like to know how everyone manages to be so brave."

"Same as you," Charlotte said. "They pretend. After a while it gets to be a way of life."

"I used to go ice climbing, and now I'm afraid of heights. I don't drive anymore because I hate owning a car. I can't pretend . . ."

Dagmar barked and hopped off the couch, bounding into the hall. The doorbell rang. Katlyn and Charlotte looked at each other. "I'm not home," Katlyn said.

"It might be Royce."

"He wouldn't ring the bell. There's really no one else I want to talk to."

"I'll get it," Charlotte said. "It's raining like hell out there, in case you hadn't noticed." He heaved himself out of the chair and headed for the hall as the bell sounded a second time.

She resented the interruption. Charlotte was one person she could talk to, even when he was angry with her. With Royce her world felt in balance and her fears disappeared. She became another person around him, a confident, capable woman with happiness in her heart. Poor Charlotte. He knew her at her worst, frayed and tattered around the edges. Broken, as if her life with Royce, or with Alan, had been a porcelain mask smashed, ground underfoot. He was right; she couldn't be trusted. She was deceptive, afraid to show her true self. Opal's stony silence taught her to be ashamed of her fears. Sometimes she buried them so deeply, even she couldn't find them. But they were there, carrying the full power of memory and she was a little girl again, powerless and confused. Only Charlotte had any patience for her when she slipped into need.

She heard voices, and then steps in the hall. She turned as a small woman bundled up in an expensive raincoat and hat stepped into the living room. She felt a shiver in her spine, as if the woman might be dangerous, and watched as the woman's eyes took in the room, the food and wine on the table, the fire. The place looked like a lovers' nest. The only thing missing was candles.

"I'm Irene Chambers," the woman said. "I'd like to talk to you, if you don't mind."

Irene Chambers. Irene. Katlyn could only stare. Irene in her living room. Irene looking her over as she lounged in her bathrobe on the couch. She pulled the robe together at the throat, but Irene cut her eyes to Charlotte, the fire, the food.

Charlotte guided her to his chair as if he were seating Irene in a restaurant. "Why don't you sit down? Here, let me take your coat. Miserable night to be out. But the fire will warm you right up." He helped her out of her coat, took her hat, as gentlemanly as Katlyn had ever seen him. She noticed his voice had dropped about an octave, almost bass. "I'm Charles Lawrence." He shot Katlyn a look and she knew she was supposed to call him Charles for the rest of the evening. "An old friend of Katlyn's."

"How do you do." Irene's look took in the kimono and bathrobe.

Charlotte hung her coat in the hall and stepped back into the living room, chattering to ward off silence. "Nothing like a good fire. I was drenched when I got here, could have been swimming in the ocean." He threw another log on the fire and Katlyn caught a glimpse of his thin, white legs peeking out from under the kimono. "I thought the rain was over for this year, but I guess I was wrong." He maneuvered the log with the poker until he was satisfied. "Can I offer you some wine? Let me get another glass. I'll be right back."

Katlyn lit a cigarette, sat up straighter on the couch and pulled the robe closed over her knees. Irene looked very Marin, smart in tailored gray pants and a pearl-colored silk shirt. And diamonds. Tiny diamond studs twinkled in her earlobes. The diamond wedding ring, but smaller than Katlyn expected. And a pale, canary yellow diamond cocktail ring as big as a marble. Only women from Marin wore cocktail rings.

Irene looked around the room, taking in everything. Definitely not Donna Reed or Beaver's mother. As prim, tiny, and cold as Nancy Reagan. Dagmar sniffed her wet boots and she absently stroked the dog's head. "That's Dagmar," Katlyn managed to say.

"Our dog was killed yesterday."

"I'm sorry to hear that. You can get quite attached to a dog." She snapped her fingers and Dagmar hopped up on the couch. Katlyn ran her hand along the dog's back until she curled up at her side.

"Here we are." Charlotte swooped into the living room with another goblet. "Red or white?" he asked Irene, indicating the wine.

"White." She looked at Katlyn. "I'm sorry if I'm disturbing your party. Royce is in Sacramento for the evening, and I wanted to meet you on my own."

Charlotte poured wine. "You're not disturbing anything. We're just passing the evening. Is Royce supposed to meet you here?"

Katlyn and Irene both looked at him. But he wasn't watching them, his attention focused on the cheese platter, which he passed to Irene. "Try some of this."

"No thank you," Irene said. "I can't stay long. Royce doesn't know I came, and I'd rather not be here when he returns." Her eyes met Katlyn's, took her in with a glance. "You don't look anything like what I imagined."

"She's really a *tabula rasa* in that outfit." Charlotte tugged at the hem of her robe. "You should see her with some clothes on."

"Charlotte!"

Irene smiled for the first time and Katlyn noticed how

striking her features were. But no matter how long and hard she stared at Irene, she couldn't imagine her with Royce. She was too small, a miniature woman, compared with Royce's long, lean bones.

Charlotte turned to Irene. "She just does that to annoy me. Katlyn actually works for me. I own Saving Grace down on Twenty-fourth Street."

"I don't think I've ever been in there."

"You should stop by some time. We have some very nice things." He touched up Katlyn's wine, then his own, and seated himself next to her on the couch, his arm over her shoulder. "So. Out in all this rain." He smiled at Irene, attempting to pull this off as if it were the most natural thing in the world.

Katlyn wanted to shake off his arm. She didn't know what he was trying to prove. The whole situation was as comfortable as flying in a crippled plane. But she wasn't sure she wanted to hold an audience with Irene alone, and she didn't know how to ask Charlotte to leave anyhow.

Irene shifted in the chair. "Now that I'm here I don't know what to say. I just wanted to see you." She took a small sip of her wine. "I listened to him on the phone. His voice sounds different when he talks to you, words like *pretty* ring strangely. He sounds like another person. That rather amazed me, how you could affect even his voice."

"I've wanted to meet you too," Katlyn said. But she was still feeling like a little girl, so silly for a woman of her size. In any awkward moment she reverted to the age of twelve. Even her body betrayed her feelings, hunching in on itself to hide her height. Short people made her nervous. With an effort, she straightened her shoulders and spine.

"Actually," Charlotte said, "I probably should be going. I'm sure you two have a lot to talk about." He stood and drained his wine. "If you'll excuse me a moment while I get dressed."

Irene watched him as he left the room and Katlyn felt herself blush. The beautiful silk kimono, the red socks, Charlotte's easy familiarity with the house. He'd played it pretty straight, not swishy at all. What else could Irene think, but that Charlotte was her lover? The other woman and her lover. God, what a mess.

"I remember when Royce bought this house," Irene said. "It's different now."

"We've done a lot of work on it." But the we seemed to stick in her mouth. How could she say we to Royce's wife?

"Beautiful job." She fingered one of the peacock feathers in the Chinese vase. "I've always thought of this place as an empty lot. Just walls and floors thrown together at odd angles. That's the way it was when I first saw it."

"I've lived here for two years now." Katlyn took a sip of wine. Take a chance, open cans of worms. "I moved in after my husband left me." The look on Irene's face told her that was the wrong thing to say.

"Well, that gives us something in common. Husbands who've left us."

She wished Charlotte wasn't in the bedroom. Charlotte was the only one who knew what the hell was going on. She heard him singing again, the only sound except for the wind and rain. "He loves you, yeah, yeah, yeah." She'd have to bluff her way through this, she just didn't have the cards. "I haven't seen Royce since last night."

Irene looked surprised. "You haven't seen him?"

Katlyn shook her head.

A small furrow appeared in Irene's forehead. "He moved some things out of the house today. He might have taken them up to Sacramento."

Katlyn smiled. Sacramento. Charlotte had said Royce was going to inform his father-in-law he was getting divorced. Something in common, husbands who've left us. "I don't know what to tell you." This woman was definitely dangerous.

Irene's look was cold and level. "Are you going to marry my husband?"

"No." But that sounded wrong. As if home wrecking were a hobby of hers, something she did in her spare time when she wasn't fooling around with Charlotte. "But I'd like to live with him."

Charlotte was singing as he stepped into the living room, "Yeah, Yeah, Yeah, Yeah." In the tuxedo and black trousers, he looked as if he were on his way to the senior prom. "Well, I'm off." He extended his hand to Irene. "So nice to meet you," as if they'd been introduced at a party.

Suddenly she didn't want Charlotte to go. She was afraid to be left alone with Irene. Where the hell was Royce, anyhow? Charlotte bent down and gave her a peck on the cheek. "I'll talk to you later," he said, and she felt helpless as he walked to the hall, donned his shoes and slicker, and let himself out the door.

"Do you mind if I look around?" Irene asked.

"Of course not." Katlyn stood, instantly aware of her height next to the diminutive Irene. She suddenly saw the point of Dr. Bodine's visit to the house yesterday. Irene's tour would tell her everything she'd need to know about their relationship, a map of their life together, everything but the wreckage in the bedroom. Days in bed. Damn, why wasn't she at least dressed for this visit?

Irene looked as if she were shopping, checking, noting furniture and appliances as if she were thinking of buying them. "Royce wanted us to move over here, did

you know that? Before he met you. We have two children, so the place is really too small. He was going to
build a room." She seemed to be talking to herself. "I
imagine he could build a room."

The idea of the two faceless children made spots of
color fill Katlyn's field of vision. She imagined the doorbell ringing again, the two children marching in as if on a
crusade. Royce's family, the tiny wife and two children,
shaking their small fingers at her accusingly. Miniature
people.

"I keep seeing little pieces of myself." Irene's hand
trailed along the top of the TV. "This used to be ours,
when we lived in North Beach. Royce made those bookcases when we lived there." She turned toward Katlyn. "I
would find all this depressing if I were you. Living with
other people's castoffs."

As she watched Irene, Katlyn realized Irene was pic-
turing this house as her own, the home she and Royce
should have lived in. No thought that this house would be
a home for Royce and his lover, until tonight. How would
Irene have decorated these rooms?

In the pantry Irene lingered to look out into the dark
rain-swept yard. "Looks like you've got a pretty big garden."

"A lot of spices and roses. I put fresh vegetables in
every year. I keep thinking about asparagus. Asparagus
takes three years to mature." Katlyn drew a nervous breath.
"In a rented house, a situation like this, you just don't
know if you'll be around in three years."

Irene simply looked at her and turned into Katlyn's
workroom. "Do you know what they used to call adultery?" she asked casually over her shoulder.

"No. You don't even hear that word much any more."

"Criminal conversation."

Katlyn laughed, a deep laugh, breaking the tension,

no longer caring how this would work out. "Oh yes." She laughed again. "I suppose that's what we're having. A criminal conversation." Yesterday an alienist, today a criminal conversation.

Irene turned to face her, the furrow appearing in her forehead again. "And you don't want to marry him?"

"I don't see much purpose in that."

"Don't you want children?"

Katlyn felt her strength returning. "That's none of your business."

Irene gave her an arch look. "A woman's heart is in her womb. If you don't have children, it's easy to remain a child yourself."

"I told you. It's none of your business," Katlyn said.

"But why destroy my marriage? Why can't you leave things as they are?"

"I'm not destroying your marriage. That's between you and Royce." And she truly believed that. Regardless of what Charlotte felt, Royce would always be married to this woman, it was stamped on her, on him. She'd be around, poking in the corners of their lives. Whether he and Irene divorced or not seemed moot.

"You're an arrogant bitch," Irene said. "I'll never understand people like you. Women like you remind me of when my kids were little. They were never interested in their own toys, only the toys some other kid was playing with."

"Royce isn't a toy." Katlyn gave her a grim smile. "But I can see how you would find that analogy appropriate. Sounds as if you've treated him like a toy all these years."

"You've got a lot of nerve telling me how I treat my husband."

"And you've got a lot of nerve coming over here."

347

Irene's face became stony. "I want you to know I'll fight this. I could make things very difficult for you."

Katlyn shook her head. "I don't think so. I never take temper tantrums seriously."

"I'd hardly call this a temper tantrum." Irene's nostrils flared. "I'm just giving you fair warning."

"I don't need any fair warnings. There's really nothing you can do to me." She drew a cigarette from the pocket of her robe, lit it, and blew a long curl of smoke at the ceiling, right over Irene's head.

"If you care about Royce at all, which I'm not sure you do, you'll find there are plenty of things I can do. I'm his wife. I'm the mother of his children. Legally, he's responsible to me. Morally, he's responsible to me. You're a whim," she waved her hand in the air, "as insubstantial as smoke."

"Funny," Katlyn said. "I don't feel insubstantial. I feel quite solid with Royce."

"We'll see." Irene waved her hand through a cloud of cigarette smoke. "I mean, there's a world's worth of rules and advice for someone in my situation. Suppose he does leave me for you. Pick up any ladies' magazine and the pages are full of articles about what to do when the husband strays. Take a class. Join a club. Find a hobby. Spend more time with your children." She turned and walked into the bathroom. "But you, there aren't really any guidelines for a person like you. You're sailing uncharted waters. What makes you think it will all work out?"

"Two very wonderful years. Two years when my life suddenly made sense. I don't know how Royce saw it, but that's how I felt."

"Two years isn't very long, you know." Irene slumped against the linen closet as if she were tired. "Things change. Time makes a difference. After a while even his sentences can become irritating, the way he phrases things. He begins every statement with 'Well, let's see,' and at first I really thought he meant that as 'Let us see.' The illusion of being included in his decision. But with him it's just a phrase, like 'you know.' It's as if he's talking to himself, or I'm invisible or something. I didn't really notice that phrase for the first couple of years, but now it's like he's sticking piano wires in my ears whenever he says it."

"It seems odd to let a marriage go over a phrase."

Irene shot her a look, her eyes narrowed to slits, and went to the medicine cabinet and began to open the door. Katlyn's hand reached out and pushed it shut. "That's enough," she said. There was nothing in the medicine cabinet Irene shouldn't see, the standard aspirins and vitamins, but unless Irene was willing to open up her own house, or be strip-searched, Katlyn saw no reason to allow her to continue peering into the corners of her life. This was her home after all, more so than Royce's.

"I was looking for his razor."

"You'll have to ask him."

Irene walked into the bedroom and sat on the edge of the bed, pushing the books and maps and clothes out of her way. "I just keep trying to see him in this house, see him here with you. Maybe if I could do that, I would understand all this better." She closed her eyes tightly, her face wrinkled as if in pain. "If I could just see him getting out of this bed, putting on his socks, walking into that bathroom to shave."

"He doesn't wear socks when he shaves." The image was ludicrous, Royce shaving in the nude except for socks.

Irene looked puzzled. "He keeps his socks next to the bed, pulls them up under his pajama bottoms and goes in to shave before he takes his shower."

SARA VOGAN

"He doesn't wear pajamas. At least not when he sleeps with me."

"Oh." She seemed to drift for a minute, lost in her own thoughts. "I see." She fingered the Michelin map, then picked it up, studied it. "You taking a trip?"

"Up the Nile and down the Congo."

"Africa. With Royce?" Her eyes shone with amazement.

"Not necessarily. I don't need Royce to go to Africa." She could see disbelief in Irene's face. Reaching into the washstand, she pulled out the Prussian officer's helmet and placed it on her head.

Irene just stared.

It was time to turn the tables, to show Irene who was in charge here. Power play this miniature woman back out into the rain. Luck changes with every spin of the wheel and Katlyn felt if she could best Irene now, in her own home, she'd have a chance to shoot the moon.

She went to the closet and stepped out of her robe, naked beneath it, just to prove the point about pajamas. "If you don't mind, I'll get dressed," she said as she hung her robe on the peg next to Royce's. Protected by a plastic bag was the beaded satin, a periwinkle blue decorated with tiny seed pearls across the bodice. The dress had taken the better part of a week to make, to fit it exactly to her body, getting the pearls to lie in the best pattern. She'd worn it only once, the night Royce took her dancing at the Top of the Mark.

Irene could watch as she transformed herself from a bedridden woman with the emotional flu to a woman awaiting her lover. Setting the Prussian officer's helmet aside, she slipped the dress over her head, no bra, no panties. She pulled herself up to her full height, lifting her breasts so they would fall into the cups of the dress. She ran her hands down along the sides of her body, shifting

350

her hips so the dress hung properly. "Would you mind," she said to Irene, "going into the living room and bringing back one of those bottles of wine?"

Without a word, Irene rose and left the room and Katlyn listened closely to see if she would just walk out of the house. But a moment later, she heard her footsteps returning and then Irene was back in the bedroom, with the two goblets and the wine bottle, Dagmar trailing at her heels.

"Make yourself at home." Katlyn smiled at the irony of the phrase. She reached into the dresser and pulled out her garter belt, which she hitched up under the dress. She decided on the seamed stockings and her fancy fuck-me shoes. In those silver spikes she was six feet tall.

Irene poured wine into both goblets, handing one to Katlyn without a word. She cleared a space on the bed for herself and sat down, watching Katlyn as if she were a television program. Dagmar hopped up on the bed and burrowed down in the pillows.

Unfurling the stockings, Katlyn pretended great interest in pulling them up her long legs, checking the seams, hooking the garters in just so. "So tell me about your marriage to Royce," she said.

"We never let our dog sleep on the bed."

"Dagmar's my dog. That's my bed. I suppose that makes a difference." She twirled her foot at the ankle, admiring her legs, before reaching for the silver shoes.

"It's Royce's house. Or rather, my father owns it."

Katlyn buckled the ankle straps. "That's true." She looked steadily at Irene.

Irene let her eyes drift away. She sipped her wine, the diamonds on her hands flashing in the light.

Katlyn turned to the mirror and began working with her hair, brushing out the long red strands so her hair would float around her shoulders. She wasn't even bluffing any longer. She could feel Irene growing smaller and smaller.

"I don't think you know what you're getting into," Irene said, her voice conversational as if they were two women having lunch. "You really don't know him the way I do. After a while you're going to get tired of saying: 'What do you want for dinner?' every night. Your head will start screaming: 'Why don't you learn to cook your own dinner?' 'Why can't we eat at a civilized time?' He's very charming in the beginning, but after a while that fades away, like the color in a shirt after too many washings."

Katlyn watched her in the mirror, waited until Irene's eyes fastened on her own. "I'm sure you're right. But the more I talk to you the more I feel we're talking about two different men. Royce couldn't cook when I met him, that's true, but now he's quite good at it. Hasn't he ever made his mussels in wine sauce for you? Or his lemon veal scaloppine? That's delicious."

"I think you're missing the point. Okay, so he's learned to cook. I'm sure he could learn to juggle or swallow fire if he wanted. But he's still Royce." She stood and paced slowly back and forth on her small feet, two steps, turn, two steps, turn, the black boots shiny and new. "I remember this very distinctly, although I'm talking about a feeling I had ten or twelve years ago. There was a series of days, months really, when I knew I wasn't opening my arms to the man of my life. I'd look at Royce and could see what he wanted and I would have a moment when I would try to rise up to what I saw in his eyes. But then I'd be too tired, too much aware of how I wanted to get on with something else."

Irene rested her hands on the windowsill, looking out at the storm, her back to Katlyn. "Finally I was just going through the motions. But then I realized the more he depended on me, the more of myself I had to give to him. That's what a marriage is, two people taking care of each other. Our futures are inseparable. We live with our choices, make the best of them.''

"A decision ten or twelve years ago might not mean the same thing today,'' Katlyn said. "And besides, I don't want our futures to be inseparable. I want to have my life and I want Royce to have his. I'd like us to be together as a matter of choice. Not obligation.''

Irene turned to face her. "Is that why you're going to Africa?''

Katlyn concentrated on her hair. She didn't have a snappy answer for that one. She wasn't going to Africa, she couldn't, but she didn't want Irene to know that. The look in Irene's eyes when she said *up the Nile and down the Congo* was an impression she wanted Irene to keep. Paris seemed pretty tame compared to Africa. Irene could go to Paris, just about anyone could do that. But she could see how the idea of Africa intimidated Irene. "I've been asked to mount a showing of my work. I need to do some research on African masks.''

"I've never known anyone who's gone to Africa.'' Irene picked up the map again, setting out on a new tack. "Certainly not a woman. Isn't it awfully dangerous?''

"You mean for women?'' Katlyn shrugged. "It's dangerous for anyone, men or women. Did you know they once had a killer hippo in Bangui? Sometimes you just have to challenge yourself, see what your limits are.'' She knew what her limits were, the same limits which kept her from boarding that plane to Munich years ago. Paris, not Africa. "As they say, you never know until you try.''

"That's a rather dilettante attitude. As if life is a smorgasbord. Try this, try that. Life isn't that way, you know. Some part of you is still married to your husband

353

and Royce can't replace him. You can't lock out that part of your life."

"Royce has nothing to do with my marriage," but she knew that was at least partially a lie. "Marriage isn't like birth or death, a one-shot situation. I don't want to marry Royce. If you don't believe me, ask him when he gets here."

Watching Irene in the mirror, she realized Irene would keep this between just the two of them. What was it she wanted?

"It might not be like birth or death," Irene said, "maybe it's more like your parents. You can't get a divorce from your parents. They're a part of your life, and so is a marriage."

"I think you can get a divorce from your parents. You can leave them behind like grade school." She pulled the brush through her hair one last time. "I was raised by my mother. My father deserted us before I was born. My mother idolized Grace Kelly, thought she embodied the modern woman. A modern woman had a career that would bring her to the attention of a man who didn't necessarily have to be the Prince of Monaco, but who would recognize her and make sure she and her children were taken care of. When that didn't happen for my mother, she was thrown back on her own resources."

She lit another cigarette, so unsure this was a wise move, but it was a chance and she believed in taking chances. "Without a father, I grew up relying on those resources. Men were secondary. Companions, friends, lovers. As far as Royce is concerned, he's my companion, my friend, my lover. I don't want him as a husband. I don't want to be his wife. I'd like us to be free to enjoy each other. I can go to Africa, keep working for Charlotte, Charles." She wondered if Irene caught that. "I can take other lovers. I've still got plenty of things to do. The list of things to do can change almost every day. I've divorced myself from my mother's values. I don't believe a man will take me to the stars. If I'm going to visit the stars, I'll have to get there on my own."

"I feel sorry for you." Irene picked up one of the books, leafing through the pages as if she were browsing in a bookstore or waiting for a bus. The only sound was the noise of the storm outside. Katlyn seated herself at the dressing table and applied foundation, eye shadow, mascara. The cigarette burned down in the silence, a long gray roll of ash, while Irene sat on the bed and continued rummaging through the books as if she were studying up to go to Africa herself. Katlyn rubbed on blusher, painted her lips with color. The cigarette was burned down almost to the filter when she stubbed it out. She stood and replaced the Prussian officer's helmet in the washstand. She put pearl earrings in her ears. Shit, what was this woman waiting for?

She decided to end the game. Every moment was perfect to try to change your luck. Charlotte was wrong. A new world every minute, why wait for the break of day? Irene looked capable of sitting here throughout the night.

Katlyn stood and poured more wine in both their glasses. "I'm going to have to ask you to leave soon." She tipped the last of the wine into Irene's glass. "I don't know what you want, what really brought you over here tonight. But I'd rather not have a scene between you and Royce when he gets back. You've got your own place to fight."

"You're destroying my marriage." The words were a hiss.

Katlyn sat on the edge of the dressing table, facing Irene with her legs slightly spread, one foot dangling in the air, the silver shoe swinging back and forth. "I'll have to ask you to leave now." She had the distinct feeling

Irene wanted to attack her, scratch her eyes out, leap off the bed like a wildcat. She could feel fear building in the base of her spine. "But don't forget, he started this affair. There's something in it for him, or he wouldn't have let it go so far."

Irene rose and made a great show of dusting the dog hair off her slacks. She looked Katlyn over, disdain in her eyes. "You're a carnival creature, a freak. Look at you, dressed like an antiquated whore. When you're done playing with him, or he's tired of you, I'll have to patch up the pieces. That's what I do. That's—that's," she stuttered with anger. "I'm his wife and I have to take care of him."

She turned on her heel and walked out of the bedroom. Katlyn listened as her steps echoed through the rooms. She heard the clang of the hanger in the closet as she retrieved her raincoat, the slam of the front door as she left the house.

MIDNIGHT

Max awoke in a cold sweat with a throbbing hard-on. The covers were twisted about his leg and his left foot knotted in a cramp. As he sat in bed massaging his toes, the bird sang in the courtyard, again and again, as if calling for a mate.

Claire falling through the air, and as she fell she whispered to him in her motherly way. But tonight he and Claire weren't alone. A chorus of women joined him leaning over the brick guard wall at the top of the seventeen-story building, murmuring their own stories. Claire sailed away in a yellow biplane.

Max got out of bed, hobbling to try to work out the cramp. It was several hours until sunrise, two more hours after that until his morning session with Thomas Pierce. Max knew he would get no more sleep tonight. He was afraid to sleep after the dream. He always started awake at the same moment, just as she drifted toward the ground and he began to scream "It's not your day to die!"

In the courtyard the mysterious bird sang again, calling, calling. He looked out the window, searching for it, a drab brown bird with such a lovely, lilting song. The wind of the storm whipped branches against his windows but he could still hear the birdcall rising on the rain. Max sat down at his piano and tried to find the notes, but as he noodled along on the keyboard he couldn't recreate the birdcall. He found the rhythm and possibly the notes, starting at G, but the sound was that of a piano and only superficially resembled the bird's song.

The bird continued singing. Max wanted to play a duet with it, the call of the bird, his response on the piano. As his hands moved across the keys the old music box tune came into his head, Beethoven's "Für Elise." The wooden music box had been their mother's, and Max loved the simple elegance of the phrasing. If he was ill, his mother would wind up the music box and set it beside his bed. That was the tune Max would hear as he drifted off to sleep. But after his mother's death the music box belonged to Claire. It was the one thing she wouldn't share with him, and on lonely afternoons she would shut herself in her room and Max, standing in the hall outside her door, could hear the faint strains of the melody. They never spoke of it and Max never thought to knock.

After listening for a while, he would grow restless and head for the backyard. His favorite place was a giant willow at the edge of their property and he would circle it, his hand scraping against the bark. As his right hand picked through the melody of "Für Elise" he tried to remember what prompted him to start the hole, what he thought he would find or discover. Perhaps he thought he would dig to China, or bury his mother, or himself. But when he heard Claire open the music box he would go to the willow tree, then the garage for the garden shovel, and take it out to work on his hole.

The hole occupied him for almost a year, even through the snowy winter. He rigged up a pulley system to lift out the dirt and protected it with a tarp. He was careful to dig around the spreading roots of the willow, wanting only to know where the mysterious hole would lead him, hoping he wouldn't kill the tree. In the spring when the rains came and soaked through the tarp, the hole became a well by the side of the willow and Max abandoned it. But when the well dried up in the summer, somehow Max couldn't bring himself to continue to dig. Instead, when he heard Claire play their mother's music box he would go stand on the edge of the hole, looking into its depths, or crawl down into the hole and look up at the sky through the small green leaves of the willow.

Max finished the phrase and took his hand off the keys. He leaned on his elbows, his fingertips touching, this-is-the-house-this-is-the-steeple. Looking out into the dark night he recognized most of his childhood memories were of Claire, cooking and digging. Thirty years ago he must have gone to school, talked to his father, read books. It was sad to think that talking to his father hadn't been a memorable event. Max's father was more sound than man, the sound of his rising in the morning to work through his exercises before using the bathroom, the sound of the front door slamming long after dark when his father came home. The sound of his silverware clattering on his plate. The sound of ice in a glass while his father sat in the living room when Max and Claire climbed the stairs for bed.

They say history is a circle, and Max knew he was living proof of that. He felt he'd disappeared from his son's life the way his own father seemed to vanish. Perhaps men are simply afraid of children, all that trust and vulnerability, all the danger in the experiments of childhood. True, he hadn't really been prepared for a baby

when Pat announced she was pregnant. But as the pregnancy advanced, he could imagine taking a child, his
child, to the circus, teaching the child how to swim.
Maybe it was time now. Conrad was no longer a baby.
Max was allowed to visit him once a month, and each
month he felt he was encountering a different Conrad.
Last time, Conrad had been playing with a Japanese car
that could be reassembled as a robot. By next month, he
could be interested in frogs or astronauts. Max could
never predict.

Maybe Conrad could fill that empty spot, like a hole
in his heart that developed after Claire jumped. Lord
knows, he'd tried to patch that hole. That was probably
why he married Patrice, a woman in his life to replace
Claire. So stupid. Patrice was the last woman on earth to
replace Claire. No one could replace Claire.

He imagined Claire and Conrad together. The three
of them playing children's games. Claire would have known
what to do, how to make a child happy for an afternoon.
How did one entertain a six-year-old? Most of his Sunday
afternoons with Conrad, those rare occasions when Patrice
found it convenient for Max to take him for a few hours,
terrified him. Once they'd played hide-and-seek in Golden
Gate Park and Max lost Conrad for half an hour. Conrad
was jubilant—such a success at fooling Max. But in all
that time Max feared kidnappers, broken ankles, drowning in a lake. He'd clasped Conrad close to him after the
boy had slowly crawled out from under a bush. Conrad
had stiffened, and Max realized Conrad really didn't know
who he was.

Max went into the kitchen for the egg timer. Claire
was dead. His mother was dead. His father too. His son
was a stranger. He'd take three minutes to feel sorry for
himself and then turn on the light and work on his paper
about American loneliness. It wasn't that he'd had an

unhappy childhood, more like not having a childhood at all. American loneliness was a vacant feeling in the midst of plenty, a loss which neither money nor love could fill. The sadness of affluence.

The world had changed so much since he was a boy. Before his mother died, Max had wanted to be a cowboy. Conrad said he wanted to be an environmentalist, a word he had difficulty pronouncing. When Max pressed him about what made him want to be an environmentalist Conrad said, "Save the whales. Harpoon a duck." Max should have let it go at that but explained what a harpoon was to Conrad. He didn't want the boy to grow up accepting every empty phrase.

"A harpoon is like a huge arrow," and Max stretched his arms out full length to demonstrate. "It's made of steel and is so big it would probably go all the way through the duck, like skewering it on a spit."

Conrad had burst into tears.

If someone else were to look at his life, they would probably rate it as a success. His practice, a son, all his debts paid off. Yet in these small hours of the morning his life didn't look so successful. Sofia's story about the Roms perishing by a blessing. He collected stories like that, he collected people and their pain. As if by collecting another's sorrows he could hold off the sorrow in himself. It had never worked. He could forget it for a while, but then, as quick and direct as a laser blast, the pain and sorrow came back. Claire would keep falling and he couldn't keep her from hitting the ground. And somehow, no matter how many he caught in mid-flight and placed solidly back on the ground, it was never enough.

The egg timer was still sifting sand through the wasp waist, but Max took it back to the kitchen. Okay, he couldn't save them all. And one can't stop one's life out of sorrow for the past.

This was as good a time as any to try to finish his paper on American loneliness. If he could finish it he would present it at a conference. The problem was that although he thought he could define the problem, he really didn't have an answer. When Sofia talked about the droughts and starvation in Ethiopia he marveled at how any American who could afford therapy could be so unhappy and depressed. Part of Sofia's problem was that she was homesick for a sense of reality America rarely confronted. Sure, droughts and blizzards affected the country, hurricanes, car wrecks, unemployment. Most of his patients could sail through those disasters, concrete problems to test themselves against. What they couldn't conquer was the pain of the past, even if the past was only last week. Americans have no sense of history and can't see outside themselves.

After pulling on a pair of thermal socks he went over to his desk and switched on the light. A neglected pile of papers took up the left-hand corner. Max paged through his notes. It had been months since he'd worked on this paper, in fact the last time had been in November, before the holidays. He'd been stopped by the six-month San Francisco spring, January to June.

On top of the pile was a note from Ned Whitman, a therapist who drank at Perry's. *Here's one for you, Max,* he'd said as they were having a drink together. *I save all my odd stuff for you.* He rummaged in his briefcase and came up with a handwritten note about a woman who worked as a teller for Bank of America and constantly had to fight the urge to leap across the counter and bite customers in the neck, like a vampire going for blood. The larger the deposit or withdrawal, the stronger her urge to bite them.

Money. Love. American loneliness.

Max doodled a snowflake next to a note.

Psychiatrists are the priests and shamans of modern America. They fill the vacancy left by the collapse of the extended family, religion, neighborhoods, and meaningful working lives. With the loss of close personal relationships, people turn to the psychiatrist to express feelings and fears they feel they cannot tell their family or friends.

And what do we know? What can we say to them? Sometimes one didn't have to say a thing, just another body there to share the pain, to diffuse its power. But after all these years he still didn't know why Claire jumped, why any of them would bottle it up so deeply only death could stop it. So we don't think of death, we don't think of pain. We think of love and money and our lives go on to their natural end.

Eskimos, living in the harshest environment on the face of the earth, understand suicide. They live together, work together, eat together, and when one of them can no longer participate in the group, that individual goes out into the snow and waits for Sila, the goddess of natural order, the goddess of thought. An Eskimo would never die because of love or money. Eskimos die because they can no longer live. The goddess of natural order receives them. Natural order. That, too, had vanished from modern American life. What was the natural order in placing one's wrist on a table saw? What was the natural order in jumping from the Golden Gate Bridge?

Soaring through the air like a bird, just for a moment. Perhaps there was that last snatch of happiness so that life didn't end on a sad or painful note, the way a person plagued with nightmares might take pills for a last, dreamless sleep.

In the flat below, Max heard Roy Becker cough, a

363

smoker's hack, then the flush of the toilet and the water go on in the shower. Roy was a bus driver and the sounds of Roy's awakening meant it was about three-thirty in the morning. As Max listened to the storm lashing against his windows, he hoped the sun would be up soon.

APRIL 11
FRIDAY MORNING

R oyce left Sacramento a little after one in the morn-
ing. Margaret had already gone up to bed, but Gerald
wanted Royce to stay for a brandy while they hammered
out the final details.

Driving in the rain-swept darkness, Royce thought
about the pioneers and their unshakable belief there would
be better land, better water, if they just kept moving on.
He'd always wondered about the families who stopped in
the middle of the country and homesteaded Missouri,
Kansas, Iowa, Nebraska. Had they ever seen the sea? A
couple of years ago, he'd hired a new printer who'd been
born and raised in Grand Island, Nebraska. Peter was
forty and had never seen the Atlantic or the Gulf. He first
viewed the Pacific only two weeks before Royce hired
him. After forty years on the prairie flats, Royce thought
Peter would be overwhelmed by the mountains and the
ocean. Peter said it looked just like it did on TV.

But the pioneers had no notions whatsoever about

what lay before them. They possessed a faith that drove them across vast stretches of land and offered no hints as to what might be beyond the horizon. Royce wished he could get in touch with that kind of faith. The courage, the patience, the faith those people held as they left everything they knew behind and set out for a life they could barely imagine. What was it like to see an Indian for the first time, a buffalo? Royce tried to remember when he first discovered the tingling pleasures of snow. Maybe it was something like that.

When he cut the engine, he sat in the driveway for a moment looking up at the house. The lights were on, even though it was almost three. He wondered if she'd left the lights on for him, or if she was sitting there, waiting. The rain drummed on the roof of the car and he watched, as if stoned, as water filled the indentation where the agate struck.

And then the front door opened and Kat came out, dashing through the rain toward the car. She opened the door to the passenger's side and was about to climb in, except there was a box on the seat, more boxes on the floorboards. "Let's get this stuff inside," he said.

She grabbed the box on the seat and he picked up another from the floor. You sure couldn't carry much in a Toyota, but he figured only one more trip to Marin and he'd have everything. He walked through the cold rain and met her on the porch. The blue dress sparkled like a star, the one she'd worn the night they went dancing. He wondered if it was ruined. "What are you doing in that dress?" he asked.

"I'll tell you all about it some day," she said. "But right now I'd rather hear what you have to say."

"Want to help me unload the car?"

She smiled. "Sure."

"Well, why don't you get into something sensible

then. You'll ruin that thing in the rain." Looking at the beaded blue dress, he saw it as a symbol. The end of the affair. The beginning of something else. He'd taken her dancing the first Saturday night after he'd told her about Irene. That was the only time he'd seen her wear it. He turned the knob to open the door, and they brought the first two boxes into the house.

The living room looked laid out for a surprise party. Cheese, wine, little containers of specialty foods. A fire blazing in the hearth. Kat in the blue dress. The only thing missing was balloons. Christ, this was home. But he didn't know where to set the box down. He didn't even know what it contained, perhaps bricks or roofing tiles from the weight of it. For a moment he thought of pitching all his boxes and suitcases into the trash, but that wouldn't do any good. A fresh start was still built on the past. Kat set her box down on the floor near the bay window, and he set his on top of it. "I'm just going to put the car in the garage," he said. "Deal with it tomorrow."

He was lucky he even remembered the garage. His thoughts kept spiraling. Gerald's handshake, Margaret's kiss on the cheek. And here he was in Noe Valley, Kat with a party all set out. In his pocket, four sets of keys. Five keys to the house in Sausalito, four keys to this place, seven keys for the shop. The two keys for the Toyota were on a separate chain. One time he'd linked the rings together, ten inches of keys.

She handed him a glass of wine when he returned to the living room. "Thank Charlotte," she said. "He catered this affair. He didn't provide me with a guest list, though."

"A guest list," Royce repeated.

"There was some wonderful smoked ham, but Dagmar ate it when I wasn't looking." She plucked a piece of wax paper off the floor, tossed it into the fireplace. "Last time I invite that dog to a party." The paper caught quickly, the wax flaming bright green.

"Where is Dagmar?" It was important to keep track. No more surprises like Wichita.

"I put her out."

"In this rain?" Royce went to the back door to let the dog in. He wanted to see every piece of this puzzle, no loose ends. Dagmar promptly rewarded his consideration by shaking water off her coat, splattering his shoes and jeans.

Royce settled back on the couch and looked around the room. This was home, and an irrational fear hit him, the first beads of sweat breaking out on his forehead, that the place was too small for the two of them, as if the meager collection of things in the car, those things still left in Sausalito, wouldn't all fit in here. But then, maybe they wouldn't have to. So far, all the plans had been his. Kat undoubtedly had some plans of her own. Africa. His scalp tingled. So much had changed, and so little of it had been discussed with her.

Kat took the easy chair on the other side of the coffee table, crossed her legs, and lit a cigarette. "Think we should talk about it?"

He let his breath out in a long, low whistle and ran his hand over his face and back through his hair. "We're going to have to make some changes," and laughed at how inane he sounded.

"What's so funny about that?"

"Well, let's see. Nothing much I guess." Normal people were sound asleep at this hour. Normal people would get up and go to work tomorrow, today. If he'd gone to work this week, perhaps none of this would have happened.

"Charlotte said you told him you were going to be

here through Friday." She pointed to the boxes. "Is that what this stuff means?"

"It's up to you now. You have to make some decisions. I've made every decision I can think of."

"Okay." She recrossed her legs. "But you've got to give me some place to start."

Royce took a long sip of wine. His bones ached. Twenty-four hours ago he and Lindy were cleaning up the broken glass. He wanted to curl up like a cat and sleep until next Thursday. But he would have to see if Irene replaced the front window yet. That was the kind of thing she always expected him to do. And Gerald would go to the bank next week, no matter what happened between now and then. If he wanted to salvage any of this, he must start now. "Okay," he said. "Like the old joke, there's the good news and the bad news."

She reached across the coffee table and refilled her wine. "Shoot."

He wasn't sure where to begin, but felt he should tackle the most embarrassing aspects first. "Although this feels like a million years ago, yesterday," he took a breath, "yesterday while you were at the pool, I looked through your desk."

"You looked through my desk," she repeated.

He nodded. "Yeah. I feel pretty shitty about that, but I did it. This whole Africa thing made me kind of crazy. I've never done anything like that before, but you threatened me, and I had this notion that if you were really going, there might be something in your desk that would tell my why."

"You didn't believe what I told you? You didn't accept my reasons?" Her eyes were wide, astonished. "You think I was lying to you?"

"Kat, we've never been very honest with each other. When was the first time I heard about your husband? You know who filled me in? Charlotte. I had to ask Charlotte what the hell's going on here."

She arched her eyebrows, drawing the skin tight across her face. "And what did Charlotte tell you?"

"Certainly nothing you don't know." The irony of all this amazed him. The first thing out of his mouth was a lie, when all he really wanted was to straighten things out, to stop the lying. "I asked him about a bill of sale I found in your desk, for a house out in the Avenues."

Her face paled as she rose from the chair to put another log on the fire. While she opened the screen, her back to him, and pulled a log out of the stack, she talked softly, dreamily. Royce leaned forward to hear. "Alan walked out on me with about as much warning as a heart attack. Remember that man up the street who died of a heart attack this winter? Everyone said he was perfectly healthy. And bingo!" She snapped her fingers. "He keeled over dead. That's sort of the way Alan left."

After adjusting the log with the poker and putting the screen back in place, she turned to face him. Royce thought she looked like a teacher addressing a classroom.

"Alan's father owned that house, and when he died Alan inherited it. Last week when I found out Alan had died, I received the title to it. Charlotte says he thought he owed me something for what he put me through when the marriage ended. But like everything else with Alan, now it's the last thing I want." She warmed her hands in front of the fire. "It was a creepy place, a museum practically. Nothing had been touched or changed since World War II. When I'd try to rearrange something, Alan would throw a fit, saying he wanted to keep it as it was in case his father got better. But we both knew his father was at the end of the line. He was eighty years old, for Christ's sake. Still, he wouldn't let me change a thing. That house never felt like a home, like this one does. And then his father died, and then Alan left me. When I met you, I'd been spending the nights in motels because I couldn't bring myself to stay there. I'd wake up at two A.M., just as the bars closed, and roam around until I couldn't take it any more. I'd call a cab and have it drop me at a motel. When you offered to let me live here, I jumped at the chance."

The truth at last. He was glad he'd spoken to Charlotte. He took another sip of wine and settled deeper into the couch. "Right," he said. "Okay. What are you going to do with the money?"

She shrugged, opened her hands. "Charlotte says to sell the house and invest the money. But in what? I can't see myself owning pork bellies or silver futures. I don't know the first thing about that crap. So I thought I'd take a trip. That, I can imagine. I felt I ought to get out and see a little of the world. That's something I've never really done, and Alan's death made me think about a lot of things I've always thought about doing and never gotten around to.

"I don't feel comfortable knowing I own a house that made me miserable and that someone else's family lives in it. I thought if I used the money on something extraordinary, I might understand a little more clearly what happened."

"Okay," Royce said again. "I talked to Gerald tonight about this place." He took a deep breath and felt the strain of this week settling in his neck and shoulders. "Gerald's not too crazy about all of this, but he's wise enough to know he can't stop history. Go ahead and take a trip, if you want. Or you can buy this house."

"Buy this house?"

Royce nodded. "Yep. But you have to make up your mind fast. He wants his money out now. He's going to sell it, and I suggested you might want to buy it. So," he rubbed his hand against the back of his neck, "I took a little flyer. Gerald doesn't care who buys it. And I thought if you really wanted to live with me, you could buy it."

She looked wary, as if she were about to step on a thin crust of ice. "Buy this place. You told him about me?"

"Of course." He was proud of the way he'd handled the subject with Gerald. Nothing sexy or sentimental, just a straightforward statement about his feelings. "He wasn't really the bastard I expected him to be. I told him about us. It took some time, some heated emotional stuff, that's why I'm so late getting back. But finally, he's a business-man more than anything else. We could keep this to-gether, but you'll have to invest your part of it."

She crossed the room and settled on the opposite edge of the couch, her arm crooked across the back. He watched as her thoughts played over her face, slight shifts in the muscles and the tones of her skin. "I've never bought a house. Alan's house came without instructions."

"We'll call a realtor. Gerald'll take whatever's fair. I don't want to screw him." A quick sale on the house would show good faith, might make the rest of the negoti-ations easier. He drew his finger along her cheekbones, watched the lights in her eyes. "He's not wild about the idea, but he recognized a bad situation. Our dog was killed yesterday, and when I told him how the whole thing came down, he could see Irene and I weren't very close anymore."

"I know," she said.

"What? What do you know?"

She waved her hand to indicate the spread on the coffee table. "Charlotte brought all this over. And while we were sitting here talking, the doorbell rang and it was Irene."

"Irene was here? You met Irene?" He couldn't imag-ine Kat and Irene talking together. He could see them like in a western movie, six-guns drawn at twenty yards.

She bobbed her head in confirmation. "I didn't much care for her."

Royce kept trying to picture Kat, in the fancy blue dress, and Irene discussing a dissolving marriage. "I'm sorry I missed that."

"No you're not. It wasn't a particularly good time."

"Did she throw any glasses at you?"

"Is she that type?"

"If Irene had a gun, it would be a very expensive little pearl-handled revolver and she'd shoot you in the ankles, cripple you for life." He wondered how that would work out in a duel, if you would survive if you aimed at the ankles.

"She wasn't packing a gun, but she certainly took a couple of shots at me."

Putting his arm around her shoulder and drawing her to him, he rested his head against the back of the couch. Even divorced, nothing would really change. He'd still be spending time in Marin, separate weekends for Lindy and Todd. He'd promised Gerald he wouldn't let that part of things slide, that he wouldn't saddle Irene with the problems of a single parent. He'd have to eventually buy Gerald out of the business, and that, plus hefty support and alimony payments to Irene, would be tricky. All that would change would be the switch from a perfect life to an ordinary one, one where money ruled.

This must be the way the end of free-fall feels. War movies show the troops parachuting out of the planes, men falling from the sky like raindrops. The chute snaps open, the men begin to drift on the air. Hit the ground, rolling. Get up and get on with the business at hand.

Kat massaged his temples. He dropped his arm to the curve of her hip, felt the cool satin against his palm. There were still so many things to do, and yet all he really wanted was to get aboard the *Singing Stars* and sail far, far away. When he sailed, watching the wind and water, his hands busy handling the boat, he felt perfectly in tune with the world. Would Nancy still let him use the boat if he divorced Irene? Probably not. That would be Nancy's idea of loyalty.

And then, as suddenly as a sneeze, he remembered the flashcards. Might as well clear everything up at once. "Kat?"

Her hands continued rubbing his temples, never breaking the rhythm. "What?"

"Bean-jam bun."

"What?" Her hands stopped, and when he opened his eyes he saw her confusion.

"Absence, sand, blue, tomorrow?"

"What are you talking about?"

"In your desk I found some Japanese, or Chinese, flashcards. In other words, I looked through your mail."

"My." She drew away from him, back to the other end of the couch. "Is there nothing sacred anymore? Is that how we're starting out? You looked through my mail?"

"None of this would have happened if you hadn't pulled that Africa stuff on me. What are you going to do about Africa, anyhow?"

"Like I said, Africa was a test. A test to see where we would end up. But I didn't expect you to look through my mail." She grabbed a cigarette and snapped the lighter angrily.

"It was there."

"That's what they say about Mount Everest. What did you expect to find? What are you really trying to do, anyhow? You look through my mail, you unplug the phone, you take off for most of the week. You even hire a goddamned psychiatrist to come over here, no less, and I have to field him for two hours." She blew a flower of smoke at the ceiling. "You send Charlotte like a messenger boy, and your wife drops over for a visit. Talk about opening cans of worms! I don't know if I'd call that passing or failing a test."

"And what about you? You're not the victim here. I am. You waltz through this as if it's the most logical thing in the world. Where's the logic in threatening to leave me if I don't leave my wife? I mean, you treated the whole thing as if we were talking about taking a vacation. As if we were debating whether we'd take a vacation together or separately." Or rather, whether they would stay on vacation, forget the real world, or come back and face the situation.

"Sometimes you have to make a few demands of this world, or it rolls right over you."

" 'Sometimes.' 'A few.' If that's your philosophy I think you've used up at least seven of a cat's nine lives on this one."

Her voice was arch. "You can still stay with Irene if you want."

"I don't want to stay with Irene. But things are going to be different between the two of us if you expect me to stay with you."

"Different?"

"Yeah. No more surprise husbands. No more newly acquired real estate."

Her look was level. "I can't do that. The world is full of surprises. Today Jody asked me to mount a show of my work. And she thought it might be a good idea if I went to Paris."

"Are we swapping Africa for Paris now?"

"In a way. I still feel I need to do something very different, on my own." Her hand chopped the air, punctuation.

"Paris." He rubbed his temples, rolled his fingers around his eye sockets.

"But listen." She took his hands between her palms. "Going to Paris doesn't have to have the same motivation as that trip to Africa. I wanted to drown myself in a new,

375

dangerous experience. That's how I saw going to Africa. What Jody was suggesting, and it made a lot of sense to me, was that I check out the designers in Paris, see if they spark some new ideas for my work. I could stop in New York, check out the competition. I've been looking at my work as a job. Maybe I should start seeing it as a career."

"What about the fucking flashcards?" he demanded. He wanted to bite his tongue. He was behaving childishly.

She drew herself up, her head turned so she looked at him out of the corners of her eyes. "The flashcards, for your information, are from Danny. You remember Danny? He owns the theater where I spend almost every damned weekend while you're in Marin. I mean, I've got to do something, don't I, while you play husband and father."

Danny. If the other man was Danny, there was nothing to worry about. Well over three hundred pounds, a face as soft as a eunuch. Royce wondered if Danny had ever had a sexual experience. And now that he thought about it, he remembered Kat told him Danny took a trip to Japan not long ago. "But what do they mean?" he asked.

"What? The flashcards?" The anger left her face, but she still held the haughty pose. "Danny's talked about going to Japan as long as I've known him. He took lessons in Japanese. They began as a joke really. The first ones were the ideograms for bats and butterflies, symbols of good luck. I couldn't figure it out, these strange little cards showing up in the mail one day. Now it's just a game we play. They're film titles. *Floating Weeds, Monster Island, Woman in the Dunes, Throne of Blood.* I'm getting pretty good at it. If I can decipher the flashcards, I send him a postcard, and if I'm right, he lets me in free."

"And that's what you do while I'm at home?"

"Yeah. Some fun, huh?" She drew closer to him, her eyes flashing different colors. "I'm a very monogamous woman. Dagmar learned loyalty from me. I never screwed around on Alan, and I don't screw around on you. Saturdays are always bad, no matter what I do. When you leave on Fridays, my spirit sinks, the bottom just drops out. I've tried everything. Work, get drunk, get stoned, do drugs. Read *War and Peace*. I've called all my friends, but a lot of people go out on Friday and Saturday nights, you know. Charlotte cruises the bars. Jody and Bruce go to parties, but I hate going to a party as a third wheel. Parties are either for cruising or couples, and when I go to a party without you, I'm neither. By Saturday evening, listening to the people start their cars and drive away, it feels like the weekend will never end. I've tried doing the laundry, but that's just too depressing, even though laundromats are usually empty. I end up at Danny's theater. It gets me through Saturday night. You can't work every minute and somehow, for me, Saturday night and Sunday morning just aren't meant to be spent alone. Do you realize how big the Sunday paper is when there's only one person reading it? Even the comics aren't fun if there's no one to fight over them.''

"I guess it wasn't fun enough or you wouldn't have come up with the Africa idea." But he knew that was mean. He was beginning to see Dr. Bodine's point about what her position might be, what her position was. This wasn't a triangle. This was a closed circle. It surprised him that he was the last to know, the last to recognize the obvious. Laundry on a Saturday night. Salesmen stranded in strange towns do laundry on a Saturday night, eat up the time until Monday.

"It just sort of hit me that I was drifting right through life, always waiting for my life to begin. When I looked back on my past, it just seemed to evaporate. When I looked at my future, I saw a blank. When I found out Alan was dead, I felt that hollow spot again, not because of Alan, but because it seemed as if I was existing outside of time, outside of life. I didn't know what would happen when I said Africa, but I felt I needed to take a chance."

He realized a vital difference in their lives. Laundry on a Saturday night. The weight of a Sunday paper to be read all alone. He was never alone and she was alone almost constantly. Something about doing the laundry on a Saturday night struck him as heartbreakingly sad. All day she worked alone, while he was surrounded by people at the plant. All weekend he was in the presence of Irene and his children while she had only Dagmar. With all that time, all that solitude, it made a certain kind of sense that she would pull up short and decide to change things, open up the circle of her world.

If loneliness is the final condition for us all, what can anyone know about anyone else? Where would love fit in if it didn't fill the void left by loneliness? Living with Irene had been like living alone. Kat's husband walked out on her. They'd been total strangers who'd thrown themselves into each other's arms to avoid the emptiness of their separate hearts. And now he had to admit that Kat had existed, at least at first, mostly in his imagination. A total stranger. But really, who is that total stranger? The person we love or the image of ourselves through someone else's eyes? Why can't we be content without leaning on another person? When had Kat become real to him? So real he felt she was the one who gave meaning to his life. If we don't share our lives with someone, how do we know we are living?

Women have children, their connection to life. Irene once said she would always have Lindy and Todd, even if he left her, even after Gerald and Margaret died, and her tone when she said that was as deep and solid as a heartbeat. He'd filled his life with Irene and his family to try to avoid the same loneliness. But it hadn't worked.

Only Kat soothed that personal spot. Irene and her family would continue to occupy his thoughts on a daily basis. But Kat's family was a string of desertions, her father, her husband. Even her mother, who couldn't be bothered to talk on the phone.

Africa. It made perfect sense for her. If all you know is desertion, the only thing you know how to do is desert. Going to Africa.

Going to Paris. Check out designers. A tone buzzed in his left ear, like a radio signal. He'd certainly prefer she go to Paris than Africa. Paris was imaginable. Africa was like going to the moon. Jody was right. Paris. Kat needed a trip like that to see herself in the context of her work, the way he saw himself through the prism of the printing plant.

He reached across the couch and pulled her into his arms. He could feel her heart beating, her moist breath on his cheek. Love could be just craziness directed at the nearest available object, a person, or perhaps a passion for stocks. It had all been a brave front, but beneath her theories about making the world over each day there was fear. He could almost touch it. Why hadn't he seen it before? "Oh God, Kat," he whispered. "I'm sorry."

"You don't have anything to feel sorry about."

"It's not that. I'm just sorry you feel so alone. I'm sorry you feel you've missed your life. I don't know if I can help you with any of that."

She looked up at him. "No one can help me with that. That's part of who I am, or who I've become. But you make me feel better about it, make it easier to bear, than anyone else ever has. That's why it's so painful when you leave for the weekends. You take that with you."

Shifting on the couch, he reached into his breast pocket and pulled out a small velvet box. "This was my mother's." He handed it to her and watched her eyes light up as she opened it, the peach and ivory cameo, the delicate profile, the woman's hair swept back, all suggested by subtle carvings in the ivory. "She left this to me when she died. It was given to her on her confirmation. Lindy was too young at the time, and Irene and my mother never got along. I don't think my mother would have wanted Irene to have it. Maybe I was saving it for you."

She fingered the pin, looking up at him, then back to the cameo. "Maybe you should save it for your daughter. Give it to her when she's older."

"She's old enough now. She suggested having lunch with you. I could have given it to her any time. But it's not the kind of thing Lindy would appreciate." Among his mother's keepsakes was a Russian lacquered box, a wedding present from his father, which he would give Lindy when she settled down a bit. "There are other things I'll give Lindy. But I'd like you to have this. Or just borrow it. I want you to go to Paris and I want you to take this with you." He took if from her and pinned it over her heart. Outside the rain was still falling, a shower now, the end of the storm.

FRIDAY
AFTERNOON

She awoke with her heart hammering in her chest and Royce snoring peacefully, curled next to her. Her heartbeats echoed through her spine, beat after beat after beat. "Royce?" She ran her hand along his shoulder, but he only moaned and buried his nose deeper in the pillows.

The clock read 11:18. She lit a cigarette, hoping that would calm her. The day was overcast, but the rain had stopped. My God, to be this frightened in the middle of the day, to feel so alone when she could feel Royce's breath on her skin. What was it that scared her so? It wasn't a dream. She seemed to have bounced from a deep, dreamless sleep into pure terror.

The mind is a monkey. We do things we can't explain as easily as we do things we don't understand. She hated the fact Royce was asleep, but even if he were awake there was nothing he could do. She was alone with her fears, and it struck her as ironic that yesterday, lying on this bed with only Dagmar for company, she was as calm as a catatonic, perhaps she'd even been catatonic. But today, with Royce here, she didn't know if she would start screaming like a sea gull or weeping. And even if he woke up, what could she tell him? How could she explain this terror?

She let Dagmar out. "Able, Baker, Charlie, Dog." Dagmar barked. That was as close as she'd ever come to speaking English. "Echo, Foxtrot, Golf, Hotel." One of these days she'd learn the rest of the army alphabet. She sat on the stoop of the pantry, huddled into her bathrobe against the cool, moist morning, while Dagmar roamed through her area of the backyard. The bathrobe smelled like sour milk, the odor of fear, an air that sprouted like mushrooms giving away her true self.

And yet Royce was here, and here she was, shaking with terror. It felt like a strong, cold wind rattling through her, bending her spirit like trees weathering a storm. She was afraid of something she couldn't name. Afraid of settling the pieces of her life? Afraid of what the future with Royce could be? Afraid of what? Wittgenstein: You don't know a thing until you can name it. Name it. Name it.

Or ignore it. That was truly the modern way. Ignore whatever is bothering you. Go jogging. Drink Perrier water. Eat to win. Imagine, a book on the bestseller list about eating to win. Fear wasn't a winning situation, definitely not a contemporary thing. There was a time when fear was an honest, honorable emotion. It brought people together, the way she'd been swept into the orbit of Warren and Dorre's lives. Sharing a fear made it less terrifying. How was it that everyone these days seemed to skirt fear? Did they really all get up in the morning, go to work, go to the gym, believe in television commercials, and live happily ever after?

Jody and Charlotte, Danny, even her mother never appeared afraid of anything. Royce. Somehow fear didn't seem to drive him. Perhaps everyone else had outgrown it. The emotional development of a twelve-year-old locked in a grown woman's body. Fear, not disappointment or anger; those were still valid emotions. But not fear. Only children are allowed to have fears.

While she'd waited for Royce last night, after Irene left, she'd turned on the news to see what damage the storm had done. She looked at pictures of downed trees, smashed bus shelters. To her amazement, three people had been killed when the aluminum sheeting protecting a building under construction had blown off and sliced through their car. No one should have even been out in that weather. Common sense would say to stay home. A healthy fear of the power of nature. Yet people, even Royce, had gone about as if the weather didn't matter, as if they were impervious to natural dangers.

Perhaps her fear and her common sense were telling her she hadn't learned anything, that she was making the same mistake. Run/hide. First the Africa fantasy, now Paris. She might as well try going to the moon. Arranging trips isn't the same as changing clothes. But maybe she could do it differently this time, not blind herself to the obvious problems, hoping they would go away.

She didn't believe in such things as searing flashes of insight or revelations. But sometimes if a problem is frightening enough, the answer lies inside of it, like the eye of a hurricane. Looking at the gray, overcast day she could sense the sun wouldn't be out today. She could sense time passing, today passing. Yesterday was gone. And with that simple acknowledgment, she realized she'd turned a corner some time this week. Always before, there was an infinite future stretching ahead of her. She now knew the future wasn't infinite but very finite. She would never see Alan again. She would never go ice climbing again. Her life was half over and she should no longer think about doing things. It was time to do them.

Dagmar came back from her morning business, and as Katlyn let her into the house she lost all sense of purpose. That was done, now what? She wished she smoked dope, like Danny. Danny stayed spaced-out every day, all day long. He smoked dope the way she smoked cigarettes. But dope just gave her a headache and never seemed to free her mind from anything. She could call Charlotte, who always had a fair share of coke stashed away and would see the whole thing as a party. But how could she explain to Royce, after all he'd been through this week, that on his first morning with her she was off to get high with Charlotte.

Too late to go to the pool and talk to Jody, and Royce was sleeping in her bed, in his house, which she was supposed to buy. Buy this house. And everything that would come after. Perhaps that was what she was afraid of, living in this house, waiting for the next visit from Irene in her pearl-gray and diamonds, the children, possibly dressed in knickers or school uniforms, and Gerald in an ice cream suit like Sidney Greenstreet always wore in the movies.

She opened the refrigerator and spotted the remaining bottle of Charlotte's wine. Strange solutions for strange problems. Champagne in bed. To hell with the coffee, to hell with Royce being asleep. White zinfandel. The label advertised it as a wine for all occasions.

Uncorking the bottle and grabbing two glasses, she went into the bedroom. She stripped off her robe and crawled back into bed. "Royce?" She poured two glasses of wine. "Wake up. Come on, baby."

He yawned and rolled around on the bed, pulling the covers after him. "What time is it?"

"Almost noon. Here." She handed him a glass of wine.

"What's this?" He sniffed the glass, rubbed his hand across his face, took a swallow. "Hell of an eye-opener."

"Champagne in bed. Only it's not champagne. But it's a nice change from coffee."

He set the glass on the nightstand. "There's a lot to do today. And Jesus, it's noon." He looked at the clock, shook his head to clear his vision. "Almost noon."

She sipped her wine, trying to believe it was champagne. But it wasn't, and there was nothing else to do but face the music. Name your fear. The newest game show. "I'm scared," she said. And as she looked in his sleepy eyes, somehow the fear seemed to lift like a mist. She knew her heart was beating, but she couldn't hear it echoing, vibrating.

"So am I," he said.

"What are we going to do?"

"We're going to start acting like normal people. We're going to get back to the rhythm of our lives." He slid his feet to the floor and moved toward the closet. After slipping on his bathrobe he took out their raccoon coat and brought it to her. "My mother believed in warmth the way Jewish mothers believe in chicken soup." He handed her the fur coat. "Why don't you put this on and sit in the kitchen while I make us some breakfast."

When she felt the silk lining of the coat close around her skin, the hollow spot housing her fear seemed to leap into her stomach, her lungs, and she blew it out in a great sigh. She was electric, neon, all the colors of the rainbow. Although it was still gray outside, she had the same feeling as when the sun peeks from behind a cloud. She knew the fear wouldn't come back, at least for a while. Perhaps they could control it together.

Following him into the kitchen she felt she was singing, the same song the wings of a hummingbird make when it hangs in the air. He poured the wine into brandy snifters and dropped the strawberries from last night into their glasses. "Cheers." He raised his glass to her. "To a new life."

There is a space she never could explain that is lost in our childhood and can only be regained through another person, deep, intimate contact where only the physical presence of someone else exists. It's the feeling of our life, not the thinking about it. As she watched Royce remove eggs, bacon, and cheese from the refrigerator Katlyn thought about Elaine. She'd wanted to stop the feeling, and the hands, as she ran her hands through the fur of the coat, the hands more than any other part of the body, even more than the sex organs, the hands are what we use to contact the world.

Warren, lying senseless in that hospital bed in D.C. But perhaps worse than that is failing to live. She swallowed hard. Perhaps all of this week's charade had been an attempt to wake herself up, to pay attention to her own life. And she'd dragged Royce into it, and Charlotte, and Irene. All those other people just to wake herself up and get on with her life. God, that was trashy. And yet, now that she'd done it, what could she say? Hey, Royce, go on home. It's okay now.

He tossed the bacon into the pan, set the fire on low. "Remember back in the sixties, you used to see a slogan: Today is the first day of the rest of your life." He took a sip of the wine. "It only took me twenty years to act on that phrase."

"Twenty years?"

"Well, let's see now. Sixteen actually." He turned to the cutting board and began chopping onions.

She laughed. "Yeah, me too." And then she felt it, as if an idea could be as physical as a hiccup. "Royce." She waited until he looked at her. "We'll work the house deal out before I go to Paris."

A look of surprise came over his face, and then he smiled. "Yeah. Yeah. I think that's the right thing to do. I could watch Dagmar, and when you get back, if you feel differently about things, I'm a free man. I can figure out what to do."

She took a sip of the wine, plucked out a strawberry and nipped at it. "Isn't it funny how good fortune can be upsetting? I mean, Alan's death isn't good fortune. I feel a loss or grief about that even though he's been out of my life for years. But that house, by way of Alan's death, has forced me to face the way I've been putting off my own life. Without that house," she shook her head, "I might have put off my life until it was over, too late to change anything."

He nodded and beat the eggs and milk into a creamy froth. "Right. I mean, here I am, about to get divorced, lose a great chunk of what I've been building up for sixteen years," he looked over at her, "and I feel I'm much more fortunate than I was last week at this time. No matter what you decide to do after Paris."

She smiled at him, although he didn't see it, his attention focused on the eggs. But some piece of unfinished business still hovered in her mind, buzzing like a gnat in her ear. Something personal and private to her. The zoo. She should go to the zoo and take a look at all those animals she wouldn't be seeing since she wasn't going to Africa. Charlotte was right. An afternoon at the zoo was all the Africa she could handle.

She watched him busily putting together their breakfast and noticed a light in his eyes she never saw on
Fridays when he had his mind on Marin. More of a
Tuesday morning light, looking forward to the week. "What
about tonight?" he said. "What should we do tonight?"

"What?" She wasn't used to thinking about Friday
nights with Royce, but of course, he would be here. She
bundled herself deeper into the coat and felt as if she
were smiling all over.

"It's Friday night," he said. "What do you want to do
with it? And don't tell me laundry. And there's tomorrow
to think about. What do you want to do on Saturday?"

She grinned at him. "I'll think about it. But no matter
what we do, it's a celebration, isn't it? We could stay
home and watch TV and it would still be a celebration."

After breakfast they dressed, the rhythms of a normal
life. Down in the garage he discovered the boxes and
suitcases still packed in the Toyota. They loaded them
into the hall. "I'll have plenty of time to put these away
later," he said.

She watched him pull out of the driveway, closed the
garage door, just as if it was seven-thirty on any Friday
morning. But this was well past noon, and a different kind
of Friday altogether. She stood in the gray day, puzzled as
to why she didn't just get on the bus and go to the zoo.
Some piece was still missing.

She looked up and just faintly through the fog saw
the pale white slice of the moon. The moon at noon. Not
even a whole moon, just a piece of it hanging above the
fog like an earring. Noon, and she couldn't see the sun,
but she could see the moon.

And somehow, without knowing exactly why, the
pieces of the puzzle fell into place. Everything begins at
home: courage, self-knowledge, charity. As well as ulti-

mate mistakes and accumulated mistakes there were old mistakes and new mistakes. One of her habitually old mistakes was to run away from any problem, any confrontation. She might as well try something new today, even if it was a mistake, a new mistake. She would run toward something. She'd go to the zoo. And she'd take Elaine with her.

She'd enjoyed her freedom too long, hadn't taken any responsibility for anyone but herself. She'd take some responsibility for Elaine, a gift to Warren and Dorre. When she left D.C. she'd run away from Warren, left him with no one to care for him, or care about him. Elaine needed care, attention, a sense of what there can be in the world, even with her handicap.

Once she rang the bell, Katlyn felt a shiver of fear. She hardly knew these people. She blushed when Mrs. Lifton answered the door. "Hello," Katlyn said. "Could I speak to Elaine?"

Elaine stepped into the hall, the red mittens over the stumps of her hands. She smiled at Katlyn, and that gave her strength. "I'm going to the zoo," Katlyn said. "I was wondering if you'd like to come along."

Elaine and her mother looked at each other for a moment, clearly stunned by the offer, but not offended. Katlyn found herself running through a list of all the things the mother had to do for her daughter, brush her teeth, comb her hair, feed her, dress her. She wondered if Mrs. Lifton smoked.

"Sure," Elaine said.

"If you'll excuse us for a moment," Mrs. Lifton said. "This is very kind of you." She smiled and ushered her daughter off. How did she wipe her ass, pick her nose, take care of her period? A grown woman as helpless as a baby.

But why had she done it? With the garage door open for all to see. Why had Warren done it? Warren had been so gentle and a gun was so violent. Why didn't he just turn on the gas?

They returned shortly, Elaine in a heavy sweater and a baseball cap, San Francisco Giants. "I have a baseball cap too," Katlyn said. "New York Yankees. The whole uniform. Number 11. I think that's a pitcher's number."

Elaine led the way down the stairs. "Where do you wear it?"

"Around the house. I bought it for a Halloween party, but you can't wear a baseball uniform every Halloween. People will think you're stuck in a rut." Katlyn decided on a cab, rather than waiting for a bus. She worried people would stare and wanted to make this as easy for Elaine as she could.

They flagged a cab on Castro and once inside, Elaine asked, "Why are you going to the zoo?"

"I was thinking of going to Africa. I wanted to see the animals. So I guess you could call it research."

"What would you do in Africa?"

"I haven't the faintest idea. That's why I finally decided not to go. But I thought I ought to check the zoo out anyhow. See if I'm missing anything."

"Why did you ask me?"

Katlyn looked at her across the backseat of the cab. "For the same reason you decided to come."

Elaine shrugged, her arms folded in her lap. "You know all that thinking I was telling you I was doing? It's hard to think all the time. I mean, there's really only so much weather in the world." She gave a short laugh. "So I kept inventing and rehashing catastrophes to keep things interesting. Krakatoa, Ice Ages, acid rain. Chernobyl. It's nice to have something else to think about."

It wasn't the best day to go to the zoo, gray and foggy, colder than over in Noe Valley. But the polar bear was having a good time. He had a silver fish which the sea gulls wanted. Tossing the fish into the deep pool, he dove in with a clownlike splash. In a moment he resurfaced, the silver fish in his mouth, and tossed it up onto the rocky ground. Sea gulls watched this closely from perches on top of the grotto. When the polar bear slid back into the pool, the sea gulls would dive for the fish. As if he could see or hear from underwater, or perhaps since this was some game they played every day, the polar bear remained under the water until a gull landed near the fish, then, with a great lunge, which sent gallons of water coasting toward the moat, the polar bear would break the surface and scrabble out of the pool, the sea gulls shrieking and wheeling away.

Katlyn listened to the sound of Elaine's laugh, watched the enjoyment on her face. There were museums and art galleries, baseball games, the track. Maybe once a week they could go somewhere. She didn't know what she would really prove by this, but somehow she had to get more involved. Show herself she wasn't totally selfish. Make up for all the selfishness in the past.

Elaine caught her staring, and with no more than a blink of an eye her face went from pleasure to an expression as blank as an egg. "They don't have polar bears in Africa," Elaine said. "I thought you wanted to see the African animals." She moved off toward the Lion House.

It made no difference to Katlyn, so she followed. She wouldn't be seeing Baffin Bay either, probably prime polar bear ground. She tried to think of animals from Central America, spots touched by the Panamanian mailboat, but only came up with parrots and macaws. Anteaters, maybe, but there was no burning desire to travel halfway down the continent to see an anteater. And animals weren't the prime reason to go to Paris.

She wouldn't be seeing Alan again either and this saddened her. The loss of a life for forty-seven dollars. All those questions waiting in the back of her mind that she was sure she would one day ask Alan. Did Guerrero really have a knife? What did he think he would need a knife for?

Katlyn didn't know if all zoos allowed swarms of chickens and pheasants and peacocks to wander through the grounds. They mingled with the sparrows and starlings and sea gulls, a flood of color crossing their path. She watched their bright eyes searching for food, keeping track of the people walking around them. Suddenly Elaine dropped to her knees, her arms coming out of her pockets. Katlyn stepped around her and saw a small white kitten, with blue eyes and the gray mask, ears, and leg markings of a Siamese. Elaine stroked the kitten with the stumps of her hands. "You're so small," she said. "Those birds will eat you all up."

A kitten. A white Siamese. Katlyn vaguely remembered Siamese didn't have to be all chocolate-brown with black markings. But she wasn't sure they were still called Siamese. Its paws were as tiny as buttons.

"I'll bet this one's a Strawberry point, or at least a Lavender," Elaine said.

"What's the difference?"

"Strawberry is the lightest." She ran the red mitten along the cat's back, causing it to arch and purr, bump its head against the toe of her shoe.

"You want that cat?" A male voice spoke from behind them. Katlyn turned and saw a zookeeper, blue uniform and small badge, looking down at Elaine with the red mittens. Elaine looked up, and Katlyn knew the zookeeper had seen the way she stroked the cat, how something was wrong with her hands. She looked at the zookeeper, and knew he knew.

Elaine began to put her wrists in her pockets, but realized it was too late. The zookeeper, an older man, spry and distinguished-looking, knelt down beside her, ignoring her embarrassment and confusion. "Some people think the zoo is for any kind of animal." He stroked the kitten, and then looked into Elaine's eyes. "Do you know Siamese cats have almost the same markings as pandas? Did you have a chance to see the Chinese pandas when they were here? The markings are just about identical. For the longest time people didn't know whether pandas were related to bears or raccoons. But I've never found anyone who could explain why they have markings similar to Siamese cats."

"We had a Siamese when I was a kid," Elaine said. She refused to touch the kitten once the zookeeper knelt down, and sat stiffly, her arms back like the wings of a bird, the red mittens in front of the pockets of her sweater.

"Somebody dropped a litter of these little guys in here. We've spotted three others," he stroked the kitten again, "besides this one. One was tiger-striped, so I guess they aren't pure bred. This isn't the SPCA you know." He looked up at Katlyn, over to Elaine again. "You could do us a favor by taking him home. You wouldn't want him to wander under an elephant's foot, or into a tiger's cage."

Katlyn could see Elaine wanted the kitten and wasn't able to pick it up. The zookeeper realized this too. "I'll tell you what," he said. "You stay right here and watch this guy, and I'll go get something for you to haul him in." He smiled at Elaine, and she smiled back, and reached out now to stroke the kitten. "I'll be right back," he said.

"Do you like cats?"

"I have a dog at home. But I like cats too." She wondered if Elaine intended for her to keep the kitten.

"I know you have a dog, a brown one. You walk her without a leash. I was just wondering if you'd mind carrying it home?"

"No problem."

The zookeeper returned with a shoe box with some holes cut in it and they placed the kitten inside nestled in a scrap of flannel shirt. He handed the box to Katlyn, but spoke to Elaine. "We give them away as we find them, that is if they're still alive. Maggie, our chimp, has one, but I think she's going to keep it as a pet. A chimp can do that. But the snow leopards got one, poor bastard. I don't know how many more are around. Take good care of him." He sauntered off with a wave.

Katlyn held the box, expecting the kitten to start meowing any minute. But it was quiet, and she figured as long as the kitten didn't make any fuss, there was no reason to go home. "Want to see the hippos?" she asked. Killer hippos in Bangui.

In front of the hippo's pool was a bench, two people seated there, talking. It took her a moment to recognize Dr. Bodine.

Elaine was ahead of her and walked up to him and said hello. "One of the zookeepers gave me a kitten." There was a wonderful smile on her face. "I don't mean to disturb you, fancy meeting you here and all of that, but," the smile faded and she looked down at her feet, "I've been thinking about some of the things you've said. And I've started trying out that stuff you gave me."

And then they were all there, being introduced, looking at the kitten in the shoe box. Dr. Bodine introduced Sofia Addisge, who was Ethiopian. Katlyn stared at Sofia, realizing this was as close to Africa as she would ever get. Sofia's eyes were warm and brown like a puppy's, and

Katlyn couldn't imagine what kind of problems this woman might have, why she and Dr. Bodine were meeting at the zoo on this cold, foggy afternoon. Sofia, a beautiful black woman, with European features. She wasn't the African Katlyn had imagined, not the Masai in the poster or Charlotte's Bantus.

"Bubbles," Sofia said, gesturing at the hippos, "reminds me of home. He's a very happy hippo. He's sired three babies."

"He must be happy," Katlyn said. "And busy."

"Katlyn's thinking of going to Africa," Dr. Bodine said.

Sofia smiled. "I'm discovering America is in many ways like Africa, a very large and complex place. Everyone hears about all the problems in Africa. When I first came here I thought there would be no problems in America. But I'm discovering there are."

Katlyn was very curious as to what problems a beautiful Ethiopian woman would discover, how she would solve them at the zoo.

"We should go," Elaine said. She winked at Dr. Bodine. "I know how you work." She looked at Sofia. "I don't want to take your time. Besides, we have to get this kitten home."

Elaine turned away toward the zebra pens and Katlyn was about to follow when Dr. Bodine called her back. He walked away from the Ethiopian woman and took Katlyn by the elbow, steering her toward the lion grotto. There was a shyness about him, a little-boy look she hadn't noticed on Wednesday. "How are things with you and Royce?"

"He's moved some boxes into the house."

"And Africa?"

"No chance. I'm just here to see what I'm missing." She gave an embarrassed laugh. "You probably think I'm really flighty, but I'm going to Paris, actually. I have a friend who has a gallery and she wants to do a show of my work. I thought I'd get some new ideas in Paris."

"That sounds very interesting. I hope you'll send me an invitation."

"I'd be happy to." She smiled. "I'd like you to see my work, not the stuff that goes on in my head," she tapped her temple, "but the stuff I can do with my hands." She felt her cheeks flush. "I didn't know you knew Elaine."

"I've been working with her for some time now."

"She's my neighbor," Katlyn said. "I decided to start over a little closer to home. One doesn't need to go to Africa to get the wheels of your life in motion."

Dr. Bodine rocked up on the balls of his feet, looked into the gray sky. "You're not going to believe this, just like running into you and Elaine here this afternoon, but," his eyes followed the strut of a peacock until it disappeared underneath a bush. "I met your mother the other day." He quickly cut his eyes away from her again.

"My mother? You met Opal?" Her emotions kept seesawing. One minute she felt she could trust this man, the next moment he felt dangerous. How would he ever run into Opal?

"If you want to start over a little closer to home, you might want to see how your mother's doing." He smiled, a grin that seemed to bear no relationship to what he was saying. "A fascinating woman, Opal. I'll tell you something. My father and I never got along. My father's dead now, and I'll never have the chance to find out what he knew, what he knew about me, about life. It's a pity and a shame to waste that opportunity."

Alan was dead too, a pity and a shame. The kitten meowed from the box in her arms. "Are you still going to see Royce?" She didn't know how she felt about that, how this man just popped into her life, her private life, and might just disappear, or reappear.

Dr. Bodine shrugged. "That's up to him. I just thought you'd like to know that about your mother." And then he looked in her eyes, the same kind of look he'd given her on Wednesday when she launched into that ridiculous story about the hijacker.

"I'm sorry," she said. "I was afraid of you, that's why I lied. Where I grew up, gambling was a way of life. I tried to shoot the moon. I hope you'll forgive me."

"That's not important." But his look belied his feelings. "If you want to make it up to me, go see your mother. Tell her the doctor sent you." And then he turned back to the bench by the hippo pond.

SUMMER

JULY 15
THURSDAY

The morning she found Lavender dead in front of the house Elaine decided God didn't want her to be happy, ever. She'd always been very careful to make sure the kitten was in the house before she went to bed. However, the last few days had been quite warm and perhaps Lavender escaped through an open window. Hit by a car and struggling home. She looked as if she might be sleeping on the sidewalk, except that one eye was popped out, staring straight up at the sky.

Elaine began to walk. Let her mother take care of Lavender's body. Her mother had to do everything anyway, she might as well dispose of Lavender. With her wrists stuffed deep in her sweatshirt pockets, she walked down to Castro. There wasn't even anyone to tell. Katlyn was in Europe. Her mother would discover Lavender on her own. Her next appointment with Dr. Bodine wasn't until the following week. The Castro Street hill loomed ahead of her and Elaine decided to climb it, something to do.

Still quite early, about eight o'clock, and another day with absolutely nothing to do. The rest of her life was going to be like this, and what would happen when her mother died? She probably would have to be locked into a home with other freaks and cripples like herself. Dr. Bodine was wrong. That Seattle hand he kept talking about wouldn't keep her from being a crippled freak. She couldn't even keep a cat.

Every morning until her mother died she would be spoon-fed scrambled eggs, just like this morning. And now she hated scrambled eggs. Mother buttoning the buttons, zipping the zippers, brushing her teeth. No one to talk to except her mother, Katlyn, and Dr. Bodine. At first she'd tried talking to some people on the street, but all except Katlyn looked at her in horror. None of her friends from school called. And now not even a cat for company.

She would never buy her own clothes or go to a dance. She couldn't eat popcorn at the movies. She would never drive her car again. She couldn't smoke a cigarette when she wanted one. No man would take her out, hold her in his arms, make love to her in his bed.

Carl had taken her out once, but only for the sex. Neither of them enjoyed it. He took her to the same motel out by the airport where they'd gone the night her father died. She wouldn't let him take off the red mittens. *In Nam,* he said, *my favorite whore was a one-legged woman. She lost the other one in a grenade explosion. That stump felt like living rock. Let me take off those mittens. I want to feel your stumps.* He'd pestered and badgered until she cried. And then, without a word, he took her home.

At the top of the Castro Street hill she decided to keep on going, her thoughts spiraling. A whole day with absolutely nothing to do, a whole life with nothing to do. A crippled freak. Why couldn't she have done it right the first time? Why had that damn postman come by? She always went in the house when she saw him coming down the block. What could she say to him? Thanks for saving my life and ruining it all in one heroic move?

Nothing but walking, walking. This part was easier, all downhill. Walking and thinking. Arguing with Mother. Coaxed and cajoled by Dr. Bodine. Patronized by Katlyn. And now not even a cat. Carl had never called again.

People bustled by in the Castro district, holding hands, holding packages. Elaine tried to keep her eyes on the ground because every time she looked up a new pair of hands caught her attention. Hands filled with flowers, groceries. Fingers covered with rings. She could still feel her fingers, an itch in her palm. Dr. Bodine explained that was called phantom pain and would go away in time. Years, probably.

Crossing Market, Elaine started up Divisidero, seeing very little of what she passed. Much later now and getting warmer. Sweat trickled down her spine, along her arms, but she didn't dare take her wrists out of her pockets. She wanted to wipe the sweat off her forehead, but every time she looked up there was someone nearby. Her legs ached, but she had no way of hailing a bus or a cab, no money to pay for it if she did. She couldn't even open the door. She couldn't make a phone call. She decided to keep walking until she dropped in her tracks. Then she'd just stay there until the police picked her up or she was raped or murdered. Nothing like that could frighten her now.

Dr. Bodine promises about his Seattle hand thing-amajig. Electronic brainwaves so she could pick up a toothbrush. Thinking's hard enough. It takes all day. You have to think every second as it is. Even in your sleep. A freak with plastic electric hands. Thinking about how to scratch your ear.

Most of the people in the nursing home had either been ill or suffered from birth defects. She knew they resented her, a strong, healthy woman reduced to a bed on their ward. The only woman who talked to her had flippers for arms. She thought Elaine was Joan of Arc. "I understand," she said. "You did it for the poor."

The average life expectancy for a woman was now estimated at seventy-two years. Fifty-four more years, probably half of that in a home with other crippled freaks. Maybe twenty-seven years surrounded by other crazies and cripples, passed from one nurse to another like a piece of luggage needing special handling. And until that time, nothing but arguing with Mother. Eat these brussels sprouts. Open your mouth and eat these brussels sprouts. No, I won't buy you a pack of cigarettes. You've got enough problems without smoking too. You're going to bed now because I'm tired and want to go to sleep. Dad would have understood. The two of them in a boat fishing at the lake, the stories he told while she drifted off to sleep. His plans for her.

Mother would never forgive her for making their life together hell. Aunt Susan came over sometimes to spell Janet, but Elaine could tell she made Aunt Susan uncomfortable. She could never look at Elaine without a slight shudder passing through her or a quick shake of her head. Elaine took to staying in a different room unless she needed something. But it seemed she always needed something, a glass of water, to go to the bathroom, a cigarette since Susan smoked. Susan performed these tasks as quickly as possible and always glanced at the clock, counting the minutes until her sister returned.

Better off dead.

She should have done it right the first time.

Mother would never forgive her.

She would never go to a dance.

A crippled freak old maid in a home.

She couldn't even keep a cat.

Elaine tried to imagine Lavender being hit by a car. Was she tossed on the sidewalk by the impact? Or had she survived long enough to try to crawl home? With her eye popped out like a big white-and-blue marble. Could she have saved Lavender's life? It was Mother's fault. She should have shut the windows. Everything good or bad that would happen to her would be Mother's fault for the next twenty-seven years.

And Dr. Bodine, the way he would pick up a shell on the beach and hold it out to her. As if she could take it from his hand and put it in her pocket. The way he skipped stones into the waves. Didn't he know how much it hurt her to see him do that? And the lies he told. Stories about Vietnam vets who'd lost their limbs. He claimed one guy lost both his legs and still played basketball. She could imagine him playing basketball, tottering around on his knees, his head arched like a dog looking at his master.

Late afternoon now and she'd crossed through Pacific Heights. She turned into the Presidio hoping the cool of the trees would dry some of the sweat. What would she do when it got dark? It had taken all day to walk clear across town, and her legs ached so badly she knew she could never walk back. She couldn't even make a phone call.

She kept looking at the bay, glimpses of the Golden Gate Bridge. And then she knew what she would do. It would be nice to throw herself off the bridge, sail into the water. It would be all over. Probably even Mother and Aunt Susan would be relieved. But as she kept walking toward the water she couldn't figure out how to scale the railing without her hands to use as a grip.

Why not just walk into the water? Let the tide carry her out to sea. That would be a good way to go, a nice long swim. The cold water rushing over her body would feel like electricity. Perhaps she could float out beyond the horizon, away from the sight of land. Just don't let anyone see, no more rescues by postmen.

She walked to the lip of the cliff and looked for a path down to the rocky beach.

FALL

OCTOBER 17
FRIDAY EVENING

During their session on September 28 Royce handed Max an invitation to an opening at Jody's gallery. Kat's work and the new designs since she'd returned from Paris in July.

The gallery was located on Union Street, not far from Max's apartment in Pacific Heights. Rather than move his car he decided to walk. Sometimes he felt a parking space within a half a mile and less than two hills away was more valuable than the Mustang. His meeting at the zoo this afternoon with Sofia had gone well, but when he left Sofia in the parking lot he noticed someone had clipped his car, scarring the paint and denting the right bumper. No note, just about five hundred dollars to get the fender fixed. This was a balancing act between his often-maligned Mustang and his insurance company. He'd already put in three claims this year.

Although he knew it was a myth, Max always felt

Friday nights were party nights, nights to spend with your friends in celebration of another week either ahead of or behind you, depending on your point of view. Clients weren't exactly friends, but he was curious about the kinds of things Kat made, the new designs since her trip to France. Fog clung to the tops of the buildings and whirled around the towers of the Golden Gate Bridge, but the neighborhood felt like the Fourth of July, windows open, people laughing and holding drinks, kids cruising in cars with the radio up so loud Max wouldn't be heard even if he sang along to the music.

He passed the Dial-A-Dance billboard. A couple in evening clothes from the forties, dancing Arthur Murray-style. Dial-A-Dance. The billboard always made him think of lonely people on a Friday night, those people who weren't at the various parties he passed as he walked to the gallery, lonely people dialing the number and holding the phone to their ear as they waltzed, tangoed, jitterbugged with their shadows, trailing twenty-four feet of phone cord. Max had called the number once and gotten a silky-voiced pitch for dancing lessons. But he still held on to the image of people dancing with their telephones pressed to their ears. American loneliness. What made it so specifically American was the technology, the telephones, table saws, cars. Not the existential inner loneliness of philosophy, but loneliness with props.

Like the man who kidnapped a woman walking down Sutter Street, manhandled her into his car, took her to his apartment on Potero Hill, and made her wash his dishes. Max had seen this clipping in the paper, noting that *the victim escaped*. What would have been next after the dishes? Sweep the floors? Wash the windows? Change the sheets?

Halloween was still almost three weeks away, but Max had to remind himself of that when he walked in the door of the gallery. He felt like the only person not in costume. Standing off to one side was a huge green satin alligator. Opal. Max took a glass of champagne from a tray and walked over to her.

"Hello, Opal. I'm Dr. Bodine. Do you remember me?"

"Of course. Do you think I'm senile?" Her voice was crisp, even through the costume, and Max could see her clear gray eyes framed by the shark's teeth in the long snout.

She raised a glass of champagne to the alligator's chin and Max noticed her lips, painted with green lipstick, framed by green makeup. "I'm glad to see you in your costume. It's stunning. First thing I noticed when I came in."

"Well, you got here just in time, because I'm about to leave."

"So soon?" When he first spied the alligator he'd hoped there had been a reconciliation between Kat and her mother. His arrival had been timed to be fashionably late, but too early for anyone to leave.

"This crowd's too young for me. I was here this afternoon helping to put all the crowning glories together. I've done my bit. Besides, I don't like the music."

Max noticed for the first time zingy rock music drifting on the air. Jan Hammer and his synthesizers, the musician for the "Miami Vice" tape he'd given Elaine. He looked around the room, spotted Kat in the flapper dress, Royce in a World War I fighter's outfit, the classic white silk scarf. Elaine would have loved this, laughed at the campiness of it all. The champagne soured on his stomach.

"How are things going with you and Katlyn?" He didn't want to think of Elaine right now.

"I suppose I should thank you. We've been seeing a little more of each other. She seems to have settled down some. I don't know if it's Royce or that trip she took, but there's some kind of a change. You can recognize she's the same person from one visit to the next."

A shout came over the ripple of voices and the hum of the music. "Cab for the alligator!"

Opal handed Max her empty glass. "Wouldn't you say that's me? Nice seeing you again." And then she walked off through the crowd, the green satin tail swishing behind her.

"Hey!" Royce clapped him on the shoulder. "I didn't see you come in."

"Hell of a party. A gala affair. But you didn't tell me to come in costume." Max noticed how handsome Royce looked in the fighter ace outfit. A thin false mustache made him resemble a matinee movie idol. Douglas Fairbanks. John Barrymore.

"Look close. Not everyone's dressed up. Just some of the heavies in this production. Let's go see Kat."

Max followed Royce through the crowd, but Max had already seen Katlyn, a waterfall of light in the center of the room, entertaining a group of people with some story. The flapper dress, her animation as she talked. Max felt he'd stepped into Movie Star Day. He noticed for the first time some of the crowd were actually mannequins.

Kat spotted them and held out her hand. "Dr. Bodine. How nice of you to come."

Max held it to his lips and kissed it gentleman-style. "I wasn't expecting so much drama and flare. I've never been to an opening quite like this."

Katlyn introduced him to an attractive middle-aged blonde in a cheerleader's outfit. "This is Jody. And all this is her idea. I was rambling on with all that stupid Africa stuff and Jody convinced me to do this instead."

Max took Jody's hand. "It's a wonderful idea. Quite a party."

"Have you seen the masks yet?" Jody asked.

Max looked around and noticed Plexiglas cases on the walls. And then he realized how the show was organized. There were only half as many people here as he'd first thought. As Royce had said, only the heavies were in costume. Standing as if transfixed in front of the cases of masks were mannequins dressed in Kat's costumes, their faces painted in abstract blue, red, and green stripes and dots, colors to match the masks in front of them. "What a terrific idea," he said.

Jody took Max's arm and leaned close to whisper in his ear. "We're selling like crazy. Charlotte and I are going to make a fortune."

Charlotte. Max had heard of him. "Where is Charlotte?"

Jody looked around and pointed out a well-built but slender man in ballet tights and a white satin shirt decorated with rhinestones and sequins. Baryshnikov. *The Nutcracker Suite*, complete with ballet shoes. Max heard them clacking as he flat-footed his way around the gallery. Max wished he would leap into the air, legs sailing him across the room. "Of course, Charlotte and I will probably have a big fight later about splitting up the commissions. But this is such fun and going so well I'm not going to worry about a fight with Charlotte. I better get back to work. But stick around. We're all going out for a drink after."

Max thought for a moment she might cartwheel back

413

to her buyers, but she simply turned to a man looking at a mask of hemp and a great crest of cowrie shells, a decidedly African influence. He watched her launch into her sales pitch.

He eased away from the center of the room and for the first time had the opportunity to really study Kat's work. Many of the outfits were clichés, but always with a special twist. A midnight-blue velvet evening gown, puffy sleeves and cut low in the front. But the startling thing was a ruff, Max couldn't call it anything else, of exotic bird feathers spilling away from the neckline. A fan of waving bright blue feathers sprouted from the shoulders. The dress was gorgeous, but Max couldn't imagine a real woman wearing it.

Some of the outfits Max recognized from his sessions with Royce. The queen costume. The harem outfit. He would miss his sessions with Royce. After six months, there really wasn't much more Max could do for him. Kat had gone to Europe and returned. She'd bought the house and Royce had managed a loan to buy the *Singing Stars*, which he docked over at Fort Mason. Officially that was Royce's home, but more practically it was a place of his own if he needed it. Gerald had been very good about things. Irene had been a bitch.

Turning his attention to the masks, he was startled by their execution and expressions. There was a definite abstract quality to many of them. He was reminded of Picasso. But where Picasso worked in line and color, Katlyn worked in feathers, shells, wood, metal, to give an eerie and different expression to each one. Some reminded him of Aztec crowns, others of Japanese Noh plays. They spoke for themselves, sitting on expressionless white heads in front of stark white backgrounds in their cases.

Nearby, Charlotte was saying, "I'm telling you, I'm going to make her into the Judy Chicago of San Francisco. You can tell she's got talent. But one of the things most people don't realize is how much of a person goes into work like this. There's not a lot left over to market yourself. That's where I come in."

Max moved on. Something caught the light behind a group of people and drew his attention. He worked his way around them and discovered a dress made of chain mail. An armored dress, simple as a dress, but all of small eyelets of metal. Armor and masks. A perfect description for Katlyn.

She was standing beside him, the shimmering flapper dress, the ostrich plumes set into her hair. "You like that?" She smiled.

"An armored dress," he said. "Get much occasion to wear it?"

"Every day." She took his arm. "There's something I want to show you."

She led him toward the back of the exhibit to a small Plexiglas case tucked behind a vase of peacock feathers. Inside sat a pair of hands, fingertips touching as if in prayer. One wore a red glove. The other hand was bare.

"I was working on these before I went to France. They're actually stuffed and reinforced gloves. I hated seeing those floppy red mittens, so I thought if I could just give her something so she'd look normal, even if she couldn't do anything with them, it might help her." She sighed and stared at the case. "But I didn't get them done. And she was gone when I came back."

"A lot of people tried to help her." He thought of his own research into the Seattle hand, their sessions, the tape player. "But once someone is determined to do something, other people's ideas can't stop them." He put his arm around her shoulder. "It's very nice of you to try."

"I decided to include them in the show as a kind of memorial. Jody didn't think it was a good idea at first. But I work so much with my hands, sometimes I even feel I think with my hands, as if they might be smarter than my head, that I felt I knew how much she lost."

"Some people don't want to live," Max said. "For some people it's the best. She knew what she was doing. The second time at least."

"God, the second time. Life can be so bewildering. I used to have a dream about the Berkeley library. I'd dream I could read all the books, aardvarks to Zurich. I could know everything about what had gone before me. But the dream turned to a nightmare when I got to the periodical room, newspapers and magazines flooding in daily. I sort of feel like that about Elaine. As if I was too slow to really understand what was happening to her. I was going to surprise her with these. Maybe if I'd told her, she wouldn't have done it."

Max took her hand. "Don't do that to yourself. You couldn't have stopped her."

"What really happened? What kind of funeral did she have? Open or closed casket? You know, Dr. Bodine, I've never been to a funeral with an open casket. Vietnam. The caskets were always closed and I used to think the army did that so we could remember our friends the way they were, before the war changed them. I had a friend who died. Her casket was closed, too. When I thought back to those boys who died in Vietnam, all those closed caskets, I remember thinking that might have been the only thing the army did right."

Max rubbed his hand across the bridge of his nose.

That day had been hell, knowing it was over, and yet having no proof he was right. "She walked out of the house and all the way across town to Fort Point, right at the base of the bridge. It must have taken her all day. When her mother discovered her missing, she had no idea where to look. We drove around for hours trying to spot her but," he shook his head. "The Golden Gate. More suicides go there than any other place in the country. She walked into the water near Fort Point and was spotted when she was already out in the current. By the time the Coast Guard got there, she'd drowned."

"Oh God. How awful."

"Maybe not," Max said. "Drowning can be quite painless. They say it can be very tranquil. It would have been awful if she'd been attacked by a shark or had second thoughts and couldn't get back."

"I can't get over her determination. I never knew what I wanted when I was her age."

Suddenly Charlotte was behind them, his arms around their shoulders. "My feet are just killing me. I've got to get out of these shoes. Come on, you two. Later we're going to a nice, quiet bar where you can neck all you want." He looked at Max. And grinned. "Or maybe I'll neck with you."

Max gave him a professional smile. "Some other time and I'd love to. But tonight I've other business." He really would have liked to have a drink with these people but knew he'd gotten dangerously close already. Time to put on the brakes.

He made his good-byes, all those promises to get together again soon. Charlotte had a watch he thought Max would love if he'd just stop by the store. Royce wanted to take him sailing. Jody would have to mount another show sooner than she expected. This one was practically sold out.

As he walked back up the hill, Max's mouth turned to desert. He needed a drink. But it wouldn't do to be caught in a bar on Union Street when he had just said he had other business. This would be a fun Friday night, alone in his apartment getting drunk by himself. Another version of American loneliness.

And that posed the fine question of the subtle difference between loneliness with props and craziness with props. The girl who peppered her high school because she hated Mondays. And the Balloon Man in LA. Max always thought of him as the Balloon Man, although since he enjoyed this example so much he was sure he'd embroidered some on it. A man on a Sunday afternoon attaching helium-filled balloons to his lawn chair, drifting up into the air in the flight path of LAX. Max always saw him with a martini shaker as well as the BB gun, sipping martinis, yelling obscenities, and firing random shots from his BB gun at the 747s passing overhead. Probably the man didn't drink martinis, a can of beer would be easier to manage. The Balloon Man was finally arrested for disturbing the peace, but Max always got a charge out of trying to figure out how the LAPD managed to get the guy down.

Friday night. If he ever became a musician, he'd always have something to do on Friday nights. Gigs to play, or at least a rehearsal or another band to check out. Before he married Patrice, he'd joined a band as the harmonica player. They never played a gig, but he enjoyed those Friday nights in a garage draped with old rugs to muffle the sound, looking forward to the jobs which never materialized. Patrice had been good for about a year's worth of Friday nights, but even she proved unable to lift his gloom, and he finally volunteered to work in an emergency ward in the East Bay. For the extra pay, he said. To get away from her, she said.

It wasn't that he expected to fall in love, or rescue a child from a burning building every Friday night. But somehow, of all the nights of the week, Fridays were the hardest to spend alone, even though he met patients on Saturdays. So a Friday night should be like a Monday night, a work night. But it wasn't. As he trudged up the hill to his apartment he knew he'd done the right thing this evening, but that didn't make him happy.

Imagine falling in love with a woman like Katlyn, Sofia, for that matter, too. Running his hands through their hair. That schoolboy crush kind of love which he always fell into when he wasn't dating a woman steadily. And these women were always talking about their problems loving someone else. Why was it so hard to love someone? Why was everyone so dissatisfied? Elaine. Claire. Patrice.

All summer long she'd managed to subvert his visiting rights. Ever since she sent those packages back in April, she'd foiled his every attempt to see Conrad. True, when Conrad was a baby, Max wasn't much interested in the hassle of visiting Patrice while she suckled the baby. But Conrad was in school now, the beginnings of a life of his own, outside of Patrice. Max wanted to stop by the school and watch him on the playground. One of these days he knew he would go up and talk to him, maybe take him for a ride in the Mustang. Would Patrice call that kidnapping?

It seemed more as if Patrice had kidnapped Conrad. In April she'd gotten a machine and had never once answered his calls. He called often, mostly to hear what the message on the machine would be. He was learning a lot about Patrice through these messages. *Ian and I are in the country for the weekend, but we love the fact you've called.* Ian? *Ian and Barbara, not to mention myself and Conrad, aren't able to answer the phone right now but if you'll . . .* Barbara? *This is Patrice Rishlow.* So she'd gone back to her maiden name. And one in Conrad's voice. *Nobody's home. Not me, or Mommy, or her boyfriend. So call back some other time.*

Call back some other time. Kids grow so fast at that age. How many inches had he grown in the last six months?

A party was going on two doors down from his apartment, and he could hear the laughter and music, the tinkle of glasses, which always amazed him, since glasses never seemed to make any noise except when being used for a party. This just wasn't an evening to spend home alone. He'd change clothes and call up Sherry, even though she bored him to tears with her stories of how many ways one could cut a radish. He simply didn't appreciate food sculpture. Food was for eating, but Sherry didn't see it that way. Still, she was awfully good when she wasn't talking. Maybe if he got laid, he'd forget about Katlyn and Royce. And Elaine.

Get laid. It wasn't the same as love, often a very loveless experience. The old people were the most touching. He'd see them leaning on each other at the hospital and his heart would warm to them, imagining their lives together before this trip to the clinic. Their wedding bands that had been on their fingers for fifty years.

Elaine. Walking into the water. Claire falling. He couldn't save them all. Why did he keep trying? Yet Katlyn made those hands, good-looking hands for fakes. All we can do is try for each other and hope if we get in trouble, someone will try for us.

The lights were blinking on his answering machine,

almost pulsing with the beat of the music from the party down the hall. *"Let me be your party doll."* The first one began "As a homeowner you know the value of roofing and insulation." He hit the cue button and wound the tape forward.

Barbara Landestoi had tried to go to the post office on her own, ended up in a shoe repair shop, and wanted him to come get her. The automatic timer on the machine placed her call at 1:42, and he wondered if she was still there, waiting for him in the shoe repair shop. But the next call was also Barbara's, and he could tell from her voice that he might as well mix himself a drink. As her voice droned on in the background, detailing every moment of her experience in the shoe repair shop, Max poured a scotch and water and began washing his dishes. *"Come on baby, let the good times roll!"* He would have to do something about her phone calls. This one was twenty-three minutes.

"I found my thrill, on Blueberry Hill." He hadn't noticed the number of calls on the machine, and when Barbara hung up he wondered if that was the last call. But the next voice caused him to shut off the water, walk back into the living room and listen closely.

"Max? I've only got one phone call down here. Isn't that ridiculous? Only one phone call, that's the law. And I get your goddamned answering machine. And they tell me that counts, this is my one and only phone call, by law, and all I can do is talk to your bloody machine. Well, anyhow, whenever you get this, if you even bother to listen back to the damned thing, I'm in jail. As they say in British novels, I've been *pinched* for shoplifting. Now, I know you probably have opinions about shoplifting, but this is neither the time or place to deal with that. I need to get bailed out. Connie's at school and he's got his own key and can get in, but he's really not good at doing anything but watching TV by himself. So I need to get bailed out. Can you come down to the jail, that's the San Francisco City Jail, just so you don't get lost, and post my bail? I'll pay you back, honest. You know what Max? I might be able to talk to this machine until you get home. I only get one phone call, but they don't tell you how long you can speak. What? Oh." There was some commotion in the background and the slam of the phone against the receiver.

He chuckled, and then a full-bodied laugh came rolling up from his throat. Patrice. Picked up for shoplifting. Pat in jail. Too much. Too wonderful for words. He wished he could remember the name of that boyfriend of hers who'd come over to borrow money. Let that jerk bail her out. He shook his head in wonder.

There were no more messages on his machine, and with that, he knew at least his problems for this Friday night were solved. He'd go over and get Conrad, take him out for a pizza, kidnap the kid, let her ass rot in jail. At least until tomorrow. She deserved it for making his visiting rights such a hassle. Boundaries are made to be crossed.

As he was changing into jeans and a sweater he heard the bird in the shrubbery again, calling. Every creature on this earth is destined for a mate. Only modern man and freaks of nature find themselves in this lonely, loveless situation. Some birds mate for life and will die if their mate is killed.

Suddenly he remembered a trip he and Claire and his mother had taken to the Everglades right before his mother died. They were in a tour boat poling through the swamps when they saw a huge, magnificently colored long-legged wading bird standing alone in a clearing. Claire asked the guide the name of the bird, and he said it was some kind of Indian crane.

But what's he doing all by himself? Claire asked.

None of the other birds will have anything to do with him. Somebody brought him back from India and he escaped. He stands in that glade all the time because he's the only one of his kind.

Max held his breath and stared at such a gorgeous bird, standing alone. He felt someone should fly to India and bring it back a mate.